The Cursed Treasure

A Travers & Redmond Archaeological Thriller

By

Desmond G. Palmer

THE CURSED TREASURE

First edition. June 4, 2022.

Written by D G Palmer.

Chapter 1

Perspiration beaded Natasha's forehead and glistened on her aching arms. She climbed to her feet and shook her hands, trying to get the numbing pain out of her limbs. There was sure to be some bruising there in the morning, but as long as the objective was completed, it would all be worth it.

When Lucas told her they'd be going to Colombia for this assignment, being in this situation was the last thing that crossed Natasha's mind. She'd been to Colombia before, but not this side of Medellin; this was like a different world. This was underground fighting, and she was in the ring.

People cheered, whilst others jeered as they passed money about, and they took bets on the outcome of the next round. Natasha tasted her blood and glanced over at Lucas, who was sitting there in a straw Panama hat, gesticulating, deep in conversation with the dreadlocked woman next to him. Natasha would have been more than a little pissed if the woman in question wasn't their target.

They called her La Viuda, the Widowmaker, and with good reason. She was the leader of a guerrilla army made up entirely of women, an army of amazons, the majority of which were survivors of physical abuse. Any potential recruits to the squad had to perform one entry test, they had to kill their husband or boyfriend before being accepted into the fold.

These acts of violence shattered families and made enemies of the parentless children that were left behind. Not all of these kids were in a position to seek revenge, however, some were young enough that in a few years they would have forgotten everything about the night mummy killed daddy. But others were only a few years away from adulthood, and when they reached that milestone, vengeance was all that was on their mind.

One such orphan was Enrique Salas. He had wanted revenge in the worse way, but when Lucas had told him that assassination wasn't part of The Acquirers remit, the young man had relented and tasked them with returning a family heirloom instead; a gold medallion with jade inlaid of opal at its centre.

Natasha could see the item of jewellery swinging around La Viuda's neck, and she wished they could snatch it and run, instead of going through this charade. But to enter the amazon's camp, which Lucas's elaborate plan called for, killing the husband as a way in was looking like a rather good deal to her right now.

The next round began. Natasha's opponent charged at her, sensing that she was for the taking. The woman's fighting name was "The Hammer", and Natasha could attest that it was a very apt one, the blows she had sustained so far certainly felt like she was being hit with one.

'Your girl is not living up to all the hype you have been giving me,' La Viuda said to Lucas. 'I don't think I'll be buying your dud of a fighter. Where you are from, she may be good, but here in Colombia, we women fight every day. When you sent her in, I said that she was too pretty to be in the ring. She should be in my bed,' La Viuda howled with laughter.

Lucas gave her a nervous grin. 'Well, if you buy her you can put her wherever you want to.'

'Only the best of my women get to share my bed with me these days, and your fighter just is not up to par. She does not have the fire to light my desire. She will probably be knocked out this round.' La Viuda turned to the woman at her side and began speaking to her, ignoring Lucas.

'I'll take that bet!' Lucas jumped at the opportunity before she could protest.

She paused for a moment, then shrugged her shoulders knowing that she'd be backing the winner, anyway. 'How much is the wager?'

'Well, there's no point in playing games. We're both adults here; how about ten thousand?'

'American?'

'Of course,' he showed her the money he had in both his inside pockets.

'Then I will gladly take your money. You have a deal!'

Finally, Natasha got the signal from Lucas she had been waiting for. Now she could fight back. All this time she'd only been able to dodge and defend, but it had all been part of the plan. To get the necklace, they had to get La Viuda at her most vulnerable, and that meant being in her hidden camp, deep in the jungle. And what better way to find it than to have her take them there herself?

It was a dangerous plan, and one that had many variables that could go wrong. It also called for a lot of trust in Lucas from Natasha. Something that she was still working on rebuilding after his affair. It had been tough to deal with. He had meant so much to her, and the betrayal had cut deep.

Her feelings for him were never totally extinguished, and the wound was healing slowly. Not only that, but the woman he had been seeing just happened to be the sister of a terrorist that Natasha had shot dead. And then there was the other thing. Something she didn't think that she would ever be able to tell Lucas. Something she hadn't told anyone, not even her parents.

All these things played on Natasha's mind, and she was barely aware of the burning rage in her stomach as she unleashed a flurry of blows on her opponent, knocking her clean out, forcing the referee to jump in between them and hold Natasha back with all his strength.

There were more cheers than jeers this time. People that had betted on the underdog won big, biggest of all was Lucas. Natasha soaked up the adulation as the referee paraded the winner around the ring, whilst the unconscious loser was brought around with smelling salts, before being unceremoniously dragged out.

Lucas looked at La Viuda with a toothy grin plastered on his face. 'Well, I guess my fighter isn't exactly the dud you thought she was, huh?'

'This was a hustle,' she spat.

'No, this was a fighter with ring-smarts watching her opponent. Learning her weaknesses and when she'd seen enough, executing perfectly to defeat her adversary. Simple as that. Smarts over brawn, every time. Now, about that ten grand?' Lucas noticed La Viuda look at Natasha with a new gleam in her eye. It was a look he himself had given her many times before; it was the look of desire.

• • • •

LUCAS OPENED THE DOOR of their hotel suite and Natasha who, since leaving the underground fighting venue, had been quietly stewing in the back of their taxicab, barged past him. She'd been biting her tongue, but now that they were away from prying eyes and ears, Natasha gave voice to what was troubling her, both barrels. 'What the hell was that?' she yelled.

'Wow!' Lucas replied, in wide-eyed admiration.

Natasha fumed as she paced back and forth. 'What took you so bloody long, huh? Having too much fun yapping away with the ladies, while I was getting my arse handed to me?'

'I mean, just wow!'

'You said it would be a quick thing. Remember that? You said give it a round. You didn't say a bloody thing about a round only ending when someone gets knocked down. That round lasted ten minutes. Ten bloody minutes!'

'You've really been putting in the work, Nat; it shows. It wasn't that long ago when little Carlos was pushing you over,' Lucas laughed. 'Remember that?'

'You were supposed to go in, sweet talk this woman, so that she takes us back to her camp and we swipe Enrique's necklace. Simple! Your words! Remember that?'

'The way you knocked her out ... bang!' Lucas did a bit of shadow boxing to get his point across, recreating the finishing blow over and over.

'That *was* pretty cool, wasn't it?' Natasha replied. She couldn't hide her pride and grinned broadly until she felt the sting of her split lip.

Lucas handed her a whisky on the rocks and told Natasha to put the ice on her lip. She took a few sips, enjoying the warmness of the alcohol going down her throat, and he massaged ointment into her sore arms. First the left and when he finished, swapped the glass over and started working on the right arm. 'Look, it was always going to be a hard sell; La Viuda is a tough nut to crack. But we did it. You put on a great show. Now, we move onto stage two, seducing the jewellery from around her neck.'

Natasha was suddenly overcome with exhaustion and shook uncontrollably, unable to formulate a coherent reply. Lucas continued to rub her arms, trying to calm her. 'It's okay,' he said in a soft voice. 'It's just the adrenaline dump. It'll pass.'

It may well have been that, but as Natasha downed the rest of the whisky, she knew that there were other involuntary feelings at work here, too. She walked over and put her glass down before turning to face Lucas and pointed at her lip. 'How does it look? Does it make me ugly?'

'Beautiful as always, Nat; don't be silly. It'll take a lot more than a little split lip to change that. How are your arms feeling?'

'Better. I'd forgotten how good your touch felt.'

His smile wavered as he shook his head softly. 'Look, Nat, what you're feeling is part of the physical aftermath of the adrenaline dump. You don't really want to sleep with me.'

'I disagree, I really, really want to,' she replied, her gaze being drawn to his lips.

'I think that would be a mistake.'

'So you don't want me?'

'I didn't say that,' corrected Lucas.

As Natasha heard that, she leaned forward and tentatively kissed Lucas. He reached up to stop her, then hesitated. Even though he didn't want to seem like he was taking advantage of the situation, Lucas couldn't resist her. The moment their lips touched; the fire rushed through their veins. They had sunk into the kiss, only breaking when he pulled her top over her head.

Natasha moaned softly as Lucas gently felt the warmth of her breast, whilst cupping her buttocks with his other hand and pulling her closer. The ardour rose quickly due to the familiarity they had of each other's bodies.

Panting as her heartbeat quickened, Natasha fumbled with his belt buckle, smiling through the hungry kisses as she finally succeeded to undo it, and slipped her hand within the waistline. Her body throbbed with desire, ached with the need to be explored.

Then there was a knock at the door.

Lucas had a half mind to ignore it and Natasha was just as willing, whispering in his ear to leave it, before nibbling his earlobe, but the knock was more insistent the second time.

'It could be her, Nat,' Lucas said as he reluctantly pulled away from Natasha. 'It goddamn better be,' he added as he adjusted his clothes and waited for Natasha to put her top back on before opening the door.

'Well,' Lucas said, seeing The Widow's associate, and welcomed her in. 'I assume you're here to take me to collect my money.'

She smiled. 'No, amigo. I'm here to collect La Viuda's new fighter.'

'What? That wasn't the deal. The wager was for the knockout, nothing else. If she wants my fighter, she has to produce the money. Cash on delivery, comprendo?'

'La Viuda will give you one hundred and ten thousand dollars, ten for the bet, one hundred for the woman.'

'Well,' Lucas smiled and rubbed his hands, keeping up his charade, 'if you put it like that, we got a deal! I'm ready to go when you are.'

She shook her head. 'No man sets foot in our camp,' she said with finality. 'The money will be brought to you tomorrow.'

'Then that's when you'll get my fighter.'

'She wants her now, tonight. And what she wants, she gets.'

'Not this time,' Lucas replied as he showed his guest the door.

'La Viuda told me whatever it takes,' the associate responded and drew a gun she had tucked in the back of her jeans. As if responding to a cue, two more of La Viuda's amazon soldiers entered the doorway, and made to grab Natasha by the arms.

'Okay, okay,' he backed away with his hands up. 'Let's all keep cool heads here, okay? Princess, you're going to go with this lovely lady.'

Natasha reluctantly stepped forward. Going alone wasn't part of the plan, this was just another one of those many variables that made it dangerous. 'What are you doing?'

'Things have changed, babe. We have to go with the flow, you know? When one opportunity is no longer available, and another one turns up, you have to take it.' Lucas hugged Natasha tightly, confusion written all over her face. 'Don't worry, Princess, I won't forget you. We'll see each other again, sooner than you think.'

'Come on,' the associate said to Natasha. 'It's time to leave.'

As they dragged away her, Natasha looked back at Lucas, expecting him to jump into action, like he usually did, but when he did nothing she was astounded.

'One last thing,' Lucas said. His sudden interruption brought a huge smile to Natasha's face. However, it soon disappeared when all he did was flip a coin to her. 'Keep it, for good luck.'

She caught the coin and looked at it as they dragged away her and bundled her into a Jeep. It was a trickster's coin; it had two heads.

Natasha had no idea what it meant.

Chapter 2

Lucas watched the Jeep until it disappeared out of view before he went back inside the rented chalet. The plan was going off script, but as long as the outcome remained the same, the journey didn't matter.

He had come to Medellin, Colombia, a few days before Natasha, since she had to attend Professor Marcus Masterson's funeral, but in that time he hadn't been idle. Lucas had been doing some detailed reconnaissance work, learning as much as he could about their target. That's when he found out about her little gambling habit and also her best fighter's weaknesses.

He had also used these extra few days to make additional preparations for just such an occasion. The thing about making mission plans are the variables—you never quite know how things will go out in the field. You can plan and plan, but it could all go tits up in a split second.

The original plan Lucas and Natasha had settled on—reluctantly on her part—was to have the archaeologist impress in the ring, and have La Viuda bring them into her camp to pay him for his fighter, Natasha. There he'd sweet talk her and steal the Enrique necklace right from her bedroom. Unfortunately, he hadn't expected her distrust and dislike of men to be so complete. The moment he saw the way she looked at Natasha, he knew he had no chance; La Viuda wouldn't be interested in what he had to offer.

Lucas's mind had instantly moved onto his backup plan, but now even that had changed.

He pulled a suitcase from underneath his bed and placed it on top, opened it flat and emptied it. Surveillance hadn't been the only thing Lucas had done with his time in Medellin. He needed equipment, and his close friend and fixer, Ellen Paige had put him in contact with a reputable dealer.

Lucas silently examined each item, just to be sure they were still in working order. Even though he had gone over the same process several times before, he knew that taking an extra bit of precaution could be the difference between life and death.

One side of the case held a camo-coloured, hooded jumpsuit with a pair of night-vision goggles. The other side had a small duffel bag containing an F-S fighting knife, a Sig Sauer P228 handgun and a HKMP5K compact submachine gun, both equipped with silencers, extra ammo, and a flash-light.

The last item in Lucas's equipment case was a tracker, which was currently tuned into the microchip, homing device which was in the coin he had given to Natasha. Both had come from Ellen Paige's stash of electronic goods. He flicked it on and smiled when he saw that it was receiving a strong signal.

It was a good thing too, considering that a vast majority of Colombia was made up of jungle regions, including ten per cent of the Amazon rainforest, over four-hundred thousand kilometres. This large area was hard to reach, the environment was also untamed, mostly unexplored terrain. Perfect for hiding away from the authorities, or for getting lost if you weren't careful.

Lucas didn't want to waste any more time and quickly changed into the camo gear. La Viuda's people had a good enough lead over him now that they wouldn't notice when he picked up their trail, but he didn't want to risk being too far behind if the signal dropped deep in the jungle.

As soon as he was ready, he ran outside and pulled the cover off of a black Honda CRF450R off-road motorbike that was round the back, and climbed aboard. Within moments, he had attached the tracker, revved the engine to life, and set off in pursuit of Natasha.

Lucas was so caught up in his preparation that he failed to notice the top-spec drone that was hovering high above him. It's lens twisted and focussed and as Lucas left, the drone slowly followed.

• • • •

AFTER A FEW HOURS OF vigorous off-road driving, the Jeep pulled in and parked amongst several other such vehicles. Natasha's body was glad to finally get a break from all the juddering about.

She stepped down and immediately stretched her back and limbs, feeling her back crack, but as she looked around, she was confronted by a bigger problem than her aching joints; the compound itself.

Natasha and Lucas had made their plans under the assumption that this "Amazon" guerrilla army was nothing but a disgruntled bunch of homemakers and girlfriends, ten or twenty women in number. But what she was seeing was easily ten times that number, and they were a well drilled female army.

Instead of the five or ten lean-to's or tents they thought might have been here, several dozen small wooden houses confronted Natasha, all surrounding a pre-Columbian step-pyramid ruin. 'You are kidding me!' Natasha said, her eyes wide. She grabbed La Viuda's associate and shook her. 'Do you know what this is? If I'm not mistaken, and I don't think I am, this was made by the Quimbaya civilisation.' She looked on in awe as her grip was finally shrugged off.

'Don't worry, you will be seeing a lot more of it...'

'Excellent!'

'...because this is your new home, Princesa.'

'Oh!' Natasha said nervously as she suddenly remembered that she wasn't on an expedition, but was here under subterfuge, pretending to be a prize fighter, until Lucas could engineer a rescue and they could retrieve the Enrique necklace. That might have been a simple enough task, once upon a time, but now that she saw the scope of La Viuda's operation, Natasha suddenly felt that their chances of success had been slashed drastically.

She glanced over her shoulder, in the vain hope of spotting Lucas, but she saw nothing but jungle. Natasha bit her lip as her heart sank.

Women turned, the ones not on sentry duty, and briefly stopped what they were doing: braiding hair, laughing, joking, and other such activities, as Natasha was led further into the compound. They looked at her, wondered why she was seeking refuge. What was she running from? What was she leaving behind? And Natasha looked back at them, wondering the same things.

They walked down the makeshift boulevard, towards the Quimbaya ruins, where Natasha now assumed was where La Viuda and her most trusted associates resided. As they grew nearer, the aroma of cooking food woke up her stomach and reminded her it had been some time since she last ate.

Someone had obviously made some nominal repairs to the ruin, to make it slightly more habitable. But to Natasha, these additions took away from the beautiful decay of the structure. The way the jungle had risen up to reclaim the space, nature hiding the secrets of this past civilisation. It lit a fire in Natasha's belly, like every new find did. If only she could bring an expedition back here and properly chart the site.

Suddenly, La Viuda, dressed in army-camo combat-trousers and a black tank-top, exited a doorway. 'I see you're already taking an interest in the compound,' she said in Spanish. 'That's good, because you're my fighter now. This is your new home, and you're going to make me a lot of money.'

Natasha smiled meekly.

'When I saw the way you demolished Hammer, it raised my blood, and I knew I had to have you.' The Widow eyed her prize fighter up and down.

Natasha smiled again. During Roman times, it was common for wealthy women to pay to have sex with gladiators. Their blood and sweat said to be an aphrodisiac. She hoped it wasn't the case now. 'I shouldn't be here.'

'Such loyalty. I hope you show me the same. Your former owner will be paid, I just couldn't wait until tomorrow,' La Viuda said as she stroked Natasha's cheek.

Oh, god! It is the same case. Where the hell are you, Lucas?

• • • •

DARKNESS IN THE JUNGLE can be an unnerving experience. With nothing but moonlight to guide you, all the noise, rustling, shadowy movements, and other nocturnal activities, are amplified by your senses, which are overworking to compensate for the diminished vision. You could be forgiven for thinking that the jungle was more alive at night than it was during the day.

When it came to disturbing night-time experiences, the dense 2.2 million square mile, Amazon Rainforest, the most biodiverse and largest rainforest in the world, was almost unbeatable. But Lucas, in his camo hooded jumpsuit and night-vision goggles, was the apex predator in this particular part of the vast jungle.

Having ditched his motorbike some two miles back, in favour of a stealthier, if slower, approach, Lucas crept cautiously through the brush. He had smelt the fires of La Viuda's camp long before he had seen them, but now, in the distance, he could see the flicking of the flaming torches in the eerie green display of his night-vision goggles. Not only that, but as Lucas drew closer, he was able to see the true scale of the compound. It was far from the hand full of hovels that he was expecting.

'Bollocks!' Lucas breathed as he crouched lower. This wasn't going to be the easy in and out job he had envisioned. Then his eyes landed on the collection of jeeps, and he smiled. 'I guess it'll just have to be a smash and grab then.'

He pulled out the tracker, shielding it's glow behind his hand, and deduced, by the direction and distance of the flashing dot, that Natasha was somewhere inside the vine and moss-covered step structure, at the back of the compound.

To Lucas, this was a good thing. It meant that he could stay hidden within the line of the jungle whilst making progress along the perimeter of the guerrilla group's enclosure. Knowing that Natasha was near, he didn't waste any time, and as soon as the tracker was put away, he set off, remaining low to the ground.

As he traversed around the side of the camp, he heard rustling close to where he currently was. Lucas stopped and drew the knife from its sheath. This would be an inconvenient time for one of the Amazon's many dangerous creatures to test their mettle against him.

Suddenly, a beam of torchlight shone from the guerrilla encampment. A sentry guard was walking towards the jungle line, no doubt drawn by the noise and coming to investigate. Lucas froze, remained motionless, and readied himself just in case she spotted him in the foliage.

She stopped momentarily and swung the light to her left. Lucas held his breath as the light passed him by mere inches. He tightened the grip on the blade's handle and prepared to strike. A few more steps and she'd be in range. He had already decided on how he would despatch the sentry. Come from behind, dig the blade in six to eight inches down from her right shoulder, then tilt it upwards hard, thus filling the right lung with blood. And since the majority of air comes out of the right lung when someone screams, if it's filled with blood, she'll let out nothing more than a few bloody bubbles.

One more step ...

The rustling sounded again. The guard swivelled and quickly shone the torch to her right. 'Quién esta?' She held her flashlight alongside the stock of her machine-gun and levelled her AK-47 at the illuminated spot. Again she asked who was there? This time, the question produced a result; two women stepped out of the bushes, hastily doing up their fatigues. The sentry sighed and relaxed, before she berated the couple for being in flagrante whilst on duty and led them away.

Lucas also sighed before he sheathed his knife. He waited until he was sure the three women were out of range, before he continued on towards his objective, the step pyramid, the Enrique necklace and Natasha.

Chapter 3

Hoping for no more distractions, Lucas quickly advanced to the point where he would start to change his direction, and head towards the step pyramid. He double checked the tracker, to make sure Natasha was still inside. The blip was still ahead of him; she hadn't been moved elsewhere.

Lucas scanned the compound for several moments, taking particular note of all the sentries, looking for an opening in the security where he could slip past. Lucas eventually spotted one, a lazy guard. She barely did half of her circuit before she would turn around and head back.

'Excellent.' There was always one that didn't pull their weight, getting by on the shirttails of others.

As Lucas berated the work ethic of some people, whilst on the other, lauding them for making his life easy, he saw a cluster of guards at the rear of the pyramid. They didn't seem to be doing the rounds like the other sentries, but they were definitely guarding something. Lucas was tempted to go and investigate, for no other reason than simple curiosity. But he knew that he had to stick to the task at hand.

The buildings of the compound were obviously prefabricated, which made sense because they were cheap and easy to build. Out here, the luxuries of life weren't at the forefront of your mind and didn't really amount to much in the grand scheme of things. As long as you had four walls, a roof and a bed, you had a palace.

Lucas sprinted quickly and silently to the nearest abode. Although it was structurally identical to all the other buildings, there was one glaring difference; whereas the others had shutters for windows, this one had metal bars instead.

He could hear movement inside as he crept beneath the barricaded window. Lucas reached the end of the wall and peered around the corner. He was right by the entrance of the house, and once again, instead of the ordinary rattan doors, like the other homes had, this one had steel bars.

'I know you're out there,' a female voice whispered from inside. 'I saw you when the guard found those women making out. Are you part of my dad's rescue team?' Lucas didn't reply. 'Or are you from another cartel, here for the drugs?'

Drugs? Shit! 'I'm not here for either,' Lucas whispered. He was taking a chance, confirming to her he was there, but the fact that she was in this prison-like building, and expecting to be rescued, gave a hint that she wasn't part of La Viuda's army. 'Who are you?'

'My name is Claudia Moreno-García,' she announced with some flourish, but she got no reaction from Lucas. 'You don't know who I am, do you?'

'Nope.'

'And you weren't sent by my father?'

'That's what I've been trying to tell you.'

'And you're not here for the drugs?

'Didn't even know about them.'

'Then why are you here?'

Lucas was about to reply, when he suddenly saw something that made his jaw drop; Natasha charging out of the pyramid, a necklace in one hand and a staff in the other. 'I'm here for her!' he finally said.

Lucas looked around quickly to see if there were any guards nearby. When he saw that there were none, he took out his flashlight and gave it a couple clicks, to catch Natasha's attention. 'What the hell do you think you're doing? And why are you carrying that stick?' He asked when she rushed over.

'Nice to see you too, Lucas! What does it look like? I'm saving my ass! And as for this, I used it to knock out La Viuda.'

'I told you I'd be coming for you.'

'When exactly did you say that?'

'When I said that I'd be seeing you sooner than you think.'

'That was your big clue was it?' Natasha rolled her eyes. 'And how exactly was I supposed to know you were going to find me in the Amazon jungle, anyway?'

'The coin I gave you is a tracker. That should have been a big clue! Two heads...two faced...deception...telling them one thing, whilst meaning another.'

'You know, Lucas, I've heard less bullshit come out of a politician's mouth.'

'Whatever! It's not my fault that you aren't as smart as you think you are.'

'I'm with her,' Claudia unexpectedly spoke up. 'That was convoluted with a capital C.'

'Who asked you, jailbird?'

'Who's that?' Natasha asked.

'Claudia something or other.'

Natasha looked through the bars and saw the teenaged girl. 'Claudia Moreno García!'

'You know her?'

'Of course. Oh, I forgot, you hardly watch the news. She's the daughter of Eder Moreno, mayor of Trujillo. She went missing several months ago.'

'Not missing,' she corrected, 'kidnapped! As you can see.'

'Anyway,' Lucas cut in as he looked around. He was sure the sentries would be on their way back soon. 'I'd love to stand here and chat, but I think it would be a good idea if we started to make tracks out of here, who knows how long The Widow will be out for?'

The answer to Lucas's question came sooner than any of them would have liked, as a decidedly groggy Widow appeared at the entrance of the ruins, alerting her troops and barking orders at them.

'I think we've out stayed our welcome, Nat,' Lucas said, grabbing her hand. 'Come on!'

'Wait! What about *her*?' Natasha asked, indicating Claudia.

'*What* about her? My bike is only for two.'

'They have jeeps!' The mayor's daughter blurted out, desperation thick in her voice. This was a chance for her to escape, and she had no intention of letting it pass her by.

'I guess you're coming along then. Step back,' Lucas ordered before shooting the padlock off and kicking the door open. 'Now where are those jeeps?'

'This way,' the diminutive Claudia said, taking the lead.

Her escape couldn't have been more timely as the first guards arrived. They opened fire at them, their bullets whizzing around the wanted trio. Lucas blindly returned fire at the same time, urging Natasha and Claudia on.

They sprinted with all their strength. Then more guards appeared ahead of them. 'Into the bush!' Lucas yelled. The two women veered into the direction of the jungle, keeping their heads down desperately trying to avoid the deadly gunfire.

Once they had the cover of nature, Lucas turned his attention to their pursuers and let loose a barrage of bullets, taking one of La Viuda's guerrilla soldiers down. He then continued after his two companions.

The guards became more cautious seeing one of their own taken out, but it didn't stop them, especially with their leader shouting at them. La Viuda would have preferred to capture Natasha and break her to her will, but if she were gunned down in the crossfire, so be it. No one plays The Widow for a fool.

'The jeeps are just around this bend,' Claudia announced. True to her word, there they were. Eight dark green army jeeps.

'I knew it was a good idea to bring you along!' Lucas and the others could see the beams of torchlight getting closer in the darkness; they had no time to lose. 'Quickly, see if any of them have their keys in.' In a pinch, he might have been able to hot wire it, but that wasn't Lucas's forte, so he was more than happy when Natasha yelled out.

They jumped into the vehicle. Lucas gave his MP5K submachine gun to Natasha and started the Jeep. He reversed hard, turning the wheel sharply whilst pressing a brake to lock the front wheels, then rapidly changed into first, followed by second gear as the frontend came around, and set off. 'Get down!' He yelled at the others as bullets pinged off the Jeep and smashed the windscreen.

Lucas hurtled towards the guards, who continued to stand in his path, firing their AK-47's. As he got closer, Lucas flicked on the high beams, temporarily blinding the assailants, forcing them to dive out of his way, and he ploughed on out of the compound.

• • • •

THE NIGHTLIFE OF THE Amazon rainforest screeched and scattered as the Jeep driven by Lucas bounced and bounded along an old, rutted track. Natasha clung on for dear life, but the trip was even more harrowing for Claudia in the back. Bullets pinged off the chassis all around her and she had resorted to laying down across the rear seat to avoid being hit, but that left her at the mercy of Lucas's erratic driving, as she called it.

'Erratic?' Lucas yelled back at her as he violently veered the steering wheel this way and that. 'Look, you're more than welcome to come up here and take over whenever you fancy jailbird.'

'She does have a point, Lucas,' Natasha added as the light from her torch jumped around. 'I'm trying to get a closer look at this staff.'

'Your stolen goods, you mean?' Lucas asked as he jerked the wheel narrowly avoiding the thick root of a nearby tree, which was sticking out of the ground.

'Liberated,' she corrected.

'Liberated for who?'

'For a museum, of course.'

'So we're doing pro bono work again, are we?'

'I couldn't leave it there! And to be honest, if I'd seen these markings earlier, I might well have used something else to hit La Viuda with. Take a look,' Natasha pushed the staff in front of Lucas.

'I'm kind of busy driving here, Nat.'

'It's the Tibetan symbol for the Mani Stone!'

'Wait...the same one in Shambala? The one you told me about?'

'Exactly! Maybe there was a piece here...which kind of makes sense when you think about the Nazca lines.'

'I've been there!' Claudia suddenly jumped into the conversation. 'They're in South Peru. Some people say that the Nazca people created them for visitors from outer space. They're pretty amazing.'

The spare tyre, bolted to the back of the vehicle, blew as their Jeep continued to be battered by gunfire unleashed by La Viuda's chasing army. The vehicle bucked like crazy as they rumbled down the trail. It was as if the Jeep were trying to shake itself apart.

Trees beside Lucas were torn up by gunfire, showering him with chips of bark. He gripped the steering wheel tight and twisted it, turning off the small trail to an even tighter one used by horses.

The Jeep slid this way and that, Lucas fighting all the time, to keep the speeding vehicle travelling in as straight a line as possible. Suddenly, the passenger side mirror struck a tree and exploded, startling Natasha as she squinted in the darkness, the only light coming from the jeeps of their pursuers, who were now in single file down the narrow trail.

'That was close, Lucas. Will you please turn on the headlights.'

'I really don't think you want to see!' Lucas, still wearing his night-vision goggles, yelled back over the noise. The mirror on his side was ripped off as the narrow road became narrower.

'Yeah,' Natasha nodded. 'Perhaps you're right.'

'Damn it!' Further down the trail, Lucas could see a half-fallen tree slightly obscuring the way. 'Duck!' He yelled. Seconds later, the windscreen was sheared clean off, showering them with glass. Lucas could feel Natasha's glare boring into the side of his face. 'Exciting, huh?'

'You know what?' Claudia yelled from her prone position on the back seat, brushing off the shattered glass. 'I think I might actually prefer to stay at the compound!'

'Fine!' Lucas said. 'If you're not happy with the rescue, you can step out anytime you want!'

'What rescue?'

A few moments later, they all heard the unmistakable sound of crumpled metal as the lead chasing Jeep, in its attempt to manoeuvre beneath the fallen tree to where it gave the most headroom, over compensated and hit another tree, temporarily blocking the route and causing a pileup.

Lucas chanced a glance over his shoulder and let out a small, celebratory cheer. Neither Natasha nor Claudia repeated the gesture. And there was little chance of it happening anytime soon, especially when the Jeep burst through a hanging curtain of vines, took to the air and splashed down in a stream, soaking the occupants, before roaring up the other side of the riverbank.

'Now, that's what I call a rescue,' Lucas stated with a satisfied sigh.

They drove up the opposite bank and through another wall of vines, into a clearing. Lucas slammed his foot on the brake and the Jeep came to a skidding halt, spitting up clumps of damp earth and throwing everyone forward in their seats.

'What the hell are you doing?' Natasha shouted as beside her, Lucas pushed the night-vision goggles up to rest on top of his head and raised his hands. Then a row of car headlights came on in front of them.

'What was that you were saying about a rescue?' Claudia said.

Chapter 4

Lucas knew the game was up and switched off the Jeep's engine. It continued to tick for a while from the thorough workout it had just been through. 'Put your hands up and step out of the Jeep,' he whispered to Natasha and Claudia.

'How could La Viuda have gotten in front of us?' Natasha asked as she slid across the driver side to stand next to Lucas before helping Claudia out.

'I don't think it is her. It could be a cartel here for the drugs.'

'Great! Wait ... what drugs?' Natasha knew that drug cartels, with their ruthless reputation, would do a lot more to her and Claudia than The Widow could have done.

They heard a vehicle door open, and slam shut. A figure walked towards them, silhouetted by the brightness of the headlights behind. Lucas had always wondered how he would meet his end. Surviving countless missions on the battlefield, and the many dangerous escapades he and Natasha had indulged in, had lessened his sense of danger. Natasha called him reckless sometimes, but to Lucas his bravery made him who he was. He didn't fear getting hurt doing something, as long as it brought him closer to his objective. His determination was unwavering in that regard.

His aim, right now, was to get Natasha and Claudia to safety, and if this person, walking towards them, got into range, Lucas would have no qualms using them as a human shield. That was, until he found out that it was the man paying their bill.

Lucas dropped his hands immediately, prompting the others to do the same. 'What are you doing here, Enrique?'

'I'm here to check on my investment; the two of you,' Enrique revealed, pointing at both Lucas and Natasha. He stood there with a pair of sunglasses tucked into the top of his immaculate safari shirt, uselessly hanging there at his chest, proof that they were on his person more as a fashion accessory, than for any practical need. He smoothed back his perfect salon-styled hair. Slender, but athletic, with looks like his, you'd expect him to be on a catwalk rather than being in the Amazon basin.

'That's bullshit! The deal was to get the necklace and bring it to you. Nothing about you coming here to get it.'

Enrique Salas held up his hands in mock surrender and smiled. 'You got me, Lucas. The thing is, I just couldn't let things end the way they did regarding the second deal.'

'What second deal?' Natasha asked, eyeing both men suspiciously.

'He didn't tell you? Well, let me; I asked him to kill La Viuda.'

'What?'

'I refused him, Nat. And I gave you the name of someone you could try.'

'Yes, Darius Solomon King. Unfortunately, he was unavailable, and since I had no other way of finding her, except you, I took matters into my own hands,' Enrique said and pointed to the night sky above them.

The others looked up, but were hard pushed to see anything, until something flew across the moon.

'There! Is that a drone?' Claudia asked.

'Exactly!' Enrique replied triumphantly. 'It's equipped with a thermal camera. I hired these men, and we used it to follow you, Lucas.'

'You piece of shit! You used me!'

'I paid you!'

'To get your *necklace*, not to help you assassinate someone!'

'Nothing you haven't done before.'

'This is different,' replied Lucas through gritted teeth.

'Because it's not for your government? Keep the necklace. Think of it as a bonus.' Enrique smirked. 'It's not mine, anyway.'

'Up yours!'

Natasha reached down and touched Lucas's balled up fist. He was about to blow, and she could feel it. 'Come on, Lucas. This isn't the time. Think about it.' Slowly her words penetrated through Lucas's red mist and relaxed his tensed arm and opened his hand. 'Well, Enrique, since your underhanded tactics have garnered the location of La Viuda, you won't be needing us anymore. I guess our business is concluded.'

Enrique took a sharp intake of breath. 'I'm afraid not.'

Lucas instinctively stepped forward and pulled Natasha behind him.

'No, nothing like that,' Enrique grinned and shook his head. 'You see, our skittish little drone pilot, was scared by the nature of the jungle and, whilst he was swatting mosquitos, decided to step on a fire-ant mound. You really can't get the staff. Anyway, whilst we were dealing with his incompetence, we lost track of you, Lucas.'

'So?'

'So, we need the location of where she is. We know it's somewhere in this vicinity, but we don't know how far and in which direction.'

Lucas let out a laugh from the depths of his stomach. 'You're kidding, right?'

'Don't get me wrong, we could find it eventually, through trial and error, but that would take time.'

'Well, Enrique, it seems to me like you're shit out of luck.'

Quick as a flash, Enrique grabbed Natasha, and he backed away, towards his men, with his prize. 'And what about now, Lucas? Have my odds gone up?'

Lucas grimaced as he looked from Natasha to Enrique, then to the mercenaries that were no doubt ready to open fire, should he make any move they didn't like. But he had to do something. He couldn't just stand there and do nothing; it wasn't in his nature.

The jeeps of La Viuda suddenly burst through the curtain of vines. Everyone was startled by their abrupt appearance, and within moments chaos ensued. Machine-gun fire roared from both sides of the clearing, flashes from the muzzles lit up the night and the smell of gunpowder filled the air.

In all the commotion, Enrique's grip had loosened, and Natasha seized the opportunity provided by the unexpected shooting to break free of him.

Lucas yelled at Claudia. 'You wanted to drive? Now's your chance! Get in the Jeep!' He told her to keep her head down and start the engine, then he ran to Natasha's aid.

Not that it was needed.

As Natasha ran from Enrique, he grabbed after her, but all his failed attempt got him was a roundhouse kick, hitting him flush on the jaw. He crashed face first onto the ground.

Enrique shook his head, trying to regain his senses, then he heard the ominous sound of a rattle. He opened his eyes and found himself face to face with the triangular-shaped head of a South American Rattlesnake. He gulped as the snake opened its mouth, revealing four-inch fangs. Enrique barely had enough time to turn his head before the rattlesnake struck, sinking its needle-like fangs into the young man's face, injecting its venom deep into his flesh.

Natasha and Lucas both heard the horrific scream, but knew there was nothing they could do to save him. They sprinted back to their Jeep, and Claudia put her foot down as soon as they jumped in.

This round of the gun battle was ending, but the trio had no interest in finding out who the likely winner would be. They wanted to put as many miles as they could between themselves and the others.

Lucas retrieved the tracker from his bag and switched it on. Still set to frequency one, which he had used to find Natasha, Lucas noted that the display said the homing device as being behind them and not where it should be, on Natasha. 'What have you done with the coin, Natasha?'

She laughed nervously. 'Well, I couldn't live with myself if I left that ruin in the care of La Viuda. So, once you told me what it was I hid it, intending to convince you to give the tracker to the authorities, so that they can get an archaeological team there, after clearing all the rodents of course.'

'Why am I not surprised?' he said with a slow shake of his head and then smiled. 'Ellen wanted them back, so I'll leave it up to you to explain.'

'She'll get it back...at some point.'

'Well, Ms Claudia Moreno-García,' Lucas said, rubbing his hands together. He was looking forward to his celebratory post-mission cigar. It hadn't been a smooth one. Little had gone to plan, but as far as Lucas was concerned, any mission you can walk away from, having completed your objectives, was a win. It didn't matter how you got it done, just that you got it done. 'As I said, that's what I call a rescue. Now, I don't suppose you know how much we're talking in the way of a reward for bringing you back?'

Claudia scoffed. 'I thought you said you weren't here to rescue me?'

'We weren't, but we did, so...' Lucas shrugged with a broad grin on his face. 'Let's go see your daddy!'

• • • •

NATASHA PADDED HASTILY across her bedroom, water dripping from her hair and body as steam billowed out of her bathroom. 'I told you I could hear my phone,' she yelled back to the shower. She dived onto her bed and grabbed the still ringing phone from the bedside cabinet.

It had been two weeks since she and Lucas had returned home to London, from Peru, through Colombia. The mayor of Trujillo, Eder Moreno, had been more than grateful at the safe return of his daughter, Claudia Moreno García, and the reward he had given them had more than reflected that; they had been awarded the Order of the Sun of Peru, the highest award bestowed by the nation of Peru to commend notable civil merit.

The discovery of the pre-Columbian ruin and presentation of the mysterious staff, the arrest of the majority of La Viuda's all-female guerrilla army, although The Widow herself was nowhere to be seen, and the destruction their poppy field, despite more than half of it having been quickly harvested, by the look of things, had all added weight to the awarding of the prestigious accolade.

Celebrations had gone on through the night, and when they returned, Lucas had been able to sell on the Salas necklace, thanks to Ellen, for more than what Enrique was planning to pay them, prompting the pair to celebrate again.

Natasha answered the phone and heard Jennifer Moore, her friend and lawyer, on the other end.

'It's done!'

'What's done?' Natasha asked.

'What do you think? Your divorce, of course.'

Natasha fell silent. A lump appeared in her throat. That was it. The marriage was over. Six years written off with the signing of her name.

'Hey? Hello? You still there, Naty?'

'Yes, sorry, what did you say?'

'You did still want to go ahead with it all, didn't you?'

'Yeah - yes, of course,' Natasha was brought back from her memories and laughed nervously. 'It was just getting to the point, with all those back-and-forth demands, where I was thinking that it was never going to happen. It's a big relief that it finally has.'

'Really?' Jennifer queried.

'For sure! Now I can get on with my life, just like he has,' she enthused.

'I don't know. It all sounds a little dubious to me.'

'What does?'

'You, Natasha! It wasn't too long ago that you wouldn't have even entertained the idea of selling Lucas your share of The Acquirers. And yet here we are.'

'Yeah, well, no point holding on to the past. I hope you got a fair price for it; It's a good business. It'll take time to build something up again, unless I can bring over some of our clients.'

'I did actually. I let it go for nothing.'

'What? Are you kidding?'

'Nope. Nada. Nothing. You idiots each signed over your share of the business to the other, so you're still partners.'

'Did he? Really?' It was a pleasant surprise for Natasha and a small smile curled her lips as she lay there on her back.

'I'm sure Lucas's lawyer is letting him know the wonderful news.'

Suddenly, another mobile phone rang in Natasha's bedroom.

'Wait a minute, is someone there with you?'

'What? No! Of course not,' Natasha replied in a high voice. 'Anyway, Jenny, I've really got to get ready for work, so we'll catch up a little later, okay?' Before her friend responded and questioned her further, Natasha hung up the phone with a sigh.

She heard the shower switch off, then it's door opening and closing. 'It was Jenny,' Natasha called out. 'The divorce has been finalised.'

'About time too,' Peter Armitage said as he wrapped a towel around his waist. 'So that means I get the distinction of being the last man to sleep with you as a married woman, and the first as a newly divorced woman?'

'I'm not some sort of prize, you know, Peter.'

'You are to me. The most precious kind of all, Natasha.' He lay down beside her and stroked her face. It wasn't long before they were kissing, and she was throwing his towel on the floor.

• • • •

LUCAS SAT ON A STOOL in the Fox & Bear bar, half watching the news. A microbiologist had gone missing and a familiar person had been put in charge of the case, Detective Chief Inspector Jake Russell. Still riding high from "his" successful recovery of the Eye of Nineveh, although people aware knew that he did little in the actual finding of the gemstone, he none the less had become somewhat of a minor celebrity, more so than the consultants, Natasha Travers and Lucas Redmond. But that had been the deal struck to keep Section Seven's low profile intact.

According to the news report Lucas continued to watch, the scientist, a Dr Karen Fletcher, had simply vanished. She was last seen, two nights before, leaving the laboratory for home, where her car was later found. She was supposed to host a meeting this morning, but never showed up.

'You seen this?' Lucas asked his friend, Trey "Cruise" Vincent.

'Kind of reminds me of something else I heard about a Canadian guy going missing not long ago. I think he was some sort of metal worker or something.'

'That's hardly the same thing. You can bet the scientist will get more media time.'

'I guess. Even though the M.O. is similar.'

Lucas scoffed. 'I'm only glad I won't be under his suspicion this time round.' He went back to watching Trey perform alcoholic magic. He'd lost track of the all the ingredients that had gone into the cocktail shaker; there had been quite a bit.

Trey shook it in the customary flamboyant manner of a mixologist, the ice sounding like dice in a cup. When the condensation built on the shaker, he popped off the cap and poured the bright blue liquid into an ice filled Collins glass.

Lucas picked up the glass between thumb and forefinger, as if the drink were as radioactive as its colour might suggest. 'What have I told you about giving me funny coloured drinks?'

Trey smiled. 'Trust me, Cap,' he replied, whilst tidying up. 'I think you'll like it.'

'What's in this concoction?'

'It might be easier to tell you what's not in it. Think it as being a Long Island Iced Tea, but without mixer.'

'Does it at least have a name?'

'It's called an Adios Motherfucker.'

'Bollocks!'

Trey smiled. 'Nope! After the adventure you just had in Colombia, I had the feeling that this is exactly what you were thinking after what happened to Enrique.'

'Well...' smirked Lucas.

Although the celebratory cigar was born during their time in the SAS, the celebratory cocktail had come later, after they'd both left the service and returned to civilian life. When Trey had seen the movie *Cocktail* for the first time, not only did he start dreaming about becoming a bar owner, but he also picked up the nickname after the star of the film, Tom Cruise.

'So, how are things with Chiara?' Trey asked.

Lucas shrugged. 'No, idea. I haven't seen or heard from her. To be honest, I don't think there's anywhere for us to go. I've packed up her stuff, just waiting for a time to get rid of it. Ever since the Eye of Nineveh mission ended, and I found out who she was, I've been thinking that the whole thing with her was a setup.'

'You think? How did you get to that conclusion?'

'Had you seen her in here before?'

Trey thought for a moment, then shook his head. 'Nope. Now that you mention it, can't say that I had.'

'And have you seen her since?'

He shook his head again. 'Okay, so what if she *was* working with her brother Baron? What does he gain from having her in your bed?'

'I don't know,' replied Lucas. 'Nothing, I suppose. It's not like there were any secrets to divulge. The only thing it really did was take me from Natasha, isolating me. It felt like it was the beginning of separating me from my support network, more than anything else, and that was far too Machiavellian for Baron.' It might not have been the terrorist's style, but as Lucas mulled things over, he knew who it did fit to a tee ... his mother, Angela Redmond.

She was the one that had made Lucas steal the Brienne letter. Kallum, Angela's flunky, had been the one to contact Ellen's perverted foster dad, Graeme; god only knows what would have happened to her if Lucas hadn't gotten there in time. He would have lost two key people in his life, the people he relied on most.

He didn't know for certain if it was her or not, but Angela had the most to gain from causing the breakup of his marriage; she wanted Lucas to join her organisation, she wanted Sebastian Jericho.

The thing was, if Lucas were being truthful to himself, he had to admit that he was more than a little tempted by the offer.

Chapter 5

The crisp autumnal air was enough to take the edge off of Lucas's liquid lunch as he walked the short distance to his car. He climbed into his black Speedback GT, a modern classic which had the underpinnings of Jaguars finest cars, and the body and shape recalling the most iconic features of the Aston Martin DB5, a modern classic in beautiful car design.

It and another car, a wine-red, Alfa Romeo 8C Competizione, had been given to him as payment by a client named Karim Abbas from Abu Dhabi, who had bought them new and had barely done three hundred miles between them, preferring not to drive the cars at all, but display them as if they were pieces of art rather than cars.

And Lucas could understand that sentiment. It was effectively what he had done with them when Ellen Paige had given him the Alfa Romeo Guilia GTA as a present. But with that car all but written off by Baron's men, when he had raced to the rescue of Natasha and Lyndsay, Lucas had to revert to the Speedback or the 8C. Today it was the British Grand Tourer.

He started the car, and the engine purred to life, bringing the smile to his face that it always did. Putting it into gear, Lucas pressed the accelerator and headed back to the office.

These were the times that he hated the most — downtime. That period in between jobs when you were waiting for the next adventure to come along. It was the time that your mind wandered, to recollect recent events and more often than not, the losses.

They affected him differently. The police that were killed by J organisation, although it was a loss, accepted a certain level of risk when they took the job. Even Professor Marcus Masterson, when he joined Section 7, knew the dangers of the occupation. It was the death of innocents that affected Lucas the most. The woman in the Savoy hotel, John and Sofia-Valentina's neighbours, the Devonshire's. In military terms, they would be classed as collateral damage. To Lucas, they were murder victims, plain and simple. Their lives ended senselessly. He was happy that justice had been delivered.

He turned into Bolsover Street, and parked in a reserved spot outside the grand, red-brick, Edwardian building, location of The Acquirers office. It had been Doctor Robert Jones that had tipped them off about the vacant office. Beforehand, they had looked at Canary Wharf, Vauxhall Bridge, King's Road, but none of them had felt quite right to Natasha. She described them as being sterile. But when she saw this one in Fitzrovia, she immediately fell in love with it. Lucas grinned as he remembered how Natasha had started planning the interior design of the place before they had even signed the deeds.

It had been Venice Jones that had assisted her. The young personal assistant had only been eighteen when she got the position, but she had impressed both Lucas and Natasha so much that it had been an easy decision to give her the role.

'Welcome back, Lucas,' she said with her usual beaming smile as he came through the glass door into the reception area. 'Your phone has been dinging like crazy.'

He patted down his pockets, realising for the first time that he didn't have his mobile with him. 'No wonder it was so quiet,' he smirked. 'I guess I've been a bit distracted lately.'

'By something or some*one*?' Venice leaned forward in rapt attention.

'What? I don't know what you're talking about,' he replied.

She looked at Lucas with a straight face. She wasn't buying any of it. 'You know exactly what I'm talking about. You, Natasha and Chiara.'

'There's no me and Chiara, just like there's no me and Natasha. It's been over two weeks since we got back from Colombia, and I've barely seen her. I guess that's how things will be now she's the sole boss.'

'Wait! You signed over your share to her?'

Lucas nodded.

Suddenly, the lift sounded. They both turned to see Natasha step out followed by Peter Armitage. They spoke briefly before they passionately kissed and bid each other farewell. Venice's jaw dropped as she looked on, whilst Lucas quietly walked off to his office.

Natasha pushed the glass door open, a broad smile on her face, and before she'd even taken a step inside, her PA was on her.

'Well, this is new,' Venice said, eager to hear the gossip.

Natasha shrugged. 'I thought it was time I started living my life. Some things aren't meant to be.'

'But then, *some* things just are,' Venice replied, briefly glancing at Lucas's office.

The words resonated with Natasha, but she didn't want to be seen as a weak woman.

'Being in love takes a lot of strength,' Venice said, seeing Natasha's hesitation. 'Showing your vulnerable side to someone you have deep feelings for doesn't make you weak, Natasha. Don't cut off your nose to spite your face.'

The archaeologist stared at her personal assistant. It was as if she could read her mind. 'I always did say that you were wiser than your years.'

'Degrees don't maketh the woman,' Venice responded and took a sip of her tea.

'Is Lucas here?'

'He's in his office. You should know, he saw you two.'

Natasha paused, took a deep breath then opened Lucas's office door.

• • • •

THE LAST THING NATASHA expected to see upon opening the door was to find Lucas clearing out his desk. 'What the hell are you doing?'

'What does it look like?' He said as he continued to remove things from his desk drawers. 'You got what you wanted, so I'm getting out of your hair. I doubt you'd want me hanging around, complicating things, especially now you have a new guy in your life.'

Natasha shook her head in disbelief as she sat on the edge of his sideboard. 'Have you even bothered to check your phone today? Because if you did, you'd have found out that we're still co-owners.'

'What?'

'You signed to me, and I signed to you.'

Lucas listened to the first couple of voice messages from his lawyer, then put the phone down and let out a sigh. 'I just assumed that...'

'That's the problem, Lucas. None of this would have happened if you had just communicated.'

'I'm not so sure it would have made much of a difference,' he said as he unpacked his things once again.

'Meaning what?'

'Nothing much, just an idea I've been having.'

'This is what I'm talking about, Lucas.' Natasha eased herself off the sideboard and took a few steps, gesticulating as she did so. 'When did it become so hard to share things with me? I know Angela betrayed you in the biggest way, but I'm not your mum. I've never given you any reason not to trust me.'

'You're right,' Lucas admitted. 'I'm sorry. I'm not perfect. I'm not a good man.'

'I never wanted perfect, Lucas. I accepted you with all your flaws.'

'Hey! You make it sound like I've got a lengthy list of them.'

'Well...' They both laughed. The mood was immediately lightened, and the old spark flickered as they looked into each other's eyes. Natasha could feel her cheeks warming up. 'So, what's this idea you've been having?

'I think my mum might have been Baron's handler.'

Natasha was more than a bit sceptical when Lucas began his hypothesis, but by the end, she thought the whole idea was more than plausible. 'I remember you said that she mentioned something about an organisation. Any idea what that might be?'

'Nope, but I know someone that does...Kallum Taylor.'

She nodded in agreement. 'Will you be able to get in to see him?'

'Who knows?' He shrugged. 'Maybe these S7 credentials will have a bit of weight.'

'Let me know how it goes.' Natasha was about to leave when Lucas grabbed her arm.

'Aren't we going to talk about this?'

'Talk about what?'

'About the fact that we almost had a thing in Colombia, and then you ghost me for two weeks, and the next time I see you, you've hooked up with Peter Armitage? Rebound much?'

'There's nothing to talk about, Lucas. What happened in Colombia was a disaster averted.'

'You don't mean that.'

'Don't I?'

Lucas suddenly wrapped his arms around Natasha, pulled her close, and kissed her passionately. She returned it with equal ardour, their hands caressed each other. Then her mobile phone rang. The sound broke the spell that had descended on both of them. 'I can't do this, Lucas. I'm with Peter now,' she said, panting slightly as she took out her phone.

'Is that him?'

She paused. 'Yeah. Yeah, it is.'

'I see. Well, I'll give you two some space,' Lucas replied as he walked out of his office.

After a few moments, to make sure Lucas was out of earshot, Natasha answered the phone. 'Hello? Alyssa? How are you? Whoa! Wait, slow down,' Natasha couldn't believe what she was hearing. 'You've found what?'

Chapter 6

Natasha sat at Lucas's desk as she listened, in wonder, to her friend, Alyssa Popescu. They had started off as bitter rivals in their early days at Cambridge, one always trying to outdo the other, but that had all changed when they were drawn to do an assignment together in forensic archaeology. Their bitter rivalry had turned into a friendly one, with respect for the other's talents forming. They had been friends ever since.

Originally from Romania, Alyssa had always dreamt about making a find of significance in her native country, and in so doing, put it on the map. The nation had a long and varied history, much like the British isles: the remains of a 35,000-year-old homo-sapien with Neanderthal morphological features were discovered in Peștera cu Oase, the Cave of Bones. Extensive Neolithic activity had also been found in the country. There had been a Roman invasion over Dacia, a former name of the region. They had rulers in the Middle Ages that were a match in heroics and notoriety for any in Great Britain.

With that kind of historically rich landscape, and given the determined nature of Alyssa, Natasha had been in no doubt that her university friend would, one day, come up trumps.

That day had arrived.

'I found Adela Cantacuzino Kogalniceanu's hidden treasure,' Alyssa revealed, barely able to contain her excitement.

'Adela?' Natasha thought a moment, then it came to her. 'Yes! I remember you telling me about her in uni. A Romanian aristocrat, right?'

'Correct! She came from a rich family and married into a rich family. She had a passion for luxury, gold, precious stones, jewellery. Adela eventually sold off her land and invested everything into creating a treasure trove.'

'And you've found it? Congratulations, Alyssa. This is what you've always wanted. You'll be having a lot of media attention, giving interviews and the like.' Something Natasha knew a little about herself when she discovered the Eye of Nineveh all those years ago.

'I have yet to make the discovery public,' she said quietly.

'Really? I thought you would have been on to reporters straightaway.'

'I would have, but we found some ...' Alyssa paused trying to find the right word, '...anomalies.'

Natasha furrowed her eyebrows. 'What do you mean? What kind of anomalies'

'I've sent you a photo of some of the gold we found. We thought they were Spanish doubloons.'

'I've seen gold before, Alyssa —' Natasha caught her breath when she looked at the photo her friend had sent. The coins were perfectly circular, which in itself was nothing strange. What was odd, however, was the image engraved on it. 'You're sure this came from the Kogalniceanu treasure?'

'Positive. I saw it in the strong box myself.'

'Fascinating,' Natasha breathed as she looked at the picture again. 'These aren't doubloons, Alyssa, they're not even

Spanish. They're pre-Colombian. This image, It looks somewhat like Viracocha.'

'And who is Viracocha? An Inca king?'

'No. A god. *The* god. To the early Peruvians he was the creator. He used stones to create the first people, but they were giants and he wiped them out with a flood and started again, only this time he used smaller stones to create man.'

'Funny how so many early civilisations have a flood story.'

'It's certainly no coincidence. It makes the idea that a place like Atlantis once existing a distinct possibility.'

'Now, that really would be the greatest of all finds. So, Viracocha, you say?'

'I said it looks like him. The styling could be Moche civilisation, which would make sense as they were known for their ceramics and gold work and that would date those coins at between AD 100 and 700. I mean I can't be sure; I'd need a closer look.'

'I was hoping you'd say that,' Alyssa said gleefully. 'I want you to come out here.'

'What?'

'No one here knows as much about South America as you do; you even had your honeymoon there.'

'That's quite a compliment coming from you.'

'I know, that's how desperate I am. Besides, I know how much you love a mystery, and the quicker I can get the provenance sorted the quicker I can announce it to the media.'

'Isn't there anybody at the museum that could help?'

'The museum didn't want anything to do with it, said it would be a waste of time and money, so I had to get private backers.'

As Natasha mulled over the offer, her gaze fell on Lucas's hastily packed things, in particular, a framed photograph of the two of them. It had been taken during their honeymoon by their friend, Carlos Sancho-Torres.

She smiled as the memories of happier times came flooding back. Her eyes focussed on the image of Lucas, on his trademark smile. It was so infectious. No matter how dire the situation they were in, seeing it always gave her butterflies and hope that everything would be fine.

Maybe going to Romania wasn't such a bad idea, especially given the palpable sexual tension between herself and Lucas. If she wanted to have a fair crack with Peter, then separating herself from temptation was the smart thing to do.

'Okay, Alyssa, I've made up my mind. I'll come over and give you a hand. It might actually be good for me to have a bit of distance from this place for a while.

'That's great, Natasha! You won't regret a thing; I'll make sure of it. And don't worry about accommodation, you'll stay with me. Just send me the flight details when you get them, and I'll pick you up at the airport.'

As Natasha said her goodbyes and ended the phone call, she took another lingering look at the photograph of her and Lucas. She couldn't help wondering how he was going to take this news, but this was how it had to be. Now that the divorce was official, now she was seeing Peter, there couldn't be any near misses like in Colombia, like what had almost happened moments ago.

Going to Romania without Lucas was for the best.

Natasha left his office, expecting to see him waiting outside. He was nowhere to be seen. She rolled her eyes, of course Lucas wouldn't be where he was supposed to be.

'If you're looking for Lucas, he's already gone,' Venice said looking up from her computer screens.

'Gone? Gone where?'

'He didn't say. But he left in a bit of a huff. It must have been a bit hard for him to realise that he no longer owned a share of the business.'

'What? No, we're still co-owners.'

'Oh. Then it must have been seeing you with that other guy,' said Venice coming straight to the point.

'His name's Peter,' Natasha responded more defensively than she would have liked.

'Lucas loves you; you know.'

'Well, he has a funny way of showing it.'

'It's obvious you still have feelings for him too, but you're just as stubborn as he is. You two are meant to be. What will it take for you both to realise that and get back together?'

'Divine intervention.'

Venice scoffed. 'Are you really into this Peter guy? Or are you just trying to get back at Lucas?'

Natasha folded her arms across her chest and shifted the weight of her stance. 'Look, I don't have to explain myself to you, or anyone else for that matter. Now get me a flight to Romania, Iasi airport.'

'Yes, ma'am. Two tickets?'

'No, just the one, I'm going alone. It's a personal matter, nothing to do with The Acquirers. I don't need Lucas.'

Venice was about to say something but thought better of it, and just nodded as she watched her employer stomp off about to leave.

Natasha paused at the door, her thunderous look dissipated. 'Look, I'm sorry I snapped. It's just...'

'I understand, Natasha,' Venice replied. 'I'm sorry too. I shouldn't have questioned your feelings for Peter.'

'I know in your heart you only want the best for me, and right now, that's Peter.'

'I *am* happy for you, Natasha. I know you're a strong independent woman, some might say stubborn at times, but just remember you've got plenty of friends. If you ever need anything, advice or someone to talk to, asking for help isn't a sign of weakness, you know, it's a sign of courage.'

Natasha turned and looked at Venice. Sometimes she felt like she was alone. Everyone seemed hellbent on getting her and Lucas back together. She couldn't help wondering if they would be just as keen if it were them that had been cheated on. 'Thank you, Venice. I'm okay, just send me the flight details when you can. I'm going home to pack.'

Chapter 7

A few minutes had passed since Lucas had received his text message. He had read it a couple of times but was still having trouble digesting the content.

I'm going to Romania to help a friend. I think we need some time apart, so I'm going alone.

Two lines. That was all he got. Two lines. That's what their six years of marriage had been reduced to.

'You okay there?' Ellen asked. She had seen Lucas's facial expression change several times whilst reading his message.

'Yeah,' he replied in a flat tone. Lucas stared down at the floor as he put his phone away. 'I guess this is it,' he said quietly. 'There's no going back for us. This is pretty much confirmation of that.'

'I take it the text was from Natasha,' Ellen sneered with a roll of her eyes.

'She's going abroad and doesn't want me going with her.'

'That's great,' whooped Ellen.

Lucas glared at her. 'You can't still blame her for your brother, Nikos? Come on, El. That was Baron.'

'It might have been him and his terror organisation that pulled the trigger which killed my brother, but he wouldn't have been there if it hadn't been for her.'

'And something could have happened just as easily on the battlefield.'

She shrugged. 'But it didn't. I mean, it's not like I hate her, I quite like her, kind of like having an older sister, which is annoying, but there's always that little thing in the back of my mind telling me she played a part in Nik's death. She kind of makes a habit of killing people's brothers, huh. How is Chiara?'

'That's not funny, Ellen. She knows Natasha killed her brother, Baron, and we have no idea what she'll do about it or where she even is. For all we know, Natasha could be in danger running off to Romania by herself.'

'Look, going off on her own was Natasha's idea. If putting space between you two is more important to her than any Chiara Harris reprisal, then let her do her thing and you do your thing.'

He looked off into the distance, then down at his wedding ring, and his shoulders slumped. He knew things would never be the same. 'You're right,' he sighed dejectedly.

'I know I am. Now get over here, we've got things to do.'

'Do?' Lucas had a momentary lapse of concentration as he was finally coming to terms with the end of his marriage.

'Come on, Lucas. Snap out of it. The best way to get things with Natasha off your mind is to keep busy, so let's get to it. You said you were going to see that piece of crap, Kallum Taylor?'

'Yeah, that's the plan. See if I can get any information about the organisation my mum is a part of.'

'Speaking of that bitch,' Ellen typed on her keyboard and brought up an image on her large screen of five huge granite stones, one at the centre with four arranged around it. A capstone rested on top of the five stones.

'What's that?' Lucas asked taking a step closer.

'These are the Georgia Guidestones, your mum mentioned,' she answered scrolling through several more images.

'Each of these four major stones are a little under five metres in height. Each side has the same set of ten instructions, but in a different language: Spanish, Swahili, Hindi, Hebrew, Arabic, Chinese, Russian and of course, English.'

Lucas read aloud, 'Maintain humanity under 500,000,000 in perpetual balance with nature. What? That can't be right. That's less than some countries.'

'It is, but think of this, there are roughly five hundred cities worldwide with a population of one million plus. Thirty-four of those are what are known as megacities, having populations over ten million. And if you add up the populations of those thirty-four, you'd get a number somewhere around 550,000,000.'

'So what happens to the other four hundred odd cities?'

'Well...they'd be gone.' Ellen rolled up another joint as she gave her lesson. 'You see, the Guidestones were unveiled in 1980, the Cold War was heating up, people were expecting World War III. There are those that believe these instructions were for a post-war dystopian world.'

'A new set of commandments for a new global society,' he mused.

'Exactly. On the sides of the capstone, another message is written in Egyptian hieroglyphs, cuneiform, Sanskrit and Classical Greek. It says, "Let these be Guidestones to an age of reason." So it kind of does have a post-war feel to it.'

'If that is the case, then a lot of these other rules would make sense. Guide reproduction wisely — improving fitness and diversity. Unite humanity with a living new language. Rule Passion — Faith — Tradition — and all things with tempered reason. Protect people and nations with fair laws and just courts. Let all nations rule internally resolving external disputes in a world court. Avoid petty laws and useless officials. Balance personal rights with social duties. Prize truth — beauty — love — seeking harmony with the infinite. Be not a cancer on the earth — Leave room for nature — Leave room for nature. So who built this thing anyway?'

Ellen shrugged and changed the image on the screen to display another granite tablet, this one showing various facts about the monument itself, including the apparent author.

'There you go,' Lucas pointed out. 'R.C. Christian. Oh wait a minute, is that pseudonyn supposed to read pseudonym?'

'Yeah, makes you think there might be other mistakes on it, but the interesting thing is the name they chose. "R.C." could be for Rose Cross.'

Lucas looked at her blankly.

'Christian Rose Cross?'

His expression stayed the same.

She sighed and rolled her eyes. 'It's another name of Christian Rosenkreuz, founder of the Order of the Rose Cross, also known as the Rosicrucian Order.'

'Do you think my mum is part of this order?'

'Who knows? We don't even know why she wanted you to ask about the stones in the first place. But if she is, she'd be among some illustrious names: John Dee, Francis Bacon and William Shakespeare, Walt Disney, to name a few.'

Lucas didn't know what to make of what he was hearing. A new Ten Commandments covering the governance and the establishment of a world government, population and reproduction control, the environment and humankind's relationship to nature, and spirituality. Learning this just made it even more imperative for him to try and see Kallum and hope he can get some answers out of him. 'What's this Rosicrucian thing about?' He tapped into Ellen's knowledge of secret societies once more, knowing that she'd lap up any opportunity to wax lyrical about the subject.

'Well, they're more esoteric than most other such organisations. Most of their teachings and doctrine revolve around philosophy, spiritualism and mysticism.'

'Okay,' Lucas said as he struggled to figure out how his criminal mother would fit into an order like that.

'Although there are many branches of Rosicrucian today, to be honest, they're not a patch of what it used to be like. Membership was strict and very secret, nowadays you can just pay a monthly fee and join up. But back in the original fraternity, initiates had to agree to six oaths: the work of the order had to remain secret. You had to promise not to wear monks robes or visual signs showing that you belonged to a secret order. On the Day of the See, all members were to gather. Before you died, you had to find a new initiate to take your place. Members would recognise each other by using the term R.C., and you had to agree that the order would remain secret for one hundred years after Rosenkreuz's death.'

'This is all well and good,' Lucas sighed, rubbing the back of his neck, 'but what has this got to do with anything? This secret society doesn't sound like anything my mum would be involved in; I just don't see her angle.'

She shrugged. 'You asked me about them and I'm just telling you.' Ellen blew out plumes of the fragrant smoke as she gathered her thoughts. 'Okay, I have an idea...a possibility...just don't take the piss, right?'

'Like I would,' he insisted.

'So, Rosenkreuz, before he started his order, when he was still in the church, he went to Damascus where he spent years learning the secret doctrine with Muslim mystics. The biggest secret being the knowledge of alchemy.'

'Changing lead into gold? Come on, that's fantasyland stuff.'

'It's not just about changing valueless metals into precious ones. It's about reversing conditions.'

'What do you mean? I don't understand.'

'People believed that if an alchemist could transmute gold, they could use that fundamental principle to change anything into anything else. The poor could be made rich, the sick could be made well, the dead could be made living, a mortal could be made into a god.'

'Now that sounds more like Angela. She already sees herself as a goddess.'

'And the idea of it was still big in the seventeenth century. Which brought me to this.' Ellen handed Lucas the Brienne Letter; the same one his mother had asked him to steal.

'Wait, you think this letter has the secrets of alchemy?'

Chapter 8

Natasha went over her checklist one last time and found that everything was exactly where it was supposed to be. The last thing she did was to pick up her passport and slip it into her purse. She let out a breath as she remembered the photo page of it had her married name, Natasha Travers-Redmond, as did her credit cards; she'd have to remember to apply for new ones when she returned.

Jenny had already said that she'd come and pick up Solo, so Natasha knew her dog would be well cared for as she hugged him and scratched under his jaw one last time. With that, she was ready to go.

After reminding Simon Rhodes, the concierge, about Jenny quickly visiting later, Natasha stepped out of Ivory House, St Katherine's Dock, and stopped short.

'Oh.' She was startled to see Peter Armitage's driver standing there, patiently waiting. 'Hello, Conrad. What are you doing here?'

'I'm here to drive you to the airport, ma'am,' the chauffeur replied and, as she began to protest, took Natasha's suitcase.

They arrived at the billionaire's, white Rolls Royce Phantom. Natasha was still objecting, stating that she had a taxi already booked, when she was confronted with another surprise. Conrad opened the door of the luxury car. As she ducked her head inside, she discovered Peter sitting there, drinking a glass of whisky.

'Hello, sweetheart,' he said as he held out a hand for her, which she took, and he then kissed.

Conrad put her case in the boot and before long he was buckled back in the driver's seat and smoothly setting off.

'When I told you I was going to Romania, Peter, I wasn't expecting you to drive me to the airport,' Natasha clarified

'The thought never crossed my mind,' he replied and poured her a glass of the same spirit he was drinking. 'Why drive you to the airport when I can have you flown to Romania instead?'

'What?' Natasha scrutinised him as if he were mad. 'You're not serious, are you?'

'Of course I am. What kind of a man would I be if I let you go off without so much as a whimper? I had business to attend to in the country next week. I've just brought it forward.'

'Look, Peter, don't take this the wrong way, but when I told you about my trip, it wasn't really an invitation...'

'And my offer comes with a no rejection clause.' He smiled. 'Besides, you will be in Iasi, and I will be far enough away, so you will have time to come to terms with the collapse of your ill-advised marriage.'

'Gee, thanks.'

'Don't worry, my dear. Things can only go up from here. I promise.'

Within forty minutes, they were pulling into a hangar at London City Airport. As Natasha stepped out of the Rolls, her mind flashed back to her harrowing ordeal with the terrorist Baron Harris.

After he had abducted her from the black-market bazaar, this was the same airport his helicopter had touched down, before he took her onto his yacht, which had been moored opposite where she stood, across Gallions Point Marina at the Royal Albert Dock.

The Rites of Spring had been its name; she'd never forget it.

Natasha's pulse raced as she recalled the way they dragged her down into the hold, thinking that this would be the place she met her end. The sound of her heartbeat threshed in her ears as she remembered pointing the gun at Baron and gently pulling the trigger.

'Hello, miss? Can I have your passport?' The flight attendant repeated her question after getting no response the first time.

'Are you okay, Natasha?' Peter asked. 'Is something wrong?'

She snapped out of her trance, blinking as she regained her senses. 'What? No, nothing's wrong,' Natasha replied as she drew her passport from her bag and handed it to the attendant.

'Oh, I am such an idiot,' Peter breathed as he stroked her arms up and down. 'This is where you had your encounter with that terrorist, The Baron; not far from where you shot him dead. Coming back here was bound to evoke some memories.'

The attendant was visibly shaken by what she heard as she handed Natasha's passport back to her.

Peter took Natasha by the hand and led her to the aircraft steps. 'Come on, my dear. We will be in the air shortly, and there is a bed in the back where you can rest.'

• • • •

A BLACK AUDI CAME TO a gentle stop at a set of traffic lights. The driver put the car into neutral and glanced out of his window; he had heard the distinctive tones of an American accent and rolled his eyes as he eavesdropped.

'Dot, listen to this,' the man said as he read from his book. 'Did you know that the Palace of the Parliament is the heaviest building in the world, weighing about four million tonnes.'

'Are you sure, Roy?' Dot replied, shielding her eyes from the summer sun as she took in the scale of the building. 'I mean, it is large, but it's only twelve storeys, nothing like the One Trade Center building.'

'Apparently, it's to do with all the stuff inside: 3,500 tonnes of crystal, 700,000 tonnes of steel and bronze for the doors and windows, over a thousand rooms, It's a lot of shit, I guess it all adds up.'

Dot wasn't entirely convinced. 'I guess.'

'I bet they don't tell you it was built using forced labour, or that it costs six million dollars a year to light and heat that piece of shit, even with only thirty per cent of it being used,' the driver admonished under his breath, 'or that Ceausescu demolished a neighbourhood to build it. Seven square kilometres! A hospital, monasteries, factories, workshops all gone, and thousands of people displaced!'

'At least the people got the last laugh,' the passenger in the back said.

The driver had completely forgotten that he wasn't alone and looked up at the rear-view mirror apologetically.

'He was executed several years before it was completed if I'm not mistaken,' she added.

'Yes, ma'am. The revolution was the end of them. They got what they deserved.'

'Sometimes a little blood has to be spilled to bring about a greater good.'

Minutes later, the black Audi pulled into the drive of the huge Marriott Grand Hotel, joining the motorcade that was ahead of them. The procession was well organised and moved at a swift pace. Soon, the rear door of the Audi was being held open by the red-uniformed hotel porter, and it was the turn of Chiara Harris to step out of her chauffeur-driven car.

She walked through the revolving door and immediately noted all the black-suited security dotted around the luxurious foyer. The ones nearest to her had distinctive bulges under their jackets, and she had to assume that all the others were likewise armed.

Before Chiara could go any further, she was met by one of the hotel staff, who held out an electronic pad. 'May I have your thumbprint, please?' Chiara complied, and her image along with a detailed description of her was instantly displayed. 'Chiara Harris?' He asked as he looked up and down, from the pad to her several times, carefully eyeing the tattoo on the back of her hand. She nodded. 'Thank you. If you wouldn't mind going to the conference room on right, someone will meet you there shortly.'

She did as she was told, but paused momentarily after glancing into the conference room on the left. Inside were not only several heads of states that she recognised, but also leaders of industry. Her sudden halt made a couple of the guards fidgety.

One of them alerted the others via his earwig, but the growing tension among the security dissipated when Chiara was met by a strikingly, beautiful, Black woman, whose sweeping, glossy dark-brown hair framed her attractive feline features: slightly up tilted, almond-shaped eyes, sweeping cheekbones, button nose above a distinctly curved mouth. She wore a red and black suit, which accentuated her lithe form, but also showed anyone brave enough to step to her, that she was not to be messed with. 'Welcome to the Bilderberg Meeting, Chiara,' said the elegant Angela Redmond.

Chapter 9

Lucas turned the unopened seventeenth century letter over and over in his hands, wondering if it really did have a clue to alchemical transmutation or even perhaps the recipe itself. The letter obviously meant something to his mother, which subsequently meant it was important to him as well. He just needed to find out why.

'Come on,' urged Ellen, 'let's open it.'

'What? No way.' Lucas defensively pulled the antique letter back. 'I promised Natasha that I wouldn't open it.'

'But she's not here to stop us, is she?' Ellen violently expelled a breath of air when Lucas shook his head. 'I knew you'd say that, and that's why I took matters into my own hands.'

Lucas glared at her with suspicion, then double checked the letter to make sure that it hadn't been slit open anywhere; it hadn't. 'What are you talking about? What have you done?'

'Oh, that's nice. I help you out and all I get is accusations. What I've done, Lucas, is this.' Her fingers danced across her keyboard and a partial 3-D image of the Brienne letter unfolding and folding appeared on the large screen.

'How did you do that? I thought you said you'd need specialist equipment?'

'Well, I wasn't just sitting here twiddling my thumbs whilst you two went travelling off around the world, having adventures and shit. We geniuses need to keep busy, or we get bored. I might not have the X-ray machine that Queen

Mary University has, but don't forget, after they finish their scan, they send the data to MIT for the image to be rendered. That's done by a computer program, my domain.'

'Okay, so what did you do then?'

'Well, since the only place to get the X-ray done was back at Queen Mary University, we decided to sneak in, pretending to be students like I did with you.'

'"We" who?'

'Me and Venice,' Ellen stated as she recounted their adventure. 'It happened when you and Natasha went off to South America...'

• • • •

TWO WEEKS EARLIER.

'Your place is amazing,' Venice Jones said as she padded around with a bed sheet wrapped around her, investigating everything that she could.

Ellen sat on the edge of her bed, preparing her customary morning joint. 'I know,' she replied.

Although they had heard Lucas talk about the other on numerous occasions, it wasn't until Professor Marcus Masterson's wake that Ellen and Venice met for the first time. Opposites certainly attracted that day. With neither Natasha nor Lucas in town, work at The Acquirers office had been slow, nothing the answerphone couldn't handle. So, Venice had taken the chance to see if Ellen was available for a liquid lunch. She had been.

That luncheon had turned into an all-day bender, culminating at a nightclub and ultimately Ellen's place. The PA wasn't the usual type she went for, but Ellen had been pleasantly surprised to discover that she wasn't as vanilla as she looked. 'What's with the sheet?' she asked, looking out from her mezzanine bedroom.

'Decency, modesty, I don't know,' Venice responded.

'There was nothing decent about what we did last night, and I have intimate knowledge about you, so you have nothing left to be modest about, babe,' Ellen said between puffs.

'That's certainly true.' Venice smiled and was about to tell Ellen to come and get the bedsheet if she wanted it, when an old, discoloured letter caught her attention. 'What's this?' She was intrigued. The aged letter seemed out of place amongst all of Ellen's high-tech equipment.

She looked down at Venice holding the letter and had a bright idea. 'How would you like to go on a date?'

Venice looked at Ellen with confusion when they arrived and found out that their date destination was Queen Mary University.

'Don't look at me like that. Haven't you ever wished that you could get out from behind the desk and do a bit of the adventuring?'

'No, can't say that I have. I stay in my lane.'

'It's no biggy; me and Lucas have done it before. We'll go in, work our way to the X-ray lab, make sure that our letter is next to be scanned, then we get out. Simple.'

'That's it?'

'Yup. Easy as that. I'll have to come back a few days later to download the data, but that should be just as easy.'

The insertion of the letter had gone as planned, with no hiccups. She had even seen the student she kissed last time so Lucas could sneak into the building. Apparently, he had been hoping to see her again, maybe take things further, but this time he had to watch Ellen kiss Venice.

Seventy-two hours later, Ellen had returned to the university without Venice, who had taken control of the office, and made it seem that people actually worked there. Ellen used the usual tactic of going through the security barrier with a group of students.

The route to the laboratory had become rather familiar to Ellen, with all her comings and goings, as had the staff. So she was more than a little surprised to see two new faces there, new faces that seemed far more out of place than she did. For one thing, their boots were far cleaner than any of the technicians she had seen previously. In fact none of them had worn boots at all, preferring to wear comfortable trainers instead.

'Hey, how are you guys doing?' Ellen said brightly. They responded with cursory grunts. One was going through the Brienne letters, while the other went through the registry of letters that had already been scanned.

She made her way directly to another terminal, and surreptitiously inserted a dongle which uploaded a program to bypass the computer's security. Once she was in, Ellen could see that the X-ray had almost finished its cycle. She started preparing to transfer the data immediately on its completion.

Even though the men weren't looking at her, Ellen could tell they were watching; she could feel it. Occasionally, she'd see movement behind her, reflected on the screen of the monitor. Ellen didn't know who they were, but a feeling was growing inside that told her she was in more trouble than she thought.

These sentiments were confirmed when the X-ray completed its scan and sounded a gentle alert. Ellen worked at lightning speed, tapping away at the keyboard, directing the vector data to the flash stick before retrieving it.

'Aren't one of you going to shut that thing off?' Ellen asked as the machine's beeping continued.

'Why don't you?'

'Jeez! I thought we were supposed to be a team here?' She moved to the machine and pressed the stop button, and the man seated closest to her rolled his chair over to the computer terminal she'd been working on. 'Hey! What are you doing?' She yelled and swiped the letter out of the X-ray machine without being seen.

'Which letter is this?' He demanded. 'Who is it addressed to?'

'How should I know? You assholes were here before me. Don't you know your jobs?' She was getting into the full flow of her bluff and glanced at the computer the man had been using. 'What have you been doing here? Synthesising the form factor won't do anything. We need to reboot the backup SMTP interface!'

The two men looked at each other before coming to the same conclusion and both drew their silenced guns, pointing them at Ellen.

She slowly put her hands up and inched back towards the exit. 'What the fuck? You know this is a university, right? Not a bank? What, you stealing test tubes or something?'

'Stop moving,' the nearest one ordered. 'I want the letter.'

'What?'

'Give me the letter.'

'What letter?'

'The "De Jong" letter.'

'Ooooh,' Ellen replied, drawing out the word. 'That letter. Well, that's right over here.' She picked up the tray of antique letters and threw them into the air, diving for the exit of the laboratory at the same time. Two shots were fired as she slid across the parquet flooring, slamming into the corridor wall. Her heart raced as she jumped to her feet and ran.

Another shot zinged past her as she left the empty corridor and turned a corner. Ellen saw a handful of students ahead, and she threw the lab coat disguise off as the idea of losing herself amongst them came to her. She just needed more.

Ellen hit a fire alarm and then another two for good measure. The shooter entered the hallway, raised his gun and took aim, but before he could fire, a tidal wave of young adults came streaming out of their lecture halls and rooms, their tutors desperately trying to get them to follow the evacuation protocols in an orderly fashion, but failing miserably.

• • • •

'AND THAT WAS IT,' ELLEN said, finishing her tale, 'I just blended in with the masses and vanished like a pro. You'd have been proud of me.' She looked at Lucas's face and saw his stern look. 'But it seems like you're not.'

'Of course not,' he yelled. 'You could have been killed.'

'And how do you think I feel when you go gallivanting around the world with your little death-wish?'

'I'm supposed to be looking out for you.'

'We're supposed to be looking out for each other.'

Lucas nodded, resigned to the fact that even though she was young, she wasn't helpless. She was smart and a lot tougher than her diminutive size would have people believe; at times, he forgot that fact himself. 'You did good, Ellen, really good. Thanks to you, we know that my mother has discovered that there are two letters, and that she needs both of them.'

'Actually, that's not all I did,' Ellen added with a grin. 'While I was fooling around with the university PC, I found this.' She sent a vector image to the huge screen.

Lucas was baffled by what he was seeing. 'What is that?'

'That, Lucas, is the letter you gave to your mum. Now we have both of them.'

Chapter 10

The Embraer Legacy 500 private jet taxied to the designated hangar at Iasi International Airport. It had been Natasha's first time on a private jet, and she had found it to be a comfortable, smooth flight. The fact she had spent most of the two-hour flight in the fully flat bed with her host, Peter Armitage, no doubt had something to do with that.

She continued to straighten herself up, whilst Peter, already back to his usual polished best, sat watching the BBC News channel. 'Anything interesting happening in the world?' Natasha asked as she put the finishing touches to her hair.

'Nothing much,' he replied.

She glanced at the TV when she heard a familiar voice. 'DCI Jake Russell, what's he up to now? Still milking his Eye of Nineveh "success"?'

'I forgot you had dealings with him.'

'Dealings? He tried to pin the theft of the gem on Lucas, so if you call that "dealings" then yes.

'What's he like?'

'He's a bit tenacious, I guess. Obstinate, maybe a bit stubborn, but they say he's good at what he does, gets the job done, sees it through to the end. Why do you ask? What's he investigating now?'

'Just a curiosity, he has been put on a missing person case. Bit of a comedown after the Eye of Nineveh heist, wouldn't you say?' Peter switched off the television as the plane came to a complete stop and the engines were powered down. 'Have you got everything?'

Natasha took a final look around and nodded. 'Yeah, I'm good. Look, Peter, you didn't have to do this, but thank you.'

'I didn't have to, but I wanted to,' he responded and took her by the arms. 'If you want to make a go of this relationship, then you're going to have to get used to gestures like this, Natasha.'

'I'm thinking maybe I can,' she smiled before they kissed. The pair then, along with Conrad, disembarked the plane, the driver welcomed the opportunity to stretch his legs.

'You've got my number, so if you need my help with anything while I'm here, don't be shy.'

'Where are you going to be?'

'I don't know, Bucharest, Timisoara. I'll be here. It doesn't matter where I am.'

'Thank you, Peter. You've already done so much for me.' Natasha had always found it difficult to ask for help. Sometimes she saw not being able to do things for yourself as a sign of weakness. And no matter how enlightened society liked to portray itself, misogyny was still rife. It had forged her into the strong independent woman she now was.

With one last embrace, Peter bid Natasha farewell and watched her leave as a member of the airport staff led her through to the exit. 'How long before we are airborne again?' Peter asked Conrad once Natasha was out of sight.

'Not long. The crew are just having a quick drink and a little food, then we'll be on our way once they get the go ahead.'

'Good. I'll be onboard. I have a phone call to make.'

'Any problems?'

Peter paused on the stairs. 'No, I don't believe so. Hitches and annoyances maybe, but not problems.'

• • • •

ANGELA REDMOND LOOKED around the table, eyed each of the faces that gazed back at her. In the other conference room, on the other side of the Marriott hotel, world and industry leaders, the global elite, conducted their secretive annual three day gathering known as the Bilderberg Meeting.

They barred journalists from reporting on the event, there were no minutes taken or summaries of discussions. Participants of the meeting were bound by Chatham House rules, meaning they were free to use the information received, but neither the identity nor the affiliation of the speaker, nor that of any other participant, may be revealed.

These conditions left outsiders speculating exactly what was being said within the walls of the meeting, the location of which changed year after year. People that were intimidated by the Bilderberg Group said that it was nothing more than decent upstanding citizens that wanted to discuss world affairs in private. Others believed that "time" was an expensive commodity for the attendees, and they wouldn't waste it on something frivolous. Then there were those that believed that this group of global elites were bringing about a New World Order.

The truth was all of it.

Beyond what people actually knew about the secret society, was something that only an exclusive number knew existed. Whilst the Bilderberg Group talked and discussed world matters, the Bilderberg Inner Circle were the ones that actively sought to bring about change and make things happen.

'With the untimely demise of Baron Harris, there was subsequently a vacancy among the Inner Circle.' Angela opened, getting right down to business without any greeting or salutation. That was the way this society operated; they had their agenda and small talk, and pleasantries were not part of it. 'With the ascendency of a new leader of the J Organisation, Alpha has extended the same offer their predecessor was given. I am pleased to say they have accepted.'

Angela Redmond pressed a button on the console in front of her and a moment later the door opened. Chiara Harris strolled purposefully into the red and gold colour co-ordinated room. The sixteen faces she didn't know turned to regard her with interest and curiosity. She confidently met each of their gazes, before Angela motioned for her to take one of the seats against the back wall, which she did.

'And now on to the next order of business.' Before Angela could continue, a short, pale-skinned man in his mid-sixties nonchalantly raised his hand. 'Yes, Upsilon?' Her tone was terse.

The eighteen members of the Bilderberg Inner Circle were only known by their code names, letters of the Greek alphabet. The seven most influential of the group were given the vowels: Alpha, Epsilon, Eta, Iota, Omicron, Omega, Upsilon. Angela herself was known as Epsilon.

For security reasons, only the one known as Alpha knew the true identities of everyone. Or so they thought. Over the years, Angela had turned her skills in thievery to espionage, as she recognised that knowledge was power. The real name of Upsilon, for instance, was Alexsadr Polishkin, sixty-five years old, husband to Zhenya, father to three girls and a boy. Making his money during perestroika, like so many oligarchs, he was a multi billionaire. His problem now however was that he was annoying Angela Redmond. That, and the fact that he believed he should be in the position that she currently occupied, and she never took kindly to competition.

'I have a question,' he said in his thick Russian accent. 'Where is Alpha?'

'Alpha is busy checking the progress of Operation Vanguard,' she replied with feigned politeness. 'If you had allowed me to finish, you would have learnt that.'

'And why are *you* in charge?'

'That's two questions,' Angela pointed out. 'Alpha has asked me to chair the meeting on their behalf.'

'I have been with the Inner Circle much longer than you. I have pumped more money into the organisation than you. I have more influence —'

'Let me cut you off right there, Alexsadr Polishkin.' There were audible gasps from the attendees when she used his real name. 'Your influence is non-existent. Your money, your power, your trophy wife, your children, everything you hold dear, will now be taken away from you.'

He scoffed. 'You know my name, so what?'

'I not only know your name, but I also know the name of your wife, Zhenya, the names of your children, Anna, Maria, Diana and Dmitri, the names of your brothers and their families, as well as the siblings of Zhenya and their offspring.' With each revelation, Alexsadr balked. As did each person sitting at the table. 'But more importantly, I know the amount your life is insured for, and the beneficiary of your will.'

'Bah! I don't have life insurance and it's common for a man's wife to be his beneficiary,' he said unimpressed.

'Wrong on both counts. At my instruction, your wife has opened a new policy in your name for $200 million. And as for your will, when you're dead, everything you own will belong to the Inner Circle, via a holding company I have set up in the Cayman Islands. Don't worry, your children will receive a regular stipend. I'm not a complete bitch...well, not all the time. If you wish to speak out against me, cross me or belittle me again, Alexsadr Polishkin, remember that I literally hold your life in my hand, *and* that of your legacy.'

Angela Redmond let out a long sigh. She didn't particularly like having to show her hand, but sometimes it was necessary for people such as these; in their boardrooms and offices. They were used to being the apex predators, the ones their subordinates turned to. Now they knew that the pecking order of this landscape, within the Inner Circle, was vastly different.

'Now, if there are no more interruptions, we will have an update on the progress of Operation Vanguard.' Angela pressed the buzzer, and the door was opened once again.

This time, however, a well-dressed man walked in. Half of his face was disfigured, with lumps and blotches, discoloured a red so dark, it was almost black as if it were frost bitten. But this wasn't from exposure, this nerve damage was from a snake bite.

'Alpha has approached an outside party to manage part of this enterprise,' Angela continued. 'If they succeed, they will be accepted into the Circle. Think of this as their interview, and so far, they are doing well.'

The man turned to address the Bilderberg Inner Circle. They didn't know his name. All they knew was that he would have something that benefited the organisation, be it financial or otherwise. Angela knew who he was, knew what he was bringing to the table. She looked for reactions from the attendees as Enrique Salas spoke.

'Operation Vanguard is proceeding as scheduled,' he slurred and wiped the spittle that dribbled from the corner of his mouth with a handkerchief. 'We will begin the next stage, "cleaning the loose ends" soon...'

Chapter 11

Detective Chief Inspector Jake Russell leaned back in his chair and let out a long sigh whilst he rubbed his eyes. It had been a tiring day so far, pawing over the witness reports of Karen Fletcher, the microbiologist that seemed to have vanished. Reading these documents was getting him nowhere, and it was giving him a headache.

He opened his drawer and reached for one of his tea bags, an Earl Grey, then he paused and checked the time; it was a few minutes after 3pm. Replacing it, the DCI picked up a chrysanthemum tea instead. Ever since he read that tea had more caffeine than coffee, Jake Russell had changed his consumption of the beverage; and he had seen a marked difference in the quality of his sleep.

There was the usual buzz and general hubbub of officers working diligently as Jake passed through the open-planned department to the kitchen area. His mind still tried to make sense of the information he had to hand.

'Alright, guv?' Detective Inspector Derek Wilkins greeted his boss and held up his mug. 'Do you want one? The kettle's just boiled.'

'That's what I'm here for,' Jake replied and tossed the small pyramid shaped nylon bag to his colleague and took a seat. A few minutes later, whilst he watched his tea brewing, Jake tried to clear one of the many things that bothered him about this current case. 'Tell me, Derek, what are the usual motives of abduction?'

'Are we still treating this as a kidnapping then, guv?' DI Wilkins asked.

'Do you know something I don't?'

Wilkins shook his head.

'Then we treat it as such until we receive information to the contrary.'

DI Wilkins cleared his throat after receiving the slight reprimand and answered his commanding officer's question. 'The kidnapping of adults is often for ransom, to obtain slaves or to force someone to withdraw money from their bank accounts. There are also specific terms that refer to certain motives of the criminal activity, such as bride kidnapping, express kidnapping and tiger kidnapping.'

Jake Russell gave an approving nod. 'Exactly what it says in the training manual. To have a chance of finding Dr Fletcher, we need to know what motivates her abductor, what does he want from her. How much does a microbiologist make, and what do they do?'

'I...I don't know,' stammered DI Wilkins.

'And neither do I, so perhaps we should educate ourselves more, and find someone that can.'

'I'll give her laboratory at St George's a call.'

'No, don't bother. We could do with getting some fresh air, and I could do with stretching my legs.'

• • • •

LUCAS WALKED THROUGH the maze-like corridors of South London's St George's Hospital. Even though the job he had to do now was an important one, getting knowledge from Kallum Taylor about his mother, Angela Redmond and her current whereabouts, he couldn't stop his mind from wondering how far Ellen had come with her rendering of the Brienne letters.

As Lucas checked his phone again, making sure he hadn't missed her call, he finally arrived at the intensive care unit where Kallum was being looked after. He pushed through the heavy blue doors. The staff were in full personal protective equipment: masks, gloves, even the plastic apron. Having seen the unmanned reception desk, Lucas approached the first nurse he saw that wasn't in a deep conversation with a colleague or rushing from point A to point B.

'Kallum Taylor?' The nurse repeated. 'I'm afraid Mr Taylor is not permitted visitors.'

'Why not?'

'His condition.'

'And what is his condition? What's wrong with him?'

'Well...I'm not allowed to tell you that.'

'But you must have some ideas?'

'Look, let me get hold of the virologist in charge, Dr Dannen. She'll be more suited to answer any questions you have.' The nurse then turned on her heel, picked up the phone at reception and dialled an internal number.

As the nurse waited for a reply, Lucas impatiently took in his surroundings. He didn't enjoy spending too much time in hospitals. To him it wasn't somewhere you visited for fun; you were going to see someone that was ill, or you were occupying a bed yourself.

Lucas knew he wasn't the only one that had these sentiments. The fact that all hospitals seemed to have the same interior designers didn't help. No matter which one you went to, the same dour neutral colours greeted you, notices postered on various walls reminding everyone of the importance of washing their hands, and others advertising that weekend's movie selections.

Behind him, Lucas could hear the nurse getting increasingly frustrated as her call continued to go unanswered. He was turning to tell her to forget about it, when out of the corner of his eye he caught sight of something, two doctors walking past in an adjoining corridor. Lucas couldn't be sure, thanks to the yellow Tyvek suit they were wearing and the surgical mask, but judging by the way one of them moved, Lucas was certain he knew who it was.

'Chiara?' The name was a breath more than anything. The second time had more conviction. 'Chiara,' he repeated, but still garnered no response. The pair of doctors disappeared from view. After checking that the phone wielding nurse wasn't paying attention to him, Lucas followed them.

He slipped around the corner, looked left and right, but couldn't see them. Then Lucas spotted them through the windows of another set of double doors. He pushed through and called her name. This time she turned around and Lucas saw different coloured eyes, a different shaped face. Despite the similar build and gait, it wasn't Chiara after all.

But something wasn't quite right. She stared unblinking at him, and what he had mistakenly thought to be Chiara's confident posture was actually a tense and rigid one. It was almost as if she were scared of something.

'You shouldn't be here,' she said, a slight tremble in her voice. 'This is a restricted area.'

'Sorry, I got lost. Maybe you can help me, though. I'm looking for Kallum Taylor? He's a patient here.'

She was visibly agitated upon hearing the name, and that discomfort only grew when an announcement came over the PA system. 'Would Dr Dannen make her way to ICU. Code Red. Dr Dannen to ICU. Code Red.'

Lucas looked at her. 'Is that call for you?' he asked. She didn't reply, just glanced at her companion, and before he knew it, a kick flashed out and struck Lucas in the head, slamming him into the wall. Before he could regain his senses, they delivered several punches to his kidneys, doubling him over.

'It has been a long time since we crossed paths, Redmond.'

Lucas recognised the French tinged accent straight away as that of the Senegalese assassin, Babou. They had first encountered each other in Peru when Lucas was on his honeymoon with Natasha, and Babou had been hired by an arms dealer known only as The Peregrine. They had come across one another many times since.

He was a formidable combatant who only ever worked with his trusted associate, Diouf. Together, they formed a deadly duo. Lucas was more than glad there was no sign of his partner right now, because at 7'4" the former Senegalese wrestler was one hell of a handful.

'Not long enough, if I'm being honest,' scoffed Lucas. 'Where's your lackey, Diouf? Did he finally get tired of hearing you yap on?'

'You have more important things to worry about, don't you think, Redmond?' Babou delivered another punch to emphasise the point, causing Lucas to splutter blood due to the continued assault on his kidneys. He dispensed of his medical disguise, revealing his usual all black garb; combat boots, cargo pants, T-shirt and shoulder holsters for his Indonesian Karambit knives.

'You know something? You're right! I still haven't decided what I'm going to have for breakfast dinner tonight.'

'Always with the jokes, huh?'

'Well, there was something else, actually.'

Babou saw Lucas's eyes dart to the right and followed them. 'Putain!' He shouted just before the fire extinguisher connected with his chin, leaving him sprawled out on the floor.

'Come on,' Lucas said, taking the doctor by the arm as they headed for the exit. 'We have to go before he gets up, or his friend comes looking for him.'

'Too late!' Doctor Dannen yelled.

Diouf's huge frame ducked through the doors and instantly surveyed the scene. He saw his comrade laid out on the floor, and the woman that had been with him. Then finally a recognised foe. The assassin lashed out with a kick, landing a size twenty-two shoe flush in the shorter man's chest.

Lucas skidded along the corridor, dragging the doctor part of the way. 'We need another way out,' he wheezed as he rubbed his chest.

'This way,' the doctor said, taking the lead. 'The emergency stairs are down the other end.'

The pair skipped past the recovering Babou, reached the end of the hall and slammed open the door to the stairwell.

'Who are those men?' Doctor Dannen panted as she threw off the protective suit before they raced down the stairs.

'Hired goons. Two of the best.'

'Well, what do they want with me? After they killed your friend—'

'My friend? Kallum?'

'Yes! They killed him. That's what that Code Red was about. It was weird. The smaller one put on surgical gloves, then he wiped something on your friend's hand, and he seized almost immediately. Blood came out of his skin, his eyes ... then they said, in a not so pleasant manner, that I had to go with them.'

'Bollocks!' Lucas spat. It had been a simple idea, come and question a man in hospital, and it had all turned to crap in a second. 'Did he say anything?'

'Kallum? No, he couldn't. He reached up for my pen. I think he wanted to write something, but they dragged me away.'

Lucas glanced at the ordinary-looking BIC biro, then his attention was drawn away as he heard the door above bang and looked up to see Babou glaring down at them.

Chapter 12

The May sun beat down on Natasha, bathing her with vitamin D. The mid-twenties temperature felt good on her skin as she stood at the entrance of the airport. She called Alyssa to let her know she had arrived, and moments later, whilst she people watched, her friend pulled up and honked the horn.

The two women greeted each other with beaming smiles and hugs. Alyssa told Natasha over and over again how grateful she was for her help, and for getting there so fast.

'Come on, Alyssa,' pleaded Natasha. 'To be honest, you're the one doing me the favour. Having the chance to see this lost treasure is a great honour.'

'And what about Lucas? I would have thought that he would be coming with you?'

Natasha had totally forgotten that Alyssa didn't know about her divorce and didn't really know how to tell her; no one was proud having a divorce on their record. But at least she could be safe in the knowledge that the break down was not of her doing. 'Well—uh, Lucas and I are no longer together.'

'Oh,' came Alyssa's high-pitched response, not knowing exactly how to react to the news.

'It's okay, it was very amicable. We've moved on. I'm with someone new now.'

'Well, as long as you're happy, that's all that counts.'

'And I am,' Natasha said, fiddling with a loose strand of her hair. 'I'm really eager to see these coins.'

'I bet you are. So what we will do is take your things to the apartment, and then head off to the metallurgical lab where we're having the unknown coins analysed.'

'Awesome. I can't wait.'

It was a short journey from the airport to Alyssa's apartment at the Lazär residence complex, in central Iasi. As they drove, Natasha saw a city that was rebuilding itself, jumping forward in leaps and bounds, confining its communist past to history, and repairing the damage of repression caused to the country under the rule of the dictator Ceausescu.

The apartment block, along the Strada Zimbului, was a stone's throw away from the Palas Mall, another testament to the cities desire for modernity, which all the citizens seemed to embrace, as long as it didn't come at the expense of nature.

The lab Alyssa had mentioned, where the unusual coins from the rediscovered treasure were being analysed, was at Alexandru Ioan Cuza University of Iasi, the first university in Romania, even though an institute of higher education had operated there since 1640.

After the unification of the Romanian Principalities of Moldavia and Wallachia by the Prince Alexandru Ioan Cuza, the inaüguration of the University of Iași, the first Romanian modern university, was to be a steppingstone to modern higher education in Romania.

Alyssa led Natasha through the grand university, parts of which resembled a museum, an opera house and yet others like an art gallery. Their destination however wasn't as lavishly decorated. Simple whitewashed walls and black-and-white tiles adorned the floor, but the decor was the last thing on Natasha's mind.

'This is it,' Alyssa announced as she knocked on the door before opening it. 'Hello? Marius? It's Alyssa.'

'I'm in here,' came the slightly muffled reply.

The lab had a bookshelf to the right of the door, which Natasha could see was filled with all kinds of textbooks on the subject, from An Introduction to Metallurgy to Extractive Metallurgy of Rare Earths. They passed equipment such as crushers and pulverisers, super agitators and balance tables.

At the back of what Natasha soon discovered to be the smaller of two labs was an office, but before reaching that room, Alyssa led them through a door on the right into the second larger lab, which also seemed to be equipped with similar but newer machines, along with hi tech computers and powerful microscopes.

'Are you still analysing the coins? I thought you would have been finished by now, Marius.'

'I did,' Marius said, leaning back from the microscope he'd been peering through and stretching before sliding his glasses in position from the top of his head. 'This is the third time I've gone through the entire process. Oh, you have company.'

'Yes, this is a friend of mine, another archaeologist. She's here to help with identifying the providence of the coins. Natasha Travers, this is Marius Anghelescu, Romania's preeminent metallurgist.'

'Nice to meet you,' Natasha said with a wave of her hand.

'You too. So, you're the one that says these coins are Moche?'

'Well, yes. I only suggested they might be, judging by what I saw from the photos Alyssa showed me.'

'That's why she's here, to get a closer look.'

'Okay, help yourself.' Marius rolled back his chair, giving Natasha space to access the microscope.

She put her eyes to the lens, and a smile slowly etched across her face. Seeing something from a lost civilisation for the first time always gave her a giddy feeling inside. She likened it to being high and history was her drug of choice. 'It seems like this is definitely a design from the Moche civilisation. This is Viracocha. You can tell by the intricate metalwork. Even though their most used techniques were derived from the preceding civilisation in the region, the Chavin culture, the Moche perfected those and invented further techniques that were still in use a thousand years later. These markings, the lines and zigzags, etcetera, also seem to be examples of a proto-language associated with the Moche too.'

'Ah the Moche, my favourite of ancient craftsmen. Pioneering electrochemical replacement plating and depletion gilding,' Marius shook his head with disbelief at their achievements, then he grinned mischievously. 'You really should see some of their other works, Alyssa, especially their ceramics.'

'Why is that?'

'Because,' Natasha cut in, 'on their pottery, the most important social activities to the Moche were documented, war, metalworking, weaving, farming and erotica.'

Alyssa groaned and rolled her eyes. 'I should have known.'

'It is like ancient pornography. There is even one of an infant breastfeeding while the parents have sex, in a way so as not to have another baby, if you get my meaning,' he winked.

'Fellatio is also represented, but cunnilingus is not,' so they weren't completely enlightened, were they?' Natasha sneered. 'Anyway, back to the task at hand.'

'To be honest, before I began my tests, I thought they were from that civilisation too. But now, I'm not even sure it's from earth.'

Natasha looked at Alyssa, who was just as dumbfounded as she was. 'What?'

'That's what I said,' Marius admitted. 'Why do you think I've gone over everything repeatedly? Turn the coin over.'

Natasha looked around for a pair of gloves. Once she'd slipped them on she tried to flip the coin and discovered how deceptively heavy it was. She turned to Marius, eyes wide. 'What is it made of?'

'That's the thing ... we have no idea. It looks like gold, has some of the same characteristics. It's malleable, but it's a lot heavier. Like the artists of Chavin, the Moche mostly used alloys because they didn't mine. Their materials contained some combination of gold, silver, or copper, which was abundant on the surface during their time.'

'So it is an alloy?' Alyssa asked.

'Yes, I suppose. But not like any alloy that's been tested, and I mean ever tested. It is not on our periodic table for a start. It has unusual levels of carbon, sulphur, gold and copper.'

'What do you mean unusual?' Natasha queried.

'Take gold, for instance. 24 karat gold has a fineness rating of 999, which is accepted as being pure gold.'

'Hold on, what's that rating?'

'Fineness. It expresses the percentage of gold to other metals in parts per thousand. 18 karat has 750, 9 karat 375. It's a much more precise scale and easier to understand. Anyway, it was thought to be impossible to produce 100% pure gold based on current technical limits. Removing tiny molecules of other material could not be done. The purest gold minted to date was in Australia. The fineness of that was 999.999.'

Natasha let out an impressed whistle.

'Hold your applause because those Peru coins have a gold fineness of 1000. I've triple checked it and the gold is as pure as you can get.'

Both archaeologists were speechless. This wasn't just the biggest find of Romania; it was probably one of the biggest finds ever. Natasha turned back to the coin, seeing the image on the reverse side for the first time.

She creased her eyebrows in fleeting recognition of the effigy and peered through the microscope for a closer look. It was as she thought, a horned and fanged head.

'What is it, Natasha?' Alyssa asked when she saw her friend's look. 'Have you found something?'

'Yeah, it's Supay. It is roughly translated into diablo in Spanish.'

'Devil,' breathed the Romanian archaeologist.

'He is the god of death and the ruler of Ukhu Pacha, the underworld.'

'So the god of life on one side and the god of death on the other. What does it mean?'

'I have no idea. I haven't seen anything like this before.'

Chapter 13

Lucas stared up the stairwell at Babou and smirked as the assassin glared back at him. There were ten floors between the two of them, but Lucas and Doctor Faye Dannen only had another five floors to go before they'd reach the ground floor and the freedom of the car park.

The one-time SAS trooper thought their escape was all but assured. Babou had other ideas, suddenly vaulting over the railing, into the vertical shaft of the stairwell. He bounded back and forth, dropping down one level at a time, twisting in mid-air to clasp the railing on the lower floor.

'Bloody parkour mother—. Move it Doc!' Lucas shouted and started making his way down to the exit, taking two steps at a time. Every flight of steps they descended, he could hear the Senegalese hitman getting closer and closer. 'Come on doc, we're almost there!'

Lucas and the Dr Dannen reached the first floor, touching distance of the car park, which they could see through the large windows. The goal was in sight. Three move flights of stairs and they'd be at the exit. But out of the corner of his eye, Lucas saw something which he had no time to react to, Babou swinging from above, slamming knees first into his already sore chest. The force and momentum of the attack sent them both smashing through the glass.

'What the hell is going on here?' DCI Russell wondered aloud as he saw two men flying through a window. One landed heavily on the roof of a car, whilst the second impressively bounced, rolled, and regained his feet.

'Look!' DI Wilkins said, indicating the shattered window. 'Isn't that Dr Dannen?'

'It certainly is. And, if I'm not mistaken, that's Lucas Redmond picking himself up off that car.'

'What's he doing here? And with the doctor?'

'That's what I intend to find out. You'd better call it in, Wilkins.' The detective stepped out of his car just as Faye exited the hospital.

Lucas groaned as he rolled off the car and got to his feet. He had been winded by Babou's attack, and the fall onto the car roof had done nothing to help except save him from cracking his head open on the concrete. He felt like he hadn't escaped injury completely, however.

'Jesus! Are you alright?' Faye asked as she checked on her saviour.

'I'll be fine, I've been through worse,' grimaced Lucas as he quickly surveyed the scene. Babou was advancing on them, a curved Karambit blade, his preferred weapon of death, in each hand. On his left, he saw the giant Diouf burst out of the hospital's main entrance. Things were looking bleak, but they would have been far worse if Lucas had not spied Jake Russell stepping out of his car. 'Don't worry doc, the cavalry's here.'

'Call me Faye. And you're Redmond?'

He nodded. 'Lucas Redmond. Okay, Faye, you see that man ahead of us by the car? He's a police detective. When I give the word, you're going to run to them and get the hell out of here.'

'What about you?'

'I'll be right behind you,' he said it more out of hope than any true conviction.

'Police!' Russell yelled as he saw the wicked-looking knives drawn. 'Stop right there!'

The chance for Faye's escape came sooner than Lucas had expected, assuming that it would be down to him to make it, but as he saw the bladed Babou turn to see who was shouting at him, Lucas sent Faye running.

The assassin caught sight of his target as she ran past him. He slashed after her, but the shoulder tackle he received from behind sent him to the ground, his blade only cutting strands of her flowing hair.

Diouf sprinted over, his long stride covering the distance quickly. Lucas slammed his fist into Babou's face, trying to keep him down and out of the combat before his giant partner got involved. Lucas glanced over his shoulder to see how far the big man was. That split second was all the time needed for the Karambit blade to cut a deep slash in the right side of his abdomen.

Lucas cried out and clasped his hand over the wound, feeling his warm blood seeping out between his fingers. In his crouched position, Babou attacked again, aiming for Lucas's groin. He knew he was trying to cut his femoral artery and make him bleed out.

In one swift move, he lifted his right leg to block the strike before he crashed his knee into the side of his assailant's head, dazing the paid killer.

Then Lucas felt the punch from Diouf's huge fist, right in his kidney. It dropped him to one knee, such was the pain driving through his body. The second blow came, but he could block most of it, as well as the third. The fourth struck hard, thanks to Babou's interference.

The knife wielder tried to get in on the act, slashing viciously, left and right at Lucas, until the unarmed man could catch one of his flailing arms and hip toss him into Diouf, hoping to take them both off their feet.

It didn't work. Babou flew through the air from the throw, but Diouf caught him with barely a step back. The giant grinned mockingly at Lucas, who swallowed, knowing he faced an uphill task.

All of a sudden, Russell and Watkins pulled up in their car. 'Get in!' Jake yelled, and Faye opened the back door. Lucas held his side as he ran for the car, jumping in as soon as he could.

He didn't see Diouf put Babou down, nor did he see the smaller of the two Senegalese assassins give chase. But he did hear one of his knives screech along the side of the police officer's car as they drove away, leaving the two hitmen watching them.

• • • •

FAYE LIFTED LUCAS'S T-shirt to get a better look at his wound. 'I'm no surgeon, but even I can see that you're going to need stitches.'

'Don't worry, I'll get it seen to.'

'Do you want to tell me what the hell that was all about?' DCI Russell asked. 'Who the hell were those two men? Dr Dannen told me they killed Kallum Taylor.'

'They're hired goons,' Lucas replied. 'The shorter one is Babou. Former Senegalese special forces, and trained in several martial arts; Pencak Silat, Eskrima and Krav Maga. The 7'4" giant is Diouf, former Laamb, Senegalese wrestler. Kallum must have known something, and his employers thought he would spill, so they made sure that info didn't get out. What were *you* doing in the neighbourhood, Russell?'

'I had some questions for Dr Dannen here, regarding the missing person case I'm on. Seems like providence was guiding us, or else we would have had another missing virologist on our hands.' The detective paused for a moment as he gathered his thoughts. 'Which makes me think that the kidnapping of Karen Fletcher wasn't financially motivated after all.'

'Tiger kidnapping, sir?'

'It would seem so.'

'What is that?'

'Tiger kidnapping is taking a hostage to make a loved one or associate of the victim do something. Taking the child of a banker in order to get them to open the safe, something like that. The only problem with that is the fact that Karen Fletcher is single and an only child. We'll look further into her parents, of course, but I'm thinking that it more than likely has something to do with her own career, especially after what just happened to you, Dr Dannen. That makes me wonder, what exactly is it you microbiologists do?'

'Well, first of all, microbiology encompasses numerous sub-disciplines including virology, bacteriology, protistology, mycology, immunology, and parasitology. I, myself, am a virologist, so I focus on the structure, classification and evolution of viruses. The ways they infect and exploit host cells for reproduction, their interaction with the hosts physiology and immunity, the diseases they cause, the techniques to isolate and culture them, and their use in research and therapy.'

'So, what Kallum had was a virus?' Lucas queried.

'Yes. It's what we call a haemorrhagic fever virus, because the clotting problems lead to internal bleeding, as blood leaks from small blood vessels in your body.'

'Sounds like Ebola.'

'There are some definite similarities: fever, muscle pains, weakness, vomiting. Ebola is only transmitted through infected bodily fluids or contaminated sheets, clothing, or other items that have been touched by them. Whatever this virus is, it's also temporarily airborne when the host dies.'

'That wasn't made public,' detective Russell stated.

'No. It was deemed unnecessary to do so as the situation was rapidly contained and revealing that information would only cause panic among the populace.'

'Do you have any idea what it is?'

Faye shook her head. 'None. But I can tell you what it isn't. It definitely isn't Ebola, and the likelihood is that it won't be any of the deadly viruses we have on record.'

'So, you're saying that it's a completely new virus?'

'That's exactly what I'm saying,' Faye said with a grim look.

Chapter 14

Alyssa was shattered by Natasha's news. 'You really don't know what it is?'

She shook her head. 'I've never seen anything like it. I have theories, of course, but that's all they'd be.'

'Well, right now, I would gladly take theories.'

'Okay.' Natasha shrugged and picked up the heavy coin with her gloved hands. She turned it back over to the side with the Peruvian image of the bearded man holding a staff and a book. 'As I said before, this represents the Maker, the Creator God Viracocha, who rose from Lake Titicaca. He who breathed life into clay and began humankind, dressed and painted those people thus creating the tribes of the Andes.'

'Right, so he made the sun, the moon and the stars and everything.'

Natasha nodded and continued. 'Now, on the reverse side,' she turned the disc over again, 'we have the horned and fanged image of Supay, the god of death and the underworld. The evilest god, ruler over demons, he leads the way along the path of the dead towards Ukhu Pacha, a place of pain and suffering, where the wicked were sent, it also had another name, Supaypa Huasin, "the house of the devil."'

'Mmmm,' Marius said with mock enthusiasm. 'Sounds like the ideal holiday destination.'

'Doesn't it just.'

'So, you're saying that we have good and evil on either side of the coin?'

'Yeah. But they didn't use coins back then, Alyssa. Their economy worked on a bartering system. So, this isn't money; I think it's some sort of token. Perhaps for priests at the temples, both gods were worshipped after all.'

'Even the devil one?'

'Well, yeah. The domain of Supay was located deep in the earth, therefore, as the god of minerals, Supay was worshipped at cave entrances among the many mountains of Peru. They would pray for him to stay away. In fact, his worship is still alive among Andean miners and excavators today.'

'You know Two-Face?' Marius jumped in. 'From Batman? He has that coin that he flips to decide the fate of someone? Maybe it's like that. Maybe the priests used it to choose their sacrifices.'

'You said yourself that it is heavy,' Alyssa pointed out. 'Can you really imagine a priest flipping it?'

'Besides, children were usually selected as sacrificial victims since they were considered to be the purest of beings. The children ranged in age from six to fifteen, and had to be physically perfect and healthy, because they were the best the people could present to their gods. Every year, one hundred children were sacrificed to Supay.' Natasha paused. Something in what Marius said resonated with her. 'Maybe it has something to do with life and death. It makes the most sense. Viracocha for life, Supay for death. Still don't know what this thing would be used for, though. If only there were some way we could determine its provenance. Maybe knowing exactly where it came from might help.'

'You've been to Peru; Do you know anyone that could give us some insight?'

Natasha thought for a moment. She *had* been to Peru. Several times. The most recent just a couple weeks ago, but the first time had been when Natasha and Lucas were on their honeymoon. They'd been convinced to re-acquire an artefact, the Slippers of Viracocha, stolen by a Peruvian gangster. The woman who had done the convincing was a village elder by the name of Feliciana Sancho. 'I think I may know just the person.'

'Foarte bine! Do you know her number?'

Before Natasha could reply, four men suddenly entered the laboratory. Natasha couldn't help but notice the diamond studded necklaces they all wore, nor the Rolex watches on their wrists. They obviously had money to burn.

'George!' Alyssa yelped, her voice had a distinct waver. 'What are you doing here? I wasn't expecting you.'

'Of course not. Why would you? I have not heard from you in days. So I came to check on my investment.' George slowly walked around the lab. One of his associates carried a bag of peanuts which he dipped his hand into every so often, cracking the shells and discarding them where he pleased, before popping the two kernels into his mouth. Now and then he'd stop to get a closer look at a piece of equipment before moving on. 'Let get down to business. Where is my treasure, Alyssa?'

'It's — it's not here,' she stammered.

'I can see that. My question was where is it?'

'We needed to do some additional testing, that's all.'

'Forget the testing. I want my treasure.'

'The treasure will be going into a museum,' Natasha stated matter-of-factly. Both Alyssa and George spun around to glare at the archaeologist, one with wide-eyed panic the other with curiosity.

'Who are you?' George demanded, rounding on Natasha.

'She's a lab assistant,' Alyssa chimed in.

'Well, little assistant, if the museum wanted the treasure, they would have funded Ms Popescu's expedition. However, I bankrolled it. Which means all finds belong to me. Do you understand that?' Natasha met his stare, but the question wasn't for her.

'I do,' Alyssa replied.

'Good. I expect to hear from you tomorrow.'

'Tomorrow?'

'Is that a problem?'

'No, not at all.'

'Foarte bine. I will be back tomorrow then. Don't disappoint me, Alyssa. Or I will be forced to end our business arrangement. And I will want immediate repayment or there will be consequences. *Dire* consequences.'

With his final words hanging in the air, George and his followers left the laboratory. As soon as she heard the main entrance close, Alyssa collapsed into a nearby chair and let out a long sigh of relief. Marius rubbed his temples as he tried to alleviate the stress that was accumulating.

'What was that all about?' Natasha asked, looking from Alyssa to Marius. 'Who is that guy?'

Alyssa put her head into her hand. 'No one of importance.'

'That was George Hincu,' Marius revealed, drawing a stern look from his friend. 'Don't give me that look. I warned you about this, Alyssa.'

'What is it? Who is he?'

'He is the Nas of Clanul Ursilor.'

'And what's that?'

'The Godfather. He is the Godfather of the Romanian mafia.'

'Jesus, Alyssa!'

'These people are involved in the drug trade, human trafficking, prostitution, extortion, fraud, racketeering, loan sharking, and of course contract killing and murder,' Marius explained. 'And that's just the icing on the cake.'

'I never intended to give it to them,' Alyssa said, shaking her head.

'What?' Marius rolled his eyes in disbelief. 'Were you just going to disappear with the treasure? Because I've heard that mafias are incredibly good at making people disappear.'

'I don't know! I was desperate. I went through every official route and they all but laughed in my face. There was nowhere else to go. I knew I was right about the treasure's location. I just needed the funds to prove it. You would have done the same thing Natasha. I know you would have.'

'I — I don't know,' Natasha answered. She liked to think that her moral compass wouldn't have allowed her to do it, but if she were put in the same situation, she might have done the same. Natasha knew that she had an inherent need and desire to prove herself in her chosen field, to show that she was correct where others were wrong. But even with this flaw, Natasha knew deep down that she wouldn't have gotten into bed with these hardened criminals. 'You made a mistake, Alyssa, a big one. I wish you had come to me sooner.'

'How could I? I have always been in your shadow. I just wanted to step out of it for once.'

Natasha knew all about being in the shadow of a rival. When she was a youngster, first starting out in fencing, there was another girl who she could never get the better of, always coming second to her. The young Natasha eventually had enough and that was when she moved disciplines and became the best modern pentathlete she could.

Natasha never let anyone get the better of her again.

'Okay, we'll get through this, Alyssa,' Natasha reassured her. She took a strand of hair and twisted it as her mind formulated an idea. 'I take it this George character doesn't know the full itinerary of what was in the strongbox?' Her friend shook her head. 'Then we'll give it to him. Minus the Peruvian pieces, of course. They're the real find here.'

'So we're okay with funding criminals now, are we?' Marius asked.

'No, but we have little choice. Unless you know of a way to get out of this without giving them what they want. They get the treasure, but we get the true treasure. And we get to keep our lives to boot.'

Chapter 15

Faye Dannen sat in the police interview room, looking around, taking note of all the acacia wood that dominated the room. The table, cupboards, door, window frame were all made of the light-coloured wood, and the ecru coloured painted walls completed the neutral decor.

It was a pleasant enough space, considering where she was. The room was quite different from what she had expected and nothing like the interview rooms Faye had seen on TV or in the movies.

Through the large oblong window, it was possible to see police detectives working at their desks. Across the open office floor, Faye saw detective Chief Inspector Jake Russell striding towards the interview room.

'Thank you for waiting, Ms Dannen. This won't take long. It's just a formality, really.' He sat opposite the doctor and arranged his papers in front of him. Russell reached over to his left and started the recording equipment. 'Interview commenced 17:18hrs. In attendance DCI Jake Russell and Doctor Faye Dannen. So, Doctor Dannen, these two men, named Babou and Diouf, who attempted to kidnap you, have you ever seen them before? Around the hospital? In the car park? Hanging around near your home?'

'No. The first time I saw them was when they appeared in the intense care unit.'

'Tell me about that.'

'Well, I was entering the ICU making my way to the special area where Kallum Taylor was under observation, when I saw the big one—'

'Uh, Diouf,' Russell said after flipping through some papers, getting confirmation of the name.

'He wasn't wearing any protective clothing, so I immediately thought he was a visitor that had gotten lost. The other one, Babou, was wearing the lab coat of a doctor I know. Even with the surgical mask, I knew it wasn't him.'

More page turning. 'That would be a Doctor Joseph Ongida?'

'Yes.'

'I see.' The DCI read more of the page. 'Unfortunately, his body was discovered in one of the hospitals refuse bins. Initial investigations suggest his head was crushed.'

Faye brought a hand to her mouth. 'Oh my god! That's terrible. He was such a gentle, kind man.'

'I'm sorry for your loss.' He gave her a few moments to recompose herself before continuing. 'So you knew they were imposters? Then what?'

'Um, they restrained me, forced me to take them to Mr Taylor.' She paused for a second. 'Now that I think about it, he had a look of terror and recognition when he saw them.'

'As if he knew who they were?' The detective wrote some additional notes.

'That's what it looked like. Then Diouf put on some gloves and grabbed his wrist, forced his hand open. Then he put a gold coin in his hand.'

'A coin?'

'Yes, or something similar. I know it sounds weird, but that's what it looked like. It was a little bigger than a two-pound coin, maybe twice the size.' She used her hands to give a rough estimate.

'For the purposes of the recording, Doctor Dannen is indicating a circular shape approximately six-centimetres in diameter.'

'It had strange markings on it too.'

'Strange? In what way?'

'The image, it reminded me of something Aztec or Mayan, something like that. There were some lines, zigzags and dots too.'

'I see.' More note taking. 'And what happened next?'

'Mr Taylor's suffering increased almost immediately. The whites of his eyes turned red as the blood vessels in them ruptured. His breathing became laboured. He began vomiting blood. Eventually, blood came out of every orifice, even out the pores of his skin. It was like he was dissolving'

Jake Russell stopped and stared at Doctor Dannen in shock as he imagined the scene.

'That's when Babou said he was taking me away.'

'Did he say where?'

'No, just that I was needed elsewhere.'

'No hint or clue as to who ordered him to take you? A phone call perhaps.'

Faye Dannen shook her head.

'Alright, Doctor, I think that just about wraps things up.' Detective Russell was collecting his papers when he remembered something. 'One last thing. Do you know any of these people?' He placed a series of photos in front of Faye, and she leaned forward to take a closer look at them.

'Not all of them. Some of them I recognise from scientific journals, but I wouldn't say I know them. They're from various subdivisions of microbiology.'

'Yes, different scientists, of different nationalities, working in different countries.'

'What's this all about?'

'According to Interpol, all these people have been reported as missing in recent weeks. But this isn't kidnapping for ransom. There have been no demands. This is something else. It seems like people in your scientific field are the flavour of the month, Doctor Dannen. We can't take these disappearances lightly, and just in case our friends decide to come and visit you again, I'll have two officers posted to you at all times, round the clock protection.'

'Are you serious?'

'Deadly serious.'

Chapter 16

With the interview completed, DCI Russell held the door open to allow Doctor Faye Dannen to exit. 'Thank you once again, Doctor. If you'll just wait in the seating area, I'll find the officers that'll be watching over you.'

Faye nodded and took a seat next to Lucas. 'Police protection, huh? He thinks they'll be back for you then?'

'It's a possibility. I think he's just taking precautions. How's your side?'

Lucas lifted his shirt to show his blood-stained bandage. 'While I was waiting here, they patched me up and I'm good as new.'

'That's going to need redressing,' Faye replied, looking at the soaked gauze. 'You should have gone to the hospital; I told you it was going to need stitches. You didn't have to wait.'

Lucas pulled down his shirt again. 'I wanted to make sure you were all right.'

'I just realised I haven't thanked you for what you did, for saving me from those men.'

'Don't mention it. I get off on getting one over those two,' he laughed.

'I can't wait to get home,' sighed Faye. 'Get out of these things and have a nice long bath. You should come over.'

'Huh?'

Her face reddened. 'For a drink, I mean.'

'That's a shame; I'm quite good at washing women's backs.'

Lucas's mobile phone suddenly rang, saving the good doctor from any further embarrassment. 'Ellen! What's going on?'

'What do you mean "what's going on?" What have you done at the hospital?'

'You still on the police scanner?'

'24/7 bae bae!'

'Alright, calm down,' smirked Lucas. 'Babou and Diouf were there. They took care of Kallum before I even got a chance to ask him anything.'

'What a shame,' Ellen replied, each word dripping with sarcasm. Some things she could forgive and forget, but putting her back in the clutches of the foster parent who sexually abused her as a teenager was not one of them. 'That douche might have been a dead end, but as usual your girl, EP, came up trumps.'

'Your program has rendered the letters?'

'You sound surprised.'

'Just wasn't expecting it so quickly.'

'What can I say? I'm a genius.'

'Okay, okay, enough of the self-promotion. Just tell me what it says.'

'I can't.'

'Why not?' Moments later, he found out when he opened a file Ellen sent to his phone. 'It's a coded message!'

'Exactly. We can assume that any single letter words would either be an "A" or an "I" but even then, we're still talking about trillions of possible combinations. We need the cypher key.'

'Any idea on where we should start looking? There doesn't seem to be a return address.'

'France or Holland, I'd say.'

'Cheers, El! I think we might need to narrow it down a...' His voice trailed off. An idea formulating in his mind. 'F. Dubois. F. Dubois. I wonder...could it be...Francois?'

'Francois Dubois? And just who might he be?'

'A sixteenth century Huguenot artist.'

'You might need to elaborate on that. Let's remember that I'm not an international art thief, like some of us, Lucas, and that I don't know anything about painting. Furthermore, what's a Huguenot?'

'They were French Protestants who believed that the Catholic Church needed a radical cleansing of its impurities, and that the pope represented a worldly kingdom, where he was worshipped as much as God. They fanatically opposed Catholicism. With the wealth and holdings of the nobility that were Protestant, the Huguenots transformed themselves into a definitive political movement. Protestant preachers rallied a considerable army and a formidable cavalry, at its height their influence grew to sixty fortified cities and posed a serious and continuous threat to the Catholic crown.'

'Okay, I get it. Different religious views. My god is better than your god, although they're the same god, type stuff.'

'That's how it may have begun, but as the French Wars of Religion raged on for its thirty-six years, the battles became more political, pitting House against House. Not only holding rival religious views but staking a claim to the French throne as well.'

'But what's all this got to do with Dubois?'

'His only surviving work just happens to be the best depiction of the Saint Bartholomew's Day massacre, the day Catholics slaughtered not just Huguenot nobility, but men, women and children in the streets of Paris.'

'Damn, that's vicious.'

'The Huguenots we're no less vicious. They killed priests, monks, nuns, attacked and destroyed sacred images, relics, and church buildings. Most of the cities in which the Huguenots gained a hold saw riots in which altars and images in churches, even the buildings themselves torn down. Ancient relics and texts were destroyed; the bodies of saints exhumed and burned. But still, Protestant minds stuck to the conviction that Catholicism was a bloody and treacherous religion; several times there were peace agreements, and edicts allowing Protestants to worship freely without persecution, and each time the new king would undo the work of his predecessor.'

'This all sounds kind of promising. I mean if I were being persecuted in those times and I needed to pass messages, I'd do it in code too.'

'Yeah, there is one thing, though.'

'And what's that?'

'Francois Dubois died in 1584; over a hundred years before these letters were written.'

'That's kind of a big detail to leave out, Lucas. I got my hopes up and everything there. I was looking forward to going to Paris.'

'Don't worry, we needed a place to begin our search and Paris is as good a place as any. But one thing keeps coming to my mind. No matter what I do, it just keeps popping into my head; why would my mum be so desperate to get a Huguenot letter?'

Chapter 17

Both Natasha and Alyssa were deep in thought as the two archaeologists left the university along with a score of the institute's students. The discovery of Adela Cantacuzino Kogalniceanu's lost treasure was indeed a great find, a valuable one to boot. But it was undoubtedly the mysterious pre-Columbian coin, made from an unidentified material that was the real find of the treasure. And both women were excited to discover its origins, its provenance.

'I don't know why Feliciana's not picking up,' Natasha huffed as she ended the unanswered call. 'She must be out.'

'And she does not have a mobile phone?'

Natasha gave Alyssa a shrug of her shoulders. 'She's the elder of a Peruvian village, probably in her sixties, possibly seventies, so I'm thinking that being in contact whilst on the go isn't high on her list of life necessities. But I do know someone out there that has a mobile phone. Her grandson.' She eagerly scrolled through her long list of contacts until she came to the one she was after. Carlos La Cucaracha.

'His phones switched off,' Natasha said shortly after leaving a message. 'I can probably guess why; he's probably busy on a job.'

'Job? What does he do?'

'Oh, he's a thief. He pickpocketed Lucas, and we ended up chasing him around Machu Picchu, but that's a story for another day.'

Alyssa was aghast. 'What kind of honeymoon did you have?'

'A really wonderful one,' Natasha said wistfully. Memories of the fun times she and Lucas had came unbidden to her mind. And this was the reason why it was necessary for her to put distance between them. The feelings and memories were slightly less intense when they were apart. She just hoped that the new ones she was making with Peter were enough to take over the ones she had of her marriage.

'You'll have to tell me about it sometime,' her friend replied, genuinely intrigued. 'Well, since we have to wait for one of your friends to call you back, we might as well get some food. You hungry?'

'Yeah, I am a bit.'

'Good, because you're about to get a taste of Romania.'

A short five-minute walk from the university and the pair were on Strada Lascar Catargi. Like most of the city, the street was lined with trees. It was very quiet, despite passing several kindergarten schools, as well as being a short walk from a busy, wide avenue. New apartment blocks stood opposite older communist era ones, a testament of the country attempting to shake off its past. Alyssa led the way down the street, where they were soon at their destination.

'Welcome to Restaurant Oscar, home of the best Papanasi in the city.'

'Papa who?'

'Papanasi. It's a Romanian dessert,' she explained, deliberately being vague.

A waiter met them at the door and directed them to a table. Once they were seated in the olive-green chairs, as Alyssa ordered, Natasha admired the decor. The colours and hues worked well, the chairs matched with wooden tables stained and vanished a dark brown. The lilac painted walls divided by grey papered feature walls all gave a sense of sophistication without any of the pretentiousness other places had.

A pianist filled the air with a piece by Liszt, making for a delightful atmosphere. The evening crowd was building, as was the buzz. Natasha smiled as she looked around at the patrons enjoying themselves.

That's when she saw the intense dark eyes of a middle-aged man staring at them from across the restaurant. She felt a slight chill and shifted in her chair, her smile vanishing. 'Do you know that guy?' Natasha asked Alyssa.

She looked in the direction indicated, saw the man with white shoulder length hair and shook her head. 'Nope, never seen him before. You've obviously picked up an admirer,' Alyssa laughed.

'You must be joking. He's old enough to be my dad. Probably older than my dad!' Natasha glanced over at the man again. 'There's something about him. He's kind of creepy.'

Just then, their order arrived. Natasha had to admit it looked delicious. Two stacked ring donuts with a donut hole on top, covered in sour cream, with blueberry compote dribbled over the top, finished with a dusting of icing sugar. She took her knife and fork and cut into the decadent looking dessert and discovered that inside the donut was soft and fluffy. Alyssa leant forward in her seat, her eyes almost glowed with expectation as Natasha brought the first spoonful to her mouth.

'That is delicious!' Natasha barely finished the first mouthful before she was taking another.

'I know! It's a cheese dough, made with something like a cottage cheese. Totally different to your western donuts.'

'That didn't stop you scoffing loads of them.'

'Oh yes! Those bags of sugar ring donuts got me through long nights of writing my thesis.'

'I'd almost forgotten that sweet tooth of yours.'

The two women descended into laughter as the drinks came and they reminisced about their days at Cambridge, the people they'd kissed, the fun times they'd had, eventually.

After a few more drinks, Alyssa had to excuse herself for a bathroom break. Natasha watched her leave, her vision falling on the white-haired man again. He was still watching her, and Natasha had enough of it.

She forcefully pushed her chair back, emboldened herself, before making her way towards the man that made her skin crawl. 'What's your problem?' Natasha asked when she stood in front of him. 'Are you some kind of pervert?' Being up-close to the man, she could see that his eyes were like two pools of black: dead, lifeless. If they were indeed windows to the soul, then this man had a void in its place. Natasha swallowed hard, thinking that maybe she should have stayed in her seat.

Without saying a word or taking his eyes off of Natasha, the man took a deck of cards out of his black, single-breasted suit and shuffled them. 'My name is Maximilian Angel,' he eventually said. Natasha tried to place his accent, American, New Orleans Cajun, probably from the French quarter.

Maximilian continued to shuffle his cards. He cut the deck rotated one half through 180° before putting the deck back together and shuffling them once more. He repeated the process several times.

Then he began to deal the cards.

Chapter 18

Maximilian Angel took the first card and put it face-down. The second card he lay across the first, all the while repeating a mantra under his breath. The next four cards were placed around the first two, at points corresponding to a compass in a particular order: north, south, west, east. Finally, four cards were placed in a vertical line to the right of the others, the seventh card at the bottom and at the top, the tenth.

'What do you know of tarot?' he eventually asked.

'Not much, just that they're used for divination and that ancient Egyptians might have used something similar.'

He nodded and waved a hand over the laid-out cards. 'This particular spread is known as The Celtic Cross, one of the most widely used of tarot spreads. This section, the cross, covers what's going on in your present. The cards in the middle symbolise you, and that which challenges you. Around them are your immediate past, your immediate future, what is on your mind and what is at the root of the situation.' Maximilian then held his hand over the line of four cards. 'This is the staff. It gives a broader context to your question.'

'Question? I'm not interested in your card game. I just want you to stop staring at me.' Natasha turned to make her way back to her seat.

'You need to see this, Ms Travers. I have questioned the cards for you, and they have answered.'

She spun around. 'How do you know my name?'

'Why, the cards of course. I know a great deal about you.'

A shiver ran down her spine as Natasha was even more creeped out, but she found herself inexplicably taking the seat across from him.

'Now, shall we begin?' Before she had even responded, he turned over the first two cards. 'My, my, would you look at that.' The cards weren't like the classic image of tarot cards Natasha had seen in movies. They were black with a pair of wings on the back. The image on the face of the card were holographic horns. Written on the bottom was The Fool, but the picture was upside down. 'This card represents you. It marks the beginning of an adventure, the excitement of the road ahead. Encourages you to approach the unknown, a need to explore.'

'That actually sounds about right.'

'But reversed, as yours was, points to the more foolish qualities of the card indicating that you are out of your depth, that you are not thinking things through.'

Natasha scowled.

'This second card is what challenges you.' He turned it over. 'Hmmm, the Five of Wands. It indicates frustration, competition, conflict. It can be healthy competition but could always cross the line and become something darker. But I think this card more likely signifies a conflict within you, your fears, doubts, voices all trying to be heard.'

'I wouldn't call it a conflict. Everybody has doubts from time to time.'

He turned over the card at the top of the circle. 'The Emperor. The position of this card, being above you, shows a strong desire to achieve your goals and get things under control. The card below you, The World reversed, indicates that you're missing something in your life, an emptiness. Which explains your constant drive to your goals.'

Natasha hated to admit it, but some of what the creepy man was saying resonated with her, even more so when the next two cards were revealed.

'Your immediate past and your immediate future, The Tower and The Lovers,' Maximilian smirked. 'You have had a recent change. A total upheaval. A life-altering event. You have lost the life you planned for, an entire future laid out. And speaking of the future, The Lovers, signal a deep connection with someone. It also represents a choice that must be made. To summarise, you are out of your depth, Natasha. Conflict crosses you. Because of your recent loss, you feel empty, and try to fill the void by going on this fool's errand.'

'I have no idea what you're talking about.'

'Really?' Maximilian took the remaining deck of cards and fanned them out on the table in front of her. 'Pick one.'

Natasha looked at the cards, then into the black eyes of the dealer, finally back down and picked a card from the far right of the spread. 'The Ten of Coins,' she read, and placed the card on the table.

'The card of abundance, or in this case, treasure.'

She narrowed her eyes as she scrutinised the tarot reader. 'You work for the Romani mafia, don't you? What's his name? George?'

'I am but a humble conduit for the spirits, child, and I must finish conveying their message.' He turned over the first card of the "staff" to reveal an upside-down image of the sun. 'The Sun reversed, in this position, means an absence of joy, a lack of love, which compounds your feeling of emptiness.

But it is of your doing. The next card, the Five of Coins. Disappointment and regret, again linking back to your recent life upheaval, and your friends are likely aware of this and the effect it is having on you. This massive change you have endured is causing you to make poor decisions.'

Natasha searched her feelings, tried to attribute what she was hearing to anything other than what was plainly obvious. Lucas was still a major part of her life.

'Now, the final two cards. These represent firstly, your hopes and fears, and finally the outcome.' He turned over the first card. 'The Ace of Swords reversed. You are being challenged mentally, but you are surrounded by a thick fog of confusion. You move slowly, watching your step as you traverse, but if you take a wrong step...' Maximilian picked up the last card, looked at it, then threw it down.

Natasha gasped. 'Death!'

He nodded. 'If you continue on this path, this is the fate awaiting you.'

She looked at the cards without saying a word. Natasha had faced dangers before, plenty of times in fact, and she had always gotten through them. But Lucas had been with her then. It wasn't him physically getting her out of the sticky situation, though that did happen on occasion. Just having him near gave her the strength to push herself further and harder than she normally would. But that rock was no longer there for her. Now she had to face the dangers on her own.

'There you are, Natasha,' Alyssa said. 'I thought you'd gone up to get us some more drinks. I didn't expect you to be here, talking to your ... friend.'

'I was just leaving.' Natasha said and rose, eyed Maximilian Angel before leaving with her friend.

'Take heed of what you've heard here, child,' he said sternly as he packed up his cards. 'Change your course, forget the treasure, for it will be nothing but a curse to you.'

• • • •

ALYSSA AND NATASHA stepped out of the elevator on the third floor of her apartment block. They had decided to walk home, hoping to burn off some of the luxurious dessert and cocktails. It had given Natasha the time to tell her friend everything that had happened in her absence, and although she put on a brave face, the whole experience had shaken her.

'Oh, come on, Natasha,' Alyssa scoffed with a shake of her head as they walked down the corridors. 'You can't seriously believe that nonsense. There are plenty of Romani fortune tellers around if you are looking to be ripped off.'

'I didn't pay him anything. He just started doing it. He even knew my name.'

'You're famous, Natasha. You were on the news.'

'In the background. I was just a consultant, don't forget.'

'Well, maybe he's a subscriber to *Archaeology Today*. He's probably a fan.'

'Yeah, possibly,' replied Natasha as she tried to sort through Maximilian's reading in her head. Suddenly, she walked into Alyssa, who had stopped abruptly in front of her. 'Hey, what's going on?'

Alyssa put a finger to her lips and pointed at the door to her apartment. It was slightly ajar. She fished into her bag and drew out a can of pepper spray. Natasha looked on with wide-eyed surprise but followed behind Alyssa as she entered.

The place had been ransacked. Not a single corner had escaped the violation. The shoulders of the two women relaxed when they discovered the perpetrators were no longer there, despite all the lights being on.

Natasha pushed open her bedroom door and saw her underwear scattered across her bed. She felt disgusted at the thought of someone going through them. She'd never been through an experience like this before and hoped never to again. It didn't seem like anything of hers was missing, luckily.

'Those bastards!' Alyssa shouted.

Natasha rushed over to her friend. 'What is it?'

Alyssa handed her a piece of paper. 'It was attached to my door with this knife.'

On the paper was a drawing of the same bear and swords image George Hincu had tattooed on his arm. 'Clanul Ursilor did this? Were they searching for the treasure?'

Alyssa shook her head. 'This was more likely a warning to ensure that I give it to them. Rahat!' she cursed. 'Marius! I need to check on him. Let him know what's happened.' The shaken archaeologist took her phone out of her pocket and dialled the number of her friend. It rang, eventually going to voicemail. She hung up and tried again. Still no answer. On the third attempt, Alyssa left a voice message.

'Now what?' Natasha asked. 'I suppose we can't go to the police with this matter?'

'No, and to be honest I don't think I can stay here tonight.'

'Me neither. So let's grab a few things and find a hotel.'

• • • •

MARIUS STARED AT HIS phone. It had rung three times, in quick succession, one after the other. He was almost certain that it was Alyssa. He looked up from the phone and met the eyes of George Hincu. 'She's going to be worried if I don't reply.'

'She should be,' George said. 'I don't want her getting any silly ideas about trying to double cross me. If you had done what you were supposed to have, we wouldn't even be having this talk now.'

'She didn't tell me where she's hidden the bulk of the treasure. Alyssa is quite rightly being cautious. Whenever she needs me to examine something, she brings it with her, and takes back with her.'

'Then why am I paying you?'

'Huh?'

'What am I paying you for?' Anger and frustration built within George as he repeated the question.

'Um ... for ... for information,' a flustered Marius replied. 'The treasure has coins from Peru, unusual coins.'

'Tell me something I don't know.'

'You know about them? How? We were only certain about their origins when Alyssa's friend got here.'

'The westerner. My associates are interested in her too. They are the ones that want the treasure.'

'And they will have it,' Marius confessed. 'Alyssa intends to bring you the treasure tomorrow. But her friend has convinced her not to give you the Peru pieces.'

'What?' The gangster slammed his fist on the table.

'She didn't think you would know how important they were. That you were only after the jewels because you could fence them and make money.'

'Stupid, interfering bitch. I'm making more money from this operation than I could ever make from selling that shit. Clanul Ursilor is going big time. And all they wanted was this treasure, in its entirety.'

'Maybe I can change her mind, make her see sense. I'll tell her that she'd be a fool to cross you. What you did to her apartment will help sow the seeds of fear.'

'What *we* did, Marius. You told us where she keeps her spare key. You should own your involvement.'

'I think I have a much better use for you.' It was a new voice — a woman's. She walked into Marius' apartment with two of George's soldiers. 'But I do like your idea of putting fear into your colleague.'

'I didn't know you were coming directly here, Chiara,' George said in a somewhat submissive tone.

'It has been decided that I am to oversee the remainder of this part of the operation. Enrique Salas has journeyed ahead to make sure everything is on schedule for the next part.'

'It will be, as long as the plates and moulds are secured.'

'How can you be sure it will be if you have yet to obtain the material? And if Natasha Travers is whispering in the ear of this Alyssa, it is highly likely that she won't give it up easily.'

'Like I said, I think I'll be able to convince her to do the right thing.'

'I agree,' Chiara nodded. 'When she comes looking for you — which she will undoubtedly do when you don't turn up at work tomorrow — and sees what I'm about to do to your body, she'll have no doubt in her mind that we are not to be messed with and will eagerly give me what I want.'

Chapter 19

Lucas held the door of the police station open for Doctor Dannen as he accompanied her out. His mind was still trying to figure out what his mum was up to, a task easier said than done. She let people know just enough, and then only what she wanted them to know.

None of it made sense, and it frustrated him to no end.

'You sure you don't want me to redress this for you?' The doctor suddenly asked, pointing at Lucas's injury. 'I can re-bandage it until you can get to a hospital?'

'What? Oh, that. It's okay, I've patched myself up plenty of times before. I'll take care of it when I get home.' Lucas drew a business card from his wallet and gave it to Faye Dannen. 'I'm sure your guard is eager to get you home, so why don't you give me a call to let me know you've arrived.'

'Thank you, Lucas. I will.' As the doctor was about to step into the unmarked police car, Lucas's phone buzzed.

'Hey, Ellen, what's up? It's done already? Yeah, I remember; the one I swiped from the X-ray. Oh, so you just needed to render it, I see. So come on, what does it say? That's it? One stinking line? "Facing behind overlooking the park of the heart". Any idea what it means? Yeah, me neither. Anyway, I'm on my way home to pack a few essentials, then jump on my train to Paris. I'll speak to you when I get there, Ell. All right, bye.'

Faye waved at Lucas as the police car pulled away. As she disappeared out of view, Lucas called himself a taxi to take him back to the hospital; there was no way he was leaving his beloved Speedback GT a moment longer there. He was already expecting a huge parking bill from the hospital and didn't need it getting any bigger.

....

IT WAS A LITTLE BEFORE 8pm, an hour or so before sunset, and it was still bright outside. Lucas loved this time of year, when the days were long; 4am it was bright, 9pm the sun was finally deciding to put its head down. Compare that to winter, where it was dark and gloomy most of the day, not to mention cold. Now that his personal life had taken a different turn, perhaps it was time to reconsider an old plan he had, and winter in sunnier climes. He had shelved the idea when he and Natasha had gotten together, but now they we no longer...

It hadn't taken long to pack. He had become a dab hand over the years at being ready to go on the next adventure at the drop of a hat. But as he did, Lucas came across a suitcase labelled Chiara Harris. He glanced around the bedroom and realised just how much of her stuff was still there: perfumes, makeup, clothes, underwear, shoes.

The sight of them made his lip quiver, and he heaved Chiara's case onto his bed before angrily tossing her belongings into the opened suitcase. Lucas smirked momentarily when he came to a particularly skimpy pair of underwear. He could remember where they were when he had first taken them off her, but he shook his head to erase the image and balled up the red lace material and threw them in the case with the rest of her lingerie.

In no time at all, Lucas cleansed his bedroom of Chiara Harris' presence. Now, he just had the bathroom to do. But that could wait a few seconds. He reached for his phone and wrote a text. "I've packed up all your shit. Pick it up from here or the nearest charity shop. Your choice. And by here, I mean with the concierge."

No sooner had Lucas sent the message, his phone rang. Unknown number was displayed on the screen. He answered it slowly, remembering the calls he received from Baron Harris, Chiara's terrorist brother. 'Hello?'

'Lucas? It's me Faye.'

'Faye? Why are you whispering? I can hardly hear you.'

'There's somebody in the house.'

'What?'

'I can hear them moving around downstairs.'

'Where are the police that were assigned to you?'

'I don't know. The car is still there, but I can't see them.'

Lucas knew that probably meant they were already dead. 'Okay, send me your address. Stay hidden, call the police and I'll be there as soon as I can.'

'Hurry, Lucas. I'm scared.'

• • • •

TWENTY MINUTES LATER, Lucas arrived in Mortlake. He parked towards the end of the street and jumped out. As much as he wanted to sprint to the doctor's house, he knew he had to restrain himself. Who knew what kind of hornet nest he could be running into?

Lucas' eyes darted all around as he purposefully strode down the quiet street until he reached number nineteen. The unmarked police car he had seen Faye and the officers drive off in, was parked directly outside, but it was empty. He turned his gaze towards the house and slowly crept up the pathway.

The door was slightly open. He eased himself inside. There didn't seem to be any signs of a forced entry. Then he came upon the first officer's body in the living room. Lucas doubted he would find a pulse, but he checked anyway. The action confirmed that the police officer was dead. On closer inspection, Lucas could see deep bruising on the man's temples, wounds that he had seen before. Diouf killed his victims by crushing their head with one giant hand, whilst choking them with the other. He recalled the first time he saw him do it when their paths had crossed in Peru. The man had struggled at first, tried to break the grip, but in the end, he succumbed to the agony.

If Diouf killed this man, Lucas was more than certain that Babou wouldn't be far behind.

His mind returned to the task at hand, and he continued his search for Faye Dannen. He had cleared the ground floor, becoming progressively convinced that Diouf and Babou were no longer here, but he continued to be cautious all the same. Better to be safe than sorry.

He noiselessly ascended the stairs, his years of special service training serving him well. The first bedroom he checked was empty. In the second one, however, was the body of the second officer. His demise was obvious, exsanguination via the knife wound in his throat.

As Lucas continued on to the master bedroom, he tried to figure out the likelihood of what might have happened.

Had the officers heard a commotion and come running? Possibly. Faye had told him she'd heard something herself and that the officers were not outside. The question now, though, was where was she?

Almost in answer to his question, as he looked around the master bedroom, he heard something in the ceiling. She had a storage loft. Lucas went back into the hallway and saw the hatch. He reached up and pulled on the latch, opening the entrance and allowing the ladder for the roof space to extend.

'Faye! Are you in there? It's me, Lucas.' There was no reply. He tried again as he climbed the ladder. 'I'm coming up Faye.'

'Lucas!' Faye gasped when she saw his head slowly appear. 'It is you!' She scrambled over, and once they had both descended, she gave him a crushing hug. 'Oh, my god. I was so scared.'

He could feel her nakedness pressing against him through the silk dressing gown she wore. It felt good, but he had to keep his mind straight. 'Do you know what happened here? Who was it?'

'It was those same men from the hospital. I had just finished my shower, getting ready for bed, when I heard it...'

Lucas could feel the shivers going through her body. Knowing that someone was out there trying to kill you is never an easy thing to come to terms with, but he was impressed with how well she was doing. 'Why don't you put some clothes on and grab a few things; I think I should take you back to the station.'

'No. The police weren't able to do anything. Can't I stay with you, Lucas? I only feel safe with you around.'

He wasn't really sure if it was the right thing to do or not, and after he thought for a moment, he decided. 'Okay, Faye. You'll be doing me a favour actually housesitting for me while I'm gone. Go get your stuff and I'll let the detective know what's happened.'

• • • •

LUCAS WAS SURPRISED that DCI Russell was all for the idea of the doctor staying with him. He thought he might have suggested a safe house or something. But no, her being with a government agent and former SAS trooper seemed to be enough to give the detective a peaceful night. All he wanted was regular updates regarding her whereabouts, and he'd let them know if there were any breakthroughs in the case.

Whilst Lucas got the spare bedroom ready, he could hear Faye talking to the hospital, telling them what happened and letting them know that she'd taken some time off.

As she finished, Lucas handed her a Disaronno on the rocks. 'You look like a liquor kind of girl.'

She took the chilled glass and swallowed a big mouthful, almost finishing it in one go. Lucas topped it up again. 'Thanks,' she smiled gratefully. 'This is a nice place you've got. Awesome view too.' She got up and walked over to the floor to ceiling windows overlooking the River Thames.

Lucas turned towards her. 'Yeah, it's not bad. For a guy with thalassophobia, I always seem to end up with an apartment near the water.'

'You have a fear of open water?'

'Yeah, although saying that, it's mostly oceans and seas I have trouble with.'

'After what you've done for me today, and seen you in action, I wouldn't have thought you were scared of anything.'

'Only a fool is fearless; only the brave face their fear.'

'How long have you had the condition?'

'Oh, a long time. Since I was a kid.'

'These kind of things are triggered by some traumatic event. Did something happen when you were younger?'

Lucas didn't reply and took a sip of his drink. That day, his mum abandoned him on their heist had left a psychological scar that would never leave him. Faye could see that it was a closed subject and didn't push for more details.

'Forget I said anything. You've been kind enough to let me into your home, it's not my business to pry.'

'That's okay,' he lied. 'Why don't you get some rest? You must be tired.'

'I am a bit,' Faye replied, setting her glass down. 'Thanks again for letting me stay.'

Lucas took another sip and enjoyed the view of her walking upstairs to the spare bedroom, then he finished his drink and tidied up before he went to bed himself.

Barely thirty minutes had passed when he heard his bedroom door open. He sat up and saw the naked silhouette of Faye Dannen in the doorway. Moonlight bathed her body, accentuating the natural curves of her body.

'After everything that's happened today, I can't be alone tonight,' she said, walking towards the bed.

Without saying a word, Lucas pulled the sheets aside. She accepted the invitation and climbed in. He put an arm around her, and Faye moved closer towards him, putting a hand on his chest. It wasn't long before that hand was between his legs, and they were kissing...

• • • •

THE FOLLOWING MORNING came and as usual, Lucas was up early. In the background, he could hear a news report come on the TV, though he was hardly paying any attention. The G20 Summit, currently being held in Jakarta, Indonesia, was in doubt with several of the attendees suddenly falling ill to food poisoning. Delegates from the United States, Russia, India and China were said to have been affected and were under observation.

Lucas picked up the remote and switched the channel. The reporter was halfway through a story about a bungled heist in Brazil. A G4 security van had been stolen in broad daylight in a daring robbery, but in their attempt to escape, the robbers lost control of the van and crashed it, leaving its contents, £1,000,000 in Brazilian Reals blowing down the streets of Rio de Janeiro. He'd already made a breakfast of eggs, bacon, sausages and tea, and was getting hungry, but his guest still hadn't woken yet.

'Faye, you thinking of getting up today at all?' Lucas said as he sat on the bed, unable to ignore the urge to pat and squeeze her naked buttocks.

She slowly roused. 'You only have yourself to blame for my tiredness. I don't know how you can be so spritely after what we did last night.'

'It's exactly why I'm spry. Come downstairs, I've made breakfast.'

'Ooo, this is new. Sex and breakfast? A girl could get used to this. I'll be down in a second.'

Lucas stood at the window, watching boats slowly going up and down the Thames. He turned around when he heard Faye coming down the stairs and saw her with the bedsheet wrapped around her like a toga.

'Really?'

'I'm trying to regain my modesty.'

'Yeah, I think it's going to take a lot more than that sheet to do—'

Lucas's sentence was cut short as he saw the red dot of a laser scope moving across Faye Dannen's body.

Chapter 20

Time slowed down as Lucas dropped his tea and moved towards Faye. The only thing on his mind was to get her out of the way of the bullet that he knew would be coming any second.

And it did.

He heard the crack of the glass as he launched himself at the doctor. Then Lucas felt the burning sensation as the slug slammed into his shoulder. He spun in the air, crashed into Faye, landing in a heap on top of her, droplets of his blood spattering her face and chest.

'Are you alright?' Lucas asked her.

'Yes—yes, I'm alright. My god, you've been hit.'

'It's just a flesh wound,' he grimaced. As he gathered himself into a crouched position, making sure that Faye stayed low and out of sight, more shots came through the window, peppering the wall behind them.

Lucas waited for the would-be assassin to reload. When the opportunity came, he raised his head slightly above the sofa he was hiding behind and glanced out of his shattered window. Nothing looked out of the ordinary until the red laser beam flashed in his vision; the assassin was on a red and white Scarab 165 speed boat.

'I see you.' A hail of bullets had Lucas ducking down again. 'Get some clothes on, Natasha. We need to get out of here.'

Faye ignored him calling her a different name, putting it down to the stress of the situation. It was almost as if he were operating on autopilot, like he was bred for these kind of occurrences.

'It looks like they may have gone,' Lucas said to Faye when she returned. 'Either that or there's a ground team on the way to clean up.' Suddenly, a drilling sound came from the front door. 'Shit! I hate being right. Get back upstairs, Faye.'

She did as she was told, whilst Lucas crawled into the open-plan kitchen and armed himself with a couple of knives. He stayed crouched and made his way across the apartment and hid behind the front door, out of the view of the large living room windows and waited for whoever was out there to breach the door.

The drilling stopped, and someone slowly pushed the door open. The barrel of a Glock slowly came into view, then the hand holding it, the arm, then finally the masked head. The assailant was dead in seconds as Lucas swiftly stepped across the person, slicing their carotid artery and driving the second blade into their sternum.

Lucas was back to hiding when the fallen assassin's comrades responded, firing their own Glocks where he had once been. In the swift seconds it had taken him to despatch the first intruder, Lucas had seen that it was a three-man team that had been sent, and now he only had two left to deal with.

They slowly advanced into the reception room side by side; guns outstretched as they swept left then right. They were being cautious not to fall to a similar attack. It didn't matter, a thrown knife sunk into the forearm of one of the men and he dropped his gun.

He screamed as his companion tried to take aim at Lucas, but he had to move when the second came spinning towards him. With no guns trained on him, Lucas closed the gap between himself and the remaining two intruders. But there was a gun he'd almost forgotten about, the sniper in the boat. Several high-powered shells penetrated the sofa as he flew past it. Lucas thought that once he was in melee range with the other two, the sniper would stop firing, but he was wrong.

As the three men moved around each other, attacking, blocking, parrying, countering, a shot would occasionally ring out and delivering more damage to Lucas's apartment. He had to end this.

He rounded on the assailant with the knife sticking out of his arm and took hold of it. Lucas delivered a kick to the man's gut and yanked the blade out. The assassin yowled in agony, but it didn't last long as it was cut off when Lucas drove the knife deep into the man's chest.

With Lucas's attention momentarily occupied, the final intruder unleashed a ferocious barrage, battering him with his gun. Lucas defended himself the best he could, but he was being forced to retreat. As he stepped back, Lucas fell over the arm of his sofa. At that same moment, a bullet from the sniper blasted into the chest of the final intruder.

Without taking any time to dwell on his good fortune, Lucas scooped up the loose gun and was about to fire at the sniper, but they had already started the boat and were making waves up the Thames.

'Faye!' Lucas called as he checked the bodies. He wasn't expecting to find any IDs, so it came as no surprise when he didn't.. He satisfied himself with collecting the spare cartridges the men had. 'Come on! We're going after that boat so we can find out who's after you.'

The doctor came running down, only to slow her progress when she saw the bodies and carnage laid out in Lucas's apartment.

'Don't look,' he said and grabbed her hand. He led her, at pace out of the apartment towards the lift.

'How can I not? It's a morbid fixation we humans have with death and violence. Even the most straight and clean-cut person will crane their head when going past a roadside accident. Besides, the death of your friend, Kallum Taylor was far more gruesome.'

'He's not my friend. I told you, I only wanted information out of him, namely the people he worked for.'

They arrived in the building's underground parking and quickly came upon Lucas's own parking spots. His Speedback and Alfa Romeo were both there, but it was the third vehicle that he approach, much to Faye's surprise.

'It's a quad bike! How are we supposed to catch them on that?'

Lucas patted the black bike. Although it had been some time since he last took it for a ride, it was sparkling, like it had just had a wash and wax. 'This is more than an ordinary quad, trust me. It's a Quadski, that's had its engine tweaked a bit. Now, get on,' he said, handing her a helmet.

Faye did as she was ordered, but as she put on the helmet on, she still had her doubts about them being able to catch the speedboat, even as he revved the engine into life.

They came out of the parking lot and immediately crossed the creek onto Lots Road, and headed northeast. They thundered past the Lots Road power station redevelopment. The former building which once powered parts of the London Underground, derelict since 2002, was in the process of getting a new lease of life much like the more well-known power station, across the Thames at Battersea was now enjoying.

As they passed the shops and residential houses, the Thames came back into view. Lucas flicked several glances at the river until he saw the one he was looking for — the red and white speedboat with the assassin at the wheel.

They were cruising along, obeying the strict twelve knot speed limit in place for this section of the River Thames. They no doubt thought they were in the clear, thinking that they had gotten away with their assassination attempt. That was great news to Lucas. It meant he wouldn't have much distance to make up.

'There they are,' Lucas said to Faye over the helmet's intercom.

'Okay, I see it, but how are we going to get them?'

They rode over Battersea bridge, slowing down slightly to watch the boat glide underneath them. Lucas finally got a good look at the person driving the boat. It was Babou.

Once they'd reached the southern side of the Thames, to Faye's dismay, Lucas turned right, heading in the opposite direction of the boat.

'Where are you going?' Faye yelled in confusion. 'He's going that way.'

'Chill out, don't worry. He's not going anywhere.'

Within minutes, the doctor found out why he was so confident, as he turned into Old Swan Wharf, beside St Mary's church. Faye squealed as Lucas headed straight on and splashed into the Thames.

This was no ordinary bike. It was a Quadski, a product of a Michigan company, and it was also amphibious. Five seconds after Lucas flicked a switch, the wheels were raised, and the bike was in water going mode. The quad had a top speed of 45mph. But 45mph on water was a lot different.

The scenery on both sides of the river flew past them, and Faye held onto Lucas a little tighter. He didn't notice as he was completely focussed on catching Babou's boat.

Just as Lucas and Faye were approaching Albert Bridge, he spotted the assassin's boat, just over a mile ahead, passing Chelsea Bridge taking the slight right hander before he would sweep left toward Vauxhall Bridge.

That's when Babou spotted the fast-moving vehicle behind him. Even though he couldn't know for sure if it was Lucas or not, because of the helmet, he wasn't taking any chances. Who else could it be breaking the speed limit with such reckless abandon.

'Putain!' Babou growled as he pushed the throttle forward.

Lucas immediately noticed the wake behind the speedboat he was chasing pick up. 'He's spotted us,' he informed Faye, who was still clung on for dear life.

He leant forward, trying to make them as aerodynamic as possible, and it was working. Coupled with the Quadski's superior manoeuvrability, they were catching up. Fast.

And Babou knew it. He tried to create a bigger wash by zig zagging down the Thames, hoping to use the waves to knock them off. But it wasn't working. So he resorted to another plan. Halfway between Vauxhall Bridge and Lambeth Bridge, Babou stopped his speedboat, then picked up his rifle. Aiming it down the river, he waited for his target to come into view.

Chapter 21

When Natasha and Alyssa had arrived at the prestigious Unirea Hotel & Spa last night, the only room they had available at the time, which came with a twin bed, was a business suite.

Although they had deliberated about going to another hotel, they had ultimately decided to pay the extra and stay put. Firstly, because Alyssa was still shaken up by what George Hincu and his Clanul Ursilor had done to her apartment, and secondly, because it had a spa.

Natasha was looking forward to trying the spa a bit later when Alyssa was awake. But while her friend was still sleeping, she took the opportunity to take a moment by herself in the adjoining office to make a phone call.

She looked at her phone and found herself almost about to call Lucas. It was a reflex reaction, something she did out of habit ... *used* to do out of habit; when she was in trouble or needed help.

Natasha looked at her now bare ring finger, devoid of the bands Lucas had once lovingly given her. She sighed deeply and scrolled down to the number she had intended to call. Shaking her head to rid herself of the memories that were trying to encroach into her mind, Natasha smiled as the phone on the other end of the line was picked up.

'Hello, Natasha.'

'Peter? Hey, how are you doing? Didn't wake you, did I?'

'I'm well, and no you didn't; I was already up. How are you? How is everything going there?'

Natasha told Peter everything. Her explanation of events began with the mysterious Peruvian pieces and her thoughts of what they could be, and culminated with their discovery of the break-in.

'You should give them what they want, Natasha,' Peter said once she'd finished. 'Give them the treasure and come to Bucharest so I can keep you safe.'

'It's cute that you're worried about me, but it'll be okay. We're going to give them the treasure this afternoon, minus the Peru coins.'

'I don't like this, Natasha. Be sensible. I've read about what these mafioso do to people that cross them.'

'But they don't even know these coins exist.'

'And how do you know that?'

'Well, I don't, but it's a calculated risk.'

'A risk I wish you wouldn't take.'

'This is who I am, Peter.'

'No, this was you when you were with Lucas, reckless. But now you're with me, you must start acting like it.'

'Excuse me?' Natasha bristled at the remark. 'If you think it was Lucas that made me the way I am, then perhaps you've still got a lot to learn about me, Peter. Look, I have to go. I'll speak to you later.'

'That was a nice wake-up call,' Alyssa said, standing at the adjoining door. 'Sounds like you're in need of a spa treatment.'

Natasha nodded with a smile and quickly went to grab a towel.

• • • •

THE SPA TREATMENT WAS exactly what they needed, and they made sure that they made the most of it. After a stint in the sauna, the two of them had a full facial and finished off the regimen with a hot stone massage. Three hours later, the two women were sitting in the hotel's Citi-Zen Bistro waiting for their lunch to arrive.

When it did, Natasha had to admit that it was a feast for the eyes, and she was rather hungry, as was Alyssa, since they'd both skipped breakfast. Alyssa had ordered a traditional Romanian dish called Ciorbā Rādāuteanā, a kind of chicken soup with garlic, sour cream and peppers, which Natasha wished she'd ordered herself when she tried some of her friend's. But she was more than happy with her own dish, Seafood Pasta with squid, baby octopus, mussels and shrimps.

'So, after this, what's the plan?' Natasha asked between mouthfuls of freshly made pasta.

'We go and get the treasure,' Alyssa replied. 'On the way, we'll drop our bags off at the university with Marius.

'Are you going to take out the Peru coins?'

Alyssa thought for a moment, then nodded. 'You're right. Those coins are the most important part of the entire find. I can't give them to George Hincu. They'll go in the museum.'

'You're making the right choice, trust me. Gangsters want money, they're not interested in historical artefacts,' Natasha stated. 'I can't wait until this is all over and they're gone, so that we can get back to studying them.'

'You and me both. This has been an episode I don't wish to repeat anytime soon.'

'Yeah, be sure who you get into bed with next time, Alyssa.'

'I can say the same to you, after what I heard this morning.'

'That was just a little disagreement. It was nothing.'

'It's really none of my business. As long as you're happy and you're not compromising on anything.'

'I'm not.'

'So, he wants children? I remember that was something both you and Lucas wanted.'

'We haven't actually talked about...' Natasha trailed off as she realised she didn't know. In fact, she didn't know much about Peter beyond his wealth, career and his love of collecting pieces of history.

Of course, it wasn't necessary to know everything about a person at the beginning of a relationship, but there were some basic things that should be covered. Knowing that you were on the same page about having a family was one of them.

'You okay?' Alyssa asked, seeing Natasha suddenly zone out.

'Yeah, I've just lost my appetite is all.'

'Well, let's not waste this then,' she said as she reached over for the half-eaten pasta.

• • • •

THE TWO FRIENDS STOOD outside the Unirea Hotel and crossed the square the hotel took its name from. They waited at the nearby tram stop, where Alyssa had just enough time to buy a freshly baked pretzel for Marius, from across the street, just before the number 9 tram arrived to take them to the university.

It wasn't a long journey, but Natasha had been lost in deep thought the entire time, Alyssa almost having to drag her off the tram when they arrived at their destination. The status of her new relationship and its future plagued her. For the last six years, Natasha had known the path she was on and where her life was going. Everything had been planned out. Lucas had wanted children as much as she had. Ideally, a boy and a girl, they had already chosen names for them. Daniel and Sophia.

Now she was in a new relationship, and she didn't know if that dream was still a possibility. Her mind drifted back to what Maximilian Angel had read in the cards about her doubt, frustration, the emptiness. She instinctively clutched her stomach.

'That's weird,' Alyssa said as they arrived at Marius' laboratory and found it locked. 'He should have been here ages ago. Come on.'

Alyssa headed to the next classroom and interrupted the lecture that was going on, much to the chagrin of the professor giving it. 'This isn't like Marius,' Alyssa revealed to Natasha after they'd finished questioning the professor.

'That guy says he's probably off sick.'

'Yes, but no one had heard from him,' she replied as she fished out her phone and dialled his number. It rang, but there was no answer. 'We have to check on him.'

'Okay,' Natasha agreed, seeing the dread on her friend's face. 'Let's go.'

As they passed the newspaper stand a little further down the high street, Alyssa came to an abrupt halt and snatched up a paper. On the front page was a photograph of Adela Cantacuzino Kogalniceanu wearing a rather striking jewel-encrusted necklace. Next to that old black-and-white photo was a modern picture of a piece of jewellery that looked remarkably similar. 'That little bastard,' Alyssa said through gritted teeth.

'What is it?' Natasha asked, and paid too much of the local currency as Alyssa walked off with the paper.

'The person I trusted to look after the strong box has broken into it and put it up for auction.'

• • • •

TWENTY SWIFT MINUTES later, they had reached Strada Oastei where Marius lived. She rang the bell, panic in her voice as she willed him to open the door. When an elderly lady exited they were able to gain entry. Just like he knew where Alyssa hid her spare key, she knew where his was kept, and within seconds they were inside.

A smell of rotting meat with fruity undertones immediately confronted them. Natasha grabbed Alyssa's arm. She knew what it meant. Talks with Lucas had educated her as well as the frequent times they had encountered death on their adventures together. It was hard for her to tell her friend that the signs were not good for the scientist, but Alyssa pulled away and moments later she screamed as they found the body.

It was a gruesome sight, and she bolted to the bathroom to throw up. Marius' throat had been deeply cut beneath his jaw and his tongue pulled through. He lay naked in repose in a pool of his own blood.

Natasha went and checked on Alyssa, who was in hysterics, almost inconsolable, blaming herself for what had happened to her friend. Even though Natasha had never been put in this situation, her line of business was often dangerous, and it had toughened you up somewhat, but nothing could prepare you for seeing your friend mutilated. That would be hard for anyone to deal with.

'This is a warning from Clanul Ursilor.'

'We don't know that.'

'Of course it is. Who else could it be?'

'Do the Romani mafia usually do things like this? Because from my understanding, this is more akin to something the South American cartels would do.'

'I did this to him. I killed Marius.'

'It's not your fault Alyssa.'

'He was only involved because I asked him.' Tears poured down her face, lamenting the brutal murder of her friend. 'I'm going to call the police,' she declared. 'I don't care about anything anymore. That bastard George will pay for what he's done.'

Alyssa took out her phone. She wiped her eyes with the back of her hand so she could see what she was doing. Then she opened her recently dialled numbers and saw directly beneath Marius' name was one Ioan Prunea.

Natasha heard her friend take a sharp intake of breath. 'What's wrong?'

'I just realised something. What if George Hincu saw today's paper as well? He might pay my friend a visit.'

'Shit! Where does your friend work?'

'Not far actually. He works at the Anastasie Fatu Botanical Gardens. Maybe twenty minutes, if we go at pace.'

• • • •

THEY JOGGED AND WALKED their way there, arriving just about the time Alyssa had said they would. The gardens spanned some eighty-hectares, having a huge variety of flowers from across the globe, as well as Romanian flora. Natasha would have loved to have taken the time to have a proper look around. She loved flowers, but she and Alyssa were on a mission.

'Come on, Natasha, it's this way to the office buildings. We should find him there if nothing has...' she stopped herself, trying not to think the unthinkable.

'Let's not even go there, Alyssa.' She didn't want her working herself up over something that hadn't even happened. 'Who is this guy, anyway?'

'Ioan? He's an ex, Ioan Prunea. He had been pursuing me since high school, but then I left for England. When I came back, I finally relented. We had some fun, a few times, but nothing too serious. The old spark wasn't there anymore, but we remained friends. I thought I could rely on him, trust him, but I guess not.'

'I'll admit, it is hard finding a good man out there sometimes,' Natasha replied thinking of her own situation.

'There he is,' Alyssa suddenly said, pointing at a handsome, statuesque man with short mousey hair. 'Ioan!'

'There was no spark?' Natasha asked in wide-eyed shock as she looked him up and down. 'No spark with him.'

Alyssa shrugged. 'What can I say?'

He turned around and beamed. 'Alyssa? I wasn't expecting you today.'

'What the hell is wrong with you?' She marched right up to him and shoved him hard. 'Do you know what you've done?'

'What are you talking about?'

'You know exactly what I'm talking about. You're such an idiot.'

'Look, if it's about the necklace I can explain. They were changing our lockers, so I had to move the lockbox. When I was taking it to my mother's house—'

'You've hidden it at Elena's?' Alyssa looked at Natasha, both knowing the danger the woman could be in.

'—there was a little accident. I mean the box they were in was all rusty anyway. I tripped, and it broke open and some of the contents spilled out. So I got you a new lockbox and transferred everything over when we saw the necklace. She recognised it from a photo my grandmother had shown her.'

'The photo in the newspaper.'

'Yes. Adela Cantacuzino Kogalniceanu's necklace. My great grandmother worked for her as a maid, apparently.'

Natasha and Alyssa looked at each other again. Maybe there was something else, a piece of information, that might have been passed down along with the photo.

'I'm sorry, Alyssa,' Ioan said. 'I mean, it was just one piece. And I would have split the money with you.'

'You are such an idiot,' she repeated. 'I might have been the one to find the lost treasure, but I was being bankrolled by George Hincu.'

'What?'

'Exactly, Clanul Ursilor. So, you haven't stolen from me, you've stolen from the mafia.'

'Shit! Shit!' His back-and-forth pacing was fuelled by panic. 'We have to get it.'

'That's why we're here.'

'Someone called me earlier, asking if I had any other pieces. I thought it was the auctioneer, but it just as easily could have been them.'

'It's possible. They've already killed someone close to me.'

'Oh, shit!' Ioan turned and began to leave. 'Let's go! My car is around the back.'

They ran to the car park and quickly found his car, a dark blue Dacia Sandero, jumped into the hatchback and set off almost immediately.

Seconds later, a black BMW gently pulled out and followed the unsuspecting trio.

Chapter 22

As Lucas and Faye rounded the bend on the Quadski, his brow creased as he noticed that Babou's Scarab speed boat seemed to have come to a stop ahead of them, near Lambeth Bridge. A second later, he found out why.

He saw the flash from the assassin's rifle as Babou unleashed a barrage of bullets. 'Duck!' Lucas yelled and veered the bike away with one hand whilst blindly returning fire with the handgun in his other.

Faye screamed as she found herself in another firefight.

Lucas headed full throttle toward the Albert slipway beside the SIS building as he heard and felt the thud of bullets striking the vehicle. The wide Quadski collided with the side of the bank, damaging the front left corner.

'Are you alright?' Lucas asked, turning to check on her.

'Yeah, I'm fine. Now what?' she asked as she watched Lucas checking on the position of Babou. He hadn't moved. He was no doubt waiting for them to come back out, so he'd have a clear shot.

But Lucas had other plans.

He flicked the switch and the wheels of the Quadski move back down. Once they were fully in position, Lucas drove up the slip, with Babou none the wiser, and joined the light traffic on the Albert Embankment and headed towards Lambeth Bridge.

It wasn't so long ago that Lucas was being chased down this very road by members of J Organisation, men of The Baron. This time, however, it was him doing the chasing, and also in the opposite direction. He paused a moment as he formulated the next part of his plan.

They were at the Lambeth Bridge roundabout, and he stood up to verify the position of the assassin. He was still there. The question was, how could Lucas get back down there?

That's when he saw something and had a crazy idea.

'Things are about to get bumpy, Faye,' he warned before he set off again at top speed. He circled the roundabout, completing a loop, exiting at Lambeth Bridge heading directly towards a purple Lamborghini. With its low nose and the quad travelling at full speed, it was no problem to launch it over the barrier of the bridge, plummeting down towards the Thames River. In mid-air, Lucas raised the wheels of the quad once more. They plunged under the water when they landed, popping up again, charging towards the gobsmacked Babou.

He barely fired off a round before Lucas was upon him, crashing into the side of his boat with the hefty Quadski. The collision forced the assassin to lose his footing and gave Lucas the opportunity to jump onto the boat himself.

He was upon Babou in an instant, tussling with him for the rifle, stopping the Senegalese hitman from bringing the gun around and taking a direct shot at him. The assassin kneed Lucas in the side, the same side he injured the day before. He sneered on hearing his opponent's agony.

Lucas repaid the compliment by head butting Babou with his helmeted head. The man was dazed, and Lucas flipped the gun around and squeezed the trigger.

Click!

It was empty. Somehow, the hitman had ejected the cartridge as they wrestled for possession of the rifle. No matter, Lucas thought. He reached for the handgun he had tucked into his belt. It wasn't there. He glanced back at where they had landed, surmising that the pistol was somewhere at the bottom of the river by now.

Suddenly, Babou kicked Lucas in the wound on his side again before delivering punches to the shoulder injury he had sustained not long ago. Blood was visible from both injuries, and they were hampering Lucas.

Babou grabbed Lucas's helmet and wrenched it off of his head, snapping the chinstrap in the process. He then used the protective gear as a weapon, striking Lucas twice with it. The third attempt was blocked by the bloodied and bruised former SAS captain, and a sequence of lightning-fast blocking and countering ensued, culminating in Babou being disarmed and thrown down.

The tide had turned, and Lucas was just about to press his advantage when he heard the sounds of sirens, which could only mean one thing: the Metropolitan Police Marine Policing Unit.

Lucas paused, looking in the direction where it was coming from only to discover that it was coming from all around, up and down the river. Unbeknownst to him however, his hesitation gave Babou time to implement his secondary escape plan, a full-face mask with a micro rebreather.

When the police boats drew near, armed officers demanding no one to move, the assassin stood up, his back towards everybody, seeming to comply. 'I'll be seeing you, Redmond,' Babou suddenly said. Lucas saw the mask he wore and made a move to stop him. The officers shouted at him to stop, and he did, knowing that it was a heated situation and there were no doubt itchy trigger fingers among them.

The shouts from the police didn't stop Babou, however, and the Senegalese assassin dived over the side of the boat, disappearing in the murky depths of the River Thames, leaving Lucas and Faye to be arrested again.

• • • •

DAVID EVANS STOOD WITH Faye, having just secured her release from a holding cell at the Marine Policing Unit headquarters in Wapping. They waited outside the second cell as a marine officer opened the door and Lucas Redmond strolled out, chin up, chest thrust out, only to be met by the chief of Section 7's disapproving glare.

'When I offered you a position with S7, Lucas,' David began as he led the pair to his company car, a chauffeur-driven Mercedes V-Class, 'I was expecting you to give it a bit more respect, and not use it as a 'get out of jail free' card.'

'I was doing my duty, protecting the good doctor,' Lucas replied, climbing into the luxury electric MPV after the others.

'By taking her on a high-speed chase down the Thames and shooting up the place?'

'Actually, after what happened to my police escort, I feel safer with Lucas,' Faye piped in.

'And to be fair, the assassin was doing most of the shooting.'

'That's beside the point, Redmond. The first 'S' in SIS stands for secret. Try not to forget that.'

'I'll do my best.'

'Good, because it's time to get to work. It's actually good that you're here, Doctor. When I got the call from Lucas, and he told me you were the virologist working on Kallum Taylor, something became a little clearer. That's why I came myself.'

'And what might that be?' Lucas asked.

Have either of you heard the news about the G20 Summit in Jakarta?

'I saw a little about it on the news this morning before my place got shot up. Something about a bout of food poisoning?'

'That's the story that's been given to the world media.'

'Okay, so what's the true story then?'

'What we know is that several of the delegates are severely ill. With what, we don't know. What I do know is that their symptoms are remarkably similar to those of the recently deceased Mr Taylor.' David Evans handed Faye a folder he retrieved from a pocket beside him.

She flipped through the files, eagerly devouring the information, occasionally mumbling to herself as she read a particularly interesting observation. Faye finally finished examining the papers and handed the folder to Lucas. 'According to all the information here, it certainly sounds like it could be the same virus.'

'You're certain?'

She nodded. 'Everything fits. The symptoms, the progression timeline.'

'So they have no hope of survival?'

'Doubtful. The thing is, we don't know what it is, and the first person that was discovered to have it is dead. We're no closer to finding out what is much less find a cure. So, yeah, I'd say that their chances of survival are pretty low.'

David Evans took a moment to let the severity of the information sink in before he continued. 'All intelligence agencies have been put on this, including us. Given the likelihood of these two diseases being the same, and your mother's association with the deceased, she has become a great interest, Lucas. We must find her, and then see what she knows about what exactly killed Kallum Taylor.'

'We've already begun that. We thought if we could find out why she wanted the Brienne letter, we might get some idea of what she's planning. Ellen was able to find out what was in the letter Angela wanted, but there were two. One is an encrypted letter, and the other has the phrase "Facing behind overlooking the park of the heart." We've got no idea what it means exactly, but I'm sure it has something to do with the Huguenots, that's why I'm heading to Paris.'

• • • •

AFTER PICKING UP A few things from Lucas's apartment, which had police crawling all over it, dealing with the carnage he'd left, as well as glazers waiting to replace the window that was shot out, David Evans had the driver take them to King's Cross station.

'Good luck, Redmond. Keep me updated with your progress and work fast. We don't know if things are going to take a turn for the worse, so find her.'

Lucas nodded, and he and Faye headed into the train station.

People milled about, looking up at the departure and arrival boards. Some ran, desperate to catch their trains, a couple argued as they missed theirs. Lucas and Faye were early for their own, which had been rearranged, due to their unexpected delay.

They used the time to have a drink and await the announcement for boarding. Lucas, ever wary, nonchalantly looked around whilst Faye checked on her colleagues at the hospital. He was looking for anyone suspicious, taking particular note of anybody who paid him or Faye more attention than they should.

Lucas saw a man with a large brown bag checking his phone. He seemed to be making a point of not looking their way. 'You want to do what to me in Paris?' He said in a rather loud voice, which made Faye blush, and as he expected, heads turned their way, even if just fleetingly. But with the phone-guy didn't so much as look up. That made him a person of interest to Lucas.

He decided not to let Faye know about his suspicions, concluding that the doctor had been through a lot already, and was now relaxing a bit, safe in the knowledge that whoever was after her couldn't possibly know that she was leaving the country. Lucas wanted to leave her with that comforting thought, whilst he deliberated how best to deal with the extra baggage.

When the time came for boarding, Lucas made sure he and Faye hung back a bit, despite her eagerness to get on board the Eurostar. 'It doesn't matter if we get on first or last,' he told. 'We have reserved seats in first class.' In truth, he wanted to see what carriage the suspicious man got on, so he could pay him a visit later on.

Faye took the window seat as the pair easily found their carriage. Lucas had offered it to her, so that he could easily watch the aisle, just in case. He was enjoying the whole cat-and-mouse game. At times he was sure that he was grinning, thinking about the whole encounter. A few times, he caught Faye looking at him with a coquettish smile, no doubt thinking that his own happy look was due to her company. Right now, he didn't have the heart to tell her that wasn't the case. There was a time when he wouldn't have cared, and he felt that if he continued on this course, that could well be the case again.

She had reminded him of Chiara so much. Same height and complexion, similar hair, that it had been extremely easy to welcome her into his bed that night. And although they hadn't really discussed it, he didn't think that Faye was looking for anything long term either, just a fun way to let off some angst. Right now, the way things were between him and Natasha, that suited him fine.

Lucas was so deep in his own thoughts that he almost missed the suspicious man enter the next carriage. Looking down the aisle, Lucas saw him talk to another man, before he glanced up the aisle, making eye contact with him for the first time, then swiftly went back the way he had come.

That was it. Lucas's interest had been piqued. I think it's time to have a little chat with him, he said to himself.

Just as he was about to stand, their dinner arrived. Chicken with coriander, Brussels sprouts, kale, almond and sultana salad and, for dessert sticky date cake with butterscotch cream. It looked and smelled delicious, but Lucas could only take a quick bite before he excused himself.

'This is amazing,' Faye told him. 'You don't know what you're missing.'

'I won't be long,' he said and headed off.

Lucas loved travelling on the Eurostar. It was a quick, efficient and stress-free way to get from the centre of London to the centre of Paris in just over two and half hours. In less than an hour they would be pulling into Gare du Nord, just enough time to find out what, if anything, this character was up to.

He made his way through the carriage, with little issue apart from squeezing past the petit train steward, a moment which they both seemed to enjoy. Lucas didn't see the man at first, but as he continued down the aisle, he saw him come out of the toilet and almost freeze when they locked eyes again.

The man turned around and quickly made his way in the opposite direction, gently pushing past people at first, but when he saw Lucas was following, he became more forceful in pushing them out of the way.

Lucas knew he couldn't continue running. They were on a train after all, and at some point the man would run out of carriages. He had started in coach three, had followed him through coach eight and nine, where the bar was, and were now approaching the rear business premier carriage, coach fifteen.

There was only one more carriage left after this one, and the way the man was looking around, desperately searching for an escape that wasn't coming forthwith.

'I'm not going back!' the man yelled as he continued to retreat down the aisle away from Lucas.

'Okay, then don't. Doesn't bother me, just make sure that you stay away from me and Faye.'

'You're lying! Of course it bothers you, it's your job. You're a police officer. I don't know who snitched, but I'm not going back to jail!'

'I don't know what you're talking about. The only thing that'll bother me is if you do something to the girl.'

'I don't give a damn about no girl. Just stay the fuck away from me!'

The few people in the carriage watched the live drama unfolding before them. The door slid open behind the nervous man, and he found himself not in another seating carriage, but in the rear kitchen galley.

By the time Lucas had entered the coach, the man had armed himself with a large knife. 'You don't want to do this,' Lucas told him in a calm even voice, holding up his hands to show that he wasn't armed. 'Put the knife down. I just want to talk.'

'I'm not telling you shit, man!' He slashed the blade in an attempt to force the ever-advancing Lucas back.

'All I want to know is who is paying you. Who's your boss? You're running out of train. There's nowhere else for you to go. You might as well tell me.'

'If I tell you, I might as well slit my throat. So, I think I'll slit yours instead!'

The man lunged, thrusting the knife out in front of him. In defence, Lucas threw open one of the cupboard doors, slamming the charging man in his shins and knees, putting him off balance. As he fell forward, he was helped on his way by Lucas grabbing the back of his head and ramming it into the counter. Blood and several of the man's teeth flew across the galley and he slumped to the ground unconscious.

Lucas kicked the knife away before he rifled through the man's pockets, looking for any ID or any clue. There was nothing except for his ticket, a burner phone and a small key, probably for a suitcase, Lucas thought.

'Oh my god!' The petit train steward gasped as she arrived on the scene.

'Do you have anything to tie him up with?'

'Yes, we have zip ties.'

'Good. Get them. You'd better call ahead and have the gendarmes waiting for when we pull in at Paris.'

She nodded and made the call to the train captain.

Lucas left the stewards to take care of things as he pushed his way through the crowd that had gathered to watch, and headed back up the train, looking for the carriage the man had been sitting in. When he found his seat, he also found a padlocked bag.

He heaved it up onto the window seat and sat down and took out the key. Just as he was about to unlock the bag, the phone rang. Lucas picked up the call but didn't speak.

'Franco? A car will be waiting for you and Malcom. Get here as soon as possible. Hello? Franco?'

On the other end he heard a voice, ragged and a touch raspy, but all the same it was familiar. A voice he thought he wouldn't hear again. It was the voice of Enrique Salas.

Lucas was stunned. He was sure that he had died in Colombia, killed by the snakebite. Yet here he was, talking on the phone. There was no doubt in Lucas's mind. Enrique was alive.

'There you are, Lucas,' Faye said, coming to a stop next to him. 'I've been wondering where you got to.'

The voice on the other end of the phone suddenly stopped upon hearing the name. There were a few rasping breaths, then Enrique spoke. 'Lucas Redmond? Is that you? The architect of all my pain and suffering. We meet again.'

Chapter 23

Crossing the roads of Iasi was like taking your own life in your hands. Natasha also discovered that being a passenger in a car could be just as harrowing given the way Ioan was recklessly speeding in and out of traffic.

But it was understandable considering the danger he had inadvertently placed his mother in.

Soon they were turning into Strada Ciurchi and pulling up the driveway of his mother's house. The car had barely stopped before Ioan had jumped out, calling for his mum.

By the time Natasha and Alyssa had joined him in the house, he had already finished searching downstairs and was just making his way up to the next floor. With the three of them splitting up and each checking a room, it took no time at all to find Ioan's mother laid out on her bed, asleep.

All the tension left Ioan's body as he let out an audible sigh of relief. His mother woke with a start, initially startled by all the faces surrounding her. Her features softened when she recognised the face of her son and his ex-girlfriend. 'Alyssa! It's so good to see you again.'

'It has been too long, Mrs Prunea,' Alyssa replied, hugging the now seated elderly lady. 'This is my friend from London, Natasha Travers. If it's okay, we'd like to ask you some questions.'

Mrs Prunea scrutinised Alyssa through narrowed eyes. 'This is about the necklace, isn't it? I told you, Ioan, nothing good would come from messing with that treasure. It's cursed.'

'Why do you say that, Mrs Prunea?'

'Call me Elena. I say that because it's true. My grandmother, Xioczana was the one who cursed it.'

Natasha and Alyssa looked at each other and knew that they were about to garner vital information. They both sat at Elena's insistence.

'Her name was Xioczana, she was born in eighteen-ninety-seven in Nasca, southern Peru.'

'Your ancestor was from Peru?' Natasha wasn't the only one shocked by the news.

'Yes, she arrived here in nineteen-fifteen, something like that.'

'She came here alone?'

'No, no, she was only seventeen or eighteen at the time.' Elena thought for a moment and then corrected herself. 'Actually, she did arrive in Romania by herself, but she left Peru two years earlier with her uncle. But something happened to him in Madrid. They were separated, and she fled.'

'Ending up here,' finished Alyssa. 'Why did they leave Peru in the first place?'

'They were on a mission of sorts. My grandmother told me she came from a family of shaman, and that they would commune with the stars for enlightenment. During the Spanish invasion, a lot of their precious artefacts were taken, and they were tasked with returning them.'

'Tasked? Tasked by who? The people?'

'No, the gods. The story is that they were visited by them in their sleep and were told that they had to make this journey across the world.'

Natasha didn't know what to make of it all. It sounded like the kind of fantastical story you would tell your child, but did it have some semblance of truth to it, and if it did, how much? 'And what about this curse you mentioned, Elena?'

'Well, I don't remember how she ended up in the employ of Adela Cantacuzino Kogalniceanu but at this time Xioczana was staying in a Romani camp.'

'It's quite possible that she saw her at some fortune telling,' Alyssa hypothesised. 'It's well known that Adela became quite eccentric after the death of her husband, Grigore Kogalniceanu.'

'Yes, yes she was. And the fact that Xioczana was said to have the power of life and death, would make her even more attractive to an aristocratic that had a love of jewels and was paranoid about losing them. So she protected them with this.' Elena walked to her dresser where she pulled open the second drawer and after rifling through some papers, pulled out a plastic sleeve inside which was an old, tattered piece of paper. She handed it to Alyssa, who had a glance and passed it to Natasha.

'This is written in Quechua, the language of the ancestral people of the Andes, a rather classical form of it,' Natasha pointed out.

'Can you read it?' Alyssa asked.

Natasha shook her head and berated herself. 'My Quechua isn't what it should be. I know it was the primary language of the Incan Empire, but it wasn't a written language until the Spanish conquest. I'm assuming this was written around that time. Some words look familiar. I guess they haven't completely changed over the centuries.' Looking up from the page, she hopefully addressed the woman who had given it to them. 'Do *you* know what this says, Elena?'

'Unfortunately not. But I remember she said it was a kind of prayer or some such thing. I do remember the name of it though, Taki Kawsay Wanu.'

'Song of life and death. Well, I think that's what it means,' revealed Natasha.

'That doesn't sound ominous at all.'

'Do you mind if we take this?' Natasha asked, holding up the decaying piece of paper.

Ioan, seeing the understandable reluctance of his mother stepped in. 'There's a shop nearby that I can get it photocopied for you.'

'That'll be perfect,' Natasha said.

Ioan took the plastic sleeve with the tattered paper and left, saying that he wouldn't be long. 'So, Ioan told us he hid the treasure here...'

'Yes, against my wishes, I might add.'

'Could you show us where? Because we need to take it away.'

'Please do! I'll be more than happy to see it gone.' Elena led them down into the basement, where she moved a few packing boxes, before getting Natasha and Alyssa to pull out a couple of loose blocks.

Getting down onto her stomach, Natasha reached into the dark and dusty recess. She searched around with her hand, pulling it out quick at one stage, hoping that the clump of fur she touched was a dust ball and not the dead mouse that she suspected it to be.

Elena handed her a flashlight. 'Ioan pushed the box in as far as he could. You will have to climb in I think.'

Natasha grimaced, but knew that she was probably right. Getting back down, she shone the light in and sure enough, there it was, back and to the right. She had to turn her head to the side to squeeze her upper torso through the gap. As an archaeologist and adventurer, Natasha had to crawl through plenty of unpleasant detritus in her time. That still didn't mean she enjoyed getting cobwebs in her hair.

She grabbed the strongbox and heaved it out bit by bit. Once she was clear Natasha shook her head wildly, convinced she could feel something crawling around in it, and begging Alyssa to help brush it out.

Shortly after they'd taken the box upstairs and Natasha had cleaned up, they reconvened in the lounge. Alyssa threw open the lid and Natasha's eyes and mouth grew wide in amazement. The contents were a light show, and the sparkling gemstones and jewellery dazzled her. But what she was more anxious to see were the Peruvian discs.

'Be careful with those,' Elena said as Natasha reached for one of them. 'My grandmother always said that she left something in the treasure so that the curse would always stay with it.'

She paused as Elena made an action of spitting, which Natasha knew was a custom to ward off the evil eye. But then she picked it up with a look of wonderment on her face and placed it in her bag followed by two others.

Alyssa confirmed that including the one at the university, which was left there for Marius to work on. There had been four of the mysterious circular tokens when she'd first opened the strongbox.

Now, with the surprisingly heavy coins weighing down her bag, Natasha looked at Alyssa. 'You're sure you still want to go through with this?'

The young Romanian woman mulled things over in her mind. Should she go ahead with Natasha's plan of just giving them the jewels, without the strange coins? Or should she give George everything? She might have given him the whole thing once, and after what they did to poor Marius, Alyssa was tempted to give them nothing but an empty box. But, as much as she would have loved to have been able to do that, in her mind she knew that was not really an option, because she'd be looking over her shoulder for the rest of her life, probably. And the reach of the Romani mafia was a long one. So there was only one real option open to Alyssa.

'I'm taking it to the police,' she declared. 'I'll explain everything to them. About us finding Marius' body, everything. And then they can deal with it how they please.'

Natasha was taken aback by her friend's decision, but she couldn't really blame her. Even though Alyssa could have gone to the police at any time, it was probably the fact that they finally acted upon their threats, and in such a brutal way, that made her question herself and decide on what to do. 'If you're really sure that's what you want to do, Alyssa, then that's what we'll do.'

Just then, they heard the front door open and close as Ioan returned, with not only the promised photocopy but also company. A man with a sharply trimmed beard, decked out in an expensive watch, and gold bracelets stood behind him. The tattoo of the head of a growling bear with crossed swords beneath it was prominent on his forearm.

The man shoved Ioan to the ground. Elena rushed to aid her son and helped him up, whilst the intruder turned his attention to Alyssa. 'I do not think it would be such a good idea for you to involve the police in this matter. Mr Hincu would not like it.'

Chapter 24

Lucas stared straight ahead as he tried to process things. Hearing Enrique Salas on the phone had completely thrown him. He was the one after Faye, the one that hired Babou and Diouf, the one that sent the thug tied up in the galley after her. Enrique was behind it all. But why was still a mystery to Lucas.

'You know something, Lucas,' Enrique rasped down the end of the phone. 'I should really thank you. Thank you for leaving me for dead. Thank you for betraying me.'

'You brought that on yourself. I told you I wouldn't help you kill La Viuda.'

'And there he is. Hello Lucas. Truth of the matter is, I'm glad you didn't, because as they say, the enemy of my enemy is my friend. And La Viuda and myself have become incredibly good friends. By pooling our resources together, we have been able to make significant advances on where each of us was before, and our poppy fields are thriving.'

'I thought those would have been destroyed by the Colombian government.'

'Oh, they were. But Viuda had already started moving crops before they arrived. After our alliance, I was approached by someone and put in touch with a group who, like us, wanted to branch out into bigger things, and also a government that just loves selling off huge swaths of their land for the right price.'

'So you've just moved her drug business and set up somewhere else?'

'Our drug business. But that's not important. Since you have my delivery man's phone, I'm assuming you have his bag too. I'm willing to make you a trade, Lucas, the life of your woman for the bag. All you have to do is simply leave it where it is and walk away. That's all.'

Lucas glanced up at Faye. The bag for the girl. He'd been after the girl all this time now he was willing to give her up for the bag? Curiosity got to him. Lucas had to know what was so valuable to Enrique.

'You know what, Enrique. Since I'm the one holding all the cards, I think I might just leave things the way they are.'

'That would be idiotic of you, Lucas. But then you are a very stupid man. Have it your way. I'll take the bag from your dead hand, you piece of shit.'

'That's not nice,' Lucas replied, getting up. He still had the phone to his ear as he took the bag and motioned Faye to follow him. When they got to the toilets, they squeezed in. 'If you carry on with language like that, I'll have to spank you like the little boy you are.'

'Okay, okay. If that's how you want to play, cabron, then that's what we'll do!' Enrique ended the call, leaving Lucas to wonder what to expect from him next.

'That sounded like a nice call,' Faye said as Lucas slipped the phone in his pocket.

'Yeah, it was. Always making friends, me. It was the guy that's been after you.'

'It sounded like you knew him.'

'Our paths have crossed.'

'Any reason why he wants me?'

'Nope, but he wanted to swap you for the bag.'

'So it's important to him, then?'

'Exactly. And I want to know why.'

They shuffled around the small cubicle, and Lucas placed the bag on the sink. He took out the small key and unlocked the brown bag. Unzipping it, he pulled it wide open and looked inside. Beneath the handful of clothes were six Bibles.

'So I take it this Enrique is a bit of a pious guy?'

'Not at all,' Lucas replied and grabbed one of the Bibles. It had been a while since he had last picked up one of the religious books, but he was sure it had been lighter than this one.

He flipped through it, and soon found out why. The middle of the pages had been cut out, and in the oblong shape were nestled four metal plates.

'What are those?'

'Pakistani rupees, Nigerian naira, Brazilian reals, Euros. They're currency plates, used to print money.'

'Whoa! Now I can see why he was so desperate to get the bag back.'

'And why we're in deep shit now,' Lucas responded. He eased his head around the toilet door and looked up and down the aisle, making sure there was no one watching, then went back inside, locking the door again. 'From what I could understand from Enrique, the owner of this bag has a friend onboard. Someone named Malcolm. They're due to be picked up by car at Gare du Nord. We have to assume that Enrique has already told them what's happened, so they'll be on the lookout for us.'

Oh great. I leave London for Paris to get away from being chased, and I end up being chased anyway.'

'It'll be okay. We'll be able to sneak out with the passengers and disappear into the crowd.'

Faye was reassured by his words but couldn't hide the fact that she was still despondent.

Lucas lifted her chin with his finger. 'Don't worry, Faye. You'll be back looking through your microscopes in no time.'

Faye leaned forward and Lucas accepted the offer of her lips, they embraced each other and kissed, as the PA declared that they were now approaching Gare du Nord station.

• • • •

LUCAS GAVE FAYE HER overnight bag and squeezed her hand to reassure her, as they waited for the Eurostar train to come to a complete stop. As it pulled into the platform, he could see the armed police waiting for their prisoner, Franco. The one called Malcolm would no doubt be keeping a low profile if he had seen them at all. So, if they were going to try anything, it would probably happen outside of the station. He knew they had the slight advantage of knowing what he and Faye looked like, but if they were anything like Franco, they wouldn't be professionals, and would no doubt be an easy spot.

First up was identifying Malcolm.

'Are you ready Faye?' On the platform Lucas hugged her, pretending to nuzzle her ear as he spoke.

'Yes,' she breathed.

People smiled as they walked around the amorous couple, believing the romance in the Parisian air had already taken hold of them. They were now the last people in the passport check line, save for the train stewards, who were still with the police. All the passengers were eagerly heading forward, desperate to begin their holiday.

But there was one man that continually looked around at every opportunity. Then he heard his phone ring and quickly pulled it free of his pocket. He looked at the name that came up, "Franco" and he turned around to see Lucas looking right at him.

'Hello, Malcolm,' Lucas said softly to himself.

The man that moments before had been stalling was now in a hurry to get through passport control. His erratic behaviour, however, was causing him even more delays as the officer had question after question for him, scrutinising every word he said.

By the time he was through, Lucas and Faye were not far behind him as he hurried off, no doubt intending to link up with the others at the car. A bad idea, as he and the doctor would soon be out of Malcolm's vision, with the ability to go wherever they pleased. In this case, doubling back and jumping on the Metro. Like he'd said they weren't professionals, probably some small-time gangs Enrique was exploiting.

As Malcolm made for the exit, Lucas and Faye watched him from the upper concourse. Once he was satisfied that they were free of their tail, they made a move towards the Metro.

But as they stepped off the escalator, they caught sight of a tall black man pushing Malcolm aside.

Faye gasped. 'Isn't that—'

'Diouf,' Lucas finished. He saw the assassin directing his men, sending them to different exits, and he picked up the pace.

They raced down to the Metro station, Lucas making them pause at the map for a second. There was no one there waiting for them in the ticket hall. But that feeling changed when they got to Line 4.

They had just missed the train, and as it hurtled past, Lucas saw it was going to the final stop on the line, Bagneux Lucie Aubrac, but yet there were two men still standing on the platform.

There were two minutes until the next train and Lucas intended for him and Faye to be on it, without the extra hassle of people following them.

Lucas whispered to Faye, told her to stay behind him as they walk towards the only other people on the platform. As he approached them, he slipped the bag of Bibles off of his shoulder. One was looking down the platform in Lucas's direction, the other standing side-on.

As soon as he was close enough, Lucas swung the heavy bag at the closet one. The air was forced out of him, and he slid down the wall, winded by the attack. The other thug, swung at Lucas, which he easily avoided. He blocked the first punch and then delivered a second. The man tried to kick out, trying to force Lucas back, but he caught the leg and lashed out with a kick to the thug's exposed groin, leaving him in a snivelling heap on the ground.

The first thug had recovered and had also armed himself with a knife. He came at Lucas, slashing and thrusting wildly. The former SAS captain avoided the untrained attacks easily, only to realise too late that he was purposefully being forced back towards the edge of the platform.

Lucas heard the announcement saying the train was one minute away, and in the split second he took to glance at the tunnel, the thug made his definite move, cutting Lucas across the chest, it would have been deeper had his reflexes not kicked in.

But the step backwards he had been forced to take landed where there was no platform and Lucas tumbled towards the track. He instinctively reached out at anything to stop himself, and he grabbed his attacker, but the thug was just as off balanced following his assault. They both fell onto the track.

The platform was slowly filling up again, and Faye screamed as she saw Lucas topple over the platform's edge. She rushed over to help, and the two men struggled back to their feet before they resumed their combat. The thug had dropped his blade, and with it, any advantage he might have had.

His face was quickly bloodied and bruised before he reached for it again. Time Lucas took to spring back onto the platform, the L4 Metro train coming into view.

'Give me your hand!' Lucas yelled at the man. He did, but as Lucas was pulling him up, the thug slashed out with the knife again. Lucas instantly let go to avoid the razor-sharp blade. The train hit the man and he fell underneath the rumbling tonnes of metal. The driver applied the brakes, the train eventually coming to a screeching halt, but it was already too late.

Faye turned her head away, as did many of the other people now on the platform, the distinctive smell of burning flesh permeating the air. She came to Lucas who checked to see if she was alright.

'Of course I am. But how are you? It looks like your wounds have reopened,' she replied. Lucas winced as she pushed on the wound.

'I'll sort it when we're out of here,' he promised. 'Where's the bag?'

'The other guy took it,' Faye revealed, pointing at the fast retreating second thug, carrying the bag, but still in some discomfort.

Lucas smiled as he took her hand. 'Let's get out of here. We can take L5 and join up with L9 to get to the hotel.'

They soon vanished into the crowd that had been bolstered by the people being taken off of the train. The L4 would not operate again for some time.

The thug found Diouf and handed him the brown sports bag. The giant Senegalese man opened it eagerly and took out one of the Bibles, then a second and a third. All the Bibles were empty. The currency plates were gone.

Chapter 25

The Clanul Ursilor member glared at each one of them to intimidate the four people that stood before him. Natasha wasn't impressed, not when she'd actually come face to face with a real bear in Alaska before, and not a man in a tattoo playing hard.

'Mr Hincu thought you might do something stupid, so he had someone follow you. When he saw this morning's newspaper, he had me follow this idiot. And here we all are, at the same address.'

Natasha snuck a look outside, and sure enough there were two cars out front, with similarly garishly dressed men milling about them.

'So, is this all the treasure?' the man eventually asked. 'You haven't put anything else up for auction?'

Ioan shook his head.

'That's everything,' Alyssa said.

'Just take it and go,' added Natasha.

'I'll take it when I'm good and ready,' the man replied as he lifted the strong box and made his way out without another word.

Elena slammed the door behind him before sitting as she trembled from the harrowing experience. Alyssa and Ioan surrounded her as they comforted her. Natasha, in the meantime, was watching the Romani mafia outside. The man brought the jewellery cache to whoever was in the back of the car. A hand reached out to check the treasure, a female hand, a hand with a tattoo of a snake bearing its fangs.

Natasha staggered back gasping as she tried to control her breathing. 'We have to go,' she whispered. 'We have to go now.'

Alyssa wrinkled her brow. 'What is it, Natasha? What's wrong?'

'Your Clanul Ursilor are working with a terrorist group.'

'What? How do you know?'

'The person in the back of the car has that organisation's tattoo on their arm, and I think I know who it is.'

Alyssa went to have a look for herself. 'Whoever it is, they don't seem to be incredibly happy. They're spilling the jewels all over the place. You say you know this person.'

'Unfortunately. I think it might be Chiara Harris.'

'The one Lucas had the affair with?'

'The one whose brother I killed. Yeah, that one.'

'Shit! Yeah, we need to leave,' Alyssa agreed. 'Hincu may not know about the Peru pieces, but judging by the way she's digging about in there, I bet she does. Do you still have your car, Elena?'

'Yes, of course. It's on the side road.'

'Okay, let's move it.'

Elena Prunea led them to the back door of her house just as someone banged at the front door. Natasha stopped her just as she was about to open it, in favour of a more cautious approach, gently opening the door and looking all around, in case the exit was being watched.

It wasn't and they all quietly left the house, getting into Elena's small Fiat Uno. As they passed the side of the house, Natasha stayed low in the backseat as she saw Chiara, her nemesis, step out of the black BMW and head towards Elena's house.

'So where are we going?' Elena asked, not wanting to think about what the Romani were about to do to her house.

'I don't know,' Alyssa admitted, and looked at Natasha.

'First, we need to get this page translated and get these pieces examined.'

'Your friend in Peru?'

'Exactly, but since I can't get hold of her, we'll have to go ourselves.'

'What? I don't have the money for that.'

Natasha smiled. 'That's okay. I'm hoping that we'll be able to get a lift. We just need to get to Bucharest.'

• • • •

ALTHOUGH ELENA WAS not a mother to either woman, she couldn't help but do the motherly thing and insisted that they eat something before she took them to the airport. They had shaomas all round, which really filled the hole Natasha didn't even realise was there.

When they arrived at Iasi airport, whilst Alyssa and Ioan seemed to be rekindling their relationship with affectionate touches, Natasha spoke to his mum, telling her it might not be a good idea to go back home for a couple days.

'It is a good time to visit my sister I think, spend a few days out in the countryside. She has some Quince trees, makes delicious juice,' Elena lent closer and whispered. 'It makes even better wine. I'll bring you back a couple of bottles.'

'I'll look forward to it, thank you. And we're sorry for all the trouble we've caused as well.'

'Rubbish, it's that cursed treasure.'

Natasha had to admit that when she had first heard the moniker, she had thought nothing of it. But after seeing Chiara, maybe there was something to it. After all, Romania would have been the last place she expected to cross paths with her again.

She wondered why she was even here in the first place, and working with the Romani mafia no less, or rather they were working for her, Natasha corrected herself as she remembered the way the man had brought the treasure cache before Chiara, almost like an offering.

Having said their farewells, in just over an hour later, Natasha and Alyssa were touching down in Bucharest Henri Coandă International Airport. It was a much bigger terminal than the one they had just left. Being the country's busiest airport, it made sense that it would have to be.

'So, Natasha, what is you plan to get us to Peru?'

'Peter, of course. I figured it would be harder for him to say no if both of us were standing here in front of him.'

'Are you crazy? You think he's just going to drop everything to take us halfway around the world?'

'He doesn't have to drop anything; just loan us the plane, and a pilot.'

'This is a stupid idea,' stated Alyssa as Natasha took out her phone.

'Hi, Peter.'

'Hello, Natasha. Have you calmed down?'

'Of course. I wouldn't be in Bucharest otherwise.'

'What? You're here?'

'Yeah, I'm at the airport, but I need to ask a favour.'

'You don't have to worry about taxi fare. I'll send my car to pick you up.'

'That's genuinely nice of you, but actually it's kind of a bigger favour than that.' Natasha saw Alyssa mouth the words "huge" and turn away.

'Really? I'm intrigued. What is it you need, Natasha?'

'A plane.'

'What?'

'I need to go to Peru.' The line went silent. 'Hello? Peter? You still there?'

Alyssa rolled her eyes. 'I told you.'

'Natasha, it will take two hours to get the jet ready. I will be there in one.'

'You don't have to do that, Peter. I know that you're busy having meetings.'

'Yes, but they are meetings that can be conducted without me. Besides, I'm curious to see what these Peruvian artefacts you mentioned are like. They must be quite something to have you travelling around the world.'

'To get the full provenance of them, we need to start at the beginning and see where they come from. That means going to Peru. We have so many questions about them, not just what they are, or what they were used for, but what are they made from.'

'I hope you are being careful with them. That you're not handling them too much.'

'Of course,' she felt like an old schoolteacher was reprimanding her. 'I'm not some newbie, you know.'

'Just making sure. I need to make some quick phone calls, then I will make my way to the airport. See you soon, darling.'

Chapter 26

Hotel Le 123 Elysees was a nice hotel in a prime location, a perfect base for people who spent most of their time away from their accommodation, experiencing what Paris had to offer. 123 rue du Faubourg Saint Honore, 8th district, was renowned for its fashion houses, antique shops, art galleries and gourmet restaurants. A few hundred metres from the Champs-Élysées, it is an area where you'd better be sure your credit card won't scream whenever it's used.

Although he hadn't stayed here with Natasha, he remembered that the apartment they had rented wasn't too far from here, a bit further down the road, closer to the beautiful Champs-Élysées avenue itself.

Once they'd checked in at the hotel, Lucas did as he had promised and saw to his wounds, with the help of Faye.

'I really think that you should get this checked out, Lucas,' she said, inspecting the stomach wound. 'It doesn't look good. It could be infected.'

'I'll get it sorted soon. As soon as we've done what we need to here.' He grimaced as he pulled his shirt down, signifying that the subject was closed.

'And what is it we need to do, Lucas? Do you even know? I'm sure dying from sepsis isn't part of it.'

'Look, nobody's dying. Okay? I've dealt with much worse things. And as for what we need to do, we go to the Huguenot church near the Louvre and ask a few simple questions.'

'And what about the plates?'

'I'm going to give David Evans a call, let him know, and see what he wants me to do. See?' Lucas grinned. 'Everything is under control.'

• • • •

THE LOUVRE, THE WORLD'S most visited museum, is home to some of the world's most famous works of art, including the Mona Lisa and the Venus de Milo. The Musée du Louvre contains more than 380,000 objects and at any one time 38,000 objects are being exhibited. The building could be considered art itself, from its beginnings as a military fortress. It was converted into the royal residence, being rebuilt in the French Renaissance style.

Along the Rue de Rivoli, opposite the Louvre, adjacent to the Cour Carrée, is Temple Protestant de l'Oratoire du Louvre. Once Catholic and made the royal chapel to the Louvre Palace by Louis XIII, it not only played host to the funerals of that self-same king but also that of Cardinal Richelieu. Looted and striped of its decor during the French Revolution, it was given to the Protestant congregation by Napoleon, who was attempting to take power from the Catholic Church and instal himself as the head of a new religion.

It was safe to say that the religious building had seen a lot in its time. Lucas just hoped that it had some secrets left to give.

'That is Gaspard de Coligny,' Lucas said as they passed a statue of a man, who had one hand on his sword and the other over his heart. 'He was the leader of the Huguenot movement until he was brutally murdered by Catholics during the St Bartholomew's Day massacre.'

'In the name of God, I suppose.'

'Isn't it always?'

'That's why people should own up to their actions. Just say you killed people of this other faith so that yours could prosper. I'd have more respect for them then. This planet needs humankind to see and do what is necessary to help it to heal. Not to sit in a wooden box asking how many Hail Mary's I need to say because I had premarital sex. People need to wake up to the fact that a burning bush isn't going to materialise and tell us what to do to make things better. We were given freewill to do it ourselves.'

'You have something against the church?'

'I just believe that it has been corrupted by man and that the parishioners are being exploited because of what they're being told.'

'I understand what you're saying. If we were made in God's image, and God is everywhere, surely I should be able to speak to him in my own way and my own manner. It's almost as if capitalism has taken over the church.'

'So many things have been done in the name of religion, both good and bad. Perhaps it is time that things were shaken up. Time that the hierarchy was written anew.'

Lucas stared at Faye, his brows furrowed. 'How exactly would you go about doing that? There are over two billion Christians, almost two billion Muslims, just over a billion Hindus.' He laughed. 'Getting them all to suddenly change their faiths and beliefs would be damn near impossible. It would take an act of God!'

Faye was about to respond, but she held her tongue as they entered the hallowed building and were immediately greeted by a rousing rendition of liturgical music from the organ.

Lucas and Faye approached the nave, then waited for the appropriate time to interrupt.

'Excuse me,' he said when the organist had finished. 'I was wondering if you could help me. I wanted to ask the pastor some questions, historical questions. I don't suppose you could tell me where he is?'

'You mean "she". Pastor Adeline is not here right now, and to be honest, history is not really her forte.'

'Not even about Huguenot history?'

The organist shook his head. 'You don't need to know the history of your faith to preach about it. People come here to hear the word of God, not a history lesson about the hardships and persecution the early Protestants suffered.'

'I see. I'm sorry for interrupting you.' With a sigh, Lucas turned; this wasn't going to be so easy after all.

'Hey where are you going? Just because the pastor can't help you doesn't mean that I can't. My name is Jacques,' he said, holding out his hand, which Lucas shook. 'I'm a bit of an amateur historian, so I know a bit about my faith. What is it in particular you want to know?'

Relief lifted Lucas's spirits. 'Actually, I wanted to know about a particular person; Francois Dubois.'

'Dubois? The artist?'

'That's the one.'

'I don't know a lot about him to be honest, apart from his painting of the Catholic massacre. Very graphic. Depicts poor Gaspard being beheaded and thrown from his bedroom window while Queen Catherine de Medici watches on.'

'That's all? Nothing about where he lived, or anything?'

'Shortly after the massacre, he left for Switzerland. His painting the St Bartholomew's Massacre is hanging in the Museum of Lausanne. There isn't much of his work left, actually. Although it's said that he used to paint down by Pont Neuf bridge.'

'Okay. Well, thanks for all your help,' Lucas said politely.

'Did you know that the island the bridge crosses, Île de la Cité, was once known as Lutetia? This was during the Roman times, before Paris was Paris. And in the medieval times it was known as the heart of the city, because is at its centre.'

'Wait! What did you say?'

'Paris was once called Lutetia.'

'No, after that. About the heart of the city.'

'Oh. Yes, on the maps of Paris, Île de la Cité, is at the centre, so the heart of the city is a very apt nickname, don't you think?'

'It's bloody perfect! You've helped a lot, Jacques. Thanks! Come on, Faye.'

The two of them rushed out, leaving the bemused man to turn back to his organ and wonder why Francois Dubois was so popular all of a sudden. This was the second person that had asked about the artist today, but that person had made the mistake of asking the pastor.

It was just a short ten-minute walk to get to Plaza du Pont Neuf, but it took a little long thanks to Lucas's laboured walking. He didn't want to say anything to Faye, but he knew something wasn't right. He could feel it. The quicker they could figure out this clue the better.

'The clue,' he groaned and struggled on through the pain. 'The clue was "The key is facing behind overlooking the park of the heart". This has to be it. If Île de la Cité is the heart, then it only makes sense that Square du Vert-Galant is the park from the clue.'

Faye nodded and looked at the small triangular park. 'I think you're right, but what about the rest of the clue? What could that mean?'

'Well, there's the "behind",' Lucas jokingly thumbed towards the statue of a horse and rider.

'Wait a minute,' Faye said suddenly getting an idea. 'You might be on to something, you know. "Facing behind, overlooking the park". It must mean the barrier.'

Lucas looked at the railing that went around the plaza and his jaw dropped. Attached to it were hundreds, possibly thousands, of padlocks. 'Bollocks! Whoever wrote this message is obviously someone that has a sense of humour.'

'What do you mean? Wasn't it Francois Dubois?'

'No, he was long dead by the time this statue of Henry IV was put up. Besides, these letters are from the late seventeenth century, so I'm guessing that these letters were passing between people using code names.'

'Encrypted letters, code names, this is real James Bond stuff, but in Elizabethan times.'

'This kind of stuff didn't start in the Cold War, you know. Julius Caesar used encrypted messages, and the Vatican has the oldest spy organisation in existence.'

'You're joking, right? But then again, it's not that hard to believe, really. So, what is it we're looking for here?'

'Beats me,' he replied with a shrug. 'The message said, "the key" so it could be a padlock with the key still in it, or it could just be a padlock on its own.'

'Jeez!' Faye whistled as she looked at all the locks. 'How are we supposed to know which one it is?'

'Check them all, I guess.' Lucas coughed and wiped the sweat from his brow. Although it was a nice afternoon, with a deep blue sky and fluffy clouds, it wasn't the sun that was making him hot.

Standing at the middle of the railing, they worked their way outwards, meticulously checking each padlock, neither one really knowing what to look for. At times it was difficult to check since couples stood in the way and came to add new padlocks signifying the solidity of their loving relationship. But they carried on the best they could, hoping rather than knowing that it was there.

This is a waste of time, Lucas thought to himself. He blinked, trying to stay conscious. He touched the wound on his side and took a sharp intake of breath as the pain shot up the side of his body. He leaned heavily against the railing, refusing to give up. Lucas stood up resolute and carried on.

Then, like a flash, it came to him. The author of these letters was from the seventeenth century. The padlock used would likewise have been attached for centuries. The majority of the padlocks here were a little over a hundred years old, World War I wives putting a love lock on their hearts hoping to see loved ones again.

Back in the late sixteen-nineties, it would have needed to be tucked away, blended in with other such items, make it look like it was a padlock serving a purpose.

Lucas made a beeline for the joints of the barrier, clutching his side as he went. Faye joined him, thinking that he'd found something. There in the corner, at the bottom, was a padlock design he hadn't seen before. It was a triangular shape, seemed to be made of iron and obviously weathered by time. Lucas smiled and knelt down, in some discomfort, to get a closer look.

The padlock keyhole was quite large, and as he rattled it, in an attempt to pull it off, it was evident that even if Lucas wasn't injured, brute force wouldn't budge it. Laying down on his belly, so as to get an even closer look, he could just make out something on the back that looked like a panel.

Centuries of dirt and grime made it a tough job to get it open. But by using his own keys to scrape away at it, garnering strange looks from visitors to the site, Lucas could finally move it slightly. Then a bit more, just enough to be able to insert his key and gain a bit more leverage to slide it down.

He had opened the secret panel.

Lucas fished out the folded piece of paper within, before getting off of his stomach and sitting with his back against the railing. He breathed heavily, unable to feel the hard, uneven metal padlocks he leaned against, and carefully unopened the paper.

He read the message once, and was reading it a second time, when he heard the first scream. Lucas looked up, his vision blurred, heart thumping in his chest. He tried to focus and saw a woman, her face in shock, looking at the blood pooling on the ground beside him. A second scream rang out as Diouf suddenly pushed through the growing crowd, snatched the paper from Lucas's weak grip, then took hold of Faye and dragged her away.

Lucas tried to react, tried to reach out for Faye, but as he attempted to get to his feet, the effort became too much for him, and he collapsed unconscious in a puddle of his blood.

Chapter 27

Everything was going as Alpha and Angela Redmond had planned. With so many components to manage, things could easily derail. But at this point in time, everything was progressing perfectly.

She took a sip of her tea and re-evaluated that notion. Things weren't exactly perfect. The Romani mafia had failed in obtaining the remaining Peruvian discs, thanks no doubt to the interfering Natasha Travers. That wasn't the only slip up she had been informed about. Angela had been informed by Enrique Salas that his courier had lost the currency plates, to her son, of all people.

Her phone suddenly rang beside her.

She waited a few seconds, took another sip of her tea, then answered the call. 'Your ears must have been burning, Enrique. I was just thinking about you.'

'I wanted to update you on the retrieval of the plates,' he rasped.

'Do you have them?'

'No, not yet, but things are on track to retrieve them. Now that we have the doctor, Lucas will have to return them if he wants her back. We also have the message he found.'

'This was good news,' Angela replied. 'Get them to George Hincu as soon as possible; production needs to be amped up, because it is time to show the world what the media is hiding. Let them know that the world is about to go through a global shift.' She drank her tea again before continuing. 'I know that you have a grievance with my son, but

I hope I don't have to reiterate that no harm is to come to him.'

'But my face...'

'Is none of my concern, Enrique.' Angela could hear his laboured breathing. She knew the rage inside him could push him to chance his luck. Angela wasn't about to let that happen. 'I don't know if you know this about me, Enrique, but I am a great lover of history. I always have been. I literally devour it. One thing that I have noticed, is that throughout history, humans are capable of doing the most atrocious acts of violence against other humans. Be it for their god, for revenge, for land, for family, nothing is beyond the scope of what a person is willing or capable of doing to another person.' Another slow sip. 'Take the emperors of China, for instance. If you were caught committing treason the most serious punishment that could be meted out upon you was called Zhulian Jie Zu. Do you know what that means?'

'No, I don't,' he breathed.

'It translates into nine familial exterminations. Basically, not only you, but close and extended family members would also pay the price for your transgressions. Parents, grandparents, children over a certain age, and if they were married, their spouses too. Grandchildren, again over a certain age, and, again if they're married, their spouses too. Siblings and siblings in law. Uncles and aunts, as well as their spouses. Cousins. Your spouse and their parents.'

'In essence, the Salas name would be wiped out. In addition, nine of those exterminations were done by slow slicing, or more commonly known as death by a thousand cuts. But I think that's going too far, wouldn't you say?' Angela paused, leaving her words hanging in the air. She let him think about what she had said, visualise it, and ultimately defeat himself, after all, your own imagination can often be your worse enemy.

'I do.'

Checkmate.

In truth she wouldn't have gone through with all that killing, but Enrique would never know that. She thought it was unnecessary, really. Once the idea was planted in his head, she would only have to execute two, maybe three, to get the point across.

'If you have such a pressing need for revenge, Enrique, perhaps you should direct it towards someone that I don't have a motherly bond with, namely Natasha Travers. I hear she is on her way to South America, probably Peru.'

'Well, I will make some phone calls and make sure she is given a proper welcome.'

'An excellent idea.' Angela hung up the phone. She finished her tea and arranged her machinations in her mind. There was only one more thing left for her to do. Angela scrolled through her extensive contacts list and selected one. When they picked up, it was a short conversation, consisting of two words; 'It's time.'

Chapter 28

Not far from Pont Neuf, in the shadow of Notre-Dame Cathedral, is Hôtel-Dieu, the oldest hospital in Paris. The ambulance crew that arrived soon after Lucas had passed out, brought him here.

The doctors had taken him in for surgery straightaway to stitch up his wound. There, it was discovered that an anticoagulant substance was inside the laceration, preventing it from healing, leaving it open to infection.

Lucas sat up with a start and blinked as he opened his eyes. It took him a few seconds to recognise that he was in a hospital, an intravenous drip protruding from his arm. He touched his wound, it felt numb, and he remembered what had happened. He'd found the old padlock with the hidden message...Faye had been there...but she had been taken.

'Faye!'

'Calm down, Monsieur Redmond,' a female voice said. It belonged to a blond middle-aged doctor who, upon entering the room, picked up the patient notes and skimmed through them. 'I'm happy to see you up, but you must not strain yourself or the sutures will not hold. Now, how do you feel? Numbness? Lightheaded, perhaps?'

Lucas nodded.

'It will pass,' she assured. 'Whatever blade caused the gash you have there, could well have been coated with some sort of anticoagulant, leaving it open for infection. Sepsis was also setting in as well.'

'Sepsis?'

'Yes, but don't worry, since we caught it early, this course of intravenous antibiotics will clear it.'

'How long will it take?' Lucas asked as he knew time was against him, especially if he was to rescue Faye from Enrique.

'Don't worry, Monsieur Redmond. You will be in perfect condition to be released tomorrow.'

'I can't stay here overnight!'

'Do not worry, your wife arrived while you were still under. She will be able to stay here with you.'

'My wife?' Lucas didn't know what to say, or even how they'd gotten a hold of Natasha. But none of that mattered right now. All that did matter was the fact that she was there to be at his bedside. He unconsciously tried to sit up straight to look his best.

The doctor was about to leave. 'Ah, here she comes now.'

Lucas knew the woman that stood in the doorway of his hospital room, but she wasn't his wife. She was someone that he had not seen in an exceptionally long time, but she had hardly changed. The same wide cheeky grin, under a mass of raven coloured hair which had a streak of white. It was more tamed now than it had been back in the day, when they were younger. She was fit and toned, though she had been a bit wiry as Lucas recalled, but she had definitely filled out as she matured from young teen into womanhood.

'Hello, Luca,' she said in an Australian drawl.

'Anne Sheppard,' he responded with a smile. It had been some time since he'd last heard his childhood friend's pet-name for him. 'Still haven't got rid of that stinking accent yet?'

'You still getting into trouble?'

'C'est le vie.'

They both broke out into a laugh before she went over to the bed and gave him a hug and squeeze, which drew a groan from him.

'Stop being a baby, Lucas,' Anne said, playfully punching his uninsured arm.

'You know, your husband has quite the singing voice. When they brought him in a few hours ago, he was mumbling something, turned out that he was singing.'

'Singing what?' Anne asked intrigued.

'The children's song, Frere Jacques. It must be one of your kid's favourites.'

'Oh, it is,' she said, her green eyes glistening.

'How many do you have?'

'Two. Luke Jr and Luisa. The apples of our eyes.'

'Aww, that's nice. Right, I'll leave you two alone, and I'll be back to check on you, Monsieur Redmond, in a few hours.'

Lucas waited until the doctor had left and closed the door before turning to Anne. 'Married? Really? And with kids, no less.'

'Yeah, of course. You forgot all our plans?'

As he thought about it, the memories flooded back. 'Oh yeah,' he breathed. 'But we were kids when we made those plans back then. I can't believe you remember it.'

'Of course I bloody do! Those were great days. The three of us pulling heists; me, you and your mum.'

'Yeah, I have to admit, they were rather good.'

'Do you remember what we used to do when we completed a job?'

'Tallied up our score card! Fastest to the target, fastest safe opener, MVT and the loser had to do a forfeit.'

'Yeah, you always won.'

'Most Valuable Thief, baby.'

'Do you know what my forfeit would have been had I won?'

Lucas laughed. 'No, but knowing you it would have been pretty fucked up.'

Before he could say a word, Anne lent over him and kissed Lucas hard and passionately. He was taken aback at first, but as images of his childhood shattered, he relaxed into the embrace and reciprocated, hoping that spending time in her arms might just be what he needed to get over Natasha.

He had once thought their friendship to be nothing more than being akin to that of siblings, under the guidance and tutelage of his mother. Even though they came from vastly different backgrounds, she went to public school and was the daughter of the billionaire Australian mining magnate, Glenn Sheppard. But despite all that, they had hit it off almost immediately. They were robbing the same house and had to help each other so they could escape.

Their hands roamed all over each other's bodies, like they never had before, seeing them in a whole new light. Anne manoeuvred under the sheets, feeling how much he wanted her, as he pulled her shirt over her head.

'What's going on?' Lucas mumbled during the few moments they broke for breath.

'Something that was inevitable, something that we've both wanted.'

Then Lucas stopped.

'How did you know I was here?' The thought came unbidden, crashing into his head.

'Are you serious? You got a sexy, half-naked raven-haired woman in your bed, and that's what's in your head?'

'I know! Trust me, I'm just as disappointed.'

'Alright. It was nothing but dumb luck to be honest. I'm in Paris on reconnaissance, and I thought I'd swing by Notre-Dame, see how the work was coming along. I swung by Pont Neuf on the way and saw all the commotion. Imagine my surprise when I saw that it was you. Now, can we finish what we started?'

They resumed kissing, Lucas's hands on separate agendas. One cupped her buttocks whilst the other was about to undo Anne's bra.

When he stopped again, much to Anne's frustration.

'Do I have to tie you down?'

'Just tell me my mum's not behind this?'

'What? No, this is all me, Lucas. I wanted this for so long, you don't understand. But we were kids back then and eventually ended up on different paths. You with your military career and me working with Angela.'

'Wait, you've been working with her all this time? You told me you were going back to Australia. You sent me letters when I was at Sandhurst.'

'And you don't know how difficult it was for me to lie to you, but Angela said that it was best for you.'

'You knew she faked her death?'

'I helped her do it.'

Lucas was completely still. 'You helped her?'

'Yeah, of course. If I didn't she could well have been killed for real. I wasn't about to let that happen, because I know that if you were there, you would have helped too.'

He couldn't say either way. The decision was taken out of his hands.

'Don't be mad at her. She did the best she could by you.'

'Bailing out on her own son was "the best" was it?'

'If she was caught that night she would have been finished. Getting caught breaking into a secret government building, for someone like her, has huge consequences. With her on the outside, she pulled some strings to help you.'

'What strings?'

'Let's just say that she has a lot of dirt on a lot of high-powered people. That can be serious leverage if used correctly.'

'And we both know that she knows exactly how to use it,' he admitted begrudgingly.

'Damn right she does.'

'So, she sent you here, didn't she?'

Anne looked deeply at Lucas with narrowed eyes, as if she were weighing up her choices. 'Yes, she did.'

Lucas pushed Anne away in disgust.

'Oi, it's not what you think! I told you, this is all me, but she sent me to help you.'

'Help me do what?'

'You're following the Brienne letters.'

'Yeah? I was trying to figure out why she wanted them.'

'I can tell you that.'

Lucas leant forward.

'The letter apparently has a counter to the curse, or at the most a location of where it's written.'

He sat back with a mocking grin and rolled his eyes. 'Jesus, Anne. Is that really the best you could come up with? A curse? Bollocks!'

'Take the piss out of me all you want, Lucas, but there's some shit coming, trust me.' The room fell silent for a moment, until Anne looked down at her baby-blue bra, then up at Lucas. 'So, are you going to finish taking this off or what?'

Lucas repeated Anne's gaze, from bra up to finally rest on her emerald eyes. 'We got this far, so I think it would be rude not to,' he said and with a flick of his fingers the clip was undone.

Before things could progress any further, Lucas's mobile phone rang. Ignoring Anne's demands to let it ring, Lucas answered it. All he heard David Evans say before the head of Section 7 hung up the call was, 'Turn on the TV.'

Lucas reached over and picking up the remote control, switched on the television.

Anne was amazed. 'Are you bloody kidding me?' she asked and put her clothes back on.

'Just hold on,' pleaded Lucas.

On the TV screen was a rotating image of the stone monoliths known as the Georgia Stones. As the camera circled the monument, it zoomed in giving views of all of the text written on them. Then a mechanically distorted voice came through, and the image repeatedly changed to match the tone of the monologue.

'The very people that we elected to put in charge of our nations have systematically lied and deceived us. They have told us one thing and done another. Sometimes they don't even tell us. Take the G20 Summit in Indonesia, for instance. At the behest of every government, the media has been telling you that an outbreak of food poisoning is threatening to disrupt the conference. Witness the truth.'

Video footage of the first sick delegates from the United States, Russia, India and China were then displayed. The number of the sick now included Pakistan, Mexico, Brazil, and Indonesia, and they all looked horrific. The whites of their eyes were red due to the ruptured blood vessels. Some were vomiting blood and others had blood seeping out of the pores of their skin.

'Jesus!' Lucas had seen many things in his life, but they'd be hard pushed to top this. He was just about to question Anne when the distorted voice spoke again.

'This is what your governments are telling you is a case of food poisoning. I can assure you that this is no such thing. It is a lethal, contagious virus. Once contracted, death occurs in forty-eight hours. How do I know this? Because we designed it. Who are we? We are citizens of planet Earth who believe it is time for a global shift. We can implement the steps necessary to make it happen.'

The image reverted to the Georgia Guidestones.

'The time for change is now. The world can no longer support the ever-increasing population. Humankind is a cancer to the Earth, a cancer that is slowly draining the resources this planet has provided us. The time for change is now. Your faith will be reformed. No longer will you need to pay to have your prayers heard. No longer will you follow outdated doctrine. No longer will you be beholden to a religion manipulated to control you. One god, one religion. The time for change is now. For this change to come about, two billion people must be sacrificed for the betterment of humankind. To those that will lose their lives, know that your sacrifice will never be forgotten, and that the world will become a more efficient, cohesive place, no longer divided, but living in harmony. The time for change has begun. Welcome to the new world.'

The message abruptly ended, and normal scheduled programming resumed.

Lucas switched it off immediately and turned to Anne. 'Please tell me my mother isn't part of this.'

'She is, in a way.'

'What the fuck is that supposed to mean?'

'The organisation Angela is a part of, *is* behind this, but she's not running this operation. Actually, she is actively trying to hamper it.'

Chapter 29

Lucas's head was spinning from all the new devastating information that he was trying to process when David called again.

'Well? What do you make of it?' The head of Section 7 asked. 'It was broadcast worldwide on every channel, even North Korea.'

'I think the world is in trouble,' Lucas replied noncommittally. 'There was no mention of ransom or anything. They seem determined to do this no matter what happens.'

'Agreed. COBRA is already devising possible outcomes. But against what? They have no idea what or who they're up against. All they have is that Kallum Taylor fellow and even dead he is still contagious; three hospital staff are infected.'

'Damn!'

'How are things with the doctor?'

'Yeah, about that...I lost her.'

'What do you mean you've lost her? Where are you, man? With the way things are looking with this virus, she could well turn out to be a valuable asset now.'

'In a hospital bed. The blade that Babou stuck me with was covered in a toxin.'

'How are you?'

'Ready for payback, sir, as soon as I get out of here.' Lucas felt the need to give his boss some good news to bring to the table and looked at Anne. 'There is another thing. I may be able to get some information about Angela.'

'That's excellent. Do whatever you can to get it.'

'I will, sir.' Lucas ended the call, put the phone down and turned back to Anne. 'Now, where were we?' He leaned towards Anne to kiss her again, but he ended up kissing air as she bounded from the edge of the bed.

'Uh uh, Lucas,' she said sternly. 'What, you think I'm deaf? Sounded like you were told to seduce me for info, the same bloody thing you accused me of a moment ago. Nah, mate, I'll answer your questions, but if there's anything else to be had, you'll have to convince me that it's coming from you, and not because you were told to get into my panties.'

'Fair enough,' he replied, 'but just—' Lucas was interrupted by his phone ringing again.

'Popular guy.'

'Tell me about it.' He answered the unknown number. 'Hello?'

'Lucas, mi amigo! I'm so glad you're not dead.'

'Enrique. You'll be wishing I was when I get my hands on you.'

'Don't be mad, amigo, especially when all I want to do is make a trade. The plates for the doctor, or should I say what's left of her.'

'You bastard! What have you done to her?'

'What have I done? No, no, amigo, what have *you* done? Imagine her surprise when I looked in the sports bag and found the plates of the Euros not there. We had to make sure she wasn't lying so ... unfortunately, my men got a little carried away. So, even after all the two of you had been through, you still did not trust her?'

'I have issues,' sneered Lucas. 'So what?'

'I am not here to judge you, amigo. All I want is the plates. Give them to me and you save another girl. Isn't that how it works, Lucas? Eaten up by guilt over your treatment of one girl, to then go above and beyond to rescue the next, as if in some sort of penance?'

'I didn't realise this was going to be a psychological evaluation. Just tell me where to meet.'

'Let's say Pont de La Concorde, in an hour.'

• • • •

DOCTOR BOUCHARD HAD refused to allow Lucas to leave, but when she had gone, Anne had left soon after, only to return with a couple boxes of antibiotics she had swiped when no one was looking. As Lucas dressed, she admired his body whilst watching the corridor, in case the doctor returned.

The SAS sure had been good for him, Anne thought as she found her gaze being drawn to the attractive attributes of his body, taking particular note of his pecs flexing as he pulled on his T-shirt.

Despite regretting rejecting Lucas's advances, that was down to the stubbornness in her, Anne was also glad that she had. She didn't want to come across as being a bit slutty, but damn he did look good. 'You finished there yet, princess?'

'Looking this good takes time, hon.'

'And how long would it take for you to *actually* look good?' Anne mocked.

'Funny,' replied Lucas, and took two of the pills. 'Now, let's make a move. It'll be close if we're to make it there in an hour.'

Anne beamed and nodded. 'Don't worry, I got wheels.'

• • • •

THE WHEELS IN QUESTION belonged to a carbon fibre and metallic, dark-purple Kawasaki Ninja H2 motorcycle. Lucas was impressed by the machine as he walked around it in admiration.

When he'd done a full circle, Anne whispered in his ear. 'I'll let you into a little secret. This isn't the street legal H2, it's the track only H2R.'

There were some differences in the build of the two bikes, but the one that was most important to Anne was the 40mph difference in speed.

Lucas looked at her in surprise, then remembered who he was talking to. 'I suppose it's a stolen vehicle then?'

'How can I steal something that belongs to me? I got the receipt and everything. They delivered it to the Nürburgring racetrack, I did a few laps, then drove off,' she said with a shrug.

Truth be told, she could easily have stolen it. When they were younger, he was definitely the MVT, but while he had been at Sandhurst Military School, then with the SAS, Anne had been perfecting her thievery skills with Angela Redmond. She was the best now, but as they say, with great power comes great responsibility. Stealing the bike for her own use would have been tacky, stealing the golden death mask of Hector, on the other hand was a triumph.

With the powerful bike between their legs, Anne and Lucas returned to his hotel room in no time. When they entered his room, it was obvious someone had turned it over. The sports bag gone.

'Are you sure this woman is worth all this hassle, Luca?'

'Yes, I am. Faye was swept up into this first because of job title, and now because of her association with me, she's been kidnapped. She's just an innocent bystander getting caught up in other people's shit.'

'Okay, then let's get her back. Where're the plates?'

'In the bathroom, behind the cistern.'

After collecting and placing them in his bag, seeing that they had time to kill before the proposed exchange, Lucas took a drink from the minibar and tossed one to Anne. He finished half of the whisky miniature in one go, as did she.

'So, you said something about Angela not being involved in this genocide plot.'

'Yeah, it's true.'

'You sure this isn't just some plot to get me onside? Tell me that my mum isn't some homicidal psychopath?'

'Angela is a lot of things...one of them being a psychopath, sure, but genocidal. Even you can't believe that.'

'I don't know. "The ends justify the means". That's what she taught me.'

'Yeah, and "by any means necessary" too.' Anne finished the rest of the little bottle of whisky and accurately threw it in the bin. 'She's probably not going to like me telling you this, but as long as you don't say anything...'

Lucas shook his head. 'Don't worry, I got your back.'

'Okay. Angela wanted the three of us to get back together. The old crew. She knew the chances of that happening were slim since you were married to someone prim and proper who knew nothing about your criminal youth.'

'Well, she does now,' Lucas pointed out.

'Yeah, and look at your marriage now.'

Although the breakdown of their marriage had not resulted from Natasha finding out about Lucas's life as a criminal, he had not told her about it out of fear that it would.

'After everything with the Eye of Nineveh was resolved, I had a feeling that she might have been involved. I didn't know how, but somehow her hand was involved. And if she wanted me separated from Natasha, then why *not* set a honey trap. And I fell for it hook, line and sinker.'

'Your mum knows you. She's been watching you for years. She knew how you would react when you received that letter with Sebastian Jericho written on it. And she put Chiara Harris right in your path.'

'I asked you about it back then and you denied knowing anything about it. You lied to me, Anne!'

'I had to, Luca. Angela swore me to secrecy and the be honest, I wanted to go back to the old days too.'

'Selfish, as always. Your feelings always come first, huh, Anne?'

'Fuck you, Lucas!' Anger flared up in her. 'I put Angela's feelings before mine, and yours for that matter. Your mum wasn't the only one that watched from afar, you know! I saw everything — shit you don't know about.'

'What are you talking about?'

Anne knew that in her anger she might have said too much. 'Forget it. All I'm saying is that I had to watch you marry somebody else because I promised your mum that I would stay away from you. And you call me selfish.'

'I'm sorry,' he said, taking a seat next to her on the bed. 'I had no idea.'

'You weren't supposed to.'

'So, what was next in Angela Redmond's master plan?'

'Have you heard of the Bilderberg Group?'

'The bunch of rich CEO's, politicians and influential people who meet-up once a year? I've heard a bit about it, not a lot because of all the secrecy surrounding it.'

'That's mostly correct, anyway. They talk about economics, trade and ways to make the world better, I guess. But someone decided that it was all well and good discussing things, but nothing would change if no one was ever going to actually try and take steps to make things happen. And that's when the even more secret Bilderberg Inner Circle was formed.'

'By Angela?'

'No, but she has worked her way up. Each member has a crack at fulfilling the agenda. The Eye of Nineveh heist was one attempt. This is another.'

'So this is the "high table" she mentioned when I saw her. Are you a member?

'No. I work exclusively with Angela. The other members of the BIC don't know about me.'

'BIC?'

'That's what they shorten the name to. Members have a ring with the letters engraved on top of each other.'

'What else can you tell me about them? What happens if someone succeeds?'

'They will become the first leader of the Novus Ordo Seclorum.'

'The New World Order.' Lucas thought for a moment. If his mother knew him, then he certainly knew her. 'She's not doing this out of any love of humanity, she's doing this so that she can be the new president, empress or whatever of this new entity, herself. How is Angela trying to stop them?'

'With you.'

'What? I'm not working with her?'

'I told you, she's knows you. She knew that your curiosity would drive you to follow the clues about the Brienne letters. Apparently, there's information there that could save a lot of lives.'

'Bollocks!' Lucas slapped his forehead. 'I forgot all about that. I haven't sent Ellen the last clue.'

'You hardly forgot, Luca. You were incapacitated. But don't worry, mate. While you were out of it, I took the liberty of sending your little hacker buddy a message.'

He gave her a stern look. 'I hope that was the only liberty you took.'

Anne laughed.

'That's not an answer.'

'It's the only answer you're getting, babe; look at the time.'

'Shit! Okay, let's do this.' Lucas checked the handgun in his bag, made sure all the clips were full, then he and Anne left the hotel room for their evening rendezvous.

Chapter 30

The flight had been a long one, fourteen hours. For Alyssa, it had felt doubly so. Being the third wheel in a private jet was no fun place to be, especially when your companions thought you were asleep, and took the opportunity to have some fun with each other's bodies. Despite the awkwardness of the flight, the Romanian archaeologist didn't regret coming along. Especially after they landed in Cusco Airport and boarded an off-road vehicle to take them the rest of the way to Ollantaytambo. The village was in the Sacred Valley region of Cusco, amid snow-capped mountains, near the Urubamba River.

The drive from the airport to the village was barely an hour, but the scenery they passed was breath-taking, and Alyssa happily snapped away with her camera. At times she caught Natasha looking solemn, and although she didn't say, it would be difficult to be with her current boyfriend sitting next to her, Alyssa was more than certain that her mood was brought on by memories of being here with Lucas, being here for their honeymoon.

'Are you alright?' Alyssa whispered to Natasha when Peter was having one of his frequent phone calls.

'Yeah, I'm fine,' she replied, absentmindedly caressing the finger that once had both an engagement ring and a wedding ring. 'I had a feeling that it might hit me, you know, the final realisation that it was all over between me and...' she glanced at Peter to make sure that he couldn't hear her before continuing. '...Lucas. It was bound to happen. I just never thought that it would be like this.'

'Like what?'

'I miss him,' Natasha whispered.

'Then you should call him.'

'What? No! This is the best thing for it...separation and distraction. The longer it continues the sooner he'll be out of my mind, and I can move on with Peter.'

'Someone mention my name?' Peter said, joining the two women.

'Oh, it's nothing. I was just saying how much I appreciate you doing this for me.'

'And I told you it's nothing. This is the life that you have to get accustomed to now, Natasha.'

'But you had meetings and other things to do. I wasn't expecting you to drop everything like that.'

'Things have been left in capable hands. I was no longer needed there. If something changes, they will call. So here I am spending time with my beautiful lady.'

They embraced and kissed, leaving Natasha with no doubt in her mind that she was doing the right thing. If this was the choice Maximilian Angel saw in his cards, then she had made her decision.

The Land Rover Discovery trundled along the dirt road bordered by the tracks of the Perurail service on one side and the Urubamba River on the other. Eventually, they crossed the rails driving pass stalls selling brightly coloured traditional clothing. The road was a long one, but it took them all the way to the brightly painted buildings of Ollantaytambo's Plaza de Armas. Natasha's smile brightened as they drew closer to seeing Feliciana Sancho again, it had been so long.

The SUV came to a stop and its passengers disembarked. Natasha whirled around as she remembered how they first came to this village, crash landing their power-glider in a field not far from the plaza. Feliciana had been waiting for them, waiting for the spirits to deliver a saviour of the village. That day she had gotten two for the price of one. And even though Lucas had been, and to this day still is sceptical about the whole belief of supernatural, paranormal, spiritual ideas, he couldn't deny that Feliciana Sancho had her prayers answered that day, as she and Lucas were able to successfully acquire the artefact known as the Slippers of Viracocha from a drug baron that had stolen it from the village.

The plaza was a hub for the village, tourists coming to visit the huge Sun Temple and Princess Baths fountain, and other Incan ruins, would be dropped off and picked up from this cobblestoned location. Only it seemed even more lively and vibrant, and Natasha soon found out why when she heard a recognisable voice and then saw a familiar girl.

'Hey! Hello, Claudia!'

The teenager was having a discussion with two builders. She tried to get them to see her vision, and although she spoke to them as if they were children, they nodded along happily as she directed them. She turned immediately when she heard Natasha, one of the two people who rescued her from La Viuda. Ignoring the two workers, Claudia Moreno-García ran to Natasha and gave a big hug.

'What are you doing here, Natasha? Where's that big oaf, Lucas?'

'He couldn't make it,' she lied.

'His loss. But I guess that means that he trusts me to get everything done.'

'What do you mean? Get what done?'

Claudia led Natasha to a banner that was about to be strung up. As it was lifted, bit by bit, the lettering eventually came into view; "Welcome to the first Ollantaytambo Carnival."

'It was Lucas's idea to bring some extra revenue for the village so that it can be properly preserved and protected. I have to admit, there's a lot to see in this place and although more visitors would be great, everything has to be done properly so that the sites aren't subject to visitor erosion.'

Natasha was having a tough time processing what she was hearing. 'Lucas had a hand in this?'

'Yeah! Feliciana spoke to him about her worries, and he called me. He knows how much I love event planning, and something on this scale would be great for my resume, and the fact that it's to do with conservation would give me even more kudos. So, yeah, I have to thank him for that.'

'He's spoken to Feliciana? I tried to call her the yesterday, but I couldn't get hold of her.'

'Yeah, that's because she probably can't get any reception where she is right now?'

'She's not here? Bollocks!' Natasha caught sight of Peter's disapproving look and unconsciously bowed her head a touch. 'Sorry, where are my manners? These are my friends Alyssa Popescu, and this is my partner, Peter Armitage.'

The American educated Claudia shook each of their hands in turn.

'I've heard a lot about your father, Ms Moreno-García,' Peter mentioned. 'Diego Moreno Mayor of Trujillo, yes? About his campaign to clean up your city. As noble as his fight is, surely after what happened to you, he must have decided to put his efforts to use elsewhere.'

'No, quite the opposite. My father does not scare easily. He is even more determined than ever.'

'I see. I guess he cares more for his legacy than the lives of his family, but you must be proud of him. Such a great man.'

Claudia's brow furrowed at the remark, and Natasha jumped in before the youngster responded. 'You said Feliciana isn't here? Do you know where she's gone?'

'Um, yeah. I guess with all the news focusing on the G20 Summit, the story about the landslide in Carajia is pushed aside.'

'What, the food poisoning?'

Claudia looked at Natasha as if she were an alien. 'Where the hell have you been?' She brought out her phone and in seconds brought up the message that had broadcast worldwide.'

Natasha and the others watched in horror. 'These days it seems better to just stay at home, because there seems to be too much madness going on in the world.'

'You can say that again,' Claudia replied. 'The even crazier thing is that this group is gathering a lot of supporters who agree with their view.'

'They do have some valid points,' Peter added.

'You can't be serious,' Natasha admonished.

'There is only a finite amount of oil in this world, Natasha—'

'But you can't be condoning genocide, Peter? They're innocent people.'

'—and unlike me, few of the rich and powerful wish to put their hands in their pocket and do some good. And to prove my point, I'd like to donate to your carnival, Ms Moreno-García.'

'That's fantastic!' Claudia squealed and gave him the bank details for the transfer. Her jaw almost hit the ground when she saw the amount deposited. 'One million dollars? Are you sure?'

'Like I said I don't mind putting my hand in my pocket for the right causes.'

Natasha tried to steer the dazed Claudia back on track. 'You were saying something about a landslide?'

'Oh, yes. I'm sure you know about Carajia.'

'Yeah. That's where the standing sarcophagi are located, right?'

'It is. But there was seven and now there are nine. A recent earthquake and landslide revealed two more, and some sort of crevice behind them.'

Natasha's eyes lit up at the sound of that. A new historical find. 'And Feliciana has gone to have a look?'

'She wouldn't be stopped. Said something about it being where she was supposed to be. She'll probably be nearly there by now. It's a nine-hour drive.'

Natasha looked from Alyssa to Peter, trying to glean ideas from them.

'I even told her she'd be better off flying part of the way and offered her the use of my helicopter. After driving with your maniac husband, I've kind of gone off driving through rough terrain, so I avoid it whenever I can.'

'I don't suppose we could borrow it, Claudia?'

'Yeah, why not? I mean it won't take you all the way. There's not enough fuel, but it'll get you to Juliaca. That's the closest airport.'

'That will be fine,' Peter said, getting on to his phone. 'I'll have another ride waiting there for us.' He walked off to get some quiet while he made the call.

'You really don't have to do this you know? You've already done so much.'

'Don't be silly, Alyssa. We've come all this way; it'd be stupid to quit now. Besides, you need the information about those artefacts, and as a bonus we get to see new artefacts right here, in their native land. How cool is that going to be?'

'Okay, yes, it will be very cool!' Alyssa replied, mirroring Natasha's enthusiasm.

Peter soon returned, having arranged everything. 'Okay, so we will have a helicopter waiting for us in Juliaca. I'm having Conrad leave with the car now, so that he can meet us there.'

'Sounds good,' Natasha replied. 'Let's go!'

Chapter 31

Lucas climbed off the back of Anne's Kawasaki as she parked her bike in Paris's biggest square, the Place de la Concorde, near the entrance to Jardin de Tuileries, the vast and beautiful public garden that was once only for royalty, before the revolution changed that.

She watched Lucas go through his things again and hand her a monocular and the gun. 'You know this is most likely going to be a trap, right?'

'I wouldn't expect anything less of him. That's why I got you as backup. He doesn't know anything about you, and he's expecting me to come alone. Just keep an eye out for anything funny.'

'No worries, just don't get your head blown off. I kind of like it where it is.'

'You and me both hon.'

Lucas walked towards Pont de la Concorde but then paused, turned back and gave Anne a hard kiss that left her slightly breathless when he pulled away. 'Just in case,' he said.

The Pont de la Concorde was a bridge that had been a few name changes in its time with each regime change. It has formerly been known as the Pont Louis XVI, Pont de la Révolution, Pont de la Concorde, Pont Louis XVI again during the Bourbon Restoration. In 1830, its name was changed back to Pont de la Concorde, perhaps for the last time.

Lucas scanned every person he passed as he crossed the wide, arched bridge. He didn't know what he was walking into, but he wanted to be sure no one doubled back and ambushed him from behind.

There was nothing there. Lucas told himself to leave his back to Anne. She had him covered, leaving him to worry about what was ahead, because there was Enrique Salas, seemingly alone, except for the female figure ahead of him; Faye.

The two of them came from the opposite end of the bridge, strolling down the other side of the crossing. He pulled her along, she obviously suffering from something hampering her movement. When they reached halfway, they came to a stop, as did Lucas.

The men glared at each other through the French evening rush-hour traffic as if it weren't there. For the first time, Lucas got a good look at the strange veil the Colombian wore, which covered half of his face. He tried to catch Faye's eye, let her know everything was going to be okay, but she wouldn't look up. Damp strands of her hair hung down, obscuring her face, and he wondered if the wetness was from fear induced sweat and tears, or from some water-based torture Enrique might have used to extract the information he desired.

Enrique indicated to Lucas that he should cross, and the once special forces captain obliged, and zig zagged his way through the slow-moving traffic. Once he had traversed the vehicles, he stepped towards them, constantly watching Faye, hoping that he'd be able to catch her eye and maybe get some sort of message across to her.

'That's far enough, amigo,' Enrique said when Lucas was about two metres from him. 'Open your coat, slowly.'

Lucas did what he was told, turning around to show that he was unarmed.

'Are you alright, Faye?' Lucas asked tenderly.

'Of course she is. You can see that. What about my plates?'

Lucas opened his bag and took out the hotel laundry bag that contained the Euro Dollar plates. He pulled one halfway out.

'Both sides,' Enrique demanded.

Lucas flipped the plate. 'Satisfied?'

'Bueno. Now put the bag down and stepped back, Lucas. I will walk forward with the girl, pick up the bag and let her go.'

'Not going to happen. You let her go at the same time, or the bag goes into the Seine.'

'What makes you think that this is up for negotiation, Lucas?' Enrique moved slightly. The hand he had at Faye's back, so that it came into view. Lucas may not have been armed, but he was. 'Now, as I said, put the bag down and step back. I won't ask again.'

It was the only leverage he had, but complying with Enrique was the only thing he could do, especially if he wanted to get Faye out of there. 'Okay, Enrique, we'll do things your way.'

• • • •

ANNE WATCHED THE SCENE intently through the night-vision monocular. They had both known that the meet was a bad idea, but there was nothing they could do about it; Lucas was intent on saving the girl, and she'd gone along with it for his sake.

So here they were, waiting for the shit to hit the fan.

'Here we go,' Anne said as she saw Lucas put the bag down and take several steps backwards as Enrique moved closer toward it.

The treasure hunter suddenly heard motorbikes revving up. She swept the monocular left and right and sighted three motorbikes roaring down Rue Astride Briand. They jumped the lights at Quai Anatole France, which brought several toots from the horns of angry drivers, the noise alerting both Lucas and Anne to the imminent danger, as the three motorbikes went into the cycle lane, moving rapidly towards him.

Lucas made a move toward the plates, but Enrique was already there, picking them up. Once he had them in his possession, he shoved Faye at Lucas and jumped on the first motorbike as it drew up beside him and took off.

'Faye? Faye? Are you alright?'

Two gunshots suddenly rang out, both striking the woman Lucas had been tasked with protecting, the woman whose life she had placed into his hands. She toppled backwards over the railing of the bridge. Lucas made a desperate emotion fuelled lunge for her.

Anne saw everything unfold before her, ending with Lucas throwing himself over the side of the Pont de la Concorde. She twisted the throttle of her motorbike and took off for the bridge, rapidly flying through the gear changes. 'Lucas, you dumbass! You better hope you're dead because if you're not I'm going to kill you myself!'

The Kawasaki roared over the bridge, passing Enrique and his trio of bikers like a blur as they travelled in the direction she had come from. He watched the mysterious black-haired woman, praying that whoever she was, she would be too late to help Lucas.

Anne parked the bike and dashed over to where the crowd had gathered to see where the suicide jumper had plunged to his death. She peered over and felt relieved when she saw Lucas dangling there.

She got the onlookers to help them in her own inimitable style. 'Don't just stand there gawping, help him up for fuck's sake!' When Lucas was finally pulled back onto the bridge, Anne gave him a hug.

'I couldn't save her,' he whispered into her shoulder. 'I grabbed her, but she slipped through my fingers.'

'Don't blame yourself, Luca, it wasn't meant to be. It's not possible to save everyone.'

'But I can make the man that killed her pay.'

'Now you're talking.'

They climbed onto the supercharged bike, Anne giving Lucas back his gun before they were racing down the pedestrian walkway, people diving out of the way of the maniac biker. Up ahead in the Place de la Concorde, Enrique and his two other bikes were being slowed by an accident that had brought the already slow-moving traffic to a standstill.

The biker who was carrying the boss saw a commotion behind him in his side mirrors and alerted Enrique, who couldn't believe what he was seeing. Who was this puta?

'That way!' Enrique yelled, pointing at the black and gold gates of the Jardin des Tuileries.

Lucas was impressed by Anne's riding ability. There was more than one occasion when he thought they might wipe out. Now he knew how Natasha felt whenever she was a passenger in a high-speed pursuit or escape.

She pulled hard on the brakes, plumes of smoke billowing out around them as they skidding into the garden entrance, narrowly avoiding the people who were already panicked by the previous three motorbikes that passed through there.

Anne and Lucas traversed the large octagonal fountain and got onto the long, straight avenue that led to the Louvre. With the three bikes of Enrique clearing the way of people ahead, Lucas could see him clearly and they were catching him, fast. He could almost feel the fear in the man because he knew he was literally running for his life.

That fear drove Enrique to desperation. He drew the gun he had moments ago used to kill Doctor Dannen and pointed it at Lucas.

With a determined look on her face, Anne Sheppard veered left and right, avoiding the oncoming gunfire. Then one of the other bikers abruptly applied their front brake, lifting the rear wheel, performing a front wheelie, which made Anne's Kawasaki to fly pass, but leaving him with a target to aim at, which Enrique's man immediately took advantage of.

'We got one on our tail,' Lucas yelled over the sound of the rushing wind in his ears.

'I know,' Anne shouted back. 'I'm not blind. I saw the bastard. I'll do my bit; you just do yours.'

Lucas drew his handgun from his holster and held the grip tightly; things were about to get bumpy.

With her head lowered, in a racing position, Anne glanced quickly over one shoulder then the other to see exactly where their pursuer was. Once she had him pegged, and whilst still trying to avoid the bullets whizzing around, she cut left, then accelerated right, taking them off the main thoroughfare of the park.

Although she had to slow slightly, since she had to contend with the obstacle of trees now, Anne was still travelling at a fair speed, slaloming between them like a champion skier. Then she noticed that the bike behind hadn't followed them off the long straight avenue into the wooded area. Their cowardice gave the upper hand back to Anne.

Lucas was a little concerned when he saw her switch off the headlight, but he didn't mention it. The fact that she was slowing down further eased his fears more. Then he realised that she was matching the speed of Enrique's man. As soon as they were level with him, and when an opening presented itself, Anne pulled out from behind the tree line and bounced shoulder to shoulder in a dangerous high-speed game.

The man tried the same trick again, braking to fall behind, but Lucas was ready this time and fired three bullets into him. His bike tumbled and flipped until it exploded in a fireball of orange and acrid smoke, lighting up the darkening French sky.

Enrique turned at the sound, wondering what was happening behind him, then he saw the headlight of the Kawasaki H2R switch on, and it grew as it gained on him again.

The bikes continued to race towards the end of the gardens, the distinctive sounds of police sirens getting ever closer. The disruption to the usual peaceful Parisian evening couldn't be allowed to continue, especially so close to one of the city's biggest tourist attractions, so the law acted swiftly.

The Louvre museum loomed ever larger as they continued to approach the historic building. Enrique and his remaining wingman negotiated the steps that led over the Avenue du General Lemonnier, forcing people out of the way. Anne accelerated hard, lifting the front end of her bike, taking to the air when she reached the top of the stairway. Whilst airborne, Lucas had a clear view of the second Enrique follower and he took his opportunity to squeeze the trigger, landing two slugs in him, sending him and his bike careening off and crashing into one of the lampposts that lined the Jardin du Carrousel, bursting into flames.

Enrique was left alone, with only his rider, but he wasn't about to let Lucas catch him. He twisted around firing shots at the determined pair behind him. 'Head to the cemetery,' Enrique shouted to the rider, their motorbike roaring under the Arc de Triomphe du Carrousel and then left onto Place du Carrousel, away from the iconic glass pyramid of the renowned museum.

Anne followed them every step of the way, matching them move for move, and still she gained on them. Until a van unexpectedly reversed out in front of the Kawasaki, both rider and passenger giving thanks for the exceptional brakes of the powerful bike.

After some not-so-gentle requests from Lucas and Anne, the van driver moved aside and allowed them to pass. The delay, however, had given Enrique enough time to make good his escape.

'Any sign of him?' Lucas asked in hope.

Anne drove at a very sedate pace, compared to what she had been doing moments ago, just so they would have a better chance of seeing anything in the side roads, but they both knew that if they carried on at this speed Enrique would be long gone.

'Wait a minute,' Anne said. 'I think I see something.' She accelerated down the road, and sure enough, it was the abandoned motorbike of Enrique and his follower.

As Lucas and Anne dismounted, they cautiously scanned the surrounding area, remaining on guard, prepared for anything. They came to the entrance of the Pere Lachaise Cemetery and found one of the gates slightly ajar. A quick glance at the timetable told them it should have been closed by now.

Lucas looked at Anne who nodded back, giving a silent agreement that she was ready to proceed. He pushed a new magazine into his gun, then edged past the cemetery gates.

Chapter 32

Natasha had done more travelling in Peru in the previous few days than she had during her many visits over the years. From Sacred Valley, southeast of the country, they had now made the flight into the northern highlands of the Andes Mountains to a village called Cruzpata.

As soon as they had disembarked, Natasha had seen the pipe-smoking old woman. 'It's so good to see you, Feliciana. We've been chasing you all over Peru.'

'Really? Stupid child, you could have just phoned.'

'I did, but I got no answer. Claudia suggested you might not be getting a good signal around here.'

Feliciana took out her phone and looked at it, then turned it around to show Natasha the screen. 'Nope, full bars, see?'

Natasha was perplexed.

'You have my new number, don't you? I gave it to Lucas the last time we spoke.'

'New number?' Natasha's palms grew sweaty, and her cheeks warmed up ever so slightly. 'You changed your number?'

'Yes, got a new phone too. You and Lucas not speaking, then?'

'It's complicated.'

'Bah! It always was between you two. But you still talked, still laughed, still loved.'

Natasha cleared her throat. 'I'm with someone else now, Feliciana. Let me introduce him to you. This is Peter Armitage.'

Hearing his name, he broke off his conversation with Conrad and walked over, extending his hand in greeting. 'It is a pleasure to meet you.'

The old woman took his hand and shook it, all the while looking at him with a creased brow. 'Well, since you have come all this way to see me, Natasha, I can only think that it must be something especially important.

'Yes, yes it is,' Natasha blurted out.

'Well, let's have some churros and you can tell me about it.' Feliciana led the way to a small rustic cafe where she ordered five of the sweet, donut like snack. Once they had all sat down and had a few bites, Natasha introduced Alyssa and explained to Feliciana all that they knew, starting with Alyssa's discovery of Adela Cantacuzino Kogalniceanu's lost treasure, and their escape from the Romani mafia. She culminated her story with the reason why she was so desperate to speak to the elderly woman. Natasha reached into her bag and fished out one of the discs.

The village elder let out a breath as she took the heavy artefact in her hands. 'Viracocha,' she whispered, then flipped it over with some effort. 'And the smaller image of Supay. I never thought I would ever see one of these in my lifetime.'

'We have more,' Natasha stated.

'Then this is the most fateful day! A recent landslide has revealed two new sarcophagi at Karina.'

'Yes, Claudia told us. She said they're in the likenesses of Viracocha and Supay.'

'Apparently so. The god of life on one side, the god of death on the other.'

'Wait, I also have this.' Natasha handed her the photocopy of Mrs Prunea's paper.'

Feliciana looked over it briefly and turned it over. 'Where's the rest of it?'

'What do you mean? That's all we have.'

'This is supposed to be a prayer. It's called Taki Kawsay Wanu, the Song of Life and Death, but this is just the song of life; the other part is missing.'

'But you know about these discs? What they are? What they were used for?'

'I do. They're incredibly old. Pre-Incan. We are talking before the Wari, before the Moche, Nazca, Chavin, about four thousand years ago, to be exact, when the world was a bit more spiritual. There was sacrifice then, but nothing on the scale it would become in later years. It is called an Aysana Kawsay Wanu. It was used as a tool for sacrifice, but the choice of who lived or died was left for the gods to decide.'

Natasha and Alyssa looked at each other. Neither one of them had ever heard of such a thing before. People only talked about the well-documented brutality of the Incas and how they would sacrifice their own citizens by the hundreds.

Natasha was intrigued. 'Do you know how it would work?'

'Well, what would happen is that the person whose life was to be weighed, would hold one of each disc in their hands and then the priest would read the Taki Kawsay Wanu, and the gods would answer the prayer with either life or death.'

'They would just die?'

'That I do not know; it could have been instant, or it could have been a slow death over several days.'

'But if it took days, how would you know which one you got?'

'Someone that was given death would cry blood because their soul knew the inevitable.'

Feliciana's words hung heavy in the air as they all tried to process how it would have been like to not only go through something like that, but to have witnessed it first-hand.

'What about the discs themselves?' Alyssa asked. 'What are they made from? I had them analysed by a metallurgist, but the substance didn't match any metal he knew of.'

'That I'm not surprised to hear, because if these discs are conduits of the god's power, then it would only make sense that the material would come from them.'

'A meteorite?'

'Or something else?'

'You don't mean aliens do you, Feliciana?' Natasha said, looking at the woman through narrowed eyes.

'You know yourself that there are many unexplained things out there. Is it any harder for you to believe than a gemstone that can call forth a tornado of fire and destroy a city?'

'You're right, I'm sorry. There are, in fact, many stories of alien visits in antiquity.'

'And the fact that certain advances in civilisation were made seemingly independent of each other, halfway across the world, is more evidence of the possibility. Which brings me to the next part in your history lesson. There is a myth that tells the story of how Supay was angry with Viracocha for giving him dominion over nothing but the dirt under his feet. They battled for supremacy and Supay lost and was subsequently banished, being sent across the Earth, but not before he could vow vengeance.'

'Where did he go?'

'I was hoping that I might find something about that when these new Carajia sarcophagi were revealed.'

'So why were you up there?'

Feliciana sighed and shook her head. 'Because the landslide not only revealed the new tombs, but it has also blocked the only way up there. I don't know how long it will take for an excavation team to come and clear the way, but it will not be quick, that I *do* know.'

Natasha was just as crestfallen as the village elder was, but she wasn't about to let things end there. If Lucas was with her now, he would come up with some hare-brained idea to get them up there. Then *she* had one of those ideas.

• • • •

ALYSSA LOOKED AT HER friend, her knee bouncing as the helicopter took off with the party once again, this time with Feliciana in addition. Natasha had got hold of all the equipment she thought that she would need and was just going through everything again to be prepared.

'Are you sure about this, Natasha?'

No, I'm not sure about this at all, she thought. 'Yeah, I'm totally sure about this. Me and Lucas have done this plenty of times.' Another lie. She had seen him do it plenty of times, and the only times she had done it was as a tandem. This would be her first solo rappel from a helicopter.

She breathed deeply and went through everything that she could remember about the equipment and safety checks Lucas would go through beforehand. The leather gloves, goggles, the safety belt, a harness and tether and finally the descent-control nylon rope. It would have been easier to just pick up a phone and call him, but that wasn't really an option Natasha was willing to exercise.

Natasha looked out of the open door of the helicopter. She could see the impressive sarcophagi standing imperiously, looking out at the valley below. 'This is it Alyssa,' she told her nervous friend as she performed one final check of the rappel seat, ring and the other equipment, pulling on the rope to double check the strength of the connection.

'You really do this?' Alyssa queried. 'You do this for archaeology?'

'Sometimes. When the need arises, you have to go that extra mile to complete a story.'

'Right now, I would not mind if this one went unfinished.'

'Don't be silly. You'll love it,' Natasha said and threw the coiled up rope out and away from the helicopter. The pilot was earning his money on this trip. The ledge the standing tombs were on didn't jut out from the wall a whole lot, so he had to keep checking that the rotor blades weren't scraping the mountain face, whilst ensuring the rope still touching the ridge.

She gave it a shake to make sure that there were no tangles or knots, then Natasha turned to Alyssa. 'Okay, you're up.'

'I still don't understand why I have to go first.'

'So that I can tell you what you have to do, of course. Now, sit down and swing your legs outside.'

Everybody looked on anxiously as Alyssa reluctantly did as she was told.

'Good. Now you're going to hold the rope with this hand at the small of your back. This is the brake hand. Keep a firm grip on it, it manages the speed of your descent. The other hand is the guide hand. What you're going to do next is turn around on the skid so that you're facing me inside the copter.'

Alyssa nodded, testing out her grips.

'When I give you the command, you're going to push away from the skid, as hard as you can, and allow the rope to pass through both hands. Keep watching the ground. When you're about halfway to touching down, that's when you start the braking process by moving your brake hand out at a 45-degree angle. You okay? Good, now when you touch down, clear the rope through the ring until it's free, and I'll be on my way down to meet you.' Natasha could see the worry on her friend's face and really wished she could do more to help her. 'You ready, Alyssa?'

'I wouldn't say I'm ready, but...'

Alyssa took several deep breaths, trying the best she could to slow her racing heartbeat. She looked at Natasha, waiting for her command. It was lucky that she gave a thumbs up because Alyssa wasn't even sure that she heard Natasha say "go" and she pushed off.

The wind whistled in her ears as it rushed past Alyssa. She screamed as she plummeted to the earth, certain that she was about to die. The ground was speeding towards at such a rate that she panicked and pulled on her brake hard. She jerked to a stop, but the force of the action caused her guide hand to lose grip on the rope. Alyssa continued to descend, but in a horizontal position.

Closer and closer she came to slamming into the earth. Natasha screamed at her to pull the brake. Alyssa was moving her hand all around, trying to get the brake to bite. Four feet from the ground she got it.

Natasha let out a huge sigh of relief when she saw Alyssa safely drop the final few feet and free herself from the rope. 'She's down. Right, I'm going. I'll let you know what I see Feliciana, I'll send you photographs.'

'Be careful,' Peter said and leaned over to kiss her. 'We'll have the pilot take us down into the valley so we can keep an eye on you.'

Natasha nodded, then got into position and pushed herself off. She whooped as she rapidly descended, fully embracing the adrenaline-seeking side of herself, ignoring the disapproving looks she knew she was no doubt getting from a certain someone. But as she said, if you want to love me you have to love all of me.

Sometimes she wondered how she would have been as a person had she met Peter before she met Lucas, because it was really his influence that allowed her to embrace who she felt she should be. And probably why her dad disliked him so much.

As soon as she landed, Natasha rushed over to check on Alyssa, and make sure that she was alright. Apart from being initially winded from the short fall, she was fine, but also stated that she wouldn't be repeating the experience anytime soon.

Natasha pulled the rope through the rappel ring and signalled the helicopter to let them know she was clear. Then she turned around and got her first proper look at the eight-feet tall sarcophagi. It was a marvellous sight. And it was an amazing feeling standing where ancient people stood before, touching the things that they had created with their own hands, using primitive tools.

There was a sacred, spiritual stillness that surrounded the site, and Natasha said a silent prayer of thanks to those that went before. Then she got to work.

'There are actually more tombs lower down,' she said.

'Obviously, the positioning of your tomb was a sign of status,' Alyssa replied with a smile. 'This is just like the times when we had a project at university.'

'You're right. I was just thinking the same thing.'

The giggling pair then moved over to the two newly discovered tombs. And sure enough, both Natasha and Alyssa recognised the images of Viracocha and Supay straightaway. The only difference to the other sarcophagi being that instead of facing out towards the valley, they were facing each other.

'Well, what do you think?' Natasha asked after starting a video call with Feliciana, who was sitting comfortably in the helicopter.

'It is amazing,' she replied. 'The colours are still so vivid. Oh, and you see, they both carry staffs indicating they are gods. Viracocha holds the Spondylus shell in one hand and the Stromboli shell in the other, which were symbols of woman and man. Can you turn to Supay, please? Ah, yes, see he holds rods of lightning, representing his destructive nature.'

Suddenly, there was a sound like stones hitting metal. 'What is that?' Natasha asked, hearing the unusual sound over the video. Then she recognised a more familiar sound of machine gun fire echoing into the valley.

The picture on the screen moved as the pilot was forced to take evasive action. Natasha and Alyssa could see the passengers being thrown about the cabin, despite wearing their seatbelts.

'There's a group of women shooting at us!' Feliciana shouted at the phone.

'Look!' Alyssa cried out pointing to the sky. They could see the helicopter veer out into the valley, then back towards the mountain. The blades of the craft struck the mountainside several times before the pilot was able to react and pull away from it.

But the damage had been done.

Loose rock was dislodged and came tumbling down on the ledge. Alyssa dived at Natasha, narrowly taking her out of the way of a particularly large boulder. But in saving her friend, they both became trapped behind a landslide that quickly blocked up their way back out with tonnes of rock.

Chapter 33

As Lucas and Anne crept into the cemetery, they immediately came upon a dead security guard. A single bullet to the head was all it had taken. Neither of them liked what they were seeing, it was dark and even if the Pere Lachaise Cemetery was empty of the living, it was like a city of the dead, the final resting place of the likes of Chopin, Piaf and Morrison. With mausoleums everywhere, it provided the perfect environment for an ambush. The good thing was Lucas expected something like that from Enrique Salas, but he wished that Anne was armed too.

Although he knew that she was more than capable in unarmed combat, taking up Jiu-Jitsu at a young age, but having two guns was always better than one.

Anne walked silently behind Lucas, stepping where he stepped. Eventually, the daunting aspect of the task before them caused her to speak her mind in a whisper. 'You sure you want to continue with this? I mean, are you doing this to stop Enrique's counterfeit money scheme, or are you looking for revenge?'

'Right now, those goals are the same.'

'I just hope that you don't let your need for revenge cloud your judgement.'

'You didn't have to come, you know?'

'Yeah, I did. Who's going to watch your back if I don't?'

The two fell silent as they heard footfall on gravel. Turning towards the direction of the sound Lucas and Anne continued their stealthy approach, only to stop again and change course when they heard Enrique shout from a completely different direction.

'I was going to kill you on that bridge, Lucas! It would have been so easy. But then I discovered something even better, the look on your face when I shot your doctor friend.'

'That's where you messed up!' Lucas yelled back, much to the chagrin of Anne.

'Shut up, don't let him bait you, or we're both dead,' she whispered harshly at him.

'No, no, no Lucas, that's where you're wrong. The look of anguish on your face was remarkable. It was almost like a piece of you was killed in the process, so much pain, anguish. And this was just someone you had only met briefly. Someone you had bedded a few times. Just imagine how you would feel when it was someone that you genuinely loved? No woman will look at me after what you did to me, and now I'm going to take away all of yours.

'I get excited just thinking about it. You should think about it too, Lucas. Think about what I'm going to do to your PA Venice Jones, what I'll do to your little hacker friend, Ellen Paige. And then there's your wife, Natasha. Oh, I will take the most pleasure form killing her. She is just as much to blame as you are. I'll be sure to do it slowly.'

'Don't you touch her!' Lucas jumped from around the side of a mausoleum and fired his gun, but Enrique wasn't there, maniacal laughter from the Colombian came from another direction.

'And what about the chica you're with, amigo? What is your connection with her? What are your feelings towards her? Should I add her to my death list? Yes, I think I will. All the women in your life, Lucas, all the women you have encountered, are fair game for me now. Say goodbye to her.'

Urged by the threat, Lucas took a quick glance over his shoulder to reassure Anne that he wouldn't let anything happen to her, but she wasn't there.

'Anne,' he yelled, panic rising within him.

Lucas broke into a run, throwing caution out the window. He looked down every avenue of the cemetery he passed, looked around every corner, calling out her name. But he couldn't see or hear anything.

Then he heard a gunshot.

'No!' Lucas collapsed against the burial chamber beside him. He looked up at the night sky with a pained expression. Then he clenched his fists so tight his arms shook as he set his resolve.

'This one was a bit feisty, amigo,' Enrique laughed. But it does not matter because they all have the same effect on you.

Lucas sprinted towards the laughter. He came to a sudden halt when he saw a body laid out on the ground beside a sepulchre. He approached slowly, dreading what he was about to see, dreading what that bastard had done to his oldest friend. He berated himself for letting Enrique get to him and cause him to think irrationally. What had happened to Anne was his fault.

He was so deep in his thoughts that he wasn't aware of Enrique's enforcer come from behind and deliver a powerful kick to Lucas's injured side, sending his gun flying. He screamed out in agony as the freshly stitched wound was attacked over and over. He could feel the warm blood slowly dripping down his side as the injury was reopened.

Lucas dropped to one knee as the assault continued. The blows rained down on him; the person trying not to give the former SAS captain a chance to retaliate. But their overzealousness did just that.

Once he was finally able to gather his bearings, Lucas caught the man's kick and delivered two powerful punches to the enforcer's exposed groin. It wasn't pretty, but right now, he didn't care. Lucas got to his feet and wrapped his arms around the man's neck, who was sniffling as he clutched his ruptured testes. He squeezed the enforcer's neck, and when he heard him choke, Lucas gave it a vicious wrench, snapping it.

He let the lifeless body fall to the ground, but before he could do anything else he heard a familiar voice behind him.

'Why don't you try that with me, mon ami?' Babou said

Lucas turned around to face the Senegalese assassin and saw him stretching and limbering up. He knew he wasn't in any real condition to face the killer, and he eyed his gun laying on the ground, several feet away.

'Really? You disappoint me, Redmond. And here was me thinking that you would want a fair fight.'

'Says the man with the poison tipped blades?'

'Ah, touché. You have me there, my friend.'

'I do, so why don't you just back up and when I'm healed up, I'll be more than happy to beat your ass.'

'You British, with the funny wit,' laughed Babou. 'No, no, I don't think I will be doing that. You see, we have the reputation to uphold. We have a contract, we have been paid, now we must fulfil that contract. Our reputation is our bread and butter, as you British say.' Babou finished his stretches and took up a fighting stance. 'Come on, mon ami, I promise to give you a swift defeat.'

It seemed as if he had no choice but to fight, despite the blood seeping through his shirt. Ordinarily, their unarmed fighting prowess could be considered as being on par with one another, but with the blood he was losing and the wild but ferocious assault he had just received, Lucas was at a definite disadvantage.

He raised his hands and prepared for combat.

Babou landed and unleashed jumping, spinning heel kick which Lucas barely saw coming. It landed flush in his chest, winding him and sending him crashing to the ground. He watched the assassin bouncing around on the balls of his feet, showing off his fancy footwork, grinning profusely.

Lucas got to his feet once more, dusted himself off, and prepared again, circling the confident hitman.

Again, Babou struck out, feinting with a low kick, only to raise his leg and hit Lucas in the side of his head, staggering him. A rapid exchange of punches between the two followed, culminating with a devastating elbow strike beneath Lucas's jaw.

He fell to the ground again. Exactly what he wanted, and where.

Lucas rolled over, coming back up in a kneeling position, pointing his gun at Babou. Surprisingly, the assassin stood there, smiling. The reason why soon became apparent to Lucas, as Diouf's giant hand grabbed his gun hand, and swung Lucas through the air like a toy, slamming him into the wall of a mausoleum. He kept hold of the semi-conscious man, crushing his wrist until he dropped the gun. Then he grabbed him by the throat and squeezed, choking him until he passed out.

Lucas slid to the floor and lay in a heap at the big man's feet. Babou came over, picked up the lank arm and checked their adversary's pulse to make sure his partner hadn't been overzealous. There was a pulse.

'Good, he's still breathing. Pick him up so we can leave. Enrique should be at the car by now. He wants to leave as soon as we're done here.'

Diouf heaved the substantial frame of Lucas onto his shoulder, and carried him, like a child, towards the cemetery entrance.

Neither of them noticed the glow of the muted mobile phone coming from Lucas's back pocket.

• • • •

ELLEN HELD HER PHONE up to her ear. Venice Jones, sitting next to her, could see the different range of emotions crossing her lover's face.

'What is it, babe?' Venice asked, rubbing Ellen's thigh.

'It's Lucas; I can't get hold of him. I've tried several times'

'I'm sure it's nothing serious. He's always leaving his phone around at the office.'

'Yeah, maybe. But he should have been expecting my call to let him know about the encrypted letter. I mean, that's what he said in the text, to let him know as soon as I'd cracked it.'

'I'm sure there's some explanation.'

'Yeah, something bad. This guy is like a big shit magnet, trust me.'

'Okay, so what can we do?'

'Nothing, I guess,' Ellen replied as ended another unanswered call to Lucas and dialled a new number. 'But I know someone that might be able to help'

'Hello?' David answered the phone after a couple of rings.

'Lucas is missing,' Ellen blurted out.

'Ellen? What are you talking about? And furthermore, how did you get this number?'

'It was easy once I found out where you lived.'

'Jesus!'

'No, Ellen, although the stuff I do is pretty miraculous. Anyway, as I was saying, Lucas isn't picking up his phone.'

'Really? I'm sure he's just fed up with your antics, as I am.'

'That's not very nice, especially after I just made your phone's digital footprint disappear. No one will be able to find this phone now. Well, except me of course. You're supposed to be the head of a spy department. These things should come as standard.'

'Well, um, thank you,' he replied slightly shamed by his earlier outburst. 'Now what makes you think Redmond is missing?'

'He wanted me to tell him as soon as I'd got a result about the letter.'

'And have you?'

'Of course, that's why I was calling him.'

'Okay, so tell me.'

'Whoever wrote the letter used a simple substitution cypher with the Frere Jacques nursery rhyme as the key, or key phrase as it were.'

'And how does that work?'

'It's simple really, hence the name. First, you write out the alphabet in its normal order, then to create your encryption key you basically delete all the repetitions from the phrase you're using, in this case you would keep the first "F" then delete the rest, keep the first "R" then delete the rest, and so forth. This forms the beginning of your key. It's unlikely that you'd have a phrase long enough that would give you an entire twenty-six letter key, unless it was a page from a book or something, so you would extend it by adding the remaining letters of the alphabet in alphabetical order, giving you a twenty-six-letter key. This key you would write underneath the alphabet you wrote, then to encrypt your message you replace each letter with the one below it. And to decrypt you would use the opposite procedure.'

'Fascinating. And what does the letter say?'

Ellen pressed a few buttons and emailed it across to the head of S7. 'You can read it for yourself.'

David sighed, opened the email, and read. '"My dear friend, Tomas. Success! It has been a long and often arduous quest that we have undertaken, but finally success has shone upon us. Further proof that our mission is a righteous one. For only the true god could have delivered to us the tools needed to finally convey his justice upon the Catholics. And their demise shall come from their own greed.

"Our friend, Armando, has returned from the New Land and he was correct; the stories he had heard about a chest of gold taken from Peru that was cursed by the natives were not the tall tales of drunken sailors, after all, but were recounts of facts. Coins he called, Moneda de muerte, given to these savages by their gods, apparently have the power over life and death, with but a touch. The Spanish took them from this land, along with the natives' gold. He was told that anyone touching the Moneda de muerte would die by exsanguination, their blood would leave their body from their eyes, nose, mouth, and even through their skin.

"Now these coins, this cursed treasure, is in the home of the Catholic Church, the Vatican, which could not be a better place for them.

"For something of this nature, there are of course some caveats which must be adhered to. Firstly, there is a heathen prayer which must be recited to awaken the power of the coins. God will forgive us this trespass, for what we do is in his glory. Secondly, and most importantly, you must not, under any circumstances, handle these coins with an ungloved hand, nor must they touch any of your naked flesh.

"Tomas, my friend, it is now down to you. Your task is to get these coins out of Vatican coffers and into the hands of the Catholic people. It is time for our sisters and brothers slaughtered on St Bartholomew's Day, and all those persecuted since that atrocity to have their justice, for it is God's will.

"I will carry out great vengeance on them and punish them in my wrath. Then they will know that I am the Lord, when I take vengeance on them.

F. Dubois"."

David finished reading the seventeenth century letter. 'We need to find Lucas. The symptoms of this cursed treasure are the same as those that killed Kallum Taylor and the dignitaries at the G20 Summit. That's too much of a coincidence for my liking. So is the fact that Angela Redmond wanted these letters. Find Lucas, Ellen.'

Chapter 34

Natasha and Alyssa coughed and spluttered as the dust from the landslide slowly settled but was still getting into their lungs as it swirled around. It was almost pitch black, only the smallest slivers of light peered through the gaps of the irregular shaped boulders. Natasha moved to one of these small spots of illumination and dug into her bag, searching for appropriate equipment. Moments later, she pulled out two headlamps, put one on herself, and handed the other to her companion.

'One thing I've learnt from The Acquirers business is to always pack for any situation, well as best as you can, anyway. I've got some water in here if you'd like some.'

Alyssa's light beam bobbed up and down profusely. She took the bottle handed to her and had two good gulps. 'I seriously do not know how you cope with all this...this stress, Natasha. If our archaeology lessons had been anything like this, I would have switched courses at the first opportunity. This is bad for my health.'

'This is what makes me feel alive, Alyssa. I'm not one for the slow lane. I love the adrenaline rush. And in this day and age, to make a new archaeological find, more than usually, comes with a rather large slice of danger.'

'Well, working with you these last few days has made me come to a decision. When we get out of this, if we get out of this, I'm applying for a teaching role. I can't do this action archaeology thing; I'd have a nervous breakdown. You are a danger-girl, Natasha Travers. I am not. Now, how are we getting out of here? Do you have any ideas?'

In the new brightness provided by their headgear, the two women were able to survey their situation. It didn't look good. Even if the boulders were smaller, they were so precariously stacked that the rocks at the top could come tumbling down at any moment. A fact Natasha chose not to share with her already stressed friend.

'Feliciana mentioned that there was a cave behind the two new sarcophagi. Perhaps we should start there.'

'Are you sure there is no other way? What if we wait here for a rescue team?'

'We don't know there will be one. We don't even know if—' Natasha became flustered as she remembered seeing the helicopter going into a dive, pulling away as it came under gunfire. 'We don't know if they made it, so it could be a long time before anyone came looking for us, if at all. I truly wish there were another way, Alyssa.'

The two women found a crevice shortly. It was roughly a twelve-inch opening, but when Natasha lay flat on her stomach and pushed in her head to look inside, she got a shock.

'Jeez! It's huge in there. It looks completely untouched too; natural formations of stalagmites and stalactites.'

'How are you going to get down?'

Natasha took an extendable grappling hook from the bag. 'Preparation is key, hon.' She pushed the bag through and heard it land barely two seconds later. Next, she dropped the rope down the gap and made sure that the hook itself was secure in the narrowest part of the fissure. Then, she got down once more and shimmied her legs into the crevice, keeping hold of the rope as her body cleared the crack in the wall and entered the abyss.

'Try not to swing when you're coming down,' Natasha called up to Alyssa as her head disappeared over the ridge.

As she reached the bottom and put her bag back over her shoulder, Natasha let her friend know it was okay to come down. Alyssa began her descent whilst she looked around, seeing if there was indeed a way out. She could see a passageway leading off, so at least there was more to see and remained hopeful that they'd be able to find a way out.

'You okay?' Natasha asked, as Alyssa finished her climb down.

'I am, thanks,' she replied as she took in their surroundings. 'Wow! If we were in different circumstances, I would have said this place is beautiful. It's like we're in something straight out of a fantasy book.'

'Yeah, I know what you mean, but unfortunately this is real life and Gandalf isn't going to appear and rescue us. We have to do it ourselves. I saw something over there, so let's try that way.'

They traversed the passage, twisting and turning. At some points it felt like they were doubling back on themselves. Natasha thought it was entirely possible as she eventually realised that they had been in a steady, gentle decline for some time.

'I don't know which part of this stuff is supposed to be fun to these spelunking people,' bemoaned Natasha as she struggled to navigate a particularly tight crevice, her arms and back getting scraped in the process.

'Says the woman that likes to dodge bullets and jump out of helicopters.'

'Not out of choice; out of necessity. There's a difference.'

'You know something that just occurred to me? Lucas and Peter are just like this.'

'What?'

'I've seen you and Peter together, and it is fair to say that he is not much of the adrenaline junkie like Lucas. He would be more like a spelunker. Slow going, steadfast.'

'I know English is not your first language, Alyssa, but your analogy stinks.'

'Does it? Or is that only because you see it for yourself too? Look, I'm not judging. I understand why you *would* date him; he is literally like the complete opposite of Lucas. You couldn't get further away from the type. I'm not saying you should be with Lucas. I'm just wondering can you see yourself being happy with Peter long term, without having to change?'

Her friend's words reminded Natasha of the disagreement she already had with Peter about who she was. There definitely were somethings that she had to consider for the future, but right now, she had more pressing things to worry about.

Alyssa slipped through the crevice with significantly less hassle, commenting that sometimes having fewer curves was advantage after all. On the overside of the crevice the cave system opened out even larger, where they found cave drawings. This discovery brought smiles to both of their faces. It was the first real positive sign they had seen that there might actually be a way out.

The two women spread out, looking for the next step on their route to freedom. But Alyssa had stopped to examine the drawings. Something struck her about an image she passed, and she whirled around, trying to look at all the others.

Natasha stopped her search as she noticed her friend's frantic movements. 'What is it, Alyssa?'

'These drawings, they're like the Bayeux tapestry. They depict creation in the eyes of the native Peruvians. Look here,' she said excitedly as she grabbed Natasha's arm and dragged her to an image of what looked like a meteor shower. 'This is the beginning. This is when the gods arrived, how they arrived, I don't know. The drawing here shows the image of Viracocha and Supay.'

'These other people must be the other staff gods from their religious pantheon,' Natasha speculated as she took as many photographs as she could.

'Exactly! These next ones depict the various myths and legends you mentioned that are associated with the gods. Here Viracocha creates the giants from rock, here he destroys them. Here he creates man. Instruction about drawing Nasca lines. And here,' Alyssa skipped past a few images to something Natasha recognised.

'The saddles of Viracocha,' she whispered.

'It's all here! Even when Supay rose up against him and they fought. According to this, it caused all kinds of natural disasters to happen, earthquakes, volcano eruptions, torrential rains, darkness. It also shows where he ended up when he was expelled from the land.'

'Really?' Natasha followed Alyssa's pointing hand and saw a drawing of Supay in amongst what looked like a strange forest of twisted trees. 'I don't get it. What's that supposed to be?'

'It's Romania!' Alyssa could barely contain herself.

'Huh?'

'In fact, to be exact, it's a forest called Hoia Baciu, in Transylvania.'

'How do you figure that?'

'The trees in that forest are exactly how they are in this drawing. They grow very strangely there, and scientists have no idea why.'

'But surely there are other places in the world like that.'

'Apparently not. But that's not all. There's one particular area in the forest called Poiana Rotunda. Nothing grows there. Again, scientists don't know why and according to the historical records, nothing has ever grown there. There's quite a bit of paranormal activity there too.'

Natasha looked at Alyssa cockeyed.

'It's supposed to be haunted,' she added. 'There are a lot of stories of people hearing things. People disappearing and reappearing years later with no idea that time had passed.'

'The god of death being sent to Europe would kind of make sense given the turmoil and violence that moulded the region centuries ago.'

'And the alien activity,' Alyssa added.

'I wonder if that's where she was going...'

'Who? Adela?'

'No! Your friend's great grandmother!'

'You mean Ioan?'

'Yes, his mother said that her grandmother, Xioczana, travelled to Romania, but she didn't know why. I must admit, at the time I thought was a bit strange that she would travel all that way for no apparent reason. But what if she did have a reason? What if she had to do something in this forest but was side-tracked by something else?'

'By what?'

'I don't know...love, maybe. She obviously never went back to Peru. We know that much because she had a family here.'

'I wonder what it was she was doing?'

Natasha barely heard her friend speak. Her analytical mind was ticking over, trying to make sense of it all. She repeatedly curled a strand of her hair around her finger as she paced back and forth mumbling to herself. 'Xioczana left Peru, went to Spain and ended up in Romania in 1915. Taki Kawsay Wanu a prayer for life and death, but its incomplete, the one for death is missing. Aysana Kawsay Wanu the coins which were used for sacrifice some lived some died by divine intervention, or maybe it was luck, or even some sort of genetic marker. I mean, the Amerindians were wiped out by a lot of the diseases the Spanish brought over when they...'

Alyssa's eyebrows drew together when she saw Natasha freeze abruptly. 'Are you okay?' She got no response and reached out to touch her.

'Huh? Oh yeah, I'm fine. I was just thinking. What if this battle between Viracocha and Supay is still going on?'

Her friend shook her head, not knowing where Natasha was going with her hypothesise.

'Viracocha created the people of South America, yes? Supay was banished from the land, yes? So, if he couldn't go back there, what if he used Europeans, such as the Spanish, to do what he couldn't and destroy the children of Viracocha?'

Alyssa nodded. 'And in retaliation, the Aysana Kawsay Wanu were sent to Hoia Baciu to vanquish him.'

'Maybe it needed all the coins to do it. Perhaps that was why Xioczana went to Italy and Spain.'

'And why she couldn't complete her task because she didn't collect all the coins?'

'What if that caused the Spanish Flu? The timeline fits. I mean that was in 1918, three years after she arrived in Romania. Someone could have found the Aysana and unbeknownst to them started a pandemic. Fifty million people died from that and there were an estimated five hundred million cases.'

'So what are you saying? We complete the task Xioczana started?'

'I think we have to. This thing about the G20, the symptoms are far too similar to what Feliciana told us, and what's on this wall just to be a coincidence. I think whatever organisation posted that message could have these coins. Fuck knows how they intend to use them, though.'

'Two billion is a hell of a lot more than fifty million, though.'

'Like I said, I don't know how they'll do it, but look at the nations affected at the G20; China, USA, Russia, India, Mexico, Brazil, Indonesia, and the EU is a member as a whole. These countries have the highest populations in the world. In total, you're looking at something like four billion people.'

'Shit. I think we need to get out of here.'

'My sentiments exactly,' Natasha replied as they both restarted their search for a way out of their predicament.

Chapter 35

The numbness in Lucas's arms was the first things he felt when he woke up. The second thing was the stinging pain in his side. He instinctively went to touch it, but found that his hands were handcuffed to a pipe above his head.

'Well, that explains that,' he grumbled. He didn't know where he was and since his current abode didn't have windows, there was no way for Lucas to tell if it was morning or night. Wherever he was, though, it was deathly silent. 'Sound proofed, probably.'

He twisted around the best he could, trying to learn as much as he could about his location. The trouble was the room had nothing, but that in itself spoke volumes. It looked like the room was new. Pristine, even. The render on the walls was smooth. There was no paint, no cracks, not even any webbing, and as he said earlier, sound proofed. It was probably an unused spare room. But where that room was, was still the unanswered question. Something that he was itching to ask Enrique the first chance he got.

Just then, the door opened. Lucas tensed himself, ready for whoever was about to come in and try to soften him up. He wasn't about to quit, and they'd soon find out that he had a lot of fight left in him.

That was until he saw who it was.

'Hello, Lucas.'

'Well, well, well, Chiara Harris. I must admit, this is an unpleasant surprise.'

She walked in and closed the door behind her. 'I see you're still getting into trouble.'

'I wouldn't feel like my day was complete if I didn't have one or two altercations.'

'Well, I think this time you may have bitten off more than you can chew, baby.'

'A bit like you, huh?' Lucas smirked.

'Don't flatter yourself. What I did was part of a much bigger scheme.'

'Really? You keep telling yourself that. You were hooked on me. Why else would you be in here now?'

'When I was told you were here with a woman, I instantly thought it was your bitch of a wife. I had intended to kill her slowly, right here in front of you. Imagine my surprise when I saw it wasn't her at all, just the next woman in line to warm your bed, I suppose. And she's Australian too. What? You couldn't get me out of your mind, Lucas? Is that why you hooked up with an Australian? Is that why you slept with my lookalike?'

'What did you say? You've spoken to her? That must mean Anne's alive!'

Chiara ignored Lucas's questions and continued goading her former lover. 'By trying to save my lookalike, did you think you were saving me?' Chiara sauntered towards Lucas until she stood beside him and gave him a loving caress, with her cheek against his. 'Let me tell you now, I don't need saving. Natasha, on the other hand, can go wherever she pleases, but she will never be able to escape my revenge. She killed my brother, and I'm going to kill her.'

'So, you were always working with your brother?'

'Of course,' she said as she walked around her strung up captive. 'The J Organisation is our family business. Do you know what the J stands for? It's Justice. Justice for the oppressed; justice for those not strong enough to speak up for themselves.'

'When exactly did this cry for justice become a shout for terrorism?'

'Terrorism? Don't listen to the media. They're as crooked and self-righteous as politicians. In fact, they're probably worse. Politicians tell you what they think you want or need to hear. The media tells you what they want you to know.'

'And you think that justifies you killing billions of people?'

'I'm not killing anyone. This isn't my gig. I'm just a soldier following orders. I'm sure you know all about that, former SAS man.'

'A soldier following orders is one thing, but when they go beyond the remit of those orders, it becomes a completely different matter.'

'I don't know where this moral attitude of yours comes from Lucas. From what I've heard, you were quite the little crim back in your youth.'

Lucas quietly fumed. 'Who told you that?'

'It doesn't matter. You know something, baby? I actually really did want things to work out with us. Of course you started out as a "mark", but I could see that having you onboard would be a great benefit to us.' Chiara stood behind him, her hot breath on his ear. 'It's not too late you know. We could pick up right where we left off.'

'Oh, god, no. First, the sex was okay, mediocre at best. I don't know if it was your brother that gave you tips, but damn, it needs some work. Second, I'm just not that into you. That bridge is gone, burnt down, then blown up, stamped on a bit, scooped up and put in a rocket then sent into space "gone".'

'This tells a different story.' Chiara grabbed his groin and kissed him.

'Nothing to do with you, love. I was thinking of my favourite football team. Or maybe I got hard thinking about killing you.'

Chiara slapped Lucas hard in pure frustration.

'Truth hurts, huh? What's the point of holding me here? When are you going to let me go?' The door opened once more, and this time it was Enrique. 'Ah, here we go, the more the merrier. Now the party can really get started.'

'Let you go? Mi amigo, you're going nowhere. For the time being, this will be your home. When my work is done, you will follow. You're my new my dog now.'

'Oh, Enrique, I'm really going to enjoy killing you. I don't usually get pleasure from doing it, it's usually a necessity of survival, but you, I'll make an exception for.'

'So funny, thinking that you're going to escape from here. Give it up, Lucas, you lost. Just accept it and move on.'

'You'll have to kill me first. You have a lot of innocent blood on your hands, Faye, for starters, not to mention the billions that you're planning to kill.'

'Planning to kill? It's already begun, Lucas. The G20 was just to get the attention of the so-called world leaders. These people don't give a shit about the slums of Brazil, Mexico,

Pakistan that are already losing people, and that's just the beginning. You look a bit confused, Lucas. Well, I'll let the person in charge of development explain the science stuff. Open the door,' he said to a guard.

Lucas shook his head in disbelief. His mind raced, tried to make sense of everything that had happened over the past few days. How could it be? 'I saw you die,' he said in a barely audible whisper.

'Did you?' Faye asked as she walked in. 'Or did you just see someone with a vaguely similar hair colour and height to me wearing my clothes? I mean her face was pretty bashed up. I don't know how you could really be sure. But I guess recognising the women you've slept with isn't really your thing. If I'm not mistaken when you first saw me, you called out Chiara's name.'

'Our resemblance is pure chance, by the way. We had no idea that you'd be at the hospital, Lucas.'

'No, we didn't,' Faye added. 'But you played your role as protector perfectly, and it allowed me to stay close, learn what you knew and pass it on to Enrique.'

'But Babou and Diouf...'

'Were my protectors, not my kidnappers. I was at the hospital testing out the final strain of the virus on Kallum. Since you knew what that Senegalese duo are, you assumed I was with them under duress. A little acting on my part sold the deal, though. Pulling the wall over the eyes of that DCI Russell was even easier.'

'The two officers he sent to watch you?'

'Yeah, I did them too. All part of the plan to stay under you protective wing, Lucas. And you came running, like a knight in shining armour.'

'A blind knight,' Chiara added.

'You know something,' chuckled Enrique. 'I'm not sure which facial expression I prefer on his face. The one when he sees a woman he has been with killed in front of him, or the expression he has when he is exposed as an idiot.'

'So, Faye, Enrique brought you in here for the science bit.'

'I think Enrique is being kind. There is a disc in our possession that is made from a space rock which contains bacteria.'

'Space germs?' Lucas scoffed.

'For your information, there are over two-hundred and fifty different species of bacteria and fungi which can survive in outer space, and that's only the ones we know about. This particular one is completely new, but we were able to create a synthetic strain, which is more potent as well as more transmissible.'

'Of course you have. You cuckoo people love to think you can improve on nature.'

'But we have. We have laced it into the currency of the of world's most populous nations. And at the rate money changes hands, it won't be long until populations decline.'

Enrique gleefully took up the explanation. 'Especially when we start visiting the poorer areas of these countries and start giving money away. It will destabilise the world economy, leaving it in the ideal position for a singular world leader.'

'So that's why you were so hot on getting the Euro plates back. So who will be this singular leader? You?'

'No, this isn't my plan. I'm just executing it, but I will be in the council.'

'Oh, yeah, that's right. You Bilderberg Inner Circle people are playing some sort of game, aren't you? Each one of you takes a turn as the head of an operation, bringing a plan for world domination to the table, and the one that succeeds will become ruler of the world or some bollocks like that.'

'How do you know...'

'Is that the look of stupidity you were talking about, Enrique? It suits you.'

'So you know about the Bilderberg Group? So what?' Chiara crossed her arms unimpressed. 'There's nothing you can do about it, Lucas. You're one little cog and this is a huge machine.'

'One little cog is all it takes to stop it dead.'

'This is a waste of time,' Enrique huffed. 'I have to get these plates to Hincu so that we can start production of the Euros as soon as possible. Doctor, would you prepare some vials for me? I will meet you in the laboratory.'

'Certainly, Enrique.' Doctor Dannen gave Lucas a final look of disdain before she left the makeshift cell.

'What about Travers?' Chiara grabbed the hooded man's arm as he was about to leave.

'She's in Peru.'

'What?'

'Yes, you let her slip through your fingers in Iasi. But I have my partner, La Viuda, there already. She shot down her helicopter, but it landed fine, although she wasn't on board. She won't get far.'

Lucas listened intently. His heart thumped when he heard news about Natasha. But what was she doing in Peru?

'Now, if you don't mind,' Enrique said shrugging his arm free. 'I have things to do.'

'And what am I supposed to do?' Chiara questioned.

'I don't know, have some fun with him or come with me. It's entirely up to you.'

'I've had my fill of Romania. I think I'll chill out here for a bit.'

Enrique eyed her intently. 'Don't do anything to jeopardise things, Chiara. You will have your revenge for the death of you brother soon. Everything is going to plan now.'

'I'm not going to do a thing, except have fun like you said. I might even go and see who this other woman is that he was with.'

'Jealous, are you, Chiara?' Lucas goaded.

'Not in the least.'

'Keep telling yourself that, love, you might actually believe it. Positive affirmation, and all that. Like me, I've been telling myself that I'm going to kill that bastard right there.' He gestured to Enrique. 'And then I'm going to kill Faye.'

'And what about me, Lucas? You can't bring yourself to kill me, can you? You still love me, don't you?'

It was like a switch in Lucas's head. A switch that allowed him to be cold, ruthless, uncaring and heartless when he needed to be. The switch that he flipped when he had to do what needed to be done to complete a mission.

The ends justified the means.

If that meant killing a woman he had kissed and made love to then, for the sake of the mission, the sake of billions of people, he would pull the trigger.

'Don't get it twisted, hon. I'd quite easily take you out too, but I think I'll leave that to Nat. I get this sneaky feeling that she'd really like to fuck you up, and who am I to deprive her of that pleasure?'

Chapter 36

After a long and fruitless search for a way out, Natasha and Alyssa's hopes of freedom were disappearing fast. Talk between them had all but reverted to monosyllabic words. The idea of having to travel all the way back to where they had first entered the cave in the hope of being rescued was looking like a real possibility. The fact that they may never be found was a daunting prospect that neither one of them wanted to give credence to. But facts were facts: for all they knew, the only people that knew they were in there could be dead.

'We might as well get some rest, before we head back,' Natasha said as she slumped against a wall. Alyssa followed suit. She was exhausted. It felt like they'd been on the go for days, and in some sense, with all the flying and crossing of time zones, they had.

Natasha took out the water and had a mouthful before handing it to Alyssa, who grunted a thanks in return. They settled down in silence, Alyssa cursing her lot, while Natasha tried to visualise the path they had taken to reach here, thinking that they might have missed something on the way. It wasn't long before both women fell fast asleep.

It was a combination of two things that woke Natasha up a few hours later. The first thing was the intermittent flashing from her dying headlight, penetrating her closed eyelids. The second thing was a sensation of wetness she was feeling in her pants.

She sat up, suddenly wide awake. Natasha patted the seat of her pants; they were indeed cold and damp. She twisted around and was more than a little relieved to see the water bottle had been knocked over during their sleep.

As Natasha reached down to right the almost empty bottle, she noticed that there wasn't a puddle of water that she would have expected from a spillage. Sure, the uncomfortable clamminess of her wet cargo pants pointed out that some of it had been soaked up by them. But in the on off light of her headgear, she could see something else.

Alyssa moaned as she was shaken awake from her slumber, only to have Natasha drag her to the damp edge of a wall, pointing at it like a madwoman.

'Look at it,' yelled Natasha. 'What do you see?'

After rubbing the sleep from her eyes, Alyssa peered at the wall. 'Well, it looks like natural bed lines, meaning it's probably a mineral calcite.'

'Which means?'

'Limestone.' It took a couple seconds for the information to sink into her sleep fogged mind. 'Limestone is a soft rock, easily broken. I don't suppose you have a pickaxe in that bag of yours.'

'No, but the coins might be able to do it. They certainly have weight to them.'

'Yeah, but we don't know how thick this could be,' Alyssa said reluctant to get her hopes up again.

'True, but I don't think it is,' replied Natasha as she poured a bit more water on the ground and showed her friend how it drained away. 'The edge is almost translucent. Just begging to be broken.'

'Okay, it's worth a shot,' Alyssa relented. 'Anything to get out of this place.'

Natasha's headgear finally gave out as she opened her bag about to take out one of the heavyweight coins. 'Here, Alyssa, make sure it's a Viracocha one.'

'I have no interest in touching the other one either, so don't worry about that.'

She shook the bag a couple of times to manoeuvre the discs into position, then Alyssa heaved one and then another out. The pair quickly got to work, picking up an efficient rhythm; Alyssa would strike, and then, since she had the only working light, she would stay steady so that Natasha could hit the limestone.

After they had both hit it two or three times, a large piece of the limestone fell away, which was accompanied by their cheers, and they heard it tumble along rock before a distinctive splash. They continued to hit it, harder and harder each time, and not so much as a chip came off. They looked at each other briefly before Alyssa got down and had a look.

'There are stairs there. It could be another chamber, but its flooded. This wall isn't thick either; barely two centimetres.'

'Maybe it was a door of some kind.'

'Could be, but I didn't see any keyhole.'

'Me neither. But there must have been a way in and out of here. I mean look at the art.'

'And the stairs. They wouldn't just lead to nowhere.'

'Exactly.' Natasha suddenly remembered the drawings, how they exalted Viracocha, showed all of his deeds and actions. Precisely the kind of things you would expect in his temple.

She grabbed Alyssa and pulled her over to one particular drawing. The picture showed a priest kneeling in front of a temple. 'We're in that temple, Alyssa.'

'This?' She looked around with disdain. 'You must be joking.'

'Don't think of the temples of later years. We're talking four thousand years ago, remember? Any valuables that might have been here would probably have been taken, definitely by the Spanish, if not before. Look at the drawings. They're like an ad campaign for Viracocha.'

'Okay, your hypothesise has merit. Now what?'

'I don't know. Kneel in front of it I guess,' she answered with a shrug.

A lightbulb went off in Alyssa's head and she turned away sharply, rushing to a spot roughly ten metres from where they'd made their hole. 'Look here,' she pointed at two slight indentations parallel to each other. 'I didn't know what it was, just thought it was a natural occurrence or something. Until you mentioned kneeling.'

Natasha inspected where Alyssa shone the light. 'I think you're right,' she nodded, looking from the smooth grooves in the rock to the wall and back again. 'What have we got to lose?'

She took a breath and knelt down in the grooves. Slowly, she raised her arms, replicating the image. But nothing happened.

'You don't think you have to recite some prayer, do you?'

'I hope not, or else we're completely screwed.'

Alyssa glance back at the picture. 'Well, in this the priest seems to have light coming out of his hands. I don't suppose you can do that?'

'Unfortunately, not.' Natasha wracked her brains. Then it came to her. 'Only a priest of Viracocha could enter his temple, so it makes sense that he would have to present something that only a true devotee would have.'

'Something like the Aysana Kawsay Wanu!' Alyssa rushed over to retrieve the discs, helping Natasha to put them on her palms, when she returned. 'Now what?'

'No idea,' she replied her arms already screaming from the build-up of lactic acid in them. Natasha pushed her hands higher still, fighting through the agony.

Suddenly, the eyes of the drawings of Viracocha glowed, as did the coins in Natasha's hands. They became light as a feather, felt like she wasn't holding anything at all. Then it happened.

Whoomph! Click! Clack!

Sounds of a mechanism waking up, then with the scrapping noise of stone on stone, dust and particles filling the air, the wall slowly raised up. They both looked on in amazement.

'How is this happening?' Alyssa said in awe, her eyes wide. 'I mean, it has been centuries since anyone last set foot in this place.'

'Beats me,' Natasha replied. The door had completely retreated into its recess, and she stood up, thankful to be able to get the blood circulating in her arms and legs again. 'One thing I've learnt over the years doing The Acquirers work with Lucas is there are some things in this world that you can't explain, and it's not our place to know.'

'And you can live with that? The not knowing?'

'I didn't say that. But if you stand around trying to figure it out, fixating on one thing, you'll miss out on the all the other glory.'

Alyssa looked at Natasha with a deep furrow. 'What's that supposed to mean?'

'It means if stand around here any longer we won't be getting out.' Natasha packed her bag ready to go. 'Besides, we don't know how much power your battery has. It could give out any moment, and I don't fancy our chances without it.'

'Good point!' Alyssa quickly took the lead and went through the opening.

Beyond the door, at the top of the stairs on either side, was a statue; a staff god.

'Viracocha. This is his temple alright. Can you just imagine how it would have been in its prime.'

'I know what you mean, but I'm sure it didn't come with a swimming pool.'

'It's probably rainfall that's seeped through the mountain over all these years. We're going to have to go down the stairs, find the entrance,' Natasha said, pointing at the inky black water.

'I'm not that strong of a swimmer. Not all of us were a modern pentathlete,' Alyssa said, staring at the still water.

'You don't have to be. Just hold your breath and we'll follow the stairs, use them to propel us along.'

'Then I think you should take the lead,' Alyssa said, taking off the headlamp and handing to Natasha. 'You lead and I'll follow.'

Natasha put it on. And stood at the water's edge, taking huge breaths and expelling them. Expanding her lungs, Alyssa followed suit. 'Okay, let's do this.' They each took a final big intake of breath, and whilst holding hands, plunged into the cold dark water.

It was hard to see in the murky depths. Their visibility was reduced to two feet ahead. The stairway was longer than either one of them could have imagined, seeming to go on forever. Alyssa felt the need to come up for air, but soon found out that was no longer an option; they were in a completely submerged tunnel. There was no going back. Panic began to set in.

She thrashed about, giving Natasha a hard time holding onto her. With a two-handed grip she pulled her close, put her mouth on her friends and blew, sharing what breath she had left. It was the only thing she could think of doing to save her friend, but now they were both desperately short of breath.

They pushed on as fast as they could. Their lungs were ready to burst. They kicked as hard as possible; the tunnel had to end at some point. But the battery in their headlamp flickered and finished first.

Natasha was terrified. Drowning wasn't as a big fear of hers as it was with Lucas, but nobody liked the idea of dying through suffocation. His thalassophobia came about when he almost drowned as a kid. He had never gone into too much detail about what happened, but now that she knew the life he led when he was younger, she could imagine that it happened whilst working with his mother.

Suddenly, Alyssa's hand went limp in hers. She was going to die if Natasha didn't drag them to safety. There was nothing she could do except fight. Natasha couldn't give up. The life of her friend was literally in her hands.

But she couldn't hold her breath forever

Chapter 37

Anne Sheppard relaxed with her hands behind her head, on the lumpy cot of her room come cell. She could feel the bump where she had been struck from the behind. The fact that she had let someone get the jump on her hurt more than the actual injury.

She had looked out of the little window in her room the moment she had awoken. All she could tell from what she saw, however, was that she was in some sort of fortress or citadel in the middle of a forest. It could have been anywhere.

All Anne could do now was wait until her host made an appearance.

It wasn't long before she got her wish. The heavy wooden door was unlocked and opened to allow a woman to enter with two armed men. Anne sat up when he saw her and scoffed with a smile. 'You look remarkably like her, the doctor, I mean. I take it that was no accident.'

Chiara smiled. 'Just a little trip to the hairstylist. The rest was god's joke on Lucas.'

'Yeah, I can see that. No wonder he was so hung up on saving this woman. You must be his ex then.'

'I am. My name is Chiara, and Lucas tells me you are Anne?'

'He's here?'

'My question is who are you to him? Are you his latest piece of tail? What were you doing with him? What are you doing here?'

Anne stared at her. 'You assholes brought me here, and that's more than one question. Besides, what's it to you who I am? He's already kicked you to the kerb. Move on sister. You're acting needy; it's not a good look.'

'That's where you're wrong. Once Natasha is dealt with, and once he realises our plan has progressed too far, he will come to his senses and know that only I can offer him a safe haven.'

'You've been hitting that cuckoo juice pretty hard, haven't you? Because that sounds kind of nuts.'

'What do you know?'

'Well, let's see,' Anne said, swinging her feet over the edge of the cot. 'For a start, I know Lucas isn't going to go anywhere near you. Unless he's there to kill you, of course. I also know that despite your accent you're not really Australian, are you?' Anne saw the flicker on Chiara's face. 'But most importantly, I know that I'll be out of here soon.'

Chiara looked either side at the guards who were already smirking, as if they'd just heard the funniest thing ever. 'And how exactly are you planning on doing that?'

'Wouldn't want to spoil the surprise.'

'You're unarmed and alone, I don't fancy your chances.'

Anne shrugged confidently. 'You'll just have to wait and see then.'

Chiara looked at her sharply. Even though she knew it would be all but impossible for this woman to escape, she was also an unknown quantity, and Chiara wasn't about to take any chances. 'Be careful with this one. Watch her closely,' she said to the guards as they left.

As soon as the door was slammed shut and locked once more, Anne relaxed. The truth of the matter was that she had no clue of the method of her escape, only that she would. Much more secure prisons had failed to hold her, so this place should be a doddle.

She rose from the bed, quickly going to examine to window more closely. Anne twisted the handle and pushed it open. It stopped almost immediately, opening only a few inches. Nowhere near enough for her to squeeze through. There must have been a catch outside.

In the back of her mind, Anne knew that it would have been too easy, and didn't allow herself to get despondent. She moved onto the next plan; smash it open. On closer inspection though, that escape route was quashed too. A little symbol in the corner of the windowpane let the thief know it was toughened glass. No way she was breaking through that.

Anne returned to the cot and made herself comfortable again. Now she was left with her final option; walk out through the door.

It was probably the easier of the three ideas, taking less effort, and that deduction included her having to take out the guards that would be at the door. But Anne always liked to challenge herself and keep her skills in tiptop condition. That's how it was working with Angela. If you let your skills drop and you became a liability, you were out. She had drilled it into Anne from a young age, and she'd never let complacency creep into her.

Time passed and Anne finally decided that now was the right moment to put her plan into action. She eased off of the bed and sauntered over to the door. Once she'd reached it, she turned her back to it, cleared her throat, and gave it three firm donkey kicks, which she was more than certain would make the guards jump out of their skin.

A guard yelled angrily through the door. 'What the hell are you doing in there?'

'What the hell kind of place you running here?' Anne yelled back. 'I need food! I'm hypoglycaemic. If my blood sugar drops too low, you'll be all sorts of trouble.'

'Shut the hell up, or we'll come in there and make you.'

This threat spurred Anne to even greater heights, banging, screaming, shouting. The guards bemoaned her actions, they themselves getting increasingly irate.

Until they heard a groan and then nothing.

'About bloody time too,' one of them said to the other, in Romanian, glad that the mad woman had finally piped down. Half an hour later, that relief turned to concern.

'We should check on her.'

'What?'

'Ms Harris said to watch her.'

'Yeah, and that's exactly what we're doing, from out here.'

'What if something happened?'

'Like what, exactly?'

'I don't know. But if they wanted her dead, they would have killed her already.'

The other guard paused for a moment. 'Fine! Go check on the crazy bitch then.'

The guard put his ear to the door, listening for any kind of movement. He didn't hear a thing. 'Step away from the door,' he called out, just to be on the safe side. He unlocked the door and with his partner covering him with his assault rifle, he swung the door open. 'Shit! It looks like she's passed out.'

The second guard entered, looking around to see what his comrade was staring at. Anne lay on the ground, face down, unmoving.

'Have you checked for a pulse?'

'No...no not yet.'

'What's wrong with you?' The older, more experienced guard questioned. 'Pull yourself together.' He put his gun down as he knelt beside the stricken woman, then checked her wrist for a pulse. 'It's there, faint, but she has a pulse. Help me turn her over so I can check her airway.'

As one pushed, the other pulled until they had rolled her onto her back. They both stopped, taken aback by what they saw. The woman's shirt had been pulled up, her breasts barely covered by the elaborately designed bra she wore.

'What the hell?' the old guard said, staring at her with his mouth open.

It was the last thing either one of them said as, quick as a flash, Anne opened her eyes, kicked one in the head then the other, before she performed a kip up to get to her feet. The beat down continued, neither guard ever getting their senses back before it was all over.

Anne rearranged her clothes, picked up the two Heckler & Koch MP7A1's and all the ammo the two men carried, then one of their radios. Finally, she crushed the windpipe of both men under her boot. Even though they were just doing their job, getting a salary, they were there to stop her. Which in her eyes made them just as accountable as Enrique, Chiara and Faye.

She quietly moved towards the door, glanced left then right, and on not seeing anything, Anne opened the door wider and stepped out. The stonework on the walls confirmed they were holding her in a medieval fortress and, judging by the accents of the guards she'd just killed, it was likely that the fortress was somewhere in Romania.

As important as that fact was, the thing foremost on her mind right now, though, was finding Lucas. This thing wasn't over yet. Angela wanted this whole scheme eradicated, and Lucas was motivated to do the same thing, albeit for different reasons. So, for the time being, he was working for his mum, whether he liked it or not. Anne liked that arrangement. She got to spend more time with him, just like the old days when her crush on him first developed.

Anne crept along with her back to a wall. She could hear voices, but it was hard to pinpoint them in the antiquated building. They seemed to bounce around like an echo. She noticed a number of electrical wires attached to the corner of the ceiling. They were passed through a hole from outside and Anne followed them, wondering what kind of modern upgrade had been applied to the medieval fortress.

She hoped that it might have been a telephone network that she might have been able to contact Angela from, but when she reached the end of the hall and looked around the corner, she had the feeling that the room was something more. Anne saw more cables running to the same room but coming from the other direction.

Anne watched two men enter, and a few moments later two men exited. A duty change. She had to act now, before the new guards had settled into whatever it was they were doing in there.

Chapter 38

Natasha kicked her feet fast to propel herself through the water with greater speed. Pulling Alyssa's unconscious body wasn't helping her cause, but if she couldn't get them to the surface soon, her friend wouldn't make it.

She did her best to hide the terror growing inside of her. Swimming into the unknown, not being able to see a thing, scared her to death. Natasha screamed. A muffled sound distorted by the water.

As air left her lungs, it was quickly replaced by rushing water. The realisation that she was going to die came to her like a flash as events from her life came to the forefront of her mind. There was a common thread among those memories. They were all of her and Lucas. And she was going to die here, and no one was going to find her, no one was going to be able to tell her parents what had happened to her. No one was going to tell Lucas that she was gone. Even if they were divorced now, her feelings for him were still there and she couldn't die with him thinking that she hated him.

Natasha willed herself on. Mind over matter. Even though she was fading, she couldn't bring herself to stop. An involuntary need to survive, fuelled by adrenaline, pushed her body to extraordinary lengths.

That was when she saw a glow through the blackness. It grew larger with every second that passed, but it was a second too long. Her vision faded as she slowly passed out. Once, twice, she lost sight of things as she fought to stay conscious.

The third black out was coming, she could feel it in her body. The fogginess invading her thoughts, expanding through her body as the blood that should have been transporting air had nothing to carry.

Then with one last weak kick of her feet, Natasha broke the surface of the water. She was on the verge of a complete collapse, but she was more than grateful for the huge mouthful of air she took in.

Under the moonlit, star filled sky, she tried her best to get Alyssa to the shoreline quickly so that she might save her before it was too late.

Natasha pulled her friend out of the water, and after not finding her pulse, she immediately performed CPR on her. She placed the heel of one hand on her breastbone, and the heel of your other hand on top of that. Then Natasha positioned her body directly over her hands and gave thirty hard chest compressions. She followed up with two resuscitating breaths.

After three cycles of compressions and breaths with no response, doubt crept into her mind. Then Alyssa suddenly choked awake, coughing up the water in her lungs. Natasha rolled her onto her side to aid with the excavation, then she flopped down next to her, relief bringing tears of joy to both of them.

'I really thought I was dead,' Alyssa revealed after a few minutes' rest. Her lungs hurt and her chest wasn't faring much better, but she didn't care. She was still alive.

'To be honest, so did I, and I wasn't far behind you.'

'And now here we are, under the moonlight. I'll never forget what you've done for me, Natasha.'

'Come on, don't be silly,' she said, accepting the tight hug from Alyssa. 'If it weren't for me, you wouldn't be in this mess. And you should know, this isn't over yet. I've got no idea where we are, so we need to sort that out and then find out what happened to the others.' Natasha soon found out that she was talking to herself when she heard the slow, rhythmic breathing coming from the sleeping Alyssa. 'Okay, I guess we've earned this one,' said Natasha, exhausted herself and she lay her head on the ground. Moments later, she was also fast asleep.

• • • •

NATASHA OPENED HER eyes, knowing she hadn't had the deep sleep that her body craved. But she rarely had such a sleep when she was forced to rough it with Lucas when they were on assignments. Because of it, however, she had learnt to function on as little as two hours rest, out of necessity more than anything else. Not that it meant she wouldn't enjoy a nice eight-hour sleep in a five-star hotel when this was all over.

She glanced beside her and saw that Alyssa was having no such problems sleeping. All right for some, she said to herself. Natasha got to her feet and stretched the kinks out of her body.

Being out in a place like this, without the streetlamps or car headlights, the light pollution that all cities had, allowed you to appreciate the night sky more. This is how the ancients could plot the movement of the stars without telescopes, how they could see planets thousands of years ago, she thought as she marvelled at the blanket of stars.

Beyond the sound of the river they had emerged from, Natasha heard the crashing of water. She hadn't noticed it earlier with all the commotion, but now that she was refreshed and somewhat dryer, Natasha was being drawn by curiosity to the sound.

She glanced at Alyssa, then rushed to follow the riverbed in the direction the sound emanated from. Basic survival says that if you follow a river, you will eventually come to civilisation. That was a fact millennia ago and it was still the same today. But if Natasha could identify where they were, she might be able to speed up the whole rescue process.

The river rounded a bend and soon Natasha got confirmation it was indeed the crashing of a waterfall she had been hearing, and she even got its name from a sign; Catarata Ashpachaca.

'That must mean this is the Utcubamba River!' Natasha shouted in excitement. 'I know where we are.' She turned and ran back to Alyssa, waking her up and letting her know that they were in the northern Amazonas region of Peru. But strangely, some sixty odd kilometres from where they had started.

'What? That's impossible. I know we did a bit of walking and swimming but to cover that distance would have taken at least half a day. There's no way we were walking that long.'

'I agree. I mean we didn't have a view of the sky, so we couldn't really take note of the passage of time, but my phone was working most of the time.' Natasha eventually shrugged and submitted. 'I'm putting it down to the ancient magic of this country.'

'Well, I for one, have had enough of the "magic" and want to go home. Where's the nearest town?'

'Not far, as it goes. We'll be on the road in no time.'

Not only were they on the road quick sharp, but the taxi driver they'd hired in town had them back in Cruzpata in just over an hour. The women paid him extra out of gratitude for a service well done. Natasha eagerly asked around for news of the helicopter and its passengers, hoping that they might have returned there. Unfortunately, no one had seen anything of them, not since the crazy woman and her female guerrillas showed up.

'La Viuda?' Natasha queried as she and Alyssa concentrated on the information the restaurant owner was giving them.

'Yes, I heard someone say that name.'

'After they had finished shooting, do you remember which way they went?'

'Si, senora,' she pointed south-east.

'Come on,' Natasha said, pulling Alyssa along.

'God, is this never going to end?'

Natasha caught up to the driver before he could leave town and paid him some more money to take them in the same direction the guerrillas had gone. Despite his reluctance, he eventually caved in, making sure they knew he was no tracker.

It was a bumpy ride, although much less than the one Natasha had been a part of when she was escaping from La Viuda. She had said that Lucas was a reckless driver, and this man was proving her right. At least she had no fear of not getting there in one piece.

Alyssa had voiced her own fear about the whole rescue plan. To her it didn't seem to be like a plan at all. 'And you think the two of us are going to mount an effective rescue against trained gun women?'

'It won't just be the two of us. Once we free them, we'll be alright. And don't forget we got our little getaway driver, Pedro, here. Besides, I know La Viuda's weak spot.'

They drove down into the valley where they could see the smouldering remains of the helicopter halfway up the valley wall. Natasha and Alyssa looked at each other. At least it hadn't exploded. The chances of the survival for Peter and Feliciana were looking up.

They drove on into the darkness, and soon came upon what looked like a small, abandoned village. Some of the homes, once filled with the day-to-day lives of its occupants, the playing and laughter of children, were now nothing more than shells of the former selves. Roofs collapsed, windows smashed, vandalised with graffiti. Only it wasn't abandoned at all. It had been taken over by the guerrilla army of La Viuda. Making sure Pedro and the Jeep remained at a reasonable distance, out of sight of the camp, Natasha and Alyssa continued on foot.

They paused momentarily at the border. Natasha noted that there weren't as many sentry guards as there had been at La Viuda's other encampment, assuming that many of the women had been slain in their confrontation with Enrique and his mercenaries. Although she and Lucas had escaped with Claudia, leaving the enemies to it, the firefight had been ferocious and casualties on both sides were to be expected.

This smaller number of female guerrillas increased their chances of success immensely. 'So, here's the revised plan, Alyssa. You're going to stay here, nice and hidden, while I go and find out which one of these buildings Peter and the others are being held in.'

They gave each other a thumbs up, then Alyssa watched Natasha as she crept into the makeshift camp.

Chapter 39

As soon as the two guards who had just finished their shift were out of sight, Anne left her hiding place in the recess, slowly and quietly making her way to the mystery room. She put her ear to the door, but the doors of the antiquated building were solid, not like they made them today, and she could hear little except for muffled voices.

Then her radio squawked into life. She couldn't understand what they said. Romanian wasn't one of the languages she spoke, but since it was a Latin language, it shared some similarities to Italian, which she could speak. Two numbers being repeated, along with a message.

They must be looking for those two guards to report in, Anne mused. It probably won't be long before someone is sent to look for them. So I'd better not hang about.

Anne took hold of the door handle and slowly turned it, trying to make as little noise as possible. The door opened a crack, enough for her to slip in unnoticed, and closed the door again behind her.

The room was at least two times bigger than the one that had been used for her confinement, and with good reason. It needed the space for all the surveillance and radio equipment. Twelve monitors, in banks of four, lined three desks, which the new rotation of guards were sat at. From her vantage point, Anne could see the monitors clearly. They were showing the feed from several security cameras, but wherever it was, looked new, sterile, not like the old citadel she was in.

Then she saw the picture on a monitor switch as a camera focussed on Lucas. He hung from a pipe, his arms above his head, as a couple of guards took shots at his undefended body.

The guard watching Lucas called his colleague, and together they laughed and pointed at him. Anne's lip twitched. She knew that if he wasn't restrained, he'd eat these drongos up without breaking a sweat. And it'd be exactly what they'd deserve.

As she looked on, slowly getting a hold of her anger, she crawled behind some cabinets and looked at the other monitor array. That's when she saw what she was after. There was a lift in the citadel. She saw people who she assumed to be lab technicians going down into this new area where Lucas was being held. All she had to do was locate it. But first, she had to deal with these jokers so that they wouldn't sound the alarm when she showed up on their screens. There seemed to be more than enough security down there to contend with as it was.

The door suddenly opened. Where Anne stood, the surveillance team couldn't see her. They had no idea she was even in the room. Her position was in full view of the door, however, and as another armed guard entered, he and Anne stared at each other for a moment before he shouted at her, raising his gun.

Anne squeezed the trigger and fired off one of the submachine guns. The bullets landed in the centre mass of the guard, throwing him against the wall. The two guards at the monitor desks fired their weapons in Anne's direction, forcing her to dive to new cover.

'So much for doing this the quiet easy way,' Anne grumbled to herself as she crawled along, bullets pinging off the metal cabinets as she tried to flank them.

The radio she had stolen came alive again; the panicked voice from one of the men in the room came over it. Great, Anne thought, they're probably calling in reinforcements. She hadn't been wrong. Soon more security arrived. The only thing slowing down their advance was the dead body at the door, but even that wouldn't stop them for long.

She looked around, tried to figure out her next course of action. As she deliberated, one the surveillance team had snuck up beside her hiding place. At the last moment, she was aware of him, and she fled, dodging his stream of bullets.

Anne returned fire, and he jumped back. She turned the attention of her gun on the window she was running toward, emptying the clip in the MP7A1 submachine gun she had in her left hand. The glass shattered, and she dived through the jagged window frame. As she passed, Anne reached out and grabbed one of the many cables running in and out of the room.

As she swung, screaming all the way, the arc of her flight was getting lower and lower, as increasingly more of the cable attachments popped free of the wall due to the unexpected duress. They weren't designed to hold a person after all.

Finally, the cable attachments held. The suddenness of it jerked her but Anne's grip was firm, and she swung towards another window, which she shot out and jumped through, releasing the cable.

It was an unoccupied, steamy shower, but Anne still proceeded with caution. The next room, however, wasn't empty.

The man that had just used the shower was in there drying his hair with a towel. He had another one around his waist, but as he turned around to see Anne pointing a gun at him, it slipped down.

Seconds later, it was on the floor, along with Anne's jaw. Just as she had used a similar action to distract the guards earlier, she now found herself in the same situation, staring at this well-endowed man, the barrel of her gun dropping.

Suddenly, a towel obscured her view, then the series of punches she received brought her totally out of her day-dream. A strong hand tightened around her throat and another one around her wrist, preventing her from bringing the machine gun into play. Someone slammed her against the wall several times, the air in her lungs being forced out each time. Anne could feel herself fading, but that didn't mean she didn't have any fight left in her.

Anne could feel his endowment against her leg, so she met it swiftly with her knee. It not only brought tears to his eyes but also got her free of his choking grasp, and with the butt of her gun, she knocked him out cold. She couldn't bring herself to kill someone that had been blessed like that.

She opened the door slowly and saw the security mobilising and looking for her. As soon as there was a chance to move out, she did, quickly and silently. Even with the whole place on alert looking for her, she still moved with caution. They could look for her but that didn't mean that she had to make it easy for them to find her.

Anne passed down several passageways, seemingly heading for the centre of the fortress. Then she saw a woman in a white lab coat, busy reading a clutch of papers in her hand, not paying attention to where she was going, because she obviously knew it by heart.

Falling into place behind the scientist, Anne followed her, making sure that she herself wasn't followed by anyone. Soon, as she had hoped, they came to the lift, but what she hadn't realised was that there were two. She waited on the edge of a corner as the lift was called and when it arrived, the woman entered, and Anne let the doors close before she approached it.

She could see from the display that it went down pretty far. As she pressed the button to call, the second one was already on its way up. She couldn't stand there in the open when she had no idea who was coming up. It could have been another scientist, but it just as easily could have been a battalion of guards to aid in the search for her.

Anne slipped back around the corner just as the lift arrived. It was two guards, but luckily, they left in the other direction, moving at double pace. When she thought they were far enough, Anne darted for the lift as its doors were closing. On the control panel were two buttons, beside the second one was a slot for a key. Damn it, she thought. Hopefully, there'll be no need to find out what was down there.

Even though the shaft was deep, the lift moved quickly, and when the doors opened on the lower landing, Anne kept flat to the wall for a second, in case there was someone there waiting to use it. When no one entered, she stuck her head out quickly before pulling it back again. She repeated the action once more, not seeing anyone but scientists in lab coats walking and talking.

Whilst in a crouch, Anne walked out, staying below the line of the large windowpanes that the laboratories had on this level. Every now and then she would raise her head to see what was going on. Glass tubes were everywhere, clear liquids percolating over fire, dry marker boards displayed equations far beyond Anne's range of knowledge.

She knew that this wasn't where Lucas was, though; he was in a room without windows. Anne continued her reconnaissance, moving further into the underground facility, soon finding an area which had a lot more guards than were present in the laboratory section.

She slipped in and planted her back against the wall. These rooms didn't have large panes of glass, just small openings in their doors. If she were to hazard a guess, Anne would say that it was a detention zone.

Anne slid around to the front of the door and took a quick look inside. A man lay on the small cot. She couldn't see his face since he was curled up, and she couldn't tell if he was sleeping or sobbing. In the next cell was a woman in a lab coat, sitting looking down at her feet despondently. She suddenly looked up, momentarily seeing Anne's face looking at her before she ducked down.

'Hey!' the woman shouted, rushing over to the door and banging it. 'Get me out of here! Hey, come on!'

Anne quickly retreated around the corner and waited.

A guard soon arrived. 'Shut your face, woman,' he snarled and banged on the door, louder than she had done. 'If you don't, I'll come in there and give you something to make noise about.'

The threat did its job and the woman immediately hushed. Anne watched as the guard kicked the door one last time before he left with a huff. Anne approached the door again, this time putting a finger to her lips to tell the woman to be quiet. She nodded and came over when Anne beckoned her.

'Are you here to rescue us?'

'Rescue who? Who are you?'

'I'm Karen Fletcher. Doctor Karen Fletcher.'

Chapter 40

Natasha didn't dare move a muscle. A guard stood only a foot in front of her, twelve little inches. She was in the shadows, but if the woman were to turn around, the chances of seeing Natasha, night-time or not, were pretty high.

The woman didn't seem to be in any rush to move on, and the reason soon presented itself, as she took a lighter from her pocket and lit the joint she'd just been rolling.

After she had enjoyed taking a couple puffs, the female guerrilla soldier finally continued her round.

Natasha quietly let the air that she had been holding escape her mouth. Her heart pounded in her chest, and she took a few moments to calm it down. It was a fool's errand really, because the whole situation was intense, and her BPM was not about to hit its normal range anytime soon.

Natasha double checked that the guard hadn't stopped again before making her move. She hadn't, so Natasha snuck around the building. When she approached the window, she had a quick look and saw two of the guerrillas in bed together. The next one had a single woman inside. Natasha's hopes of this being a quick task disappeared. It was never going to be easy; she had only formulated the plan up to the point of finding the others. Getting them out was a completely different matter.

She moved onto the next abode and found more sleeping soldiers. Then across on the other side, a bit further down, she saw what looked like a storage unit, a small warehouse, but it was the only place she'd seen so far that had a guard. 'That must be where they are being held,' she whispered.

Natasha strained her head, trying to look down the side of the building to see if there was a way to get in through the back. It looked like it was, and either way, it was a better option than the head on frontal approach.

Sometimes she couldn't believe the crazy things she got up to these days. She was sure if her dad knew, he'd have a heart attack. At least he wouldn't be able to blame Lucas, but he'd probably put it on him anyway, even if it was Peter she was trying to save.

When she was sure that no one was watching, Natasha dashed across the street to the nearest building to the destination warehouse. The only problem was that it wasn't particularly close, and she'd have to cover the thirty-metre distance of open ground between them. But there was nothing else she could do.

Natasha psyched herself up, the adrenaline pumping through her body. Then she set off. She had always been an athletic person, from her fencing days in private school before transitioning to modern pentathlon, to her weekly squash matches with Jenny and her MMA classes. She'd always been sporty, and she was glad for it right now as she sprinted the distance in a matter of seconds, stopping herself short of slamming into the wall of the warehouse, and not even breathing hard.

Slowly moving to the back of the warehouse, away from the guard at the entrance, Natasha looked for another way in. There didn't seem to be one. There was no back entrance, only the several windows that the building had. But surely none of those would be unlocked.

The windows were high up, making it impossible for her to just look in. Jumping was also out of the question as that would surely make too much noise. Natasha looked at the windows in her vicinity, scanning for possible handholds to pull herself up. It didn't take long to find one that had a bit of an edge to put the tips of her toes on as well.

She stepped forward, and putting her toe firmly on it, pushed herself up to the window ledge, grabbing on with her fingertips. After a second, she pulled herself up the rest of the way. Someone had hammered a plank of wood across the window, and the same had no doubt been done to all the others too. That ruled them out as an escape route.

But there was a skylight.

Before Natasha could even contemplate finding a way up there, she wanted to make sure everyone was alright. The first person she saw was Conrad, because he was pacing back and forth. The pilot was there also, talking to Feliciana. Good, the village elder was okay, too. But there was no sign of Peter. She moved her head all around, even pulled herself higher up, just in case he was sitting underneath the window. But he wasn't there.

That was probably why Conrad was so agitated. Where was he? Was he dead...?

Natasha suddenly felt two hands around her ankles, then found herself on the ground at the feet of the joint-smoking guard.

'And who do we have here?' the guard said in Spanish as she leered at Natasha.

The guard from the front of the warehouse came rushing around to the back, drawn by the sound of a commotion. 'La Princessa,' she breathed when she saw Natasha. 'La Viuda is going to want to see her straightaway.'

'Even though she said not to interrupt her?'

'Trust me. She has a personal issue with this woman.'

'That's a shame. I was hoping that I might have been able to show her how things were done in camp.'

'Cover my position while I take her to see her,' the warehouse guard said and picked Natasha up in a firm grip and dragged her away to another building.

The guard knocked on the door.

'I told you all that I was not to be disturbed!' La Viuda yelled in response.

'I'm sorry, Viuda, but we found a trespasser that you are going to want to see,' the guard said.

'This had better be good. Come in,' she commanded. 'Oh! Oh, you have done very good indeed,' Viuda gushed when she saw Natasha struggling to break free.

She stopped wriggling the moment she saw who Viuda was with. 'Peter?'

'Natasha! I am so happy to see you alive. We all feared the worse when the landslide happened.'

'And I thought that you were dead when I saw the chopper go down.'

'The pilot did an excellent job of landing, even with the damage.'

'And now you're sitting here playing cosy with the woman that shot you down?'

'I am trying to negotiate a price for our release.'

'Hey, Princessa, that price just went up, thanks to you turning up here.' La Viuda grinned, then she addressed the guard that was still waiting for orders. 'Take him back to the others. I have some catching up to do with our new guest.'

Natasha swallowed hard. She knew exactly what that meant. But this was exactly what she was hoping for though, because La Viuda's weakness was Natasha. She had seen it when they were alone together in the old encampment, the way she had looked at her, how she had touched her. But Natasha had escaped before anything could happen. Now she was back, and Natasha was planning on using La Viuda's obvious attraction for her to escape again.

'Oh, Princessa,' Viuda breathed as she stroked Natasha's cheek. 'I hoped our paths would cross again. But I never thought that it would be so soon. When I heard you were on your way back to South America, I knew I had to be the one to give you the best welcoming possible.'

'Someone told you I'd be here? Who?'

'Enrique Salas, of course. Thanks to you and Lucas, we discovered that we have a lot in common, namely that we both want the two of you dead.'

'Enrique? He's still alive?' Natasha still remembered his scream as the snake bit into his face. 'But he wanted you killed?'

'And it seems that your husband's betrayal and the disfigurement to his face caused by Travers and Redmond mean more to him than me killing his father. And the way things have worked out, it seems like we will both be having our revenge very soon.'

'What do you mean? Is Lucas here, in South America?'

'In Romania, I believe.'

'Romania? Shit!' Natasha wondered if Chiara had anything to do with getting him there. 'But why is Enrique even in Europe?'

La Viuda sneered at her, 'We have expanded our criminal empire. Not only do we deal in drugs, which is almost back up and running, despite your efforts,' she goaded, 'but we have gotten into the counterfeit money business. He had the bright idea of using the Romani mafia since they are never thought of as being counterfeiters, and it has worked perfectly.'

'Fake money?' Natasha questioned, completely flummoxed. 'Enrique is already rich from his father's inheritance. Why would he need to make fake money when he has the real thing?'

'That is none of your concern, Princessa. Right now, the only thing you should be concerned about is how you are going to make up for all the trouble you have caused me. After all, I paid for you, and I still own you.'

The smile on La Viuda's face sent a shiver down Natasha's back, which she did her best to hide. If her plan was to work, she had to play up to her captor.

Natasha smiled back. 'I'm sure that we can figure something out. Something that we can both benefit from.' She pulled her long curly hair free of the band that was holding it in a ponytail and flipped it to one side, as she gave her best look of seduction before she sashayed over to the nearby two-seater and sat down, slowly running a hand down her thigh as she crossed her legs.

La Viuda watched every moment she made with a look of desire, and she licked her lips before she poured them both a drink, then joined Natasha on the chair. 'So, Princessa, what did you have in mind?'

'I don't know. I'm new to this. You'll have to show me,' she replied as she arched her back and trailed a finger down her neck towards her cleavage.

A grin broke out on the guerrilla leader's face. 'New? It seems like you have learnt quite a bit since our last encounter, Princessa. Then you were innocent, but most importantly scared. Now you act like a whore! Now I will have to break you, to mould you back into that scared little flower that was ripe for plucking. Only then will I be able to enjoy you, Princessa.'

Natasha's coquettish smile vanished as she suddenly had difficulty breathing. Her chest was tight as a feeling of dread washed over her.

'You shouldn't have come back,' La Viuda said and grabbed Natasha by the wrist. The glass fell to the floor, spilling its contents as it rolled away from the furore. She dragged her prisoner down to a kneeling position in front of her, before she slapped her across the face, still retaining control of her wrist. 'You should have stayed dead. Even though things might have changed, I still get to have a bit of fun with you. And baby, I'm going to have so much fun. You're going to pray for me to kill you.'

Natasha was rocked by another slap, still being held up like a rag doll. Despite her fear, she could still catch Viuda's comment about things changing. Did that mean that Peter had made a deal with her to spare their lives? She tried not to think about the possibility, didn't want to get her hopes up.

Viuda's free hand went around Natasha's throat, and she was slammed to the ground. The South American took a position on top of her, bending down to lick her face as she tried to break her grip. The hand around her throat squeezed tighter to stifle her attempts and let her know who was in control. La Viuda moved her head to kiss Natasha, the choking grip holding her prey in place.

Then there was a knocking at the door.

La Viuda screamed at whoever was there. 'What is it?'

The door opened, and a guard dragged Alyssa inside, throwing her to the ground, along with Natasha's bag. 'I found this woman at the boundary of the camp.'

'Well, well, well,' La Viuda said, eying up her new prisoner. 'It looks like we'll be having a party tonight.'

Chapter 41

The name was familiar to Anne, and it took a few moments to remember where she'd heard it. 'You're the microbiologist that went missing? I remember seeing it on the news.'

'Yes, that's right. I got home from work, then everything went black, and I woke up here, wherever here is. There are a few of us, all taken in similar circumstances. Mostly scientists, microbiologists, but there are some people from other backgrounds. There was a blacksmith, Canadian I think, but they killed him.' Karen Fletcher became hysterical as she remembered the man that passed away.

Anne hushed her and looked around to check she wasn't drawing attention to them. 'What do they have you doing here?'

'They gave us an unknown, fast-acting bacteria. Told us they wanted us to replicate it, make it stronger, turn it into a virus that was easily transmissible but also had an extremely high mortality rate. And we did it. We created something that could be passed on through touch, bodily fluids, and when the host died, they were still infectious, and the virus becomes airborne until the next host.'

'I'm confused. How can you turn bacteria into a virus? Aren't they completely different things?'

'They are. Bacteria are a living, single-cell organism. They generate energy, make its own food, move and reproduce. Viruses, on the other hand are sub-microscopic. They can only grow and reproduce inside host cells they have infected.'

'That doesn't explain how you changed a bacterium into a virus.'

'We didn't, per se.'

'Look, just get to the bloody point. The longer you take the more chance there is of guards returning.'

'Bacteriophage,' Karen blurted out. She continued when she noticed the blank look on the face of her would-be rescuer. 'Since bacteria are a living single cell, viruses can live in them, hijack them, so to speak. Usually the virus would kill the bacteria, but the virus we have developed only piggy backs on it, using it as a delivery system, and spreading, multiplying by the thousands, leaving the host cell and infecting the victims other cells, once the bacteria has infected the body.'

'Jesus! I take it something like this could kill billions, right?' Anne asked, remembering the Bilderberg Inner Circle broadcast she and Lucas watched about their intention to reduce the world's population.

'Definitely, but it would be almost impossible. Once an infected person is hospitalised, then the spread is cut. The quicker they're isolated the quicker it will stop. There would be some deaths, many, but not billions.'

'And what if this little virus you made was put on something, like say money?'

'Then the spread would just continue. As the money is spread from person to person so will the virus be. You isolate and hospitalise the patient, but the source of the infection, the bank notes, would still be out there. Unless all the money which carried the virus was destroyed, then it would just continue to spread like nothing we had ever seen before.'

That explains why Enrique went through so much trouble for those plates, Anne thought.

'There is one thing,' Doctor Fletcher added. 'In its liquid state the virus can be destroyed by fire.'

'Burn up the lab and burn up the virus. Good to know.'

'Are you going to get me out of here? They don't know, but I've been secretly formulating an antidote for the virus.'

'Is that so? You really have been a busy little bee, haven't you? Do you have it with you?'

'They always search us before we enter and exit the laboratory, so I have it hidden inside my mattress.'

'Okay,' Anne nodded and looked at the electronic lock on the door.

'Each guard has a key-card on their belt,' Karen revealed.

'Then it looks like you're going to have to bring your friend back.'

The doctor understood and as Anne headed back to her hiding place, Karen made noise just as she had before; kicking the door and shouting to be let go.

The guard soon returned, his face dark like thunder. 'You just don't listen, do you? I warned you what would happen if you didn't shut up, didn't I?' He fumbled with the key-card on its retractable lanyard and swiped the terminal. The door buzzed, and the bolts clunked into their housing. Then he swung the door open. 'Now I'm going to give you something to scream about, you annoying little bitch.'

He swung his submachine gun behind him and, with a malicious grin on his face slowly entered the doctor's cell.

She stepped back until she hit the wall, no escape possible. She glared at him, her bloodshot eyes wide, filling with tears, fearing going through the same ordeal again.

Then there was a pop and a warm liquid splattered here face. When she opened her eyes, the guard was dead at her feet, his blood dripping down her face.

'Okay, let's go,' Anne said, the barrel of the MP7A1 in her hand still smoking.

The doctor was about to gladly follow when she remembered the antidote formula and she threw over the mattress of her cot, revealing a tear in the middle of it. She fished out some scraps of paper and joined Anne at the doorway. 'I'm ready.'

'You sure that's all of it?' Anne asked.

'Yes, four pieces of paper joined together to make the strain,' she demonstrated before putting them in her pocket.

'Excellent.' Anne raised her gun and squeezed the trigger twice. Karen Fletcher's look of shock was met by the cold glare of the person she thought was there to save her. 'Someone has plans for this, so I'm afraid I can't let this little golden egg of yours get out into the world just yet.'

Making sure that she had all four pieces of paper, Anne secreted them away in a pocket before she restocked her ammo by taking what the dead guard had, along with his submachine gun.

She looked up and down the corridor before she stepped out, closing the cell door behind her. Anne was about to continue her search for Lucas when the other kidnapped scientists came to their doors to see what was happening.

'What's going on?'

'Are you here to rescue us?'

'What's happened to Karen?'

'Who are you?'

'I'm nobody,' Anne replied, and continued walking past them all. 'I'm not even here. I'm a figment of your collective imaginations.'

At the end of the corridor was a door operated by key-card. After checking to see if anyone was hanging about on the other side, Anne swiped the card and the door slid open. She slowly walked through, taking one measured step after another, when an alarm suddenly blared out.

'Crap! I guess they must have found me,' she said and smiled up at the security camera. Now that she no longer needed to take things slow and easy, she picked up the pace, one gun slung across her back the other held in her two hands.

A door opened on her right, and she riddled the guard that came out with bullets. The body crumpled to the ground, but Anne was more interested in someone else. Down the hall, Faye Dannen came running out of a room, a pile of papers in her hands.

Perfect, thought Anne, and took aim. But as she pulled the trigger, her hand was kicked sending the bullets up into the ceiling. The same guard continued their assault, charging and slamming her against the wall, and punching her several times in the kidneys, until she brought an arm down to block, and brought the gun butt sharply under his chin. As he staggered back, she fired the gun at his chest.

Anne turned her attention back to the fleeing doctor and was about to give chase when she heard Lucas call her from the room beside her.

'Jesus!' Anne breathed as took in the sight of the beaten captive. 'You've looked better.'

'Cheers! I see you've been making friends, as usual.'

'Well, you know me, I try my best, but it seems like we've outstayed our welcome, so maybe we should leave this party.'

'Agreed!'

Anne instantly searched the bodies for the keys to unlock the cuffs around Lucas's wrists, bringing each other up to speed on what they had learnt in the meantime, everything except what she knew about the anti-viral, the kidnapped doctors, or the fact that she had killed one of them.

Once freed, Lucas rubbed the circulation back into his arms, then took the gun and ammo offered to him by Anne, who followed it up by kissing him. 'I'm glad they didn't kill you.'

'You and me both, baby. Right then, here's the plan: blow up the labs, get this disc thing, warn Nat and kill everybody. We also have to find out where the counterfeiting is being done. That's where Enrique went.'

'Sounds good! Simple, straight to the point...I love it! I saw the doctor making a run for it just now.'

'Then I think we should go say hello.'

Lucas and Anne left the room, following the direction she had seen Faye Dannen leaving. The two of them were going against the tide of scientists running for the exit, so their progress was somewhat hampered, but so was that of the doctor's, and she was rather more timid than the two armed professionals that were in pursuit, pushing people aside.

'There she is,' Lucas yelled over the continuing alarm. Faye was easy to spot as she ran up a flight of metal stairs and along a gangway. Lucas was tempted to take a shot, but there were too many bodies in the way, stopping him from getting a clean shot. Anne didn't have the same dilemma and fired. The shots missed and before she could re-aim and fire again, Lucas pushed her aside.

'What the hell are you doing?'

'What does it look like? I'm doing what you seem incapable of doing, taking out Faye.'

'There were innocent people in the way.'

'Were there? Because I just saw people complicit in creating a deadly virus.'

Lucas didn't reply.

'You can glare at me all you want. Just because they don't have a gun in their hand doesn't take them off the list of the guilty. I'm interested to see how you react if we come across Chiara.'

'I'll put her down.'

'We'll see about that. Just make sure your hesitations don't get me killed.'

Just then there was a barrage of gunfire, hitting scientists and blowing plaster onto Lucas and Anne who ducked for cover, returning fire when they could.

'We're cut off,' Anne shouted. 'We won't be able to make it to the stairs.'

'Then we'll have to hope that there's another way up somewhere down here. Come on!'

The passage led down five flights of stairs to another passage and three more flights of stairs. They were chased all the way down, stopping now and then to return fire. Two guards were hit and toppled down the stairwell. They had no idea how many guards were following them, but they hoped they would find a way out soon; both of them knew that their ammo was running low.

Anne opened the door when they finally reached the bottom and they found themselves in what looked like a small power plant.

'It makes sense that a facility like this would have its own off the grid power.'

'For sure. Now, if only there was some way to blow it up,' grinned Anne.

'Fuck it! Shoot everything,' Lucas said as they shot out the control panels and piping before engineers that had been working deeper in the power grid room suddenly charged at them. Anne cutting them down swiftly without giving Lucas a chance to protest.

The doors they had entered by suddenly slid open as the chasing pack of guards arrived. The first two to enter were the first two taken out by Lucas and Anne, the two bodies acting as a wedge between the doors, stopping them from closing fully. The room filled with smoke fast, sparks flying from all the damaged equipment, becoming a hazard to everyone in the vicinity.

'We need to get out of here,' Lucas shouted over the machinery sparks and gunfire.

'No shit! Any ideas?'

'We do what we do best.'

Anne smiled, and the two master thieves disappeared into the smoke and steam, tiptoeing through the darkness, their actions obscured from the advancing guards that were trying to find them. If they would have been more experienced, the guards might have known that they would have better luck doing what Lucas and Anne did and stayed low beneath the raising smoke.

Like the tag team that they once were, Lucas and Anne worked fluidly, not missing a beat. In a matter of seconds, they had dispatched two of the men, sweeping their legs from beneath them, and shooting them, whilst the remaining two fired blindly into the growing smoke, before they too were felled by a spray of bullets.

As the long-time friends restocked on ammo, there was a muffled boom from further in the power room where the engineers had been working. The dark room was suddenly being lit by the orange, yellows and reds of fire.

'We need to move. Now!' Lucas yelled.

They dashed out of the power grid room, leaping over the bodies, which blocked the doors open. More explosions could be heard below them, each one louder and bigger than the last. An explosion that rocked Lucas and Anne as they escaped up the stairs blew off the half-opened doors, and flames licked the walls. Even from this distance, they could feel the heat rising.

There were significantly fewer people obstructing them as they headed back to the stairs Faye had left by. There were still armed guards to contend with, but they did not hamper Lucas and Anne as they dealt out a hot death for each of them.

The metal gangway clanged under foot as the pair raced to the door. On the other side was the residential area of the underground facility. It was much more habitable compared to the rest of the cold and sterile decor of the place.

They walked through the carpeted area prepared for anything, guns at the ready. The room was oval shaped, with a lowered soft seating space. Several doors led off to other rooms, and they decided the split up to check them quickly since time was against them. They didn't know how long it would be until the entire place would blow-up.

Lucas kicked open the first door he approached only to find an empty office. But on closer inspection, he discovered it was Enrique's office. A large map of Romania on the wall confirmed what Anne had told him about their location. As much as he would have liked to have gone through everything that was on the desk, Lucas knew it was a luxury he didn't have and remained on task.

Scattering papers as he searched, Lucas paused briefly when he saw a headed letter from a place called the Republic of Nauru, but before he could read it any furthermore explosions reminded him of what he was supposed to be doing.

He continued to look, picking up one paper after another and discarding them quickly once he thought it was useless. He kept going until he almost discarded another page, stopping himself when he found out that they were the deeds to a warehouse in a place called Iasi. That in itself meant nothing but the map on the wall had two cities circled, Targu Neamt and the second one being Iasi, a city which had an airport. Perfect for getting the virus-coated money across the world.

Lucas's train of thought was shattered by the sudden sound of a gunshot.

Chapter 42

La Viuda circled Alyssa like a condor about to swoop down on its prey. The terrified Romanian archaeologist remained on the ground where the female soldier had thrown her, too shaken up to move.

Natasha was scared for her also. She knew full well that her friend was way out of her comfort zone and was no doubt on the verge of a nervous breakdown. She tried to make eye contact, finally succeeding, and tried to give Alyssa some reassurance that they would be okay, but she wasn't convinced that her friend believed it.

La Viuda knelt down her face inches from her new captive's, a motion which startled her. 'Como te llamas?'

'She doesn't speak Spanish,' Natasha jumped in.

Viuda smiled as she stroked Alyssa's cheek. 'Is that so? She'll be speaking it fluently by the time I'm through with her.'

'I can translate if you want me to, La Viuda.'

The mercenary leader looked at Natasha and laughed. 'And you think I trust you? No, little Princessa, I don't. But I will get what I am owed from you, after I see what your friend has to offer first.' She got to her feet and then told Alyssa to stand up, which she dutifully did. 'What is your name?' La Viuda asked in heavily accented English. Alyssa answered. 'Why you here?'

'I'm just a lost tourist who wants to go home.'

'Tourist?' Viuda laughed again. 'You are with this puta. Do not play games with me, or you will get what she will get.

I think you would be better for you to be on my good side, no? You will be looked after and protected, not like her.' La Viuda shoved Natasha with the bottom of her boot to drive her point home.

Alyssa gasped at her friend's treatment. She had been through so much already, but nothing had made her tremor as much as she was now. 'Okay, okay. I'll do as you say.'

'Good. Now why you here?'

'I found something, discs with images of gods, in my country, that we traced back to Peru and we wanted to find out more about them. They're in the bag.'

La Viuda opened the bag and looked inside. 'Ah, I have seen this before.'

'You have?' Natasha asked in Spanish. 'Where?'

'Yes, Enrique has one. It has Supay on it, just like these two.' She held the bag open in front of Natasha. 'Take them out, both of them.'

Natasha looked at the bag, then at the huge grin on La Viuda's face. It was as if she knew what she was demanding of the woman at her feet, knew that she was effectively telling her to commit suicide. The grin on Viuda's face quickly turned into a scowl as Natasha refused to comply.

'Fine,' the soldier said and went to a drawer beside the two-seater and pulled a handgun. If only Natasha had known that it was there next to her when she was seated, this whole mess could have been dealt with swiftly. 'If you will not do as I say, then I will just have to kill you.'

Natasha sat on her haunches and shrugged. 'It doesn't matter. I'd be dead either way.'

A flash of anger crossed Viuda's face, then changed tact. 'And what of your friend? Pick them up or I kill her.'

Alyssa didn't need to speak Spanish to know that things were bad. A gun pointed at your face spoke volumes and transcend any language.

'Alright, alright, just don't hurt her.'

'What are you doing, Natasha?' Alyssa was distraught when she saw her take out the first Supay disc.

'If I don't, then she'll kill you. I can't let that happen.'

'And I'm supposed to be okay with you killing yourself to save me?'

'At least this way we'll have time, forty-eight hours to figure something out.'

'Maybe you haven't noticed, but we're prisoners here.'

'Yes, yes you are,' La Viuda added, understanding little bits of the conversation. 'And do not forget who is in charge. Now pick it up, Natasha!'

Reluctantly, she did what was ordered of her and dipped her free hand into the bag. Natasha hesitated when her hand came close to it. She had to will herself to pick up the artefact. But she did.

La Viuda had been watching with wide-eyed anticipation. And when she saw her enemy kneeling before her, holding two discs that would be the death of her, she broke out into laughter. 'Oh, what a glorious night! I have truly not felt this excited since I killed my husband. And I get to watch you suffer, Princessa. You should have just submitted to me like your friend here.'

The guerrilla leader put the gun in her pocket, dropped the bag and grabbed her second prisoner, drawing her close until their lips met. Her hands were all over Alyssa, mauling her body, squeezing her breasts hard, which garnered groans of pain from her victim, but they just seemed to spur La Viuda on.

At first, Alyssa thought that she might have been able to play along, feign interest in La Viuda but the task was too hard. She stared at Natasha with a vacant look in her eyes.

Natasha couldn't watch this brute abuse of her friend any longer. She quietly got to her feet, and with the deceptively heavy Aysana Kawsay Wanu still in her hands, went to strike La Viuda. But the female guerrilla briefly opened her eyes, to see if Alyssa was enjoying herself, only to see her victim looking pass her.

La Viuda's dreadlocks flipped to the side as she reacted, evading the bulk of Natasha's attack, but still receiving a glancing blow from the mysterious objects. It shook her, but she didn't drop. Viuda swung out blindly with a wild backhand, catching Natasha flush on the cheek, causing her to taste her own blood.

The two women squared up to each other, Natasha versus La Viuda. Blood from the guerrilla fighter's head wound streamed into her left eye, making it hard for her to see out of, reducing her vision of attacks coming from that side.

Natasha saw the left eye blinking and immediately knew the issue her enemy was having, and there was no way she wasn't going to take advantage of it.

It was a quick and brutal fight, the likes of which Alyssa had never witnessed before, especially one involving her friend. Each part of their bodies were used to strike the other. Every piece of furniture was used as a weapon to beat the other into submission, something neither woman did, but neither could they keep up with the physicality.

La Viuda staggered back, dropping to one knee after receiving a combination of blows from the equally tired Natasha. It had become a battle of attrition to see who's will was stronger. The guerrilla leader glared at the woman walking toward her and knew that she had nothing left to give to the fight. But she wasn't about to lose to her either.

Alyssa screamed and lunged at La Viuda as the criminal reached into her pocket, about to draw her gun. She grabbed her wrist with both hands, desperate to stop her from pulling out the weapon. But Viuda was stronger than her and coupled with a few well-placed punches to the ribs, she was able to pull out the handgun.

However, Alyssa hadn't let go of the wrist she tenaciously held, not allowing the gun to be aimed, as they tussled for it. Natasha was on the way to aid her friend when the gun suddenly went off.

There was a look of surprise on all three of the women's faces, even more so on Natasha's as she felt the bullet enter her flesh and she fell to the ground.

Alyssa's eyes bulged, and she reeled backwards at the sight of Natasha being shot. Her sense of shock was soon replaced by an anger like she'd never felt before. Her nails bit into the palms of her clenched fists, her heartbeat pounded, her nostrils flared and as Alyssa's eyes narrowed, she swung at La Viuda with all her strength.

The punch connected squarely on La Vuida's jaw. It caught her completely off guard. The last thing she was expecting was an attack from the nervous Romanian, but it sent her sprawling to the ground, and the gun flying.

La Viuda recovered and was upon Alyssa before the stricken woman reacted. She wrestled her to the ground, pinning the smaller woman beneath her. Trapping a hand under her knee whilst keeping hold of the other, she began to unbutton Alyssa's blouse.

'It is just you and me now, no more Princessa. You struggle now, but soon you will learn to appreciate my touch...no, you will learn to beg for it.' She bent down intent on mauling her prisoner once more.

'That's not going to work, La Viuda. I'm not done with you yet.'

The mercenary paused, hearing the familiar voice. She slowly looked up to see Natasha slumped against the two-seater, pointing her own gun at her, and smiled a crooked smile. 'Amor y balas, Princessa. As I have lived, so I die. At least I know you will be right behind me.'

'I look forward to disappointing you...again.'

Two shots from the gun were enough to end La Viuda's life.

Chapter 43

As Lucas went to the right of the oval room, Anne silently, instinctively, slipped off to the left. With gun in hand, she opened the first office and smiled. Providence was shining on her today. After a quick look over her shoulder, Anne walked into the room, closing the door behind her.

'Hello, doc. Fancy meeting you here.'

Faye had been bent over, searching in the drawers of her desk, but on hearing the Aussie drawl she shot up straight in her chair, like a kid caught doing something wrong. Doctor Dannen stared at the intruder. 'Just who are you? Enrique told me that Lucas had been sighted with a black-haired woman, but Jesus, you've become a real pain in the ass, and we don't even know why.'

Anne grinned. 'I'm just the wrong lady at the right time.'

'And what exactly is that supposed to mean?'

'It means that you're shit out of luck. You're plans to depopulate the planet end here. Well, actually, your contribution to that insane plan will still go ahead,' Anne aimed her machine gun at the doctor.

'Only someone that is unenlightened would say that,' Faye said as she became more relaxed, almost forgetting the gun was even there as her mind focussed on her grand crusade. 'The world needs our help. Human beings have plundered the resources of this planet to the point that by the year twenty-fifty, they will be exhausted. And because of the negligence of humankind, many animal species have seen their numbers halved, and many more on the brink of extinction.'

'So, you've taken it upon yourself to be the saviour of the Earth?'

'Me? No, I'm just someone that could see the bigger picture and took the opportunity given. If you stop us now—'

'Lady, there's no "if" about it.'

'If you stop us now,' Faye reiterated, 'the plan might change, but the goal will remain the same. We will win in the end.'

'Only when we allow it when the time is right.'

Faye examined Anne closely. Things slowly made sense to her. 'Who is this "we" you're talking about?'

'Now, that would be telling.'

Faye continued to study Anne. 'You were never here by accident, were you. You're working for someone within the Inner Circle, someone that wants their own plan to succeed so that they'll be the one to head up the New Enlightened Order. I'm right, aren't I?'

Anne had been standing in a relaxed pose with both her arms and feet crossed, listening while leaning against the doorframe, smiled. 'You got me.'

'I knew it,' Faye replied, leaning forward in her chair. 'Alpha was always under the impression that because everyone in the Inner Circle has the same agenda, that no one would make a power play. As much as I would have liked him to be right, human nature tells a whole different story. So, who is it?'

'I don't think they'd appreciate their identity being revealed just yet.'

The doctor shrugged. 'No matter, when Alpha finds out, they will be as good as dead.'

'And how exactly is he going to find out? You certainly won't be around to tell him.'

'What if I were to switch allegiance? I am the top scientist in my field. I could be useful.'

'Viruses aren't our thing.'

'In that case, maybe you should know that there is an anti-viral for this new strain that we have developed.'

'An anti-viral?' Anne replied, playing along.

'Yes, one of the kidnapped scientists secretly created the formula. I found out about it, but never told anyone, not even Alpha, just in case.'

Anne nodded, impressed by her foresight. 'The only problem is that I've already spoken to Kathy Fletcher and taken the formula from her,' she said and held up the pieces of scrap paper for the doctor to see.

'I see, but you should know that one of those scraps is a fake secreted into her mattress while she was working in the laboratory.'

Anne studied her hard, lifting a single eyebrow and cocking her head.

'It's true! I'll show you,' replied Faye when she saw her expression, and immediately reached into the open drawer, an action that resulted in a quick and deadly response from Anne, who fired a single bullet into the doctor's head.

Anne went around the desk and checked the drawer. 'Well, would you look at that, you weren't lying.' She lifted the page, which looked like the complete formula, and saw the 9mm beretta underneath. 'Tut, tut, tut, bad doctor.'

Anne folded the paper, then slipped it in with the others; she'd leave validating the authenticity of the equations to someone else.

Suddenly, the door was kicked open and Lucas stood there with his MP7A1 at the ready. When he saw Anne had everything in hand, he relaxed and joined her as she continued to rifle through the late doctor's drawers.

'I see you found the doc,' Lucas said in a cold manner. The idea that he had been used grated with him.

'Yeah, she was reaching for this,' Anne flipped the handgun on top of the desk, then she held up a zip-lock bag. 'I also found these. Don't know if this is the artefact they told you about, but its heavy, and the writing on the sheet looks Mexican or something. I don't know.'

'Yeah, you might be right. I may have found out where Enrique has his counterfeiting business; a place called Iasi.'

'Then let's go, this place sounds like it could go off at any time.'

'You're right. Come on, there must be another way out nearby. It'd explain why the Dannen came this way.'

They checked two of the three remaining rooms, one had their personal affects, along with a fragrance that Lucas recognised to be the one Chiara used, the second room they looked in was an armoury which had them both salivating. Lucas picked up some extra clips and explosives, whilst Anne was drawn to the bladed weapons, in particular a pair of rapier swords.

As they restocked, Lucas heard a faint humming coming from the final door. As he went to investigate, he found out too late that, although its facade was identical to the others, it wasn't a door to a room, but the door to an elevator.

Babou and Diouf stood in the lift staring at Lucas, all three men momentarily stunned. As the former SAS captain lifted his gun, Diouf's long leg flashed out and kicked it aside, sending the stream of gunfire, meant for him as his partner, into the wall.

Anne, hearing the machine-gun go off, stuck her head out the door to see what was going on and pulled it back in time to avoid Babou's drop kick. She backed into the room, her finger on the trigger, sending bullets through the doorway, penetrating the wall across the hallway in a tight grouping.

As soon as the gun clicked empty, the Senegalese assassin dived into the room, sprung off the ground and planted both feet into the chest of Anne, sending her flying over the table. 'We meet again, Cherie.' Babou smiled. 'At least this is a much better location for a rendezvous, non? You look much more at home in these surroundings compared to a cemetery.'

'So, it was you that hit me over the head?'

'Guilty. I would have much preferred to have just killed you, but my employer wanted you alive.'

'Then it looks like I owe you one.'

Anne launched herself over the table, feet first. Babou blocked the attack, and she quickly followed it up with another strike and another. The assassin was a match for her offence, countering when he could, and eventually sweeping the legs from under her. She rolled away to come up with another plan of attack.

• • • •

FOR SUCH A BIG MAN, Diouf moved with incredible speed, slipping behind Lucas, and using the strap of the machine-gun to choke the smaller man. It wasn't very often that Lucas faced someone that was not only bigger than him, but strong too, and he was very thankful for that fact.

Due to the taller man's reach advantage, Lucas knew he wouldn't be able to stay back and pop off shots off at will, neither would he be able to out power him. He would have to get dirty. But as he liked to say, the end justified the means.

As Lucas continued to be strangled from behind with the gun strap, the giant Diouf twisting it ever tighter, he felt himself fading from the lack of oxygen. Then out of pure desperation he finally fought. It wasn't pretty, but it was effective. Lucas stamped on Diouf's foot with as much strength as he could muster. To finish his retaliation, and break the stranglehold, he brought the heel of his boot up into the man's groin. With a howl of pain, Diouf let him go, only to pick him up again and throw him against the wall before he rubbed the feeling back into his testes.

Lucas landed hard and although he was shaken, he was also stirred into action, this giant was going down.

• • • •

'YOU ARE NOT BAD, CHERIE. Incredibly good in fact, you have some moves. It is a shame that I have been paid to do a job, else I think that you and I could have had a lot of fun together.'

'I thought you said Enrique wanted me alive?'

'Yes, unless you tried to escape, of course.'

'Yeah, I'm not one for being caged up.'

'I completely understand. We have the spirit that needs to be free.'

'Well, I do. You just do the bidding of the person who pays your bills.'

'Touché, Cherie, but we all need to make a living. Now, don't worry, I will make this a quick death. It is the least you deserve, considering your fighting skills, although I still say it is such a waste to kill such a fine woman.'

'You know, Babou, you haven't actually seen my fighting skills. I just wanted to see what you had.'

Anne threw herself at the assassin, who instinctively raised his hands to block a high attack. But instead, she only grabbed his head and unleashed a series of knees to each side of his body. Eventually able to read her repeated moves, Babou caught her leg, lifted her up before he slammed her on top of the table. But still she fought on, driving the point of her elbows into his trapezius muscles until he let her go.

He jumped back, rubbing his shoulders whilst he watched her lie on her side, propping her head up with her hand. 'Very well, Cherie, now we do this the hard and messy way.' Babou unsheathed his two Karambit knives from their shoulder harnesses and advanced on his prey.

Anne rolled onto her back before doing a kip up to get to her feet, then somersaulted over Babou's slashing attacks, grabbing a sword as she dived through the doorway and into the oval room. She turned around to face Babou in a fencing position, sword at the ready. 'You sure you want to do this? Your two little pricks don't add up to much.'

• • • •

DIOUF WAS STILL RECOVERING when Lucas went on the attack once more. His focus this time was on the massive assassin's knees, kicking the sides of his legs at every opportunity, trying to chop the big man down, who winced as each strike landed. After several hits, Diouf tried to dodge the kicks as they came in, but to little avail. If he stepped back, then Lucas's attack just hit the inside of the other leg. If Diouf raised the leg, then his shins took the damage.

His only other choice was to step in closer, reduce the range of his kicking. But the dirty tactics of Lucas had him second guessing, had him blocking low in case of another groin assault. The cumulative damage from the kicks was taking their toll however, and as Diouf lunged in, his left leg wobbled and gave way, dropping him to one knee. The perfect height for Lucas who unleashed a barrage of punches to the head of the massive assassin, who tried desperately to block.

The glint of a blade suddenly flashed in the corner of Lucas's eye, and he barely ducked out of the way of Babou's slashing attack as he came to the aid of his partner. The sneak attack brought a look of derision from the former SAS captain.

Anne lunged at the lively hired killer, thrusting several times with the rapier she'd picked up. The pinging of metal on metal sounded, as there was a rapid exchange of blocks between the two.

Then there was a huge explosion.

All four of them were knocked off their feet by the eruption. Then the doors that Lucas and Anne had originally passed through blew off their hinges as a great jet of flame burst through. The temperature suddenly rose, and Lucas and Anne looked at each other, then at the armoury, knowing that time for escape was running out; when the fire hit that room, there was enough explosive to take out whatever was left of the underground facility.

The sudden ding of a bell sounded, and the two old friends had just enough time to see the elevator doors close, taking Babou and Diouf to safety.

Chapter 44

Alyssa had seen more fresh dead bodies in the last few days than she had in all the previous years of her life. It was something that she didn't think that she could ever get used to, especially when the corpse was draped over her legs.

She squirmed out from underneath La Viuda's body and rushed to Natasha's side, collapsing on top of her and giving her a huge hug. 'I thought you were dead, Natasha! When I heard the gun go off, I thought that was the end. And all that blood...'

'It's okay. I was hit in the thigh.'

'But still, we need to get you to a hospital.'

'I think I have more important things to worry about, don't you?' She looked at Supay's image facing up from the disc beside her.

Alyssa followed her gaze. 'Shit! I'd forgotten about that. What are we going to do?'

'We're going to concentrate on getting everybody out of here first,' Natasha replied, pulling herself up onto the sofa. She ripped off a swathe of the spread that covered it and tied it tight above the bullet hole. 'Come on, we're going, but I'm going to need your help.'

With Natasha's left arm draped over her friend's shoulder for support, the two women headed for the exit. Before they reached it, the door was flung open as the first responders arrived. The two guerrilla fighters saw the dead body of their leader, but before they had time to do anything else, two precision shots fired by Natasha took them down.

The pair slowly navigated their way past the dead soldiers, pausing briefly to look outside and plan their route. They looked at each other, knowing that the odds were against them, knowing that it wasn't going to be easy, especially with Natasha's wound. But neither of them were ready to give up just yet.

'Okay, so we'll swing to the right, avoid the central area of the encampment, and just keep heading towards the warehouse. Let me worry about everything else.'

Alyssa nodded, and with a final deep, empowering breath, she opened the door wide and set off, Natasha hopping as fast as she could beside her.

Moments later flashes from the muzzles of machine guns periodically lit up the night sky. Natasha and Alyssa were thankful that the aim of the gunwomen was hugely compromised in the dark, as they moved ever closer to their target, the warehouse where Peter and the others were being held captive.

'You're doing great,' Natasha encouraged as they navigated around to the side of one of the small houses, stopping so Alyssa could catch her breath.

'Thanks, but when did you get so heavy? You're killing me.'

'We're almost ...' One of the guerrilla soldier's came running around the corner, surprised to see them standing there and lifted her AK-47. Natasha reacted quicker, putting a bullet in her chest.

Suddenly, bullets peppered the wall above them, showering the women with splinters of wood. Twisting around, so that she could face behind, Natasha aimed at the muzzle flash, using it as a reference point, to estimate the shooter's torso, and quickly fired. She took down another one.

The pair set off once more. Shouts from the guerrilla fighters were growing louder as they closed in on the hampered escapees. But as they did, Natasha and Alyssa were getting closer to the warehouse. Until they found out that it wasn't the guerrillas that were closing on them. Guessing that the two friends, after killing La Viuda, would attempt to rescue the rest of their party, a group of the soldiers had been sent to bolster the security there. The two archaeologists were closing in on a larger guerrilla unit. It was a trap.

'Bollocks!' Natasha gritted. She checked to see how many bullets were left in the beretta and didn't like what she saw. 'We're going to need to come up with something.'

'What do you mean?'

'There's seven of them and I've only got five bullets left.'

'So what are we going to do?'

Natasha tried to zone out all the surrounding noise; the pounding of her heart, the pain in her leg, as she thought. Then she remembered the skylight. 'If you can get around the back, you should be able to climb up.'

'What? Are you nuts?'

'Nope, it's the only way.' Natasha looked over her shoulder, hearing the rest of the guerrilla pack behind them. 'And you'll have to move because they're looking to sandwich us in.'

'But what about you?'

'I'll be fine. I'll find somewhere to hide until you make enough noise and commotion to get them do something. And once they open the doors, I'll come shooting.'

Truth be told, Alyssa wasn't completely sold on the idea, but the confident look on her friend's face galvanised her resolve. 'Okay, I'll do it. But how am I supposed to get there in the first place? I can't just walk up to them and ask to be let by.'

Natasha smiled, but knew that Alyssa was right. She scanned the ground, looking for some good-sized stones. It wasn't hard to find a few. Peru was a mountainous region, after all. Leaning heavily against the wall of the home they were hiding behind, Natasha threw the stones at a building away from the warehouse. The first one was short, the second pinged the window, but didn't shatter it. Some of the women's ears pricked up when they heard it. They didn't act upon it, however. The next stone thrown hit the wood. The final stone smashed the glass.

The guerrilla soldiers jumped into action, readying their machine guns and advancing toward the direction of the broken glass. At the same moment, Natasha and Alyssa made moves too; Alyssa sprinted in a crouch around the side of the storage building, whilst Natasha hobbled into the nearby brush, unaware of the amount of blood she was still losing, thanks to the pinpoint focus she had on the task at hand.

Alyssa tiptoed around to the back of the building, glad that it wasn't as big as some of the American barns she saw on tv. Coming in at roughly three metres in height, she felt she was more than capable of scaling the back wall, providing she could find adequate hand and foot holds.

Though nowhere near the action woman that Natasha had become, Alyssa had to do a fair bit of scrambling up cliff faces in the past, searching in caverns and finding relics, so she wasn't a complete novice at climbing, and made a strong start.

As she passed the window, the moon cast her shadow on the floor of the warehouse. Conrad noticed it and pointed it out to Peter and the others, who were all standing around, hearing the gunfire and wondering what was going on outside.

They all looked up and saw Alyssa looking down at them. She was struggling to open the old dormer window, grime and disuse making it almost impossible to budge. Alyssa slumped back, panting heavily from her exertions.

She wiped the sweat from her brow and caught sight of the beam of light from a torch swinging left and right, not far from where she had been standing with Natasha. The light stopped for a few seconds before it continued, following something on the ground, unerringly towards Natasha's hiding place.

Alyssa's heart raced as she saw the guerrilla closing in on her friend's position. Then she had an idea. Just as Natasha had broken a window to distract the guards, perhaps she could do the same in return.

She signalled for the others to move from beneath the skylight before she got to her feet and stamped on the window, two attempts being enough to smash the glass. Alyssa achieved her goal, but didn't think through the consequences of her actions.

Someone pointed a torch in her direction, lighting her up in the darkness. Shouts in Spanish quickly followed, then the hail of gunshots came. She ducked to avoid them, but in so doing lost her balance and toppled through the broken window.

Conrad, Peter's driver, was the first to react, dashing to the centre of the warehouse, arriving just in time to break her fall. He set her down, and she squeezed him tightly, before divulging Natasha's plan to their companions. She couldn't help but notice Peter's face light up when he got confirmation that she was still alive. Alyssa wanted to see her friend's reaction when she told her.

Outside, Natasha had overcome an anxious few seconds. When the cigarette smoking, torch wielding guerrilla had walked towards her, following a trail of her blood, she had thought that it was all over. But Alyssa had acted quickly with her diversion, smashing the skylight. Then Natasha's heart jumped into her throat the moment she saw Alyssa fall through it when the soldiers shot at her.

The way she fell, she thought that her friend might have been shot. But minutes later, as per the plan, a loud ruckus emanated from inside the warehouse. Alyssa had told the others. She was alive! Natasha smiled, eyes glassy, and as she blinked the tears away, she prepared for the next part of the plan.

There was a problem, though. With La Viuda dead, the group had no leader. But judging by the way the woman with the torch barked out orders to the others, Natasha guessed that she was picking up the mantle and positioning herself as the successor. Only thing with that was La Viuda had been the one in league with Enrique Salas. She had been keeping the hostages for him as part of their partnership. From what Natasha could hear, this new woman seemed to be a bit more of a hardliner, in the sense that the group had been founded to escape the abuse of their husbands and boyfriends, men were the enemy, and they shouldn't be working with them.

Natasha's eyes opened wide when she heard the woman's command. 'Enciende el fuego! Quemalos!' She intended to burn them alive.

Even if she didn't have enough bullets on her, there was no way that she was going to stand by and let that happen, but what could she do?

As two women returned rolling a barrel of petrol towards the storage building, she knew it was now or never. Natasha acted, struggling to her feet, a plan formulating in her mind. She didn't like it, but in the last few days, she'd had several plans that she didn't particularly like, but had no choice but to go through with them, anyway. This was one of those times.

She took aim at the barrel, shooting it three times in quick fire action. Unlike in the movies, however, it didn't explode. 'Bollocks!' Natasha screamed and ducked down the side of a shack as the guerrillas turned around.

Torchlight shone in her direction as the hovel was pelted with bullets. Natasha kept herself as small as possible, shielding from the deadly spray of lead. She had two bullets left, and she intended to take at least one of them with her. In her mind, she was already dead, thanks to the Supay discs. Punching her ticket now, in a shootout, would be a better way than to suffer a slow and excruciating death over several days. She did have one regret; that she didn't have the chance to say goodbye to Lucas.

Natasha waited, took a deep breath and jumped out, squeezing the trigger of her gun.

Blam! Blam! Click!

The bullets found the target, the face of the woman with the torch, the woman that at that moment had been blowing smoke out of her mouth, holding her smouldering cigarette butt between her fingers. The force of the bullets threw her head back, her hand flew up, the cigarette left her fingers, landing in the pool of petroleum, igniting it with a whoosh, and seconds later, the barrel exploded, shooting up into the air.

The remaining female guerrillas screamed as they were covered with flaming petrol. Some ran around like human torches, others rolled around on the ground desperate to put out the flames. That's when Natasha noticed that, despite her efforts, the warehouse had still been set alight because of the proximity of the barrel when it went off.

She rushed over as fast as she could with her injured leg, yelling over the roar of the flames and the crackle of the fire, smoke billowing into the air. One of the guerrilla women had the keys to unlock the padlock and chain that secured the doors of the building, but how she was supposed to search their bodies through the flames was beyond her.

Suddenly, Natasha heard the revving of an engine and headlights speeding towards her. She thought it was more of La Viuda's troops, and looked around for a weapon, but let out a huge sigh of relief when she saw it was Pedro.

'When I saw that barrel go up, I thought you might need a getaway car,' he said.

'Dude, you just earned yourself a fat bonus!' Natasha said and slapped him on the back. 'You got something to get through this warehouse door?'

He told her he did and patted his steering wheel, at which point she jumped in next to him as he reversed his Jeep, then pressing the horn continuously, he drove straight through the wooden doors skidding to a stop inside.

'Get in!' Natasha shouted.

As soon as they were all onboard, Pedro put his foot down on and sped out of the storage building, the flames crackling up its sides, spreading uncontrollably. They drove away at high speed, and as they crossed the river those that were looking saw the roof engulfed in flames as the warehouse collapse in on itself.

Chapter 45

More explosions rocked the underground facility, causing large chunks of debris to fall to the floor. On more than one occasion, Lucas and Anne were forced to jump clear to save their skin.

'We can't keep doing this,' Anne said to Lucas.

'Neither can we stay here,' he replied. 'There's no telling when this place will go up completely, but I'm guessing that it'll be sooner rather than later.'

'Then you'd better stop dilly dallying and hurry up with your escape plan then.'

'My plan?'

'Yeah, of course. You're the only bloody SAS captain around here, so get to work, captain,' she said with a salute.

Lucas knew she was scared, but she hid it well. She always had. The space heated up as the flames grew in intensity, a fact that played on his mind. They were far below ground, yet they were breathing perfectly fine, and the fire was burning away, growing and building, not only because there was fuel, textiles, furniture, flammables, but there was also air.

He scanned the area, looking for the vent. But before he could finish his search, the elevator dinged as it returned. He looked at Anne, who was just as surprised as he was.

'Maybe they're not such bastards after all.' Anne smiled and approached the lift. The doors opened, and she immediately sprinted in the other direction, diving for Lucas as the explosives in the car went off.

'You were saying?' Lucas asked Anne as she lay on top of him.

'Well, I can admit that I was wrong, and as much as I'd love to get hot and sweaty with you, this isn't quite the setting that I had in mind for it.'

Suddenly, there was a sound of grinding metal and what remained of the mangled elevator car dropped slightly, kicking up a cloud of dust, the electrics giving off sparks in their death throes. But as the dust plume cleared Lucas saw possible salvation. Part of the lift shaft had been destroyed, blown away by Babou and Diouf's final attempt to kill them.

Lucas sat up with Anne sitting on his lap. 'Is that excitement because of this position or because you've found a way out?' she asked.

'Both,' he answered and untangled her legs from around his waist. He had a closer look at the elevator shaft, silently weighing up their chances of using it. Another series of explosions made up his mind.

'So, what you got?'

'Look up there,' he said, pointing at the gap above the top of the buckled lift. Anne could see that the back of the shaft had a hole. 'I think that could be an escape stairwell in case the lift got stuck. We'll have to climb through the car to get to it, but it should be okay.'

The lift suddenly dropped a few more inches, more sparks flared off, then fire roared up the shaft only to die down again.

Anne glanced at Lucas, before she tentatively looked down the shaft; it was nothing but a flaming pit. 'You've got to be kidding me, right?'

Lucas shook his head. 'I'll go first. If it can take me, then it'll definitely be fine for you.'

'And if it doesn't?'

'Then I'll be dead, and you'll have time to find the air shaft.'

'Nice. You sure know how to keep a girl's spirits up.'

Lucas grabbed Anne and drew her into him with little resistance. He stared into her green eyes a moment before kissing her. They deepened the kiss. Her tongue gently stroked the roof of his mouth, which sent shivers through his body. 'How are your spirits now?'

'Anxious to continue this in a more civilised surrounding.'

Lucas grinned and prepared himself to enter the half-destroyed lift.

He tested it first with a foot, placing it inside the lift and pushing down with his weight a few times. When it didn't move, he turned to Anne and smiled triumphantly. Then Lucas edged inside, as it was tilted slightly, it was possible for him to crawl up the side wall of the elevator, just enough for him to reach the escape hatch in its roof. Lucas forced it open after several attempts.

His movements inside the lift suddenly made it drop a few more inches.

Anne gasped audibly and covered her mouth with embarrassment. Lucas glanced at her, surprised by the little outburst, then turned his attention back to the hatch. He was glad that he continued his exercise regime even after leaving the SAS, because it was going to take a bit of brute strength to get up there. The way the lift was reacting to any little juddering motion, Lucas knew he wouldn't be able to use momentum to assist him in the pull-up.

He reached a hand up and once he had a firm hold, lifted his legs. Lucas hung there, steadying himself so there was no swing, then brought his second arm. As he exerted his strength, pulling himself up in a straight, unwavering line, his muscles tensed, glistening in the flickering light of the fire. The confined space was boiling hot, drying out his eyes. But he had no intention of giving up for a little discomfort.

With his hands planted after pulling himself up, Lucas now pushed himself the rest of the way until he could bring a leg up through the hatch as well. It was a slow, controlled action, which Anne looked on with more than a little awe.

As Lucas manoeuvred himself and brought his second leg through and finally stand atop the tilted, wrecked elevator, it slipped again, blasting up another, intense column of fire, which almost threatened to engulf the car.

'Are you okay?' Anne asked as explosions beneath her own feet let her know that she herself was in a precarious position as she felt the heat of the fast-encroaching flames behind her, the sunken seating area already swallowed by the inferno.

'Yeah,' he answered. 'Good thing I don't have any hair, or it would have been singed. Other than that, I'm good.' Lucas slowly made his way over to the blown-out wall. He stepped off the lift onto an exposed metal beam, and as he braced himself on the edge of the hole, he leaned his head in.

Lucas grinned widely as he held himself back from hooting and yelling. 'Anne, there's a staircase. Come on up.'

'Yes!' She punched the air in jubilation and stepped into the lift.

Not being as tall as Lucas meant she had to jump up a few inches to reach the open hatch. Standing directly beneath it, she crouched down and, with an explosive push, jumped for the opening, reaching up to grab the ledge.

The lift dropped again, and then again as another explosion shook the facility. The lower the car went the more the fire pit extended around it. The walls of the shaft were already charred and blackened with smoke. Anne felt the metal of the elevator heating up through her gloves and noted the discolouration.

She pulled herself up, feeling the muscles in her arms almost sigh with relief after finally getting to rest. But not much.

A sickening, ear wrenching screech of metal against metal reverberated throughout the tight enclosure of the shaft, as the lift car finally gave out and plunged into the fiery depths.

Neither Lucas nor Anne said a word, they just reacted to the situation. Anne dashed towards the wall, and jumped, using the upright to boost herself higher, hoping that it would be enough. Lucas anchored to the stairwell side of the wall with one hand and reached down with his other hand for her to grab. He held on tightly to her forearm as she swung below him, grasping on with her two hands.

The elevator disappeared into the flaming pit, which happily devoured it, increasing its intensity, its flames licking at the sides of the shaft and stretching out for Anne.

'You can pull me up anytime now,' she said bluntly.

• • • •

SPRINTING UP THE ESCAPE stairway was a huge test of endurance for Lucas and Anne, especially after what they'd been through, but they had no choice; the BIC's underground laboratory was blowing up all around them. The higher the pair ascended, the more the devastation seemed to be. Fire was everywhere. The acrid smoke choked them, neither one knowing what chemicals would be mixed up in it. But at least they both knew that it wouldn't be the Bilderberg Inner Circle's deadly virus.

'As long as that intel was legit, this fire should vaporise all traces of that virus,' Lucas puffed, desperately trying to ignore the lactic acid build-up in his thighs as they finally reached the top of the stairwell.

Anne nodded noncommittally and checked her pocket out of Lucas's view to make sure that the antidote formula was still there. It was.

Putting his shoulder into the exit door, Lucas forced it open, and they squinted their eyes as sunlight streamed in, along with smoke which was billowing around in the air. The underground explosions had taken their toll on the old medieval fortress, too. Deep cracks were evident on the walls and ramparts.

Lucas and Anne found themselves at a helipad and quickly surmised that Babou and Diouf probably had a helicopter waiting to whisk them away. That Chiara's office was empty, meant she had been in the copter already, and the two assassins had been sent down to collect Faye Dannen.

They had escaped the underground facility, but they knew that this wasn't over yet. This was a two-part operation, and they still had the money counterfeiting side to bring down. But first, they needed wheels.

The two of them sprinted along the ramparts, down the steps of each level, until they were one floor above the courtyard. Lucas had spotted a single vehicle left, a security van with recognisable livery, and the driver was about to climb into his seat.

Without a second thought, he sprinted down the battlement towards the van and dived headlong at the driver, catching him completely unawares and crashing the man into the side of his vehicle. Lucas dragged him up by his collar, about to give him a knockout blow, but it wasn't necessary, and he let the unconscious man slump to the ground.

'Strange place for a security van,' Anne commented. 'This doesn't look like a place that needs a money collection service.'

'And no security firm I know uses a Mercedes V-Class,' added Lucas, remembering the vehicle as the same make and model the head of Section Seven was driven around in.

Anne jumped into the driver's seat and marvelled at the interior and the van's cockpit. She was like a kid in a store and couldn't help pressing buttons, and inadvertently brought up the GPS. 'Hey, guess where this guy was going?'

'Where?' Lucas asked as he relieved the man of his mobile phone before getting in the van.

'Iasi.' She turned around in her seat to have a look at what he was transporting and found several secured boxes. Climbing into the back, she unlocked the nearest one and looked inside. Tightly packed in polystyrene, were vials of a clear liquid. 'Shit. It's the virus. I guess we didn't get it all.'

'Well, I guess we'll just have to go in his place and explain why he wasn't able to make the delivery himself and burn it up with the fake money.'

Once Anne had re-secured the package, she jumped back into the driver's seat and set off. Beside her Lucas was calling a number he'd dialled in. A few seconds later the call was answered.

'Ellen Paige's phone.'

'Venice? What are you doing answering Ellen's phone? As I recall, you work for me, not her. Where is she? Put her on.'

'Um, she's a little busy right now.'

'What?'

'Lucas? Where have you been?' Ellen berated, taking the phone from Venice.

'Long story. Right now, I need you to patch me through to David.'

'Okay, hold on,' Ellen replied and got to work. It wasn't long before she was back. 'Go ahead, Lucas. The line's secure.'

'I'm glad to hear that you're not dead, Lucas.'

'Well, they came close a couple of times, but this isn't a social call. Enrique is behind the whole thing. Enrique and the Bilderberg Inner Circle. They've developed a virus more lethal than Ebola and more transmissible than SARS, and they're putting it on counterfeit currency.'

'Damn it!' David could see the pieces of the jigsaw falling into place. Things that once seemed like unrelated, individual snippets of news, were turning out to be all linked.

'The crashed security vans in Brazil and India. They happened in the poorer parts of town, overcrowded slums, where free money would be snatched up without a second thought.'

'Well, the laboratory has been destroyed, but I've got a van of the virus. Perhaps you can find someone to reverse engineer it or something.'

'That's great news! Ellen cracked the cypher, by the way. Apparently, the Huguenots were going to use some cursed discs from Peru to poison the pope and destroy Catholicism.'

'I think I have one of those in my possession, and that's what Faye Dannen used to create this virus.'

'She's part of the scheme?'

'Was. The kidnapped doctors were used to help her, but she was the one in charge of developing it. With the labs taken care of, we're on our way to do the same to the printing operation.'

'I'll get in contact with my opposite number and have them send you some backup. Wait a minute, did you say we? You linked up with Natasha?'

'No, it's an old friend.'

Anne glanced over at him indignantly and mouthed the word old.

'Actually,' Ellen interrupted, 'Natasha is in Peru. I tracked her before it went dead.'

'What the hell is she doing there?'

'It's the discs. Venice said that she went to Romania because her friend found some South American coins amongst a lost Romanian treasure. She must have figured out that they were from Peru.'

'Typical,' Lucas huffed. 'She's a real shit magnet. Call Feliciana and Claudia, see if either of them have heard from her, Venice can get the numbers from the office. It'll take a few hours to get to the destination. Get me on this number when you've got an update.' Lucas ended the call.

'I hope you're getting well paid for doing all of this,' chuckled Anne.

Chapter 46

Pedro was more than happy to drive Natasha and her rescued friends to the nearest airport in Carajia. It had turned out to be a lucrative opportunity for him, ending up being paid more than he would usually make in several months.

Peter and Alyssa had both insisted that they took a detour to a hospital first, so that Natasha could receive the treatment that she desperately needed, despite her protestations.

The doctor had examined her immediately and soon returned with a diagnosis. Luckily, the bullet had passed through her thigh, not causing a great deal of damage and missing the bone, the wound only needing stitching and dressing.

Once that was done Natasha was given a blood transfusion to replace the blood that she had lost. She hated being a bother to everyone, but because she had helped to rescue them, no one held it against her.

'Relax, Natasha,' Feliciana told the archaeologist as her enthusiasm threatened to run away with her. 'You can tell me all about the caves after you've rested.'

'I don't ... I don't need to ... rest,' stammered Natasha. 'I'm fine ... really. Where's Lucas? Tell him to ... charge my phone ... so I can show you ... the pictures I took.'

Feliciana and Alyssa glanced at each other, relieved that Peter had gone with the others to sort out transport back to Ollantaytambo, as they watched their friend doze off.

'Even in this situation, her first thought is for Lucas.'

'It's not a big thing,' replied Feliciana. 'She didn't even need surgery. It is probably all the stress of the day that has made her mind tired.'

Alyssa looked at the village elder, not sure if she should say anything about what happened. It wasn't really her place to, but she couldn't let things lay. 'Something happened, something dreadful. Before La Viuda was killed, she ... she forced Natasha to take the Supay discs, told her she would kill me if she didn't, made her hold them in both hands. The woman knew what it would do, knew that it would kill Natasha.'

Feliciana comforted Natasha's distraught friend and tried to hide her own anxiousness. 'It's not a complete death certificate. Yes, by using only Supay's disc's, she has become an offering to the god of death. It can be reversed, though.'

'What do you mean? Natasha can be saved?'

'Yes, but it will be difficult because you do not have all the necessary components.'

'Just tell me how.'

'You will need the missing prayer, all the discs, and you must complete what Xioczana did not.'

'Vanquish Supay? Surely, that can't be real?' Alyssa looked at the old woman cockeyed and wondered if she may be a bit senile.

'Of course it is. I'm surprised that you would even doubt it. But as I said, you do not have the components, nor do you know where to look.'

'We know Supay was banished to a place in my country. Hoia Baciu. It's a forest that is said to be haunted.'

'And you question the validity of Supay? All the death and destruction that has ravaged Europe is no doubt because of his influence.'

Alyssa had to admit it made sense, she and Natasha had come to the same conclusion, but it's one thing to listen to stories told to children, about strigoi and Baba Yaga, in order to scare them, but it's a completely different thing to think that a devil of some sort had been walking amongst people, spreading disease and starting conflicts. 'I don't think that we will have enough time to find the discs that were lost,' Alyssa said with a long face.

'In that case, we must do what we can to make her passage to the next life as manageable as possible.'

Alyssa nodded silently and remembered what Feliciana had told them about the sacrifices, how they would cry blood first before the symptoms escalated. She didn't know how she would cope when she saw that happen to Natasha.

Just then Natasha's phone rang as it finally got enough charge to bring it back to life.

'Hello? No, this is Alyssa Popescu. I'm afraid Natasha can't come to the phone right now. She's ... she's in hospital. What did you say? Lucas has a disc like mine and he's in Romania? Right now? Miss Paige, that is the best news I have heard all day!'

• • • •

DAVID EVANS RECEIVED the information regarding Natasha but chose not to divulge it with Lucas, because he didn't need his agent to be distracted. He had called his Romanian opposite and had been put in contact with Filip

Lakatos of SIAS, special interventions and actions, Romania's special police unit. The apprehension of people like George Hincu and his Clanul Ursilor was what the unit was created for, so they were more than happy to receive the intel from the British Government.

When they arrived at the rendezvous point, they weren't so pleased when they were told about two civilians that would not only be part of the operation but also be taking point. Eventually, it was revealed that they were both ex SAS, however, and they were a little less aggressive towards the two strangers.

'Look,' Lucas began at the ops briefing, 'We're not here to step on any toes, and we're definitely not here for a secret evaluation, or to tell you how to do your jobs. All we want to do is put a stop to Hincu's money printing business. As high a prize as his head may be, the priority is to destroy the counterfeiting production and all moneys therein. Is that clear?' The members of the masked police unit nodded. 'Good. One last thing. There are likely to be vials of a clear liquid around the factory, under no circumstances are you to get any of it on your bare skin. That goes for the money as well.'

'So we can't take any of it for our bonus?' one of the men joked, which brought laughter from the rest.

Lucas, however, was not amused. 'Sure, take as much as you want, if you want to end up like the dignitaries at the G20, or those poor bastards in Brazil, Mexico and India.' A hush descended, and they could hear only whispers about those death tolls. 'That's what I thought. Now, who's on drone duty?'

The images from the drone showed that the task wasn't going to be a simple one to complete; the factory, an old communist era one left abandoned until it was purchased by a South American, was vast, and the amount of Romani enforcers on patrol suggested that things were going to get messy.

'You sure you don't want to leave this up to them?' Anne thumbed towards the SIAS unit.

'This fight started with us and that's how it's going to end.' He strapped on a bulletproof vest provided by the police and then checked the weaponry. 'Besides, I'm hoping that Enrique will be in there too, because I've got a bullet with his name on it.'

'Well, since you put it like that, I'd like to have a few words with that asshole, too.' Anne looked at the Glock-17 in her hand, feeling the distribution of its weight before putting in its holster, then took up a HK-MP5 that the unit, and most other police forces used, secretly wishing that it was an MP7A1, her new favourite submachine gun.

In no time at all, the moment of the assault had arrived. An objective had been laid out. A small team would feign an incursion from the west of the factory, drawing men towards them. Then they would retreat out of danger, regrouping later. Whilst on the east side, the remainder of the assault team would gain entry of the factory and systematically work their way through until the counterfeiting presses were found, then the SIAS pyrotechnic unit would do their thing.

Anne listened to Filip issue the orders to his team, rolling her eyes when he'd finished. She glanced at Lucas and could see that he was on the same wavelength as her, thinking the same thing. He nodded and indicated with his head for her to get in the van.

When she was aboard, Lucas pulled the SIAS commander aside. 'There's another way to do this, Lakatos; go through the front door, snoop around and electronically paint the printing rooms if you've got the equipment with you, a small tracker or something.'

'Yes, we do, but there is no way I'm going to send any of my men on a mission like that. You can forget it.'

'Well, it's a good thing I wasn't asking you to. We're on a tight timeframe here. Hincu is expecting a van of the virus, so me and Anne will deliver it to him. Just make sure your men are in position on the west and east sides of the factory.' With that being said, and taking the bulletproof vests off again, Lucas and Anne drove off in the van, heading towards the factory two blocks down the road.

• • • •

LUCAS PULLED UP ALONGSIDE a service entrance with its wide corrugated door. The armed guard that had been giving him directions came to the driver's side and was a little taken by surprise to see Lucas there.

'What happened? We were expecting this shipment ages ago, and where's Nickolas?'

'He didn't make it. The whole place has blown up.'

'So, who are you?'

'I'm one of Enrique's men. He told me to deliver this and link up with him here.'

The man laughed. 'He must not think much of you, my friend.'

'What do you mean?'

'He has already left. The other three vans made their delivery and pick up and he went with one of them.'

'Where were they going?'

'Like I get told any of that stuff. I'm in the same boat as you, way down on the food chain, but what I've heard is that is that two were being flown out and the other two were supposed to be driven out. Anyway, you'd better stop yapping and get those crates inside.'

Lucas jumped out and made his way around to the back of the van. When he saw that he was out of the view of anyone that might have been watching him, he opened the rear of the van, where Anne had been hiding.

'We should just bug out, Lucas,' Anne said flatly. 'There's no point hanging around here if the contaminated money is already in the wind. And we don't even know where Enrique is.'

'We can't do that. This place still has the facilities to print more deadly currency with this van of the virus, so we need to take it out, simple. As for where Enrique is, I might have an idea for that. It's a bit of a long shot, but at this point, we have to try anything. Now, get going and good luck.'

'What? No kiss?' Anne said sarcastically.

'Get the job done and it'll be waiting for you.'

Lucas watched Anne slip into the one-time communist building and disappear into the shadows, something she was extremely good at. He then picked up one of the secured crates and headed through the door the guard had indicated.

Chapter 47

Armed enforcers did their rounds, prepared for something that none of them ever expected to happen. Why would they? The people of Iasi didn't know what was really going on inside that factory, and they'd be shocked if they ever found out what was going on right under their noses. Extortion, racketeering, prostitution and people smuggling was one thing, that was the bread and butter of the Romani mafia but being involved with the global conspiracy to exterminate billions of people with counterfeit money, laced with a virus was something completely different.

Lucas followed the instructions the guard outside had given him and eventually found the storeroom where the crates of the virus were being held. He couldn't believe how much they stockpiled there. Even with the laboratory itself gone, they'd be able to continue producing the contaminated money for a long time.

He gently placed the box down and opened it. Underneath one of the polystyrene boxes, which protected the vials, was a small explosive. Lucas took it out, made sure that it was still on, and planted it among the crates. He didn't want to risk his crate being moved elsewhere, because this room had to be destroyed.

Having finished in there, Lucas moved on to his next objective; finding out where the three shipments of money were going. He walked out purposefully, his MP5 slung over his shoulder, looking and acting like any other enforcer, giving off the impression that he belonged there. That was how you blended in.

As he walked, nodding at passing guards, his eyes scanned left and right, taking in the whole operation. For a criminal organisation that had never ventured into this territory, they seemed to be doing an extremely professional job of it. Someone had put a lot of time, effort and money into the operation. Dedication too. The more Lucas thought about things, from what he knew about Enrique Salas, the more he suspected he wasn't the mastermind of this elaborate scheme at all.

He had money yes, but only recently, after the death of his dad, and was it enough to build an operation like this? Maybe the BIC had some sort of fund that he could dip into. Who knew? But the effort and dedication this would have taken was way beyond what Enrique would have been prepared to put in. Then there was the fact that this would have taken years in the planning, the finding of the disc, the kidnapping of the scientists, the counterfeit plates. These things take time. It wasn't something that you would get up one morning and say I'm going to take over the world today.

Lucas had concluded that just as Hincu, and the late Faye Dannen worked for Enrique, he in turn worked for someone else, someone that sat at the Bilderberg Inner Circle table.

One thing that he could be sure of was that it wasn't his own mum. Anne had been sent here to help stop this plan, and she still worked for Angela Redmond. But he wondered if Anne knew who else was sitting at that table.

He had been blindly walking about the factory deep in his thoughts when he saw a blur out of the corner of his eye. Something had dropped from the rafters then was gone. It could only have been Anne. The little magpie still had skills. Lucas carried on with his own search. If she had decided to come down to ground level, it meant that she was close to finding the printing equipment.

He went upstairs and saw a small cabin office on the above level and went up to check it out. As he went up, a man with a sharply trimmed beard and gaudy jewellery passed him on the stairs. Keeping up his charade of being a guard on duty, Lucas nodded at the man, who didn't return it.

Lucas walked along the gangway and reached the office. He took a quick look around and checked the door. It was unlocked. He slipped in and closed the door behind him. Three walls of the square office were mostly made of glass, so Lucas knew he had to move fast before anyone spotted him. Luckily, he found something of interest almost immediately; it was a list of currencies. Some had ticks and were struck through, some only had ticks. The ones that had both were the Brazilian Real, the Mexican Peso, the Indian Rupee and the Nigerian Naira. The ones that had just ticks were the Chinese Yuan, the United States Dollar, the Euro and the Indonesian Rupiah.

It only took him a few seconds for him to realise what it meant. The ones that were struck through were all the countries that already had the infected money, the ones with the ticks were the ones in transit. Next to each of them there was also three letters, IAS or OTP. But before he could figure out what it meant, he heard the sound of a gun being cocked.

The man he had passed on the stairs was standing at the door, pointing a gun at him and holding up a mobile phone in his other hand. 'I thought you looked familiar, Mr Lucas Redmond.' On the screen was a photo of Lucas. 'I am George Hincu, and your days of causing us trouble are over, my friend.'

'Well, I feel like I'm on a roll, to be honest. I mean I've taken out your little lab. Now I'm going to do the same to this factory, then I'm going to pay Enrique a visit and finish him once and for all.'

George Hincu turned to the two enforcers behind him, and they all laughed. 'And how exactly are you planning on doing any of that? In case you haven't noticed, my Clanul Ursilor brothers are all over this place. How do you think you are going to escape?'

Lucas smiled. 'In ways you couldn't begin to fathom.'

There came the sudden unmistakable sound of automatic gunfire from outside the factory. Hincu and the others turned around, giving Lucas the split second he needed to make a run for it, diving through the window on his left and sprinting down the gangway. Hincu and his men fired on their escapee, who ducked whilst making his getaway, returning fire blindly over his shoulder as he did so. It wasn't long before there was an explosion within the factory as the bomb Lucas had set went off.

Hincu screamed at Lucas as he charged after the man that was on the verge of ruining his payday. More gunfire could be heard coming from the opposite side of the building, followed by more explosions. Shouts of 'Politisti,' could be heard. Hincu's Romani mafia were in a panic even though they had the numbers. Hincu positioned his two men to cover his back, whilst he made his escape, telling them not to move.

The SIAS were doing a thorough job on the mafia. Any of them that didn't surrender were cut down with bullets. Lucas was impressed with how they handled themselves, knowing the trials and tribulations they would have had to endure to reach this level of professionalism.

His own skills were no less than what they were when he was an active soldier, thanks to the fact that he kept his physical activity high, and thanks to all the turbulent places he had been paid to visit in his Acquirers role, Lucas was able to keep his marksmanship pretty high.

As he made his way quickly back to the van, where he was supposed to meet-up with Anne, Lucas was tackled from the side. His gun went skittering across the stone floor. The enforcer that had the idea was trying to beat down on Lucas, smothering him with punches so that the saboteur could not retaliate. But most of the punches were being defended by Lucas, and the man didn't know that Lucas was not working alone.

Anne introduced herself by delivering a step kick to the side of the man's head. Before he even knew what had hit him, he was out cold.

As Lucas pushed the man aside, Anne looked on in mock disappointment. 'Tut, tut, tut. Am I always going to be the one saving you? Because if I am, I might have to start getting a salary for it.'

'Whatever,' replied Lucas. 'I take it you found the currency printing rooms?'

'Of course. Found, tagged and soon to be destroyed.'

'Good. I found their stash of the virus; that's up in smoke too. But Hincu has done a runner.'

'We going after him?'

'I think we'll leave Filip to clean up the rest of the mess; we've got the vans that have already left with tainted currency to deal with.'

'Yeah, I remember, but how are we supposed to find them?'

'Two were being flown and two were being driven out. This mafia guy had a list of currencies on his desk. Four of them had ticks beside them, of those four, had three letters beside them; IAS and OTP.'

'Airport codes.'

'That's what I thought. IAS must be for Iasi, but I've got no idea what the other is.'

'It's Bucharest. Otopeni Airport,' replied Anne and saw Lucas's surprised look. 'What? I get around.'

'So I've heard.' Lucas took out the phone he'd taken and called Ellen. 'Anyway, the vans that were flying out from Iasi are probably in the air by now. We may be able to ground the ones at Bucharest...'

'But that still leaves the ones being driven. Ours is one, but where's the other one?'

'Ellen? I need you to do something for me.'

'No hello? No how you doing? I've got something to tell you.'

'I don't have time, Ellen. You still got the tracker on my phone, right?'

'Yeah, but it only works if it's switched on.'

'Bollocks!'

'But if it's not, I can do it remotely.'

'You can? Do it, but when I get back, you and I are going to have a talk about privacy.'

'Well, I'll start my defence by saying that if I couldn't switch it on, you'd be up shits creek. Why isn't it with you?'

'I think Enrique has it. He got a laugh out of trying to torture me by killing women I knew in front of me, so I'm trying a hunch that he'd take my phone for the contact details.'

'You might actually be right; the signal is moving. It looks like it might be heading to Bucharest.'

'Awesome! Now check the flights that have departed Iasi in the last couple of hours, probably private jets.'

'Hold on. Okay, there have been three flights. One to Indonesia, one to Ukraine and one to Germany.'

'It's the Indonesia and Germany ones. Get on to David and have him isolate those planes as soon as they land. Also, tell him to ground all flights from Bucharest to Washington and Beijing. And tell him I need a helicopter.'

Chapter 48

Lucas was startled, but also impressed by how quickly David Evans had arranged a copter for him. The head of S7 was certainly using up a lot of his favours with SIAS. It wasn't long before Lucas was in the air, Anne opting to remain with the van and follow him once the factory operation was complete, so she could verify that everything was destroyed.

The helicopter pilot knew the best way for a car to get to Bucharest from Iasi, it was a five-hour journey, and despite Enrique having a few hours head-start, Lucas's tracker indicated that they were almost on top of him, just outside the Romanian capital.

With the use of a monocular, Lucas spotted the phoney security van driving along the wide highway. 'There's that little shit,' breathed Lucas. Now that he was within sight of Enrique's, the next problem was how to stop him. He had thought just to come alongside it and shoot out the tires, but seeing how the van would be full of tainted money, the chance of the goods scattering was too high for Lucas to risk it. He had to get aboard and stop it.

After instructing the pilot, Lucas checked his handgun, tucked it into his belt and slid open the side door. The pilot shook his head in disbelief as he saw Lucas step out onto the skid, at which point he brought the helicopter down in altitude, chasing after the van with the fake decals.

The sight of a low-flying helicopter shocked many of the drivers, some dangerously slowing down on the motorway to get a better look, especially when they could see that a man was standing outside. When they were positioned above it, Lucas indicated the pilot to lower him down. That's the moment Enrique's van swerved back and forth as soon as the occupants noticed what the helicopter was attempting to do.

The pilot pulled up sharply when it missed the van's roof because of their evasive driving. He almost missed again, but the driver got himself blocked in by two slower moving vehicles. Lucas grabbed the chance to make the leap onto the roof, and just as the pilot pulled away, the driver of the van rammed one of the cars out of the way.

Lucas lost his footing and rolled off the right-hand side of the van's roof. At the last second, he snatched hold of the railing which ran around the roof's edge. Wind battered him, the driver accelerating to top speed again. Once he was sure of his grip, Lucas drew his gun and hammered at the large, tinted side window. The driver immediately swerved towards another car to squash Lucas between the two of them.

The driver of the small hatchback turned her steering wheel hard to the right when she saw the van on her left suddenly veer towards her. But in her panicked state she was unaware of the car on her right and performed an unintentional pit manoeuvre on it, spinning it and ultimately flipping the car over. With the sound of screeching tyres and crunching metal chassis', Lucas watching a smoking pileup of vehicles behind them.

Hanging there, he took the gun and shot out the driver's side mirror, warning him against attempting to do that again. It took another two strikes on the window for him to shatter it. He brought his leg up, kicking in some of the glass that remained, and climbed inside the van.

Lucas instantly felt a pain shoot up his leg as it was hit by something hard. As he toppled into the vehicle, he was struck again. This time he could see that it was Enrique attacking him with a tyre wrench, a crazed demented look in his eye.

The enraged man charged again, Lucas rolling over the shrink-wrapped blocks of money to avoid being hit. He reached for his gun, which had fallen from his hand when he collapsed into the back of the van, but Enrique hit it away with his metal rod and with a grunt brought the wrench down on Lucas's outstretched arm.

He yelled in agony and kicked out at the mad Colombian, tripping him up, sending him sprawling on his back. Lucas pounced on him like a tiger, driving his forearm into his face. As he was about to repeat the attack, he saw that sweeping the feet from under Enrique had inadvertently brought him close to the gun.

Enrique took up the gun and laughed wickedly. 'At least you'll part this world knowing that I'm going to kill every woman you have ever come into contact with, even if I won't have the pleasure of making you witness it. Goodbye, Lucas.'

Enrique had the look of victory on his face, but Lucas had a tenacious attitude that wouldn't give up. As Enrique squeezed the trigger, Lucas flashed out a leg, kicking the money block that his would be executioner balanced on, sending his aim wide to the right, the bullet shattering the window.

Seizing his chance, Lucas picked up a solid block of money, and first knocked the gun away then proceeded to repeatedly bring it down onto Enrique's face. So tightly packed we're the blocks, that they were like being hit by bricks.

Several of the shrink wrap layers ripped on the block he was using as a weapon, and he tore at the rest until he could get a handful of the virus tainted money.

'You wanted to make this money so badly, Enrique, so why don't you keep it!'

Enrique tried to stop Lucas from ramming the US dollars down his throat, but he wasn't strong to stop the determined former SAS Capetian. He choked on the wad of the poisoned notes in his throat. But it wouldn't be that which finished Enrique. His eyes haemorrhaged and became bloodshot, as he ingested the notes along with a high dose of the virus. Tears of blood ran down his face, the injured side becoming redder as blood streamed from his pores. Enrique's face was a mask of red. Blood gurgled from his mouth. He tried to reach for Lucas. He didn't know if he was begging for help or if he was trying to take Lucas with him into the depths of hell.

Either way, he wasn't about to let his touch reach him. Lucas picked up the gun and pointed it at Enrique. He stopped immediately and dropped his hands. It was a cry for help. Lucas squeezed the trigger.

'Pull over on the hard shoulder now, or you can join your former employer,' Lucas said to the driver, who was more than happy to do as he was told.

Chapter 49

The buzzing sound woke Lucas from his light sleep, and he rolled away from Anne Shepard's naked body. The mission had been completed, they had both survived to tell the tale, and as was often the way, the gratitude of being alive after facing danger on numerous occasions, rose the amorous feelings within and they were both happy and eager to expel that need with each other.

Lucas reached over and gently stroked Anne's firm buttocks as she slept soundly.

He picked up the vibrating phone, glad he could retrieve it from Enrique's security van, and looked at the name on the display. 'Natasha? Is that you?'

'Lucas...husband...I need you...where are you...why did you leave me?'

'Natasha? Are you okay? You sound kind of weird. What's going on?' Lucas asked as he walked over to the window of his hotel and looked out over the city of Bucharest at night.

'I have never...felt emptier...than I do without...you.'

'Why are you saying this? What's happened?'

Another voice suddenly came on the phone. 'Hello? Is this Lucas?'

'Yeah, Alyssa, right?'

'Yes. I take your friend Ellen or Mr Evans hasn't told you anything?'

'Told me about what?

'Listen, this is going to sound a bit weird, but are you still in Bucharest?'

'Yeah, I am. How did you know?'

'Do you have the disc with the Peru images on it?'

'Yeah, I do, in a bag waiting to go back to London with me. Why?'

'Excellent! I need you to meet us at Otopeni Airport as soon as possible.'

'What's going on?'

'Natasha has been poisoned by the original strain of the virus that killed the people at the G20 Summit.'

'Fuck!' He looked around for his clothes.

'It's a very old bacteria, thousands of years old, but here's the funny part: you need to send it back to where it came from.'

'And where's that?'

'The god of death.'

Lucas was silent for a long moment. 'Are you taking the piss?'

'I truly wish I was. I'm as sceptical as you are, but if it really is the only way to save Natasha, I'm willing to give it a try.'

'Okay, I'm on my way.'

Lucas rushed out, not knowing that Anne hadn't been asleep at all.

• • • •

LUCAS GREETED ALYSSA at the airport entrance, and they headed directly for the tarmac where a medical helicopter waited, surprised that she even had a military escort with her.

'That is thanks to David Evans. He arranged a plane to take us from Lima direct to here. Peter wasn't thrilled about the arrangement, though. He was blocked from boarding, to control any possible spread. He threatened to sue them as well, then he said he would pay their government just so that they would be fired.'

'I always knew that dude was an asshole.'

'I agree with you. Did you remember to bring the disc?'

'Yeah, it's right here.' Lucas held out the artefact and Alyssa opened Natasha's bag for him to drop it into. Then they both climbed aboard, and the helicopter took off.

Lucas had witnessed Enrique go through the excruciating pain of the virus with little to no emotion, but this was different. This was the woman that up until very recently had been his wife. The woman that he had planned to have a family with one day. Now that he saw her lying there, in the back of the helicopter, with all kinds of tubes in her veins, trying to replace the blood that was continuously leaving her body, but failing to succeed.

Even her bloodied face couldn't diminish the gleam of her smile when she saw Lucas. 'I don't regret...much in this life...but you are...the one thing...that I do regret...Lucas.'

'Don't try to speak, Nat.'

'I have to...I want you to know...that I'll always love you...even when I die.'

'You're not going to die. I won't let you.'

'It's not up...to you. My fate...is in the hands...of the gods now.'

'Then I'll just have to give them a gentle nudge then.'

Natasha smiled at Lucas, then suddenly began to sing over and over again. 'I am the fool on the fool's errand, and so are you.'

Lucas looked at Alyssa neither one of them wanting to state the obvious, that perhaps they were indeed on a fool's errand.

• • • •

THE HELICOPTER LANDED on the edge of the Hoia Baciu forest, as close as they dared. Nobody wanted to accompany Lucas in. Each person aboard the transport had a different story to tell about the strange forest. Tales of children disappearing only to reappear years later still looking the same, people hearing voices and following them into the forest, never to be seen again. And then there were all the UFO sightings.

Lucas took the stories with a pinch of salt, rolling his eyes as they finished their retelling. He was glad to get away from them in the end, so he didn't have to listen to any more of their tall tales.

Natasha was unhooked from all the medical equipment whilst Lucas put on protective gear since he would have to carry her through the forest to their finishing point, Poiana Rotunda, an area of the forest where nothing grew.

Alyssa explained to Lucas what he had to do once he arrived at the clearing. He nodded his head, but was still uncertain that any of it was going to work. The way he saw was that Natasha had chosen to spend her last moments with him. It didn't matter to him if they were on a wild goose chase or not, the fact of the matter was that she wanted to be with him. Not Peter or anyone else, but him. And he would always be there for her if they were together or not.

'This is the spot,' Natasha said as they entered the small clearing. All around it were misshapen trees, the likes of which Lucas had never seen before.

'This place doesn't seem to be all that haunted after all,' Lucas shrugged. 'I haven't seen a single thing that couldn't be explained away.'

'That's because...we haven't started...yet.'

Lucas frowned at her as he helped her to sit in the approximate centre of the rotunda.

'Now...take all the...Aysana Kawsay Wanu...and place them around us. The large images of Viracocha and Supay must face up and be side by side.'

Lucas did what he was told. 'How do you know all this?'

'It's just there in my head, like it has been there forever,' she replied, genuinely perplexed. 'Now we read the complete Taki Kawsay Wanu.'

'What? I can't read that.'

'Just follow what I say.'

Lucas did as Natasha asked. The sound of old Quechua was spoken in the mountain region for the first time. They completed the prayer, and just as Lucas had been expecting, nothing happened. He looked at Natasha, seeing the hope drain away from her, as the realisation hit her; she only had hours left to live.

He threw his arms around her, wishing that there was more he could do to comfort her in the last moments of her life. Then he heard a whispering come from the forest. It grew louder and louder until it reached a point when they had to cover their ears. The audible pain was penetrating their heads, both of them screaming in agony.

Within the tree line, red and orange lights suddenly flickered into existence in the darkness. They surrounded them, blinking repeatedly, like pairs of eyes watching the two of the former couple. Lucas was about to reach for his trusty gun when Natasha stopped him, shaking her head.

The discs around them grew brighter and brighter. The red and orange seemed to get larger only for Lucas to realise that they were soaring towards him and Natasha, only to then retreat. It happened repeatedly, until the red and orange lights no longer advanced, but rather stayed back and rotated around them so fast that they were just a blur.

A beam of light then flew from each Aysana Kawsay Wanu disc, penetrating and passing through Natasha, leaving a faint glow. Pulses of light then emanated outwards from the circle of discs, slow at first then faster. Then they returned until the beams of light from the discs shot straight up into the night sky.

Then everything was quiet.

The lights were all gone, as were the sounds. But most intriguing of all was the fact that all the discs were gone, too. Lucas wondered what he had just seen when he turned to Natasha to see her smiling at him and saw that she wasn't bleeding anymore. But before he could say anything, as they reached out for each other, they both passed out.

Epilogue

Lucas watched Peter Armitage leave the hospital bedroom and walk through the ward towards the lifts. As soon as Lucas saw him enter it when the doors opened, he strolled into room ten.

'Lucas!' Natasha said with excitement as she tried to sit up.

'Hey, come on, Nat. You don't need to sit up. Come on, relax.'

'Fine,' Natasha relented and lay back down. 'There, are you happy now?'

'Very,' he smiled. 'How are you feeling?'

'Good, actually. I can't wait to get out of here and get back to work, to be honest. There must be a back log waiting for us.'

'I'm sure Venice has everything under control, even if she has been spending a lot of time with Ellen.'

'What? Those two...? Well, they do say opposites attract.'

'Definitely! Look at us.'

'True.'

Lucas took a moment to find his words. Natasha silently watched him and couldn't help but notice that something was on his mind. 'What's wrong Lucas?'

'I was just wondering, do you remember when we were going to Hoia Baciu?'

'Vaguely. I was pretty much out of it, though. Why do you ask?'

'So you don't remember any of the things you said?'

She shook her head. 'I didn't make a fool of myself, did I? Say something stupid?'

He let out an exaggerated chuckle. 'No, not at all, just some shit about you being the empress of Peru or some shit,' Lucas said.

'Well, that I can live with.' She yawned.

'Maybe you should get some rest. Sleep well, Nat.' He helped tuck her into the bed. Natasha rolled over to hide the tears that were welling up in her eyes as Lucas left.

• • • •

ANNE LET OUT A HEAVY sigh as she continued to watch the news. She arrived at Angela Redmond's gated mansion, in Little Venice moments earlier, and her host had immediately directed her attention to the news report currently on her tv.

'It's a complete mystery, Susan. The doctors here in Rio de Janeiro are just as perplexed as the ones in Nigeria, Mexico and India. The people that were infected with this deadly virus, the ones that hadn't passed away from it, suddenly made an instant recovery. They were no longer showing any signs of the virus at all. The patients, however, remain in hospital receiving blood transfusions, replenishing what they had lost. But this situation has the potential to usher a problem. Because of the amount of people infected and needing blood, doctors fear that the possibility of running out of blood supplies is extremely high. They are urging people to go to their local practices and donate blood...'

'Well, that's completely useless now, isn't it?' Anne said indicating the formula she had taken from Karen Fletcher. 'I know you wanted to have the first anti-viral on the market and sell it, but I guess this puts an end to that idea.'

'Maybe,' Angela replied, picking up the scrap of paper from her desk. 'Maybe not. Who knows? The vials of virus you took from the van are being analysed to see if they are still viable.'

'Let's hope so.'

'How are things with Lucas? Has he thawed at the idea of coming back into the fold?'

'I don't know,' Anne shrugged. 'After what he did in Bucharest, I've been ignoring him. I'll let him stew a bit longer before I answer any of his calls. No doubt he's at Natasha's side.'

'Not if Peter's already there.'

At that moment, Angela received a message on her phone, which she read aloud. 'Urgent group meeting in five minutes.' She looked at Anne and stood up from her chair. The pair walked towards her vast bookshelf and stopping in front of it. Angela twisted the stone of her ring, then pressed it and the bookcase slid apart, revealing a staircase to a hidden complex.

It was Angela's nerve centre, where she conducted all of her clandestine activities, her own personal ones and those as a member of the Bilderberg Inner Circle. She took her seat and faced the three-monitor setup on her desk. Anne remained out of view, studying the images of all the BIC members. Each one had lines of red string leading to other images of their immediate family, as well as close associates.

Anne stopped at a picture of Natasha Travers and followed at the thread leading to it.

'I must apologise for this unscheduled meeting,' Alpha said as the remote gathering began.

'I'm sure I speak for everyone here, in saying how sorry we are at the failure of Operation Vanguard,' Upsilon said. 'It was an exceptional plan.'

'Thank you all. Yes, it was. Which brings me to the crux of this meeting. Operation Vanguard was indeed a master plan. Years in the making. And it was foiled by this man.' A picture of Lucas appeared on their screens. 'This is Lucas Redmond, a former SAS captain, and for Operation Vanguard to have failed can only mean one thing; someone among you talked.'

A general murmuring of disbelief ensued from most of the eighteen BIC members.

'Are you sure of this?' Iota, a Japanese woman asked.

'My adviser, Mr Angel, brought the possibility of it to my attention. I will find out who it is eventually, unless, of course, that individual wishes to save me the time and effort by coming forward, in exchange for leniency of course.'

'We are all of the same mind here, Alpha,' Omega, a slim American man said.

'Obviously not all.'

'I find it extremely hard to believe.'

'As did I. Perhaps they have their own agenda. But it does not matter. The person who will next have the chance of bringing about the New Enlightened Order will soon be made, but in the meantime, Lucas Redmond is to be at the top of all of your agendas. If he crosses your path, he is to be eliminated. That is all.' With that, the Bilderberg Inner Circle meeting was ended.

Angela Redmond looked into the ether, her mind ticking over, scheming and plotting, digesting everything that Alpha said. The fact that the meeting was even held had calmed Angela. It let her know that her identity was still clean. Angela Redmond was still dead to the majority of people in the world. She turned to Anne. 'It's time to tell him,' Angela stated.

Anne nodded and took out her mobile phone.

• • • •

TRE VINCENT STARED at Lucas as his captain finished recounting the events of his latest adventure. 'Don't look at me like that,' he said. 'That's exactly how it happened. Don't believe me? Ask Natasha.'

'Well, I'm not saying it didn't happen like that. I'm just saying that it's one hell of a story that's all.'

'No need to tell me, and I'm the one that went through it.' Lucas sipped the cocktail his friend had put in front of him. 'So what's this drink called?'

'Devil's Soul.'

'Mmm, not bad. I'd say it's up there with some of your best concoctions.' Before Lucas could take another sip of the dark orange liquid, his phone suddenly rang. 'Anne! I'm glad you've finally returned my calls. Look, I'm so sorry about what happened in Romania. One minute I was in Hoia Baciu, the next I'm waking up in my own bed. I have no idea how I got back here.'

'We'll get to that. But you owe me, big time, and I'm not only talking about the hotel bill I was lumbered with.' Anne took a deep breath to calm her boiling blood. 'I'm calling to tell you you've made it onto the Bilderberg Inner Circle's radar.'

'It's nice to feel wanted.'

'I'm serious, Lucas. That virus scheme, Operation Vanguard, was the brainchild of BIC's numero uno, Alpha, and he's taking you spoiling his plans very personally. He wants you dead.'

'Wouldn't be the first guy,' scoffed Lucas. 'So, who is this sensitive soul, anyway?'

'I saw him for the first time today. I couldn't believe it at first, to be honest. BIC's Alpha is Peter Armitage.'

'Well, that explains that. I always knew that motherfucker was an asshole, but I didn't think that even he would be capable of global genocide. The question now is, how am I supposed to tell Natasha without sounding smug?'

End

Travers & Redmond
Will Return
In a New Adventure Coming Soon

A Word From Desmond G. Palmer

Thank you for reading THE CURSED TREASURE. The adventures continue in THE ACQUIRERS series, fast paced archaeological thrillers that take Natasha, Lucas and all of you around the world.

If you've enjoyed the book, I'd be very grateful if you could leave a review. It only needs to be a few lines. Not only does it keep me honest, so I don't stray from what makes these books a fun adventure romp, but it lets the algorithms know that people are reading them, and they'll push the books to likeminded readers.

Don't forget to join my Newsletter List. I won't bombard your inbox with emails, but you'll get a free book, PERIL IN PERU and you'll stay up to date with everything that I'm doing. All you have to do is scan the QR code to go to the sign-up page. Onwards & Upwards!

Scan The QR Code To Join My Newsletter List

And Get A Free Novella, Peril In Peru

Don't miss out!

Visit the website below and you can sign up to receive emails whenever D G Palmer publishes a new book. There's no charge and no obligation.

https://books2read.com/r/B-A-JGOH-DXMYB

BOOKS 2 READ

Connecting independent readers to independent writers.

Printed in Dunstable, United Kingdom

63741566R00224